PRETTY *Heartache*

BRITTANY TAYLOR

Pretty Heartache
Brittany Taylor
Copyright © 2024 by McGregorInk LLC
ISBN: 979-8-9908842-4-3

Cover Design by Amanda Shepard of Shepard Originals
Editing by Vicki James
Proofing by Tiffany Hernandez
Formatting by Brittany Taylor

**Want to be notified of Brittany's upcoming releases?
Sign up for her newsletter here**
https://www.brittanytaylorbooks.com/contact

For the girlies who constantly feel they have to move faster, go bigger, and do better just to keep up.
This one is for you.

CONTENT NOTE FROM THE AUTHOR

Hello dear reader!
Pretty Heartache is a high angst, emotional read. **Please be aware** this book contains scenes and topics which may be sensitive to some.
Topics include alcohol addiction, drug addiction and drug use, as well as scenes and discussions of physical and emotional domestic abuse.
I sincerely hope you enjoy Micah and Adeline's story.
Thank you and happy reading!
Xoxo,
Brittany

"Love takes off masks we fear we cannot live without and know we cannot live within." — James Baldwin

ONE

ADELINE

Eleven Years Old

Summer is my favorite time of year. The two and a half months between the last day of school and the first of the next grade are pure bliss. Ice-cold lemonade, lounging by the pool, sunburnt skin, and the way my chest bubbles in anticipation. The anticipation I get every time I see _him_.

I used to dread summer. The few short months only gave my father more opportunities to criticize me. To remind me of all the ways I'm a disappointment and how he wished I were never born—a fact he's never shied away from making public knowledge. But for the past two years, I've waited impatiently for summer.

I no longer have to hide in the spaces I know my father will have a harder time finding me. I no longer have to lurk around the house in a constant state of nervousness, waiting for the moment my father walks in the door, blaming me for existing in his world and stealing his oxygen.

School always provided an eight-hour window away from the tension at home, but during the two and a half months it was stripped away, I was left to my own devices, fighting for my own survival.

Until a few summers ago.

I haven't been completely free from my father's wrath, but trips to the pool and the way he makes my heart race at the sight of him are the perfect distractions.

"Do you think I can get a tan this time without burning first?" Ember, my tan-obsessed best friend asks me. She sprays her arms, dousing them in the brown liquid coming from the bottle gripped between her hot pink-painted fingernails.

There are only three weeks left of summer vacation before we start the seventh grade, and Ember has made it her number one goal to get the deepest tan she can manage before we return to middle school.

"Doesn't that stuff *attract* the sun?" I sniff, the scent of my sunblock flooding my nostrils. My mother always insists on me wearing it, reminding me of the dangers of developing skin cancer at a young age. Ember doesn't seem concerned. The risk of cancer is worth it if she looks like she's been baking in the sun all summer long.

"Yes, Adeline," she retorts with a grin. She smooths her hand over her left arm, rubbing it in. "That's the point."

"Well." I sigh, squinting up at the sun through my sunglasses. "I guess it's a race to see who wins. The tan or the burn."

Ember laughs and playfully slaps me on the arm before sitting back in her chair. We both sit in silence and people watch. It's our favorite thing to do when we come to the Cambridge Country Club pool every day.

"You should get used to tanning if you want to become a model," Ember says, breaking our silence.

"Models don't need to be tan." I think back to all the ones I admire. Even my mother when she used to model. I want to be just like her when I'm old enough. My mother became a model when she was only fourteen. I've begged her for years to let me start at the same age she did, but she won't let me. Not until I'm eighteen.

Only seven more years.

"You're going to be a beautiful model, Adeline." Ember smiles. "You're already beautiful, but you get what I mean." She tilts her head and studies me. "It's those cheekbones. You've got good cheekbones."

I smile inwardly and allow us to sit in silence once more. But our relaxation is temporary.

Ember squirms beside me, buzzing with excitement at the prospect of seeing the boy she's had a crush on all summer long. Teddy Long is sixteen years old and the hottest lifeguard at the club. According to Ember, that is.

I giggle as she adjusts the straps of the bikini—the one her mother allowed her to wear—the moment Teddy emerges from the locker room before climbing the small ladder and taking his seat.

She blows out a nervous breath between her glossed lips. "I'm going to talk to him today." Her eyes are trained on Teddy, but mine are on someone else.

The one person I've been anxious to see all summer walks out from the club bar wearing a suit, as always. The white shirt under his dark blue blazer is unbuttoned halfway. Typical for him. Unusual for the country club poolside bar, because while everyone else is in their swimsuits, Micah looks like he's just walked out of an important business meeting.

He's tall, dark-haired, and has these blue-gray eyes that shoot straight for my heart every single time they swing in my direction. It's a bolt of lightning I chase every year.

Micah Lucas Harding. I feel his name on my lips as I mouth them to myself.

"Micah and Archer are here?" Ember asks, turning her head in their direction. I must have said his name out loud without realizing it.

My cheeks heat. "They are?" I play off her question as if I didn't just say Micah's name out loud. I lower my sunglasses and shimmy my shoulders against the back of my pool chair, but Ember isn't in the dark about my feelings for my older brother's best friend.

"You just said his name out loud, Addy." She giggles.

"No, I didn't." I inhale a deep breath, thankful my eyes are shielded by my sunglasses and Ember can't call me out on my obvious lie.

"Whatever." She sighs. "You don't have to pretend for my sake. I know you look forward to seeing him every summer. You've known him practically your whole life, but now that he comes to the pool every year during the summer, you can't stop talking about him. I just think it's silly you have a crush on someone over ten years older than you."

"You have a crush on Teddy, and he's in high school," I argue, twisting my face into a scowl.

"Shh," she hisses, whipping her head to the side and dramatically lifting her sunglasses to shoot me an angry glare. "Do you think you said it loud enough for the whole club to hear you?" She nervously shifts her eyes up to where Teddy is sitting in his lifeguard station. Completely oblivious to our conversation. And us. "Besides," she adds. "Teddy is only a few years older. Micah is *twelve* years older than you."

I bite the inside of my cheek. Ember is right.

With my sunglasses still shielding my face, I watch as Micah walks alongside the edge of the pool beside my brother. He's talking animatedly, waving his hands in front of him and laughing. He grins, displaying his perfect teeth. They stop at the bar and both lean against the counter with their elbows as the bartender drops full glasses of beer in front of them.

My warm chest fills with oxygen at the sight of Micah. The sun hits his dark brown hair when he tilts his head back to take a sip of his beer. But the oxygen is sucked back out from my lungs the second two women walk up to Micah and Archer.

I ignore my brother and the woman draping her arm across his back. Instead, I hesitantly shift my attention to Micah. The blonde woman standing between Archer and Micah turns her entire body to Micah, giggling as she drags her finger down his cheek. He leans into her gesture, his mouth spreading into an even wider grin.

My stomach sours. I'm green with jealousy. I feel it in my gut, growing like long strands of ivy.

I haven't seen Micah all summer. I prepared for today. With my eyes still shielded, I look down at the pink bikini I took hours to pick from my drawer. I chose this one because I'd seen a model wearing a similar one in my favorite magazine.

I swipe my tongue across my lip, licking off the pink lip gloss I'd put on an hour ago. I feel stupid for thinking Micah would ever notice me. In a way, he does. He's my older brother's best friend, and I'm his best friend's annoying little sister.

But that's all I'll ever be in his eyes.

We haven't even spoken yet this summer, and I'm already feeling foolish. But even though I know he's only my brother's best friend, I look forward to these moments, because even the rare, ten second high I get from being acknowledged by Micah Harding is worth the wait.

I risk a chance looking at him again and swing my gaze back up to the bar.

Archer and the girl clutching his hand have already left the bar, leaving Micah standing with the girl he's with. They're still deep in conversation, not paying any attention to anyone else.

I inhale a deep breath and sit up from my lounge chair. My skin peels off the plastic as I swing my legs over the edge and slip into my sandals.

"I'm going to the bathroom to fix my lip gloss," I tell Ember.

I can't tell whether she's asleep or still watching Teddy.

I don't have to wonder long when she turns her head slightly. "Are you truly going to fix your lip gloss, or is it because Grant is heading in our direction?"

"What?" I turn to my left just in time to see Grant doing just that, heading in my direction. I stand and swipe my pink, sequined makeup bag from the ground at my feet.

"Both." I quickly stand.

"You know he's only mean to you because he has a crush on you," Ember says. "All the boys are like that. If they tease you, they like you."

I open my mouth to argue, but maybe Ember is right. My dad isn't always the nicest to me, yet he says he still loves me. Maybe the same could be said for Grant. Though my stomach doesn't agree. It wobbles, and the thought of talking to Grant right now when I feel the way I do for Micah makes me nauseous.

Without answering Ember, I straighten my back and hold my head high, keeping my eyes focused on where I'm headed: toward the bathroom, away from Micah and the girl he's with. But I only make it a few feet along the perimeter of the pool when I realize I need to pass Grant to get to my destination.

I clutch my bag and start to turn on my heel, but I'm too late. Grant is already standing in front of me.

"Where are you headed, Addy?" he asks, lifting his chin as he grins. He reaches out and curls his finger around one of the ends of my braided pigtails.

"Leave me alone, Grant," I force out between my clenched teeth, and jerk back. His hand falls away from me.

He looks the same as he did during the school year. I've known Grant ever since we were in kindergarten, and he stole my favorite pink, feathered pencil with the unicorn eraser.

His cheeks redden and his dark eyebrows knit. "That's not very nice. I'm sorry if I hurt your feelings, *Addy*."

"Stop calling me that." I steel my voice, narrowing my eyes.

His attention falls to my makeup bag clutched in my hand. "You look pretty in pink." His gaze roams over my body.

Maybe there's truth to what Ember is saying. Maybe Grant does like me. He hasn't stopped teasing me since we were five years old.

I swallow. "Thank you."

"Yeah. Whatever. Don't take it to heart. I was only being nice because no one really likes you except for Ember." He quickly glances over my shoulder.

I turn, following what or who has grabbed his attention, only to see Micah is walking toward us. The woman he was with is no longer beside him. Neither is my brother.

I snap my head back to Grant. Water splashes on my feet from swimmers in the pool. I didn't realize how close to the edge we are.

"I don't get it," Grant says, curling his lip as his eyes dance across my face. "Who wears makeup to the pool, anyway?"

"I like it." I grip my makeup bag even tighter. My nails cut into the sharp-edged sequins.

"Yeah," he scoffs, his eyes falling to my mouth. "We all know the real reason you put it on."

"Everything okay, Addy?"

My heart beats erratically at the sound of his voice. I immediately feel his tall frame fill the space around me, and I look up to find Micah standing next to me, trading glances between me and Grant.

I want to ask him how his summer has been and how he's

been since he lost his father a few weeks ago. I didn't make it to the funeral because my father didn't want me to be seen with the family. He and Mom left me at home with my father's secretary. When Archer told me he wished I was there but understood when our father told him I was away at summer camp, I didn't bother correcting him. When I asked how it went, Archer told me it was a bunch of rich, old people gathered around to celebrate a man who didn't deserve it, so I didn't miss anything by not going.

He was wrong, though. I missed seeing Micah and being there for him, even if I am his best friend's annoying little sister.

My cheeks flush with heat when my eyes fall to Micah's cheek and I remember how a woman's finger grazed it only minutes ago. I tighten my grip on my bag for different reasons than my reaction to Grant.

I look into Micah's blue-gray eyes. "I'm fine." I give Grant a side glance, then turn in the other direction. "I was just on my way to the bathroom."

"What?" Grant jerks his head back. "So, it's okay for him to call you Addy but not me?"

I roll my eyes, wanting to get away from Grant and my embarrassment. I cross my arms over my chest. "Micah is my brother's best friend. He's been calling me Addy for years. You and I aren't friends."

"You're right." He quickly flicks his gaze to Micah before looking back at me, his eyes flashing with anger. "We aren't."

"Are you sure there isn't a problem?" Micah asks, his brow furrowing deeper.

"Yes, Micah. I'm fine." I hate that I sound annoyed, but I can't help it. Grant has gotten under my skin.

Micah gives me a nod before taking a step back, away from Grant and me.

I spin on my heel and take a step in the opposite direction. I briefly glance up to see if Ember saw my interaction with Grant and Micah, half expecting her eyes to be glued to the drama, but she's no longer laying back in her chair. Now, she's leaning against the lifeguard stand, looking up at Teddy, *flirting* with him. She whips her hair and gives him a grin that stretches up to her eyes, and it reminds me of the woman Micah was talking to earlier.

Embarrassment fills my chest like a balloon ready to pop. I hold my breath as tears sting the backs of my eyes. I hate that Micah just overheard Grant talking to me the way he did. And that Micah tried bailing me out. I know I'm only eleven, but somehow, I feel more aware of my age around Micah.

He's protective of me, in a big brother sort of way.

I hear footsteps behind me as I make my way to the opposite end of the pool. Swimmers and waitstaff pass by me along the edge of the pool. My feet grow closer to the edge the more I try to avoid bumping into them. I look down and unzip my bag when I feel a finger tap my shoulder.

"Hey, Addy."

I'm already spinning around before reality sets in.

Grant. Again.

"What do you want?" I ask him, tired of his teasing. "I told you to leave me alone."

"The pool is meant for swimming, *Addy*," he mocks, the corner of his mouth curling into another evil grin. "Don't you think it's about time you actually swim?"

Then his hands are on my shoulders.

A gasp catches in my throat when I'm pushed back into the pool. My sandals scrape across the concrete before my feet slide out of them and into the water. My scream is muffled the second my head goes under.

Water rushes in my ears. The sound of the people outside

and the swimmers surrounding me are silenced while I sink to the bottom.

The dying grip I once had on my makeup bag loosens, allowing it to float to the surface. Instinct tells me to immediately kick back to the surface. My lungs burn from the air caught in my throat, shocked from Grant's shove. I open my eyes and allow the water to burn, mixing with the tears I already know I'm shedding.

Is it possible to die from embarrassment? How did this day suddenly turn into a nightmare?

I stay under the water as long as my body allows.

The world is quiet and still down here. I'm completely alone. I imagine the grin of satisfaction on Grant's face. I imagine Micah wrapping his arms around the woman at the bar. I imagine Ember flirting with Teddy, not caring that I haven't returned from the bathroom yet.

My chest squeezes, and my lungs burn as raw as my eyes.

I may only be eleven, but it feels as if all my dreams have been shattered in this moment. I don't want to face the world. I wish I could hide from this one and emerge in my own. One where I'm in control. One where I'm a successful model, living far away from all the elites who feel superior.

People surround me in the pool. Their headless bodies kick and swim around me, but I'm completely alone. Dark spots fill my vision, and my head feels light. I feel weightless and free under here.

Bubbles escape my mouth while my lungs attempt to hold onto the only bit of oxygen left in them. I point my toes and prepare to kick to the surface when two arms wrap around my waist from behind. I'm suddenly pulled and dragged to the surface, and I let my arms fall to the side, surrendering myself to the world above. A sob escapes me one last time before I'm suddenly gasping for air once I break the surface.

After swimming away from the person who pulled me up, I blink and spit water out as I swim to the edge, then I pull myself out of the pool and hang my head low. I crawl on my hands and knees, coughing and gasping for air. My lungs and chest are still burning, and when I gather the strength, I finally look up, fully expecting to see Teddy beside me... but it isn't him.

It's Micah.

His soaking wet hair sticks to his forehead, and his blue suit clings to his arms. Somehow, the water has made his blue-gray eyes shine brighter than I remember. Or it could be that this is the closest he's ever been to me. His hand gently rests on my bare back and suddenly, I'm fully aware of it. It's as if a million sirens are going off as a million arrows are pointed to his hand on my back.

His hand. On my back.

"Are you okay?" he asks.

But I can't speak. The words get caught on a cough. I simply nod, squeezing my eyes shut as I keep looking at the ground.

"Okay," he says. When I don't say anything, the tone in his voice changes. "Then, what the hell were you thinking, Addy?"

I look up sharply. Anger flashes across his too gorgeous face. Despite my entire body burning, my heart still beats erratically at the sight of him.

He's too old for you, Adeline. Obviously. You can't like him.

"What?" I rasp. My throat burns. "What do you mean?"

His hand falls away from my back, and he moves to sit beside me. Micah bends his legs and rests his elbows on his knees, hanging his head low as the muscles on his back move dramatically. He's still working to catch a breath of his own.

"I heard you scream, and when I turned around you slipped into the pool. I was expecting you to come back to the surface. When you didn't, I went in after you. I thought you were drowning." He wipes his hand across his forehead, pushing his wet hair back, then turns to look me in the eye. "You know how to swim, Addy. What the fuck?"

I narrow my eyes, anger building inside me. I've never heard him talk to me this way.

First, Grant. Now, Micah.

Tears slip from my eyes, but I wonder if they're even visible, considering I'm already wet. This isn't how I expected my first conversation of the summer with Micah to go. My heart broke for his, and when I look into his eyes, I search for the sadness—sadness and loss for losing his father—hoping I'll catch a glimpse of what it looks like to love your father enough to be fractured by their loss.

Instead, all I see is fury and anger in his eyes, and my heart breaks again.

"You're a jerk." My chin wobbles as tears flow down my wet cheeks.

"Right." He scoffs, pushing his soaking wet hair off his forehead. "I jump in the pool to save you, yet I'm the jerk."

"You are." I stand, curling my hands into tight fists.

Micah stands, too, placing his hands on his hips.

I look down at my bikini, making sure it's still intact. Thankfully, it didn't come loose or shift when Grant pushed me in, so I tuck my wet hair behind my ear and cross my arms over my chest, every emotion flooding to the surface. Somehow, I bite back the tears stinging my eyes.

"Maybe you should pay more attention where you're walking when you're around the pool," Micah scolds, narrowing his eyes.

"I was pushed in," I force between gritted teeth.

"What?" He takes a step forward, his eyes softening. "You were pushed in? I didn't see." His eyebrows dip in concern. "Addy, I swear, I thought..."

I look over his shoulder as Archer and the girl he was with

earlier move to stand behind Micah. The woman Micah was with earlier is only one step behind. All three of them look at me, with Archer's eyes bouncing between Micah and me.

"What the hell happened?"

I don't answer my brother. My entire body is on fire with embarrassment. I want to hide. I want to run far away from eyes who look at me like I'm someone to be doted on. I want to escape eyes that look at me with pity. Like I'm some little girl who's just had her heart broken. Which I am, and I have.

I look Micah in his blue-gray eyes, and my heart aches for someone who can never be mine. Will never be mine. It's a foolish dream for a foolish girl like me.

"Thank you for pulling me out." I harden my gaze and curl my fingers into fists. "But I don't need you to save me. I don't need anyone to save me."

I turn on my bare heel and leave the country club as fast as my feet will carry me. If this is how the rest of the summer is going to go, seventh grade can't come fast enough.

TWO

ADELINE

Ten Years Later

"Ms. Mayfield? Are you in here?"

I snap my head up to the door with wide eyes. My heart is still pounding, the echoing sound vibrating up to my ears. I clear my throat, willing the words to make their way out of my mouth. "Be right out."

Looking down at my shaking hands, I frantically rub the blood from my fingers. It's no use as most of it has already dried. With unsteady hands, I reach behind my neck and unclasp the diamond necklace wrapped around it. The chain pools in my palm before I drop it into the toilet. It sinks quickly to the bottom, and I shut the lid before pulling on the lever and flushing it without another thought. The bit of wet blood remaining on my fingers smears across the silver handle. My chest squeezes when I tear off a fistful of toilet paper and frantically scrub the handle until the blood disappears.

"Ms. Mayfield?" my assistant Ruby repeats, her voice muffled by the bathroom door.

"One sec!" I croak a little louder while moving to the sink.

I rinse my fingers, watching the remaining bit of dried blood under my fingernails. I dab at my nose and sniff. The pain radiates along the side of my face and nose, reaching behind my eye.

Taking a deep breath, I steel my chest and look up. The bruises aren't showing yet, but they're beginning to bloom, nonetheless. A bright red mark covers my entire cheek. I scrunch a piece of paper towel and dab at the little bit of blood still dripping from my nose, then reach into my small makeup bag still sitting on the edge of the sink.

After squeezing out a large glob of foundation, I smear it across my face, careful not to press too hard against tender skin. I grit my teeth through the pain, spreading out the foundation as fast as I can. My hands are shaking uncontrollably, as if I've injected coffee directly into my veins. I'm running on pure adrenaline.

"Ms. Mayfield," Ruby says again. She pounds on the door. "Please, let me in."

Heat spreads across my body. After applying the liquid foundation, I sloppily dab my brush into my setting powder, hoping it'll mask the splotches of color on my face.

"I'm..." I swallow back the tears that sting the back of my eyes. "I'm almost done."

My words come out choppy and unbalanced. I'm almost finished applying the powder when Ruby turns the handle on the door and pushes her way into my trailer bathroom.

I take two steps to the side to let her in, but I keep my head down, not wanting her to see me just yet. My long, brown waves create a curtain that shield me from her.

"I told you." I drop the brush in my bag and pretend to be looking for another makeup tool. "I'm almost finished."

"Adeline." Her voice is soft, but fear creeps in.

I can't look up at her, because when I do, it will make this moment real. It will solidify the fact that my boyfriend just barged into my trailer, falsely accused me of having an affair, simply because he caught me talking to one of the photographers from the production crew. Then before I could comprehend what was happening, his hand connected with my face. The snap and crack of the force behind his hand meeting my face ripples through my body once more, the memory refusing to leave.

I fell to the floor to him hovering over me, spewing threats about how he has the power to ruin my career if he were to ever catch me again. I stayed curled on the floor until I heard the metal door of my trailer slam shut, and the silence that ensued sucked all the air out of the room.

"Adeline," Ruby repeats from behind the door.

"Seriously, Ruby," I warn her. "I'm fine."

"Are you sure?"

Zipping up my makeup bag, I keep my focus on what I'm doing. Ruby is standing in the doorway of the tiny bathroom, and I need to reach my overnight bag in the common area of my trailer.

"Yes," I say while I blink back the tears. "I just... I need to go."

Simple and direct. It's the truth. I don't know what I plan on doing or where I'm going. I just know I need to keep moving.

"What?" She gasps. "Why? You have a photoshoot in two hours. Hair and makeup are waiting for you. You can't leave." I hear the panic in her voice, but I still don't look up. I shield the side of my face from her as I push past, clutching onto my makeup bag. I know if I look at her, I'm going to fall apart. I'm going to allow reality to set in, and I won't let it. At least not now. This isn't the first time Maddox has hit me. The first time was last week, the day after he proposed to me.

I thought when he'd pushed me against the wall after an argument over where we were going to eat for dinner was going to be the one and only time. Apparently not.

Maddox has been my manager for a year, and my boyfriend all for a total of one month. For months, he spent his time convincing me to give him a chance. He wooed me. Our days were filled with endless flirting and him showering me with gifts —the diamond necklace being the latest in celebrating our one-month anniversary.

But it was all a ruse.

A ploy to control me.

I feel foolish. Duped. Conned. Embarrassed. And I can't imagine what our lives will look like if we continue down the path we're taking. How worse will he get? Will he turn out just like my father? I've lived through a life of abuse, and I refuse to stick around with Maddox to find out how the rest goes.

"Because..." I choke out, answering Ruby, swallowing the lump of regret threatening to claw its way out of me. "I just can't do this anymore. At least not now."

Once I'm past her and step into the tiny hallway, I make a sharp left and eye my bag sitting where I left it. Well, sort of. Now, the contents are spilled out, all the way from the table to the floor. Underwear, shirts, and pants are strewn about haphazardly. I blink away the vision of him hurling my bag at the wall before he charged toward me.

My teeth cut into my cheek until it stings. The sensation propels me to keep going. Shame slams into my gut for allowing my relationship with Maddox to get to this point.

"If you need to cancel this interview, I can reschedule with the crew," Ruby blurts out, and I hear the fear in her voice. "I can find Maddox and—"

"No!" The word falls from my mouth as sharp and fast as a bullet. I spin around to face her with my hands curled into tight fists at my sides. "Do not find Maddox."

My sharp response is followed by an equally sharp gasp

coming from Ruby's lips. Her soft brown eyes immediately widen, and my stomach flips.

She brings her hand to her mouth before she reaches out to me. I shy away from her, not wanting to venture down this road. The one where she feels sympathy for me as if I'm some weak, broken woman.

I lift my hand and cover my cheek, as if it'll take us back to ten seconds ago before she saw what Maddox has done to me.

"Adeline..." She frowns. "What happened?"

"Nothing. I—" I gently press my palm against my skin, then resume cleaning up my clothes, fisting each item and shoving them into my bag. "I don't know."

I truly don't know. Flashes of the words Maddox spewed in my direction play in my mind. Every word and every touch he threw in my direction is like a pile of mixed puzzle pieces. None of the pieces fit, and I'm too distraught to try to put them together and make sense of it. All I feel in my gut is the need to get out of here, far away from Maddox, this trailer, and my life in Los Angeles. This isn't me. This isn't the life I wanted for myself. I'm better than this. At least I want to believe I am.

My dream to be a model and get out of my parents' house has been a goal for as long as I can remember. But now, my modeling career is crumbling in front of me. How can I possibly stay here after what he's done? How can I continue this career with him still in it, representing me?

Karma has come for me. I've always been in a rush to get on with my dream, never thinking about the price I might have to pay to get it. I've wanted to become a model since I was four years old. My first memory is sneaking into my mother's closet and digging through her vanity. I found her favorite, crimson red lipstick, and sloppily swiped it across my mouth. I was smoothing it across my tiny lips for the hundredth time when she walked in, catching me red-handed.

From then on, she was convinced I'd never let up on my dream to be just like her. Professionally, at least. If it weren't for my mother's insistence on waiting until I was eighteen, I would have done everything I could to make it happen before then.

I'm silently cursing myself for allowing myself to get to this point, where my career is literally dissolving in front of me. I allowed myself to fall for my manager and his sweet words. Now, this relationship is costing me everything: my career, my physical health, my emotional health, my reputation.

Once I have all my belongings shoved into my bag, I zip it shut and leave it on the table to gather the rest of my things from the bathroom. I wind the cord around the base of my curling iron and feel my assistant behind me. My chest vibrates, and I know my body is crashing from the adrenaline. For the past ten minutes, I've been running on autopilot, not allowing my situation to sink in. I'm in fight or flight mode, quietly deciding to fly.

I feel Ruby's eyes burning a hole on my back. With a shuddering breath, I finally gather the strength and courage to look up.

My eyes meet hers in the reflection as she moves to stand beside me. Her soft, beautiful face gives me comfort when inside, I feel broken.

Not broken for ending my relationship.

I'm broken at the fact I've allowed him to manipulate me and my career. I've lost out on this key photoshoot opportunity. Even if this one wasn't for a major publication, it was publicity. Publicity I desperately need. I've been a model since the day I turned eighteen. It's been three years since my first magazine featured photoshoot, but every day has been a struggle to be seen. Days turned into weeks spent jumping from one job interview to the next. I didn't want to ride on the trail my mother left behind or rely on my name to push me through my career. I wanted my talent to propel me, but it's impossible when you fall for someone whose sole mission is to hold you back.

I thought what Maddox held for me was love, but this isn't love. It never has been.

Resting the heels of my hands on the edge of the sink, I hang my head low. Tears sting the back of my eyes. The warm liquid spills over my lashes and warms my already-heated cheeks. I inhale a shaky breath, my sobs working their way up my throat. Ruby places her hand on my back, and her touch radiates across my body, and the floodgates burst open.

"He wasn't always this way." My chin quivers and my stomach flips. "Only... there was this change in him, like the flip of a switch. It was so fast and so sudden. I didn't see. I didn't know it would—" I can't finish. My words linger in the air, dissolving through the thick oxygen filling this tiny bathroom.

"It's okay, Adeline," she soothes as she runs her hand gently down my back.

I finally turn my head and look up at her. "Promise me you won't tell anyone," I whisper.

"Adeline." Her soft voice wraps around me like a blanket.

"I don't want this to become a headline," I say in a rush, twisting my fingers. "I don't want to read some distorted version of the truth." I inhale a shaky breath. "I just want to go. Quietly."

I look back down and stare at the sink and the single drop of blood still resting in the drain.

When did I become this person? When did I become the model who fell for her abusive manager? Being with him is costing me everything.

Every dream I've ever had has disappeared.

At some point during my sobs, with Ruby's hand on my back, something in my mind clicks. Reality crashes into my thoughts with unrelenting force. I'm not this person, and I won't allow this to become my life.

I can't explain it, but this place doesn't feel like home. I always believed I wanted to leave my life back in Boston. I wanted to run away as far and as fast as I could. The shadows and recessed corners of the place I used to call home were hanging over me like a dark cloud. My heart was begging to see more of the world, but now that I'm here, on the opposite side of the country, I've never felt more isolated and alone. I don't recognize the woman I've become.

A comforting warmth spreads across my chest at the thought of returning to the East Coast. An inexplicable pull tugs at my chest, like an echo vibrating through my bones.

"You're coming back, though, right?" Ruby asks, her copper eyebrows knitting together. "I can black out your calendar for a while, but eventually..." Her voice trails off, then her eyes find mine. "You have a photoshoot scheduled in two weeks. You'll still make it then, right?"

"I, um..." I inhale a deep breath and inflate my lungs until they burn before I release it. "I can't answer that right now."

"Oh, honey." She places her fingertips gently to my cheek, but I hiss and jerk back. Her mouth twitches with pity and sadness, and the hole in my heart grows wider. Ruby has been a great assistant and friend these past three years. I hate that I'm leaving her this way, but there's an understanding in her eyes that reassures me.

"I understand." She nods.

"Thank you. I'll keep you updated." I nod, patting my cheek to dry the tears soaking into the makeup I put on only minutes earlier. I'm thankful she doesn't hold my lack of commitment against me. I hate not giving her a concrete answer, and the uncertainty of not showing up for future photoshoots scares me.

The fear of letting go of what I hold dear to me weaves into my broken heart.

I move past Ruby again and stuff my makeup bag and curling iron into my duffel.

Closing my eyes means I only see a road with no direction, no ending. But the thought of coming back to work and facing Maddox makes my stomach coil. It aches like a spring resting at the very bottom and twisting into knots, the sharp edges cutting into my flesh like barbed wire. The uncertainty of the future is scary, but the promise of returning to this life, the version I'm living in now, is even more terrifying.

I steel myself. Invisible armor wraps around my heart, giving me the strength to keep moving. It's what I've always done.

Slinging my bag over my shoulder, I push through my trailer door for the last time and call one of the only people I've been able to rely on.

THREE

Micah

The pubs lining the small streets of London can often be mistaken for Boston's. If I'm drunk enough, I'll forget which country I'm in. At least until the bartender or stranger sitting at the end of the bar yells across the room, their distinct accents reminding me of where I really am.

Despite me being born in America to American parents, sometimes I feel like I was born in the wrong country. Fuck, sometimes I think I was born into the wrong family. The motto 'the grass is always fucking greener' is constantly playing in my mind, everywhere I go, because no matter where I am, I'm always questioning if I should have been born into another family.

Maybe it's because I've never fully belonged. My older brothers are mine but not fully. Half their blood has always been loyal to their mother. I have vague memories of her when I was younger. She was kind and treated me as her own during the times I was away from my own mother.

While I had my own loving mother, she always treated me as the outcast. Her treatment by the Harding line bled into me and how I was treated by anyone sharing my last name.

No one wants to be loved out of obligation, but that's how my father's love for me operated. That's how *he* operated.

He's been dead for ten years now, rotting as a corpse in the cold, damp ground where he belongs. But sometimes, when I look in the mirror, I see his piercing eyes staring back at me, and the older I've become, the more I swear I look like him.

I fucking hate it.

My phone vibrates in my front pocket, intensifying the hard on pressing against the zipper of my dark blue suit. This wasn't the plan, but sometimes my dick decides to go rogue, abandoning all reason.

"I want you to taste me. Right here." The woman in front of me falls against the crusty, faded wall of the dirty stall we're standing in. Her voice is flat, and every few words, I swear I hear a distinct Boston accent, reminding me I'm not thousands of miles away from the home I dread coming back to every week.

The woman spreads her legs and slides her hand down the length of her stomach, then lifts her skirt, displaying her bare pussy to me. Her breasts are shoved together by the tight, black corset wrapped around her frame, the tops of them spilling over. My eyes follow her arm down to the hand she has pressed against herself. She parts her folds with her fingers, telling me exactly where she wants me to taste her. She massages her clit as she bends her left leg, hitching it up to rest her foot on the roll of torn toilet paper. Her foot slips, and she stumbles forward, gripping onto my waist to keep herself from falling face first onto the sticky, beige, tile floor. Her long fingers grip onto the lapels of my suit, crinkling the smooth fabric. Righting herself, she giggles as she straightens her back, lazily wiping flyaway strands of her curly hair away from her face.

She giggles again, hiccupping as she falls back against the wall. It's comical to see her in front of me. She's a stranger, pawing and clawing at another stranger. I wish I was more into this than I am.

My dick twitches, with another vibration rippling from my pocket.

"I'm really drunk." She covers her mouth, unable to contain her laughter.

"I gathered as much." I sigh. "Do you normally drink on the job?"

"Not always." She giggles—again—and tosses her head dramatically from side to side. "Usually, I can get away with it, though. Especially on nights that are slow. You walked in at the right time. I was beginning to get bored." She leans forward, half closing her eyes. Her mouth comes close to mine, but I stop her before she gets too close.

"Do you think because you own this bar, it means you can drink on the job whenever you want?"

"Maybe." She shrugs on another hiccup. "My boyfriend is never here and doesn't care that I drink with the other customers. And while I might not officially own this bar, you could say I do." She leans forward again.

I fall back against the door of the stall as she lifts her face to mine, biting down on my lip. She winds my tie around her small hand, keeping us only inches apart. I brace myself against the dirty walls of the bathroom stall, and she looks up at me with drunken eyes that are swimming with heat.

After swiping her tongue across her lips, a heavy breath and deep moan passes her mouth as she slides her other hand down the front of my pants. Instinctively, I grunt when she wraps her thin fingers around my hardened length over the fabric of my suit.

"What do you mean you don't officially own this bar?" I ask, closing my eyes and clearing my throat, telling myself to focus on the task at hand. I can't allow myself to get distracted. Not yet.

Business first.

Pleasure second.

I'm here for work, but it doesn't hurt to have a distraction. Anything to get my mind off how fucked my life has become.

"Technically, my boyfriend owns it, but I pay the rent." She winds her hand tighter around my tie. Her voice is heavy and weighted, and the sour scent of whiskey blows across my face.

I roll my eyes, irritation bubbling under my skin. It seems the business side of the encounter with the bartender of this pub is quickly fading. She isn't the one I'm supposed to be talking with.

"You told me you owned this place when I walked in."

She flexes her hand around my tie, tugging me impossibly closer, and I hold my breath, wondering how I'm going to get out of this situation. I shouldn't have come in here with her like this, but my head, heart, and dick are in a persistent battle. Three sides refusing to surrender easily.

"I didn't lie." She giggles with a glint in her eye. "Like I said, technically, I do own it."

"But you don't," I say, my eyes bouncing across her face. I press my fingertips into the dirty plastic walls. The incessant vibration from my phone has finally stopped, but my dick is relentless. It wants to be inside something. Anything to make me forget the horrible, wretched human being I've become.

"Are you disappointed?" She pouts. "Does that change things?"

She tries to pull me closer, but something in my brain has flipped. My stomach sours. Suddenly, the memories I work to bury in the dark recesses of my brain have come out to play. They taunt me, refusing to retract the claws they've sunk in deep.

"Come on," the woman begs. "Don't get soft on me now. My boyfriend won't be back until later tonight. I'm a quick fuck." She slips her hand under the waist of my pants, cups my length, and starts rubbing.

"Stop," I grunt, pulling her hand out from my pants. "I didn't come here for you. I came for your boyfriend."

She cocks an eyebrow, crossing her arms over her chest with an exaggerated huff. "Then, why are you in here with me?"

"That's not what I meant." I sigh and dig into the front inside pocket of my suit jacket to pull out my business card. I pinch it between two fingers before handing it to her. Her dark eyebrows knit, eyeing me curiously as she snatches it from me and holds it annoyingly close, as if she can't read it unless it's three inches from her face.

She snaps her head up, wide-eyed as she sucks in a sharp breath, realization dawning on her.

"You're a Harding," she whispers shakily.

Her face has paled. The loose, curly strands framing her face cling to her damp cheeks. I'm not as intoxicated as her, but suddenly, I'm aware of the alcohol we shared before deciding to come into the bathroom. The dingy walls close in around us, and the air is tight.

"I am." Like the prick I am, I hold out my hand in some sort of mock greeting, as if she wasn't just attempting to stick her tongue down my throat or fondling my dick a few minutes ago. "Micah Harding."

She doesn't take my hand. Instead, she lifts her worried, pleading gaze. Her face has softened.

"I know who you are and what you being here means. I promise, I pay the rent," she squeaks between her pale lips, as if her explanation will make a difference. "I give my boyfriend money every week so he can make the payments. The pub's been struggling, but we have plans to fix it. That's why he's not here tonight. He's talking with a strip club owner here in the city to see if he's willing to invest."

I lean forward, bringing my face close to hers to look into her eyes, keeping my hands pressed to the walls. My tie is now unraveled from her hand, no longer binding her to me.

"Your boyfriend may be going to the strip club to network, but if he isn't using your money to pay the rent for this shithole, then I doubt his networking is strictly business related."

Her chin dips to her chest as she swallows, placing her hand on her stomach. I can't tell if it's the alcohol making her nauseous or that my speculation has made her put two and two together. Her brown eyes flicker back and forth as she keeps her head down. My business card slips from her hand, landing on the floor beside the mildew coated toilet.

Call it being numb.

Call it unfeeling.

But business is business.

I've come to terms with this being part of my job. Hardings have always been known for their ruthless business tactics. Ever since our father died ten years ago, and my older brother Lennon took over the company, the sharp bitterness that once haunted our family is gone, but we still have a reputation. A reputation for buying companies a second before they're seized by the bank or the city. It doesn't matter who is at the top or the face of the company, the nature of the beast never changes. To the city, this is an ugly business.

For a moment, I dig deep, scrounging up even the slightest bit of pity or remorse.

The woman standing in front of me doesn't know her boyfriend hasn't made a single payment for this shithole in months, or that he's been stealing her money, most likely to pay for strippers at the club he's been going to every week. Or that he's keeping a secret he doesn't care will cost him his business or relationship.

Even if I weren't numb to the emotions that go with this job, the sympathy I'd have for this woman wouldn't go very far. She was willing to cheat on her boyfriend before she found out who I was.

"Harding Holdings has bought your boyfriend's business out," I say, matter of fact. My words linger in the tight, damp air. "I'm simply here to deliver the message out of courtesy."

"Courtesy?" she practically spits with anger, but her face is still pale. "You call this courtesy?"

"Yes. You should consider you and your boyfriend lucky this place didn't go straight to the bank. They wouldn't have been as kind and considerate."

She laughs, lifting her chin and squeezing her eyes shut, a loud cackle escaping her throat before she slowly narrows her eyes on me. Leaning forward, her hooded eyes stare straight into mine. "You call this being kind and considerate?"

"Don't take it personal. It's just business."

Our connection to the major banks lends Harding Holdings the privilege of knowing what businesses are set to go into fore-closure, giving us the opportunity to buy them before the bank seizes them. We pay a slight premium for snagging them early, but with our wealth and success, it's a small price to pay.

"If you were strictly here for business, you wouldn't have come in here with me. Why did you?" she asks.

I give her a blank stare, suddenly aware of my breathing. The claws inside my mind sink deeper, refusing to retract. Flipping this woman's world upside down may have been business, but following her into a dirty stall and hoping for a quick fuck isn't, but the reasoning behind my decision is something I refuse to acknowledge.

Declining to answer her question, I bend down and pick up

the business card I'd given her and hold it between us, the gold lettering glimmering under the dim yellow hue of the light above us.

"My boyfriend's apartment is upstairs. He'll be homeless if he loses this place. But if I had your job, I guess I would have to tell myself the same things you do just to be able to look in the mirror without hating myself."

Heat simmers under my skin, bubbling and boiling over. Darkness clouds my vision. Suddenly, it's as if thick, gray clouds have surrounded me, drowning me in their darkness. I clear my throat, unwilling to let it take hold, once again.

Memories and images of the man I used to be flash through my mind. Time is a construct I haven't been able to understand. The life I once had seems so far away, yet there are parts of me left dormant, like a pile of ash at the bottom of a fire, the slightest bit of smoke drifting from it. But the smoke isn't enough to relight the fire. It exists only to remind me of what once was. Of what's lost.

I stare at the woman in front of me. The way my father taught me.

"You might want to tell your boyfriend it's in his best interest to call me before he shows up for work one day and finds himself without a place to go, aside from that strip club he seems to love so much."

She doesn't take the card. Instead, her hand flies to her mouth. I didn't notice before, but her skin has turned from ghost white to a pale green, clammy, glistening in the faded light. The echoing thud of the classical rock song playing from the bar fills the stall we're standing in.

A grumble climbs up her throat, then she shifts on her feet and lurches forward. Panicked, I reach behind me, fumbling to find the handle to the stall. My back is pressed against the door, leaving no room for me to move. I press myself against the door as much as humanly possible and turn my head to the side. I can't find the lock. Unsure of what to expect, my heart pounds, knowing I'm stuck. I peek to the side just as her eyes widen and her hand flies away from her mouth.

Vomit streams from her open mouth as she bends over. A mixture of dark yellow, brown liquid and red chunks cover my brown suede shoes. Wrapping her arm around her stomach, she hurls again, the sound causing my stomach to wobble.

I hold my breath, listening to her throw up the three vodka sodas and five shots of whiskey I watched her down an hour ago. Her sickness comes in waves, the thick liquid splashing onto my ten thousand-dollar pants before she suddenly stops. Her body heaves, and for a few moments, she remains looking at the floor, with her hands pressed to her knees and her hair curtaining her face as she catches her breath and regains her bearings.

She spits the remnants of the vomit dripping from her mouth before she finally looks up at me with a dazed expression. Color has returned to her cheeks. Her eyes are crystal clear and more sober than the entire time we've been in here, as if she's suddenly no longer drunk.

I scrunch my nose, the sour scent of her bile filling my nostrils. I don't miss my business card back on the floor, sitting beside my feet, now coated in vomit.

Sloppily wiping the back of her hand across her mouth, she takes a step back with a sneer, trading glances between my face and my now vomit-covered shoes.

"Something tells me it won't be difficult for you to replace those." She points to my feet then turns her anger on me. "Now, get the fuck out of my way so I can get back to work."

I shift to the side and raise my hands in surrender, giving her enough room to reach the handle of the stall door. She squeezes through the small opening, while I stand still, listening to the door to the bathroom swinging open. The thumping music grows louder before it quiets again.

I place both of my hands on my face and breathe out. Pushing my hair back in disbelief, I look down at my feet.

"Fuck," I breathe out. This must be the messiest confrontation I've had. My role in this business has always been to deliver the bad news, but it's never landed me in a dirty bathroom stall, covered in vomit.

I pull my phone out of my pocket and type a quick text to Lennon, telling him the job is done. Afterward, I check and see that I have three missed calls and a text from my best friend Archer.

Archer: I need a favor.

Of course, he does.

I stare at those four words, the claws in my mind expanding again. They still have their grip on me, not willing to concede or let up.

My mouth waters for a drink, and my brain begs for the promise of being numb. Leaving the stall, I straighten my tie and tear off a fistful of paper towels to clean off the extra vomit covering the toes of my shoes. Frustration festers. I toss the paper into the trash bin and move to the sink to wash my hands, but the sharp glint of the damaged mirror hanging above the sink catches my eye. It's barely clinging to the wall, hanging cockeyed by the top left corner. The corners are faded and out of focus.

The claws latch on, sending a searing pain through my mind, down to the muscle still beating in my chest.

I stare at my reflection with hate-filled eyes, wondering if I will ever be able to look at myself in the same way I used to, before my life became unrecognizable. When I wasn't increasingly becoming the one person I never wanted to become. To a time when I didn't look at myself with resentment.

My reflection stares back at me, and it's all it takes.

I lift my fist in the air and drive it into the mirror. Sharp pain immediately meets my knuckles. The glass fractures and splinters out like a web, my fist at the center of it. Blood clings to the mirror as I lower my hand and ignore the pain shooting across it as I grind my teeth. The pressure builds in my temples, and it feels as if my brain might explode. Spreading my fingers, I hold my hand in the air and study the cuts. A line of blood spills down the ridges of my knuckles and over the peaks of my hardened veins. I don't feel the sharp pain from the cuts. My skin is numb to the damage I've inflicted.

I'm wondering what other parts of me have become numb, but those thoughts don't stay around for long.

They leave me the second I leave the dingy bathroom and shattered mirror behind.

FOUR

ADELINE

Frigid, cold air bites my skin as soon as I step out of the car. Despite the cold, the familiar sea salt taste hits my tongue when I open my mouth and breathe out. A cloud spills from my mouth, leaving a trail as I whip my head to the side and watch the taillights of my ride disappear around the corner and out of the neighborhood.

I swallow the lump in my throat and wrap my arms around myself. I'm glad I decided to wear a sweater. Aside from the one I had buried in the bottom of my bag I don't have a single piece of clothing to prepare me for surviving winter in New England. It may be nearing the end of March, but the start of spring doesn't hit for another month. Boston is still in the throes of winter.

A crisp breeze rolls in, causing the bare trees to sway. Their branches bend and creak, singing a song to anyone willing to take the time to listen. The air washes over me as if it were welcoming me back with open arms. My chest squeezes. I don't want or need its welcome. It's a simple reminder of what I was escaping when I left.

Over the past three years, I've kept my distance from home

and immersed myself in Los Angeles, putting as much distance between my family and me. It was an easy decision... but coming back here wasn't.

Tears sting the back of my eyes when I realize the scenery and community may have changed, but one fact remains: I never escaped the abuse. Only this time, the abuse came from my boyfriend instead of my father.

I've been hurt at the hands of two men who were supposed to love me... so they claimed.

I ghost my fingers along my cheek, thankful the pain is now gone. It could be the pills I swallowed on the flight over finally kicking it, or the injury inflicted by Maddox isn't as bad as I first thought. I haven't looked in a mirror since I was standing in my trailer, staring back at Ruby standing behind me with her look of pity. I have no idea if the bruising is still present. Years of covering myself with the right combination of creams and powders has allowed me to perfect the art of concealing any evidence.

A shiver ripples down the length of my arms, and I wrap one around myself, gripping onto my bicep as I look up and down the street. Aside from the wind and singing branches, it's quiet. Peaceful, even.

Large, brick houses covered in vines of ivy line the wide, cobblestone street, each one set far back off the road, their yards separated by tall, black, wrought-iron fences.

Although this neighborhood isn't the one I was raised in, it looks eerily similar. My stomach wobbles as I take in each picture window and each aged-brown brick. At first, I want to believe I'm imagining it. My eyes dance from house to house, hoping to pull some difference that will solidify my decision to go through with this. I fight the urge to leave and find some-where else to go. But I remember my brother's text. The one telling me this was the best, safest place for me to stay. No one would know I was here or bother to ask why. He told me I could stay here as long as I need to, no questions asked.

I didn't tell my brother my reason for running away.

Archer and I are somewhat close, considering we're twelve years apart, but we've never been close enough for him to ask questions that require him to dive into the details of my life. To him, I'm a happy-go-lucky twenty-one-year-old living out my dream. It's all he needs to know.

Part of me still harbors bitterness for him not standing up for me. I used to dream he'd show up and demand to take care of me the way he knew our father couldn't. He wasn't naïve to our father's abuse. But I guess the old saying rings true: ignorance is bliss.

Archer ran away and assumed the dynamic at home would change, but he never stuck around to check if it did. He never looked back.

I tried to do the same.

I rub my arm and take a step forward. My foot lands on the stone-paved driveway. This house isn't surrounded by a large, wrought-iron fence. Instead, the stone driveway winds up the front lawn, stretching all the way to the house resting at the top of the hill. From where I'm standing, I can't see the entire house. My feet slowly carry me closer to the large, brick exterior.

I tighten my grip on my duffle bag when the house comes into view.

It's massive.

A large balcony sits off to the side of the house, facing the garden in the side yard. Brown, dried-out flowers and leafless branches cover what look like they used to be rows of garden boxes, as if the plants dying inside them have been rotting there longer than I've been alive.

As with some of the other houses, rich green vines of ivy cling to the brick exterior, sprawling over some of the windows along the top floor. A paved-covered patio in different stone than the driveway lines the front of the house. Complete with two old wooden rocking chairs.

One is empty.

The other isn't.

I stop in my tracks at the sight of him.

I hold my breath, concentrating on keeping my chest moving.

I wasn't expecting to see him here; at least not today. Archer told me he would leave the key in the black mailbox beside the front door.

He's slumped in the chair, his tie loose around his neck, practically unraveled down to his stomach. With his long legs parted, his hands dangle between his thighs. The dark blue suit he's wearing stretches across his muscles. Dark hair peppers the sharp line of his jaw, and his bottom lip is parted slightly to allow tiny breaths to pass through. His brown hair is a disheveled mess, with pieces clumped together, proving it must have been styled with some product before.

His eyes are closed as if he's in a deep sleep.

"I know, I know," he mumbles. "The grass needs to be cut, but I'd rather you didn't walk in it."

Half of his face is shielded from view, and he doesn't move from his spot. If I didn't already recognize his voice, I'd wonder if it came from someone else other than him.

I rub my toe across the long blades of green grass. "Your garden on the side of the house is more of an eyesore than the length of the grass. Don't you think you should be more concerned with getting that cleaned up?"

He finally moves. Slowly.

One eye pops open, followed by the other. Shifting in his chair, it rocks as he repositions himself. Relaxing against the back, he peeks up at me.

His eyes are familiar. The same blue-gray eyes I used to dream about. He's the same man I remember, but he's different.

He's a far cry from the Micah I saw that day at the pool.

Years later, I remember laying in my bed at night, reading the headlines sprawled across social media.

MICAH HARDING, YOUNGEST SON OF BILLIONAIRE JAMES HARDING, SENTENCED TO TWO YEARS IN PRISON AFTER ARREST FOR DRUG POSSESSION AND DRUG TRAFFICKING.

"Addy." He sighs, pulling himself up by resting his elbows on the arms of the chair with a groan. "I didn't realize it was you."

"How would you?" I ask, shrugging, playing off the use of my childhood nickname. "Seems I caught you at a bad time. Do you normally sleep on your front porch?"

The corner of his mouth curves into a half grin. Three lines dip between his lip and his cheek. "No, this would be a first." He rests his head back against the wood and peers up at me with a narrowed gaze. "Just a late night."

"Oh." I nod, tucking my lip under my teeth, unsure what to say. The last time I spoke to Micah Harding, I was a broken-hearted, eleven-year-old girl, who was embarrassed and ashamed that Micah felt the need to save me when I didn't need saving.

Now, here he is again, offering me a place to stay. Saving me.

"I've just flown in from London." He rubs the heel of his hand over his eye. "Once I landed, I had something to do for work."

I frown. "I'm not sure how that led to you sleeping on your front porch, but you don't have to explain anything to me."

I step back when he quickly stands and sways on his feet, and I immediately smell stale alcohol. I scrunch my nose as he looks up at me.

"It's not me. Well, I drank a little too much, but it was the first time in a long time. Besides, the smell isn't from that." He points to his feet. "Hazards of the job."

The bottoms of his blue slacks are covered in visible stains, and the toes of his brown suede shoes are discolored. From what, I don't know. All I know is that it doesn't smell good, and it isn't any of my business.

"I believe you." I nod once, and swing my gaze to the house behind him. "Archer told me it was okay to stay here, but if it's not..." I hitch my thumb over my shoulder.

"No," he rushes to say. "You can stay here. I told him it was okay."

"Okay. Um, thanks." I awkwardly tug on the ends of my sleeves, digging my nails through the fabric into my skin.

It's strange seeing Micah this way. Talking to him this way. Last time I spoke to him, I was dripping wet in my perfectly pink bathing suit. The one I wore just for him.

He's changed now. Not only are there a few more lines in his forehead and the corners of his mouth, there's a pain in his eyes I don't remember being there. The gray has darkened, as if they're carrying the weight of ten years more experience.

"Here." He moves, running his hand over his hair again. "We'll go inside, and I'll show you the house."

"Is this yours?"

"Yeah," he says over his shoulder while digging his keys from his pocket. "I bought it a few years ago off this family who inherited it from their grandfather. He was in his nineties and lived here alone. The family had no interest in keeping it or fixing it up. That's why not much has been done to it."

"But you've owned it for several years?"

"Yes." He sticks the key into the lock, and my eyes fall to his hand. Dozens of cuts cover his knuckles. Dried blood lines each cut. I try to peek at his other hand to see if it could be swollen, but I'm unable to catch it before he's pushing the door open.

It's not until he steps inside do I realize I don't know Micah at all, outside of public knowledge. I know he's a billionaire, he's thirty-three, the youngest of three brothers, and he's my brother's best friend, as well as a recovered drug addict —all traits I could easily find if I were to do a simple online search.

Before that fateful summer I turned eleven, Micah had always been a part of our lives in some capacity, though I only ever saw him every now and then when Archer decided to bring him over to our house. After the summer he pulled me from the pool, I never saw or spoke to him again.

When I step inside the front entryway, and the door shuts behind me, I make another realization.

I've never been alone with Micah before.

The absence of sunlight pronounces his features. He's taller than me by nearly an entire foot, and aside from the putrid scent of alcohol covering his feet, he appears clean. Well, sort of.

I break my attention from Micah long enough to take in my new home. The inside looks nearly as neglected as the front. Marble tile stretches across the large space. Several doorways leading to different parts of the house cover all sides of the room. On the far side of the foyer is a long, wooden staircase—modest for this style of house, but quintessential New England, just the same.

I tilt my head to the ceiling, eyeing the glass chandelier hanging above. The brilliant stone glints and shimmers with the morning sun peeking through the heavy, gray, cloud-covered sky. The large picture window above the door allows a few streams of light to pour into the eerily quiet house. I lower my gaze and find myself staring back at my reflection. A gold, inlaid frame mirror hangs on the far wall.

I suck in a sharp breath, not wanting to look at myself too long. I snap my head away and dart my attention to Micah, who's standing in front of the staircase, watching me.

He nods his head. "The kitchen is down this hall and to the right." Placing his foot on the first step of the stairs, he points down another hallway. "There's a bathroom down there, and an office. I haven't had a chance to clean all the boxes and papers out of there yet, so you won't get much use out of that room."

I follow him up the stairs, each plank of wood creaking beneath our feet.

"There are four bedrooms up here, but three of them don't have drywall, and parts of the floor are missing."

"Sounds like this house needs a lot of work. Are you sure it's livable?"

"It's fine." He waves me off. "I know it isn't as put together as the house you grew up in, and I'm sure it isn't as glamorous as the places you're used to staying at as a model but—"

"Being a model has nothing to do with it, and neither does the house I grew up in," I cut in.

I hate that he assumes to know me when he hasn't talked to me since I was a little girl. He doesn't know the abuse I endured in the fancy house he claims I grew up in.

I clear my throat. "I just mean I'm perfectly capable of living here. A few boxes and broken floorboards don't scare me."

He stares at me until a small smile grows on the corner of his mouth. "Of course."

Spinning around, he heads down the long, wide hallway. My feet land against the matted blue and gold rug, stirring up an oddly comforting, warm scent. Like walking into a bookstore stocked with hundreds of old, aging books. I wrap my hands around my duffle bag and follow Micah into a bedroom. He scratches at his chin as he surveys it before turning back to face me, and watches me as I take in the room. I drag my finger across the dust coated dresser as I cross the room and sling my duffel over my head before dropping it onto the queen size bed pushed against the largest wall.

"Wait." I turn to face Micah. "If this is the only room that's livable, where are you sleeping?"

"Um." He drops his keys onto the dusty dresser I dragged my finger across. "I haven't stayed here yet. I travel quite a bit for work, so I haven't had a reason to stay here overnight."

"Not even when you're in town?"

"Nope." He shakes his head and blows out a heavy breath. "If I do, I just stay in a hotel or at either one of my brother's houses. Gives me the chance to spend time with my nieces and nephews."

"Hmm." I smile, planting my hands on my hips. "At thirty-three, I figured you would be a bit more settled, married with kids... that whole bit. Sounds as if not much has changed in ten years."

He delivers me another blank stare, the heavy pain returning to his blue-gray eyes. They cloud over, and my heart hammers in my chest, even though I can't pinpoint the reason. It could be nerves from today bubbling to the surface, or it could be that my comment has crossed a line into the personal zone. Our conversation up until now has been formal, as if he were a landlord showing his new tenant around.

Micah's dark eyebrows twitch, and his eyes roll away. He slips his hand into his pocket and crosses the room overlooking the front of the house. "A lot has changed in ten years, Addy."

I cross the room to join him and look out the window, noting the massive houses lining the street, bits of them visible through the bare trees.

"You're right—a lot has changed in ten years." I clear my

throat and swallow down the memories of being back in Boston, then turn my head and face Micah's that's only inches from mine. "No one calls me Addy anymore. Just call me Adeline."

I leave Micah and stand beside the bed to pick up an old alarm clock sitting on the nightstand. The time is off by over an hour, so I correct it before setting it back down.

"How much do I owe you for staying here?" I ask him.

He moves to stand at the foot of the bed. "You don't have to pay me." He leans forward and grips the footboard. "*Adeline.*"

His muscles strain under the sleeves of his suit. His noticeably deeper voice at the use of my full name has a chill prickling down the back of my neck.

I inhale a deep breath, forcing as much oxygen into my lungs as possible before blowing it out. "I can't stay here for free."

"Yes, you can. I don't need your money, and I don't want it."

"I know you don't need the money."

"I'm doing this as a favor for Archer. Really, I don't need you to pay rent. Especially when this place looks like it hasn't been touched since the revolution."

I can't deny that his admission of only letting me stay here as a favor to my brother stings. I try not to take it personally, but it's hard when I feel I've been reduced to the clothes on my back and the belongings I was able to shove into my duffel bag.

"I refuse to stay here without earning my place." I cross my arms over my chest.

"Fine." He digs into his back pocket and tugs his wallet free. Slipping a black metal card between his fingers, he holds it out for me. "Take this."

I give him a sarcastic laugh. "How is giving me money letting me earn my keep?"

"I need to get this place fixed up. I have no intention of keeping it."

"You don't?"

"No." He shakes the card at me, urging me to take it. "It's kind of what I do. I buy places with the intention of fixing them up, then sell them at peak market value."

"Oh." I frown, looking around the room. Sadness fills my chest unexpectedly. I can't explain it.

"You can earn your keep by buying whatever you want to fix this place up. Archer didn't tell me how long you plan on staying. I'm sure you have a life to get back to so if you can't finish, it's fine. Just do what you can whenever you have the time. I can take care of whatever is left."

I open my mouth, the words resting on the tip of my tongue, begging to spill. I want to tell him the truth, but shame fills my gut. Suddenly, the spot on my face where Maddox struck me last seems to swell. It feels as if it's flashing like a bright red beacon, even if the bruise may be gone.

I want to tell Micah I don't have a set date in mind to leave. I wouldn't know where to go even if I wanted to escape. I tried calling my best friend Ember, but she hasn't returned my call. I only tried her after I called Archer the second I stepped out of my trailer back in Los Angeles. With him living overseas and constantly working all over Europe, he didn't have a place for me to stay. After hanging up, he said he'd get back to me with a solution. When Ember didn't answer, he'd called me back telling me he'd found a place for me to go. A place with Micah.

With no other choice, I took him up on his offer. Archer didn't ask questions then, and neither has Micah now.

The confession rests on the tip of my tongue, but I force it back down. Voicing the truth only solidifies my reality. The truth is easy to ignore when you refuse to speak it into existence.

I take Micah's card and drop it on top of my bag.

"I guess we have a deal, then," I tell him.

He eyes me up and down as he rakes his fingers through his

messy hair. "I know you're twenty-one now, and you probably have a million other things you'd rather be doing. Going out with your friends or partying. I understand if you don't want to do this. No one is forcing you."

"No." I choke down the emotion building in my throat. "I told you I want to earn my keep. If this is what it takes, I'll happily do it."

I've never given much thought to interior design, and I'm probably the least qualified to take on a project such as this one, but I'm in no position to be picky. I've spent the past three years keeping myself busy, creating a life that looks drastically different from the one I was raised in. And when it came down to it, it led me right back into the arms of someone with just as much dangerous power over me as my family.

Despite only being blocks from my parents' house, I feel as if this place is still giving me the opportunity to start fresh. At least I can use it as a jumping point to give me time to figure out where to go next.

"Good, then it's settled." He nods as a vibration sounds off in his pocket. He clicks on his screen and reads a message before looking back up at me. "I've got to go take care of some business."

"Okay," I say nervously.

"Your copy of the house key is on the dresser." He points to the keyring he dropped on top when we first walked in.

"Thanks."

"I don't plan on coming back tonight, so you'll have the whole place to yourself."

I close my mouth and swallow my nerves. I don't know why, but I'm conflicted. The thought of staying in a strange, cobweb-covered house, completely alone, has every nerve firing on all cylinders. I give Micah a simple nod, resisting the urge to ask him when he *will* be back. I know he doesn't live here, but I wonder how often he comes by.

Once he's standing at the threshold, Micah stops and turns long enough to nod at the card still sitting on top of my duffel. "Don't be afraid to use that card for things other than furniture and décor. You can use it to buy groceries or whatever else you might need. The refrigerator is completely empty."

"I can buy my own food, Micah." I ignore the way his gaze makes me feel, as if he's shining a spotlight on me. My heart races, and my palms grow sweaty.

"Right." He taps his fingers on the doorframe, his gold watch glinting in the mid-morning sun peeking through the faded curtains. "Enjoy your new home, Adeline."

Then he's gone, my full name spilling from his mouth and dropping like a heavy stone at the bottom of my stomach.

I sit on the edge of the bed and allow the silence to wrap itself around me. It comforts me like a warm blanket. This house carries a history with it; secrets and memories buried within the faded walls. There's something comforting in knowing I'm alone with them, both inside and outside.

When the thoughts become too much, I quickly stand and swipe the keys from the dresser, leaving Micah's credit card sitting on top of my bag. I shut the door to my new bedroom behind me and set out on my first mission in my new life.

Food.

FIVE

Micah

Freshly showered, with my pain pills kicking in, I shut off the engine and slide out of the driver's seat. It's been a long time since I've driven my own car, and when I first decided to drive this morning, I immediately regretted my decision, but it was too late to turn around. I drove into the city with a pounding headache and the need to vomit.

I haven't been this hungover since I was in my early twenties. With a headache from hell, and my eyeballs ready to pop right out of the sockets, I remember why I stopped drinking years ago. Before my life turned to absolute shit. I kept my drinking under control for quite some time after I was released, but as the days of being back in not only the real world, but my world—the Harding world—all I could think about was the sweet relief I would feel once I took a drink of whiskey.

I took last night a little too far, though. Further than I have in years. The high and numbness I get from drinking simply isn't worth the aftereffects.

I downplayed my night to Adeline. It was embarrassing enough to have her find me passed out on my front porch. Especially after not having seen or talked to her for ten years. I didn't give much thought to seeing her again... until I saw her.

Although she was wearing a long, thick sweater and loose joggers, I could tell she wasn't the eleven-year-old girl I remembered. She's now a full-grown woman.

After I toss the keys to the valet out front and stride into the lobby, I ride the elevator up to my brother's office, with my hand pressed against the wall, and my head hanging low. It's an agonizingly slow ride, and when the lift stops and pings, I push off the wall and step out, bypassing all the secretaries at the front desk along the way. I don't plan on staying here long, considering I have a client meeting in Barcelona tomorrow morning. I need to head over to the airport hangar to catch my flight if I'm going to make it with enough time to sleep.

I weave my way back to my brother Lennon's office. His longtime secretary Olivia sits behind her large, oak desk, tapping away on her computer.

"Good afternoon, Mr. Harding."

"Is it afternoon?" I ask her, flicking my wrist to eye my watch.

"Well..." Olivia giggles and shrugs. "It's five minutes after noon, so I consider it afternoon."

"Oh, you scared me." I place my hand on my chest, worried I've wasted my day.

"Sorry." She winces.

"Do you mind telling Lennon I'm here? He's expecting me."

"Of course." Olivia presses her finger to the intercom, and Lennon is quick to respond, telling me to head back to his office.

I push through the large, mahogany door, then allow it to shut behind me.

"Uncle Micah!" My eight-year-old niece Lucy comes running over to me, her long, brown, curling pigtails bouncing with every step. She quickly wraps herself around my waist.

"Shouldn't you be in school?" I tease.

"Daddy picked me up early because I have to get a filling today." She unravels one arm from around my waist long enough to pull back her cheek, showing me the left side of her mouth. "Right here."

I laugh.

She squeezes me again and rests her chin on my stomach before looking up with the largest grin. "I asked Daddy if I could have a telescope, and he said I'd have to wait for my birthday, but my birthday isn't until after science camp this summer, so there's no way I can get enough research done in time. I'll be way behind."

I can't help but smile at her enthusiasm seeing me and the way she talks a mile a minute without taking in a single breath. The growing dimples in her cheeks and the light in her eyes temporarily fill the gaping hole I have in my soul.

"Woah." I dip my eyebrows and dart my narrowed eyes to my brother sitting behind his desk. "You won't get her a telescope? It's educational."

"That's what I said," Lucy whines. Her arms are still wrapped around me, her hands grasping onto my gray blazer.

"Lucy!" Lennon scolds, narrowing his eyes. "You can't run to your uncle every time you feel like you aren't getting what you want. It doesn't work that way. Your mother and I have already had this conversation with you. Science camp doesn't work with our schedule. We'll be gone most of the summer."

"I know." She pouts, pulling away from me. "Sorry, Daddy. I was just hoping Uncle Micah would be able to help."

"Hey, Luce," I say, hooking my fingers under her chin. "You know I'm always here to help with whatever you need." I give her a wink and nod toward Lennon. It causes my head to pound again, but I ignore it. "I'll see what I can do. I promise. Okay?"

She claps her hands together and points them to her chin.

She gives me another large toothy grin, even though half her teeth are missing. "Thank you, thank you, thank you." She wraps her arms around me one more time. "You know you're my favorite uncle, right?"

I laugh. "Duh! Of course, I am." I lean down and press my finger to my lips. "But it's our little secret, right?"

My other brother Jude is just as amazing of an uncle to Lucy, and I've heard her say the same thing to him multiple times when she thinks I haven't been able to hear, but I love these moments with her.

"Yep." She smacks her lips and nods enthusiastically.

"Hey, Lucy, girl." Lennon moves around his desk and stands beside his daughter. "Do you mind sitting with Olivia for a few minutes while I talk to your favorite uncle? Your mom shouldn't be much longer. She's on her way to pick you up to take you to your dentist appointment."

"Sure." She walks over to the chair in the far corner and grabs her pink bag. "Love you, Daddy. Love you, Uncle Micah."

We both tell her we love her, too, and wait for the door to shut.

When I'm alone with Lennon, I blow out a heavy breath and sink into the chair across from his desk. I hang my head back and run an exhausted hand down my face. Feeling Lennon move around the room, I sit up and watch him return to his chair behind his desk, across from me.

"You shouldn't make her promises you can't keep," he mutters, sifting through the paperwork on his desk.

"I didn't." I cross my leg and rest my ankle on my knee.

"Laurel and I already talked with her about this. We're planning on spending the entire summer in Paris. It's not because we don't want to get her one, it's just that we don't want to give her hope when going to science camp isn't a probability."

There's an edge to Lennon's voice, and I see the annoyance in his glare.

Dressed in his usual all black suit, his face is set into a hardened expression—the same expression he gives the rest of the world. But not to his wife. Or his brothers.

Today is different. I see the frustration behind his fixed jaw and pulsing temple.

"It's not like Lucy is asking for a castle." I scoff. "It's a telescope, Lennon."

"That's not the point." He pinches the bridge of his nose. "You would understand if you had children of your own."

I curl my hands into fists. The cuts from punching the mirror last night crack, and a sharp, blistering pain sears across my knuckles. Pressing my mouth into a tight line, I breathe out heavily through my nose, causing my nostrils to flare.

"Is this why you called me down here?" I ask, cutting him a glare. "To talk to me like Dad would and scold me as if I were still a fucking teenager? I must not understand anything because I don't have children of my own, right?"

Lennon's eyes widen, and his chest stills. He takes a moment before sighing and closing his eyes. He reopens them, this time looking at me with pity. If there's anything us three Harding brothers have in common, it's all in our desire to be the furthest thing from our father. But every day I look in the mirror, the more I see him staring back at me.

It makes me fucking sick.

"I shouldn't have said that. I'm sorry."

I don't speak a word. I simply uncurl my fists while the pounding in my head continues.

"You look like shit," he adds.

Straight to the point. My oldest brother never misses.

"Thanks," I mutter, running my finger over one of the cuts.

"Do those cuts have to do with you punching a bathroom mirror at Harley's Club last night?"

"What?" I ask, wondering how in the hell he knows where I got these cuts from.

He tosses me a piece of paper from his desk. I catch it, quickly reading over the list printed in black ink.

"What the fuck is this?" I ask, confused. I toss the paper back on his desk.

"I got a call this morning from the insurance company who cover Harley's Club and its owner Jeremy Turpin," Lennon explains. "Jeremy claimed you and his girlfriend snuck off into one of the bathrooms in his bar. He says you stumbled out with those cuts on your hand, and when he went in to open the bar up this morning, the mirror was shattered, and there was vomit all over the floor."

"How would he know it was me? The mirror could have been broken at any time, and I'm sure dozens of customers go in there to throw up. The place is a shithole."

"He has you on camera, Micah."

"He has enough money for a security system, and so what?" I look out the window and shake my head before swinging my attention back to Lennon. "I can't believe the insurance is even bothering to cover that place, or that Jeremy is worried about it, considering he's losing the place. But I guess it's whatever. I'll pay the bill."

"That's not the fucking point." Anger flares his nostrils, and he's no longer trying to hide his annoyance.

I roll my eyes. We're back to this again.

He leans forward and jabs his finger at the invoice. "Whether you like it or not, Jeremy is still the owner of that bar and is free to make an insurance claim if he wants. We haven't closed on the property, and the bank sure as fuck hasn't seized it yet. Don't you think you were being a little selfish last night?"

"Selfish?" I raise my eyebrows.

"You put our company at risk! I sent you there as a courtesy to the owner. Instead, you're caught on camera practically undressing his girlfriend in the hallway before leading her into the bathroom to fuck her. Then you walk out after destroying property, with your hand all fucked up."

"I said I would pay for it, Lennon." I narrow my eyes, tired of my brother looking at me as if I'm something that always needs to be fixed or taken care of. Like I'm some liability. All I've ever done these past three years is fought to get back on track. But it's difficult to get back on track when you're the reason for the derailment. I did this to myself. I'm the only one to blame.

"I thought we were past this."

"Past what?" I ask, venom sitting on the tip of my tongue.

"I don't deny our father fucked all three of us in ways we can't comprehend. With Jude, he had a drinking problem, but he overcame his demons and put his past behind him. When you were caught with all those illegal prescription drugs, I thought I was doing right by you the first time ten years ago. The judge was willing to give you a slap on the wrist by giving you a small fine. But this last time..." He sighs, resting his elbows on his desk and massaging his temples. "I hired the best lawyers to talk down your sentence, and as much as I despise doing it, I tried to use our family name to lessen your penalty. I tried to negotiate your sentence down to rehab, but the judge wasn't having it. He said your offenses were too extreme, even for setting bail, and if he didn't send you to prison, it would have sent a message that money can buy your way out of facing the consequences."

"I know you did what you could." The idea that I have a felony attached to my name for the rest of my life turns my stomach sour.

"So, stop living in the past, and move on!" he yells.

"I'm not one of your children, Lennon," I bark back. I know I fucked up. Every day, I wake up knowing I messed up my life with one singular decision. It flipped at the turn of a dime.

I look at my brother, angry he doesn't understand that the trauma of prison doesn't simply fade with time.

"No, you aren't one of my children," he seethes, his eyes bulging. "But I am your big brother, and I've done nothing but try to protect you. Your sentence could have been a lot worse than two years, and I won't deny that the stunt you pulled last night worries me that you're traveling down the same path. I missed the signs the first time. I don't intend on doing it again. Because next time, it won't just be two years. It'll be more, and I'm afraid my hands will be tied."

I roll my eyes and squeeze my hands into impossibly tight fists. I want to drive one of them into the fucking wall when I hear shit like this.

"You don't need to worry about me," I force out between gritted teeth. "This isn't like that."

"How can I trust you?" He narrows his eyes. Despite my brother's hard exterior, I see the love and fear he has for me, but it's misplaced. I wish I could take it away from him. I wish I could tell him the truth, though the truth breeds contempt. It's better to remain in *this* truth than to live in the alternate one. For all of us.

"I think it's time you take a break." Lennon disrupts my thoughts. The nonchalance in his voice makes me think he's been planning on having this conversation with me for some time. The smooth, effortless way the words fall from his lips are as if he's recited them in his head for longer than I care to know.

"I don't need a break." I rest my hands in my lap and straighten my back in my seat. I'm losing my grip, once again.

"You do." I can see the fight in him to stick to his guns. "Ever since you were released, I've given you the benefit of the doubt. I figured it would be great for you to dive back into your work, start over with a clean slate. Same as before. I gave you another chance, and I saw change. I saw you'd finally grown up. You weren't the same, troubled, twenty-something you were back then, and handling our accounts overseas has always been your strong suit. But your work has been slipping, and the last thing I want is for you to get in trouble again, find yourself going back to prison, or worse, in a situation you or I can't talk our way out of. My power only reaches so far, Micah, and I refuse to wield it as our father did. Last night is proof you need a break. I don't blame you for struggling these past few years. I can't imagine what you went through once you were released, but I can't, in good conscience, allow this to keep happening."

I open my mouth to object but stop short. I don't have it in me to argue with my brother, and maybe that makes me weak, but it's easier than trying to convince him otherwise.

"Why don't you take this time to fix that house you bought out in Cambridge years ago? You've always said you never had the time to remodel it, and it was just sitting there when you were gone, untouched."

"I have someone working on it," I mumble, not wanting to dive too much into who, exactly. "Besides, I don't plan on keeping it. Not anymore."

I keep my words short and clipped. I'm trying to stand my ground, digging for reasons to throw back at Lennon as to why he should keep me at work, but I come up blank. Instead, I find myself talking about this house. The house that used to mean more to me than it does today. But I fucked up, and it cost me everything. My future. My life. Everything.

"It's a shame you aren't going to keep it." Lennon frowns. "But I understand. I think, anyway."

"Yeah." I nod, chewing on the inside of my cheek. I don't

like thinking about the past. It stirs up dark feelings, and dark feelings lead me to recklessly trying to fuck women in dirty bathrooms, only to end up with vomit all over my shoes, and staring back at my father's reflection in the mirror.

"How long am I supposed to take this break?" I question him.

"However long it takes you to release whatever it is that's trying to pull you back." He drags his finger on the arm of his chair in circles before looking me in the eye. "You don't have to become that person again, brother. It isn't you. Whatever it is that's trying to pull you back there, let it go."

I give him a sarcastic laugh. Easier said than done.

Lennon is wrong. It's not that I feel like I'm being pulled back. The truth is I feel cheated. Cheated out of the life I deserved, and every day I'm reminded of the price I paid for it all to mean nothing. I'm not living the life I wanted for myself because of the choices I've made in the past. I'm not living the life I envisioned because every day, more and more, me and the rest of the world see James Harding.

I stare at my brother, completely at a loss for words. There's nothing I can say to change his mind or make me hate myself any less than I already do.

"Fine." I stand, buttoning my suit jacket and moving around the chair. I rest my hands on the back and grip the leather as I lean forward and look him directly in the eye. "Since you seem to know me so well and claim to know what's right for me, why don't you let me know when it's appropriate for me to come back?"

"Micah..." He holds his hands out. "Come on, man. Don't take it personal. This is for the best."

"Yep." I push off the chair. "That's what I'm here for. To always do what's best." I spin on my heel and head for the door.

"Micah! You're my brother, and I love you. I just –"

The door closes behind me, quieting my brother's booming voice, shutting him out.

I wish it were as easy to block out my past. Maybe then it would stop haunting me.

SIX

ADELINE

The musty smell emanating from the sheets invades my senses. I really should have given them a wash before deciding to climb under them for a nap.

Exhaustion hit me as soon as I unloaded the last grocery bag, and my eyelids grew heavy. All I wanted was sleep. It feels as if I haven't slept in years. I want to believe it's due to the time change, but I think it's a combination of my world crashing down around me.

Leaving Maddox.

Being back here in Cambridge.

Seeing Micah.

All of it has been overwhelming.

With the curtains shut, I've pulled myself into darkness. Drifting in and out, I turn on my side and hope to fall asleep again, but my mind wanders again. This time, to Micah. I've spent part of the day replaying this morning in my mind. Seeing him again after all these years. I don't know when he plans on returning to the house. I didn't want to ask. I haven't been able to stop thinking about the pain I saw in his eyes.

Ten years have passed between us, and he's no longer the same man who saved me from the water.

My heart twists and aches. I need to shut my brain off. Frustrated, I toss the sheets aside and place my bare feet on the hardwood floor, and a shiver ripples up the length of my legs. The cold air fills the room, and for a moment, I consider scrambling back under the musty sheets just to stay warm but decide against it. I grab my phone from my nightstand. There's a missed call from Ember and a message from Ruby asking if I made it to Boston safely. I quickly respond to her and decide to call Ember later. I'm thrilled at the prospect of seeing my best friend, but something buried deep in the back of my mind keeps me from responding right away.

Dropping my phone back on the table, I spin around and strip the sheets from the bed. I leave them in a pile on the floor, debating whether it might be best to just toss them or if I should search the house for the laundry room to wash them. I decide to leave them there and start exploring the room.

Along with a dresser on the far wall, a small, round table sits in the corner beside a large, overstuffed, green velvet chair. Crossing the room, I run my finger along the bookshelf lined with dozens of old books, weathered spines, and faded covers. Every single one looks like it wasn't printed this century or even the last.

I open the closet to find it filled with undisturbed clothes. Above the row of hanging clothes is a long wooden shelf at the top lined with old cardboard boxes. Standing on my toes, I attempt to pull one down, but I can't reach. I stretch as far as possible, using the tips of my fingers to scrape the lip of the box. My entire body tenses as I look down and lift one foot to rest on a wooden shoe rack pushed against the side wall. It wobbles under my weight, but I'm able to grab the edge of the box and begin to slide it back off the shelf, but then my hand freezes when I hear a loud noise come from another part of the house. I hold my breath as goosebumps crawl their way down the back of my neck.

I quickly step down, abandoning the box. My heart races, picking up with every shallow breath I take in.

Crash.

Another loud bang.

Pressing my hand to my chest, I tiptoe across the room to grab my phone from the nightstand, and with a shaking hand, press my thumb to the screen to unlock it. Slowly, I walk to the door, praying my steps don't give me away. My chest squeezes, hoping another board doesn't creak under my weight.

Crash.

My breath shoots to the back of my throat and I start panicking. Every possible scenario plays in my mind.

Maybe there's a broken window or hole in the side of the house that's allowed an animal to come inside. Maybe someone else has broken in. Micah said he wasn't coming back, so it shouldn't be him.

Did Maddox follow me once he'd discovered I left? Did he press Ruby to find out where I am?

I quickly try to rationalize the answer to these questions. Although I told Ruby I was coming back home, I never gave her the address to Micah's house, so even if Maddox somehow figured out where I was, I don't think he would find me this quickly.

I don't *think.*

Keeping my thumb hovered over the emergency call button, I step into the hallway. When I reach the top of the stairs, I peer over the railing and see the entryway is empty. I take the first step at the top of the stairs, and the floorboard whines underfoot. I wince, pausing and holding my breath.

I wonder if I should call out to whoever is making the sound in the kitchen, but I don't. That doesn't sound smart.

When the noise continues, I continue to make my way down the stairs until I reach the entryway. I reach for an umbrella hanging by the front door and hold it up. I'm not exactly sure how much damage it will do to the intruder—probably not much, but it's the best I've got.

Making my way down the hall, with my umbrella ready for attack, I follow the continued slamming and rustling sounds of kitchen drawers and cabinets. I round the corner and jump at the sight of the man standing in front of the refrigerator.

"Holy shit!" I yelp, jumping back. My eyes widen in shock. The umbrella falls from my hand, bouncing and crashing at my feet. I bring my hand to my chest, certain I'm having a heart attack, and my phone slips from my hand, dropping on my toe before landing on the old tile floor. I bring my hand to my mouth to stifle another scream.

Micah shuts the cabinet door and spins around. His wide eyes land on me before moving to the umbrella beside my feet.

My entire body bursts into flames and I'm suddenly aware of what I'm wearing. Rather... the *lack* of what I'm wearing.

I pick up my phone to see the screen is cracked, but otherwise, it still works, so I drop it on the counter, catching Micah's hardened stare.

His blue-gray eyes slowly slide up the length of my bare legs to my favorite faded Nirvana sleep shirt. Although I'm wearing an unlined bra underneath, I'm sure my nipples are peaked, poking against my shirt. This house doesn't seem to stay warm.

My cheeks bloom with heat, and my arms shoot to cover my chest and hardened nipples.

Micah's gaze finds mine again.

I blow out an exasperated breath and look around the

kitchen. "What are you doing here, Micah? You scared the shit out of me."

"Sorry." He sighs. "I figured you heard me come in."

"No." I shift on my feet, the cold air clinging to my legs. "I was upstairs taking a nap. Besides, you told me you weren't coming back."

"I wasn't." He runs his hand through his hair.

His jacket is laid out on one of the barstools, which he moves and places on the counter before sliding to sit on the stool while I move to the other side of the island, using it as a shield.

Resting his elbows on the counter, Micah brings his hands together and rests his chin on them.

I arch my eyebrows. "Everything okay?"

He blinks. "Yeah." He nods. "My trip to Barcelona was canceled, so I figured I'd come here and check on you." He stares at me with half-saddened eyes.

"Check on me?" I point to my chest.

He simply nods, but a small smile plays on his lips.

I find myself smiling, too. This is the most we've ever talked.

I gesture at the room. "Didn't exactly sound like you were coming to check on me."

"Oh, right." He nods, twisting to look around the kitchen. Nearly all the cabinets are left open, and some of the drawers are sticking out. "I was looking for something to eat but realized I don't know where anything is."

"You didn't think to check the refrigerator?" I chuckle. "I went grocery shopping earlier."

"You said you were buying your own food. I figured it wouldn't be polite to eat yours." He shrugs. "I remember sticking a jar of peanut butter and fluff in one of the cabinets after I bought the house, but I couldn't remember which one."

"I'm not exactly an expert on expiration dates, but I doubt a year old jar of marshmallow fluff isn't breeding mold by now."

He nervously scratches the back of his head. "I guess it was a gamble I was willing to take."

I grin. It's silly to me that a man with all the money in the world would resort to searching for an old jar of fluff.

I lean forward and rest my arms on the counter. My eyes are now in line with his, but there's still a good two feet of distance between us. Although he scared the shit out of me only minutes ago, I now feel comfortable enough to relax. I also realize this is the first time I've held a normal conversation with someone outside of Maddox and Ruby. The longer I was in my relationship with Maddox, the more I began to walk on eggshells any time I was with him. And even though I absolutely love Ruby, she's been more like a mother than a friend. Ember has been my best friend for as long as I can remember, but distance and life has made it difficult to stay as close as we were as kids. I didn't realize how small my circle had become in Los Angeles.

"You're allowing me to stay here, Micah. You can eat the food I bought. Besides, I was feeling hungry myself. Well, at least I was before you scared the shit out of me."

I stand and straighten my back, waiting for his response. As though it's suddenly awake, my stomach grumbles in response.

Micah winces and tilts his head to the side, shaking it with a small, playful smile on his lips. "I don't know. I was really craving some peanut butter and fluff."

"Wait." I eye him suspiciously. "If you were looking for the peanut butter and fluff, what about the bread? It's not exactly a sandwich without the bread."

He scrunches his nose and scratches at the stubble lining his jaw. "This plan wasn't well thought out, was it?"

"Not really." I laugh—this time a genuine, full laugh, causing me to smile.

"It's okay." Micah digs his phone from the jacket of his suit. "I can order a pizza or something."

He opens an app, diverting his gaze. I bite my bottom lip, deciding what to do.

"No!" I blurt out. He looks up from his phone. "Let me make you dinner." I pause, swallowing as heat spreads across my half-naked body. I've never been more thankful for the cover of the counter I'm standing behind. "As a thank you."

He falls back into his seat and eyes me. "Did you buy bread?"

SEVEN

Micah

Fuck me.

When I showed up here after my brother basically fired me, I didn't expect to see Adeline wearing nothing but an old Nirvana T-shirt, her long, bare legs on display.

Heat shot straight to my groin, and my cock twitched.

She's my best friend's little sister. These aren't reactions I should be having when I look at Adeline. The last time I saw her, she was the sweet eleven-year-old, yelling at me for embarrassing her in front of the entire country club. She's two years younger than the age I was when we last saw each other. I begin doing the math in my head, having never thought about it before. I'm twelve years older than her. My mind is at war with itself when she opens a cabinet and reaches for two plates. Her T-shirt rises, exposing the bottom curves of her round ass.

I avert my gaze and pick up my phone, pretending to scroll through social media. Silently telling myself to calm down, I bounce my leg nervously under the counter. As if she has sensed my reaction, she places the plates in front of me.

I look up as she crosses her arms over her chest again, hiding her pebbled nipples.

"Um, I'm going to go change." Her cheeks redden. "I'll be right back."

I grin. "Okay."

She disappears, and when she comes back, she's wearing the sweater I saw her in this morning and a pair of shorts. I sigh with relief, even if the shorts still show off her toned legs.

Flashing me a quick closed-mouth smile, she grabs the loaf of bread and the new jar of peanut butter from the cabinet before dropping them near the plates she set out. She opens the fridge and pulls out a jar of strawberry jam along with two sodas.

I catch the can she slides over to me before she starts on our sandwiches.

"I didn't buy any fluff," she says while tearing off the seal to the peanut butter. "I hope you like strawberry jam."

"Strawberry is fine. I'm surprised you didn't buy fluff. Peanut butter and fluff sandwiches are a New England staple."

She shrugs, digging the butter knife into the peanut butter and smearing it across a slice of bread. "I never ate them too much when I was a kid, and they aren't exactly popular out in LA. Or the diet of a model."

"Yeah, I never really eat them when I'm away from home," I say, watching her squeeze the two slices of bread together.

She cuts the sandwich diagonally down the middle and passes the plate to me. I don't start eating immediately, instead waiting for her to finish making hers.

"Do you still do a lot of traveling?" she asks, smearing a large glob of jam onto her bread before she pauses and looks at me. "I mean, I'm only going off what Archer used to tell me."

"I do." I nod, careful with my words.

I don't want to dive into my history too much. Our conversation has been lighthearted, considering we haven't spoken in years. When I left Lennon's office, I considered where to go. My plans to travel to Barcelona for work may have been suddenly squashed. Technically, I still could have gone—perks of having an endless amount of money at your disposal—but my conversation with my brother soured the idea of traveling. I couldn't stay at Lennon's after our talk in his office. I didn't want to barge in on Jude and Victoria, considering they're adjusting to life with a newborn when they already have three other children at home.

I love my brothers, but sometimes when I'm around them, they are constant, living reminders of where I should be at this phase in my life. The path I could have taken had I not fucked it all up.

It's as if we were all walking down the road side by side until, one day, I'm suddenly staring at their backs. Both are married with children now. Lennon is head of the company. Jude is doing what makes him happy, helping Victoria run her bookstore while dabbling in construction every now and then.

"What's your favorite place you've ever been to?" Adeline asks, interrupting my thoughts.

She pushes her plate to my side of the counter, then walks around the island to join me before sliding into the barstool beside me.

I don't have to think long on my answer. "Ireland. When I was twenty-five, Archer and I took a few weeks off work and decided to backpack our way across the country. We made it a point to hit every single tourist attraction but got lost along the way in a small village. They had the most welcoming people. It ended up being the best trip I ever took. I think because, for once, I was traveling for fun, not work."

"I've always wanted to go to Ireland." She grins, picking up half of her sandwich.

I do the same, taking a bite. The combination of flavors hits my mouth in a way I don't expect. It's comforting and delicious. I can't remember the last time I ate this for a meal.

"You should go," I tell her around the peanut butter glued to the roof of my mouth.

She shakes her head and looks down at her plate. "I don't really have the time or money for a trip like that." She looks up and smiles. "Maybe one day."

"If you ever had the opportunity"—I swallow another bite—"where would you want to go?"

She doesn't hesitate in her answer. "The cliffs of Moher." She's clearly been dreaming about this for a while. "And don't tease me, but the Blarney Stone."

I roll my eyes. "Such a touristy thing to do."

"I know, I know." She sweeps her tongue across her lip to collect a dot of jam. "I just think it would be fun."

"I assumed you would have had time to travel."

"Why would you assume that?" Her perfect eyebrows pinch together.

"Don't models go to Paris and London? Places like that."

She considers my question while picking at a crumb on her plate. "I didn't quite make it there yet." She gives me a weak, unamused smile. "After I left home and headed out west, I tried my best to follow in my mother's footsteps. She refused to help, not offering me a foot in the door or connecting me with anyone in the industry. I guess because she didn't want me to end up like her." Her eyes shift, avoiding looking at me as she mutters under her breath, "Whatever that means." She inhales a deep, cleansing breath, finally bringing her gaze back to mine. "Anyway, after I left home, I fought tooth and nail to get to where I was."

I raise my eyebrows. "And where are you now?"

She cracks a smile that stretches all the way to her eyes. "Now, I'm sitting here eating peanut butter and jellies with you."

I laugh, and after that, we sit in silence, taking a few more bites of our sandwiches before drinking sips from our sodas.

"It's funny." She eyes me over her sandwich as I take another bite. I hadn't noticed the way her eyes shimmer under the dim light. A mixture of caramel and brown, with flecks of sage green.

"What's funny?"

"Watching a billionaire eating a peanut butter and jelly sandwich." She giggles.

I chuckle, too. "I may be a billionaire, but my mom raised me to never take the small things for granted. Although she wanted it to be known I was my father's son, she never shied away from raising me as normal as possible. You didn't exactly grow up in a modest household," I point out. "Your father was district attorney. I'm not sure what the lifestyle of a model is like, but I'm guessing it isn't too far off from the life you had here, right?"

Her eyes shoot to her right. They soften, and from where I'm sitting, I can see liquid building along her dark lashes. The curves of her cheeks blush with pink again, but this time it isn't embarrassment. There's sadness in her expression. She looks down at her plate as pieces of her hair slip from behind her ear, shielding parts of her face from me.

I resist the urge to reach out and tuck them back.

She sniffs, turning her head back to look at me. "No, it wasn't much different."

I consider my next words. I didn't question Archer when he asked if his sister could stay here at my house, but now that she's sitting in front of me, and she's gotten my mind off my own shit, I decide to ask her.

"So, what brought you back here?" I ask. "What brought you back home?"

She sighs and looks down at her plate. She's only taken one bite out of her sandwich. "I needed a break, that's all."

The irony isn't lost on me.

I didn't choose my break from work.

Adeline chose this.

Somewhere deep in my chest, I know her reason runs deeper than what she's willing to divulge, but I don't press her for more information.

"I guess you could say I'm on a break as well."

"Oh." She blinks, seeming unsure of what to say. "I hope it's a break you wanted or needed."

"Maybe." I glance out the window overlooking the back-yard. It needs a lot of work. Lennon was right when he suggested I needed to fix this place.

But the claws in my mind remind me why I haven't yet.

Despite having never truly stayed here, this house repre-sents the death of a dream, which is exactly what it looks like: Death.

"I haven't decided yet," I add.

I turn back to Adeline. She doesn't continue the conversa-tion, allowing us to eat in silence until we've both finished our sandwiches. When both our plates are empty, she carries them over to the sink. She gives them a rinse before loading them into the dishwasher, and I try my best to keep my eyes away from those damn long legs and how her shorts ride up the backs of her thighs as she bends, but it's difficult.

She drops the plates into the slots before she uses the side of her foot to kick the dishwasher door closed.

"Have you thought about what you want to work on first?" I ask, leaning forward and resting my chin in my hand.

"I'm not sure." She pauses. "Is there a room or a certain area you've wanted done or one that's more important to you?"

"No." I lean back on my stool and raise my arms above my

head. "Not really. You can start anywhere you'd like to." I loosen my tie, then completely remove it to wrap it around my fingers and lay it on the counter in a neat circle.

I catch Adeline looking out the window at the backyard again. "I think I'll start with the room I'm staying in. I'm going to go out and get some new sheets and things tomorrow."

"Not bad."

"It feels like it's the easiest task to tackle. That, and considering it's the room I'm staying in, I think it's best. Other parts of the house may require a construction crew."

"They will, and I can get that figured out." I didn't plan on getting involved with the reconstruction of the house, but I don't want Adeline staying here for a long time with over half the house unlivable. I know parts of it can be dangerous.

I stand and push my stool back under the counter, then grab a towel and quickly wipe down the counter, feeling Adeline watching me again, her stare burning a hole in my back.

I stop and I smile. "Let me guess. You think it's funny watching a billionaire clean a counter."

"A little," she agrees, sheepishly.

"Do you not remember the year Archer and I worked at the bar down at the country club?"

"No." She shakes her head. "I'm sure your father loved that. And mine."

"Oh..." I hang the towel back on the hook above the sink. "My father loved it so much he had me fired one week from the day I started, which was exactly how long it took him to find out I was working there." I think back to a few short days of living a semi-average life. "It was the summer before I went off to college. I was eighteen... so you must have been six."

Wincing, I spin around to face Adeline. She's now standing in the doorway, leaning against it with her shoulder.

It's strange looking at her now as a full-grown woman and

bringing up stories like my trip to Ireland and the few short days I worked as a bartender.

Adeline's perfect dark eyebrows arch across her tan forehead. "I was six. No wonder I don't remember it."

"Right." I nod.

The air between us tenses, and suddenly, I feel awkward. Self-conscious, too. They're foreign feelings.

Adeline points her finger straight up. "I'm going to go take a shower and wash the sheets before I go to bed. I know you said you don't normally stay here, but are you planning on it, because I can sleep on the couch?"

"No." I wave her off. "I don't have any clothes here, anyway."

I'm lying. I stuffed a few boxes of clothes in the closet of the bedroom the week after I bought this house. I brought them here on the off chance I ever decided to stay.

But I don't want to make Adeline feel uncomfortable because of the way she constantly lets her hair fall over her face as she tries to not so subtly hide her sad and distant eyes from me.

"Okay, well, it's your house, so just let me know whenever you want to stay, and I'll sleep on the couch."

"Absolutely not." I shoot her a glare, sharpening my voice. When she jerks back, I realize how my tone must have come across. "I just mean I won't put you out. I'll sleep on the couch or something. Besides, I don't have your number, anyway, so I wouldn't be able to warn you."

"Right." She nods, wringing her hands while she remains leaning against the doorframe between the kitchen and the hallway.

I tug my phone from my pocket and unlock it before handing it to her. She types her number in and calls it.

She ends the call and holds her arm out, passing it back to me. "There, now I have yours."

"Cool." I slip my phone back in my pocket and swipe my tie from the counter. "Well, thanks for dinner."

She giggles. "You're welcome."

The sparkle in her eye tells me we're thinking the same thing.

Why does it suddenly feel like this isn't my house? And why do I suddenly feel awkward for telling her thank you?

I've so easily forgotten she's my best friend's little sister. I'm only remembering it now as I find myself staring at her long, toned legs, once again.

"I should go," I force out.

She springs off the doorframe and moves out of the way. I slip past her and head down the hall.

With my hand on the doorknob, I stop, remembering something she said earlier. "I almost forgot. If you plan on washing those sheets, the laundry room is down in the basement, but you might want to be careful."

"Careful of what?" she asks, her eyes widening with fear. Her full, smooth lips part as she takes in what I assume to be a nervous breath.

"There's plenty more cobwebs down there than there are up here." I glance around at the ceiling before locking eyes with hers. "You may want to watch out for all the spiders. It's probably where they live."

Her mouth drops, and she shivers. I bite back a smile, thankful to get my mind off the thoughts invading it. My hand twitches, and I tighten my grip on my tie.

After I make my way down the walkway and sit in my car, I stare at the front door of my house. I imagine Adeline still standing in the entryway, thinking about having to go down in the basement. Shame settles in my chest. I shouldn't have said it, and I feel guilty for leaving her that way, but I needed to get out of there, and I couldn't leave thinking about how she'd reached up to grab the plates from the cabinet.

My thoughts were headed in a direction they certainly shouldn't have been going.

Without a place in mind to stay tonight, I force myself to start the engine and put the car in reverse anyway, and by the time I turn off the street and out of the neighborhood, I wonder how long my resolve will last.

EIGHT

ADELINE

I've spent the past two days completely remodeling my bedroom. After Micah told me about the spiders in the basement, I didn't bother wasting my time on the sheets. The bare mattress didn't have any stains, so I resorted to laying out a few of my T-shirts and sleeping in my sweater.

The next day, with Archer not answering his phone, and Ember in New York City for work, I was forced to call for rideshares and spent several hours going to different stores, stocking up on the necessities. I grabbed an entirely new sheet set and a new rug for the bedroom, along with shampoo, body wash, and a can of bug spray for the house. I refused to use Micah's credit card, not giving him the satisfaction.

But with the way he dropped the bomb on me the other night about the spiders, I was tempted to buy out the entire hardware store's stock of spider killer and charge it to his card.

With my arms loaded with clothes, I slowly walk down the stairs to the basement. The musty, acrid air hits my nostrils the same way it has all week. I drop the clothes onto the top of the washer before moving the curtains I tossed in earlier to the dryer. After loading my clothes in and starting the machine, I grab the can of spider killer and spray another nest I spot in the corner.

If I didn't need to live here, and if Micah didn't own this place, I probably would have burned this house to the ground by now. I've never been a fan of bugs, and I loathe spiders entirely. I wonder if Micah assumed I'd hate them or if he somehow remembers me hating them from when I was younger.

"Adeline!" Ember's voice calls from outside.

The washer door snaps shut, and I look up. A small, narrow window sits between the joists above the brick wall surrounding the basement.

"Ember?" I yell back.

The house is large, but the window near the washer sits at the front of it. Shadowed by grass, there's no way Ember can see me, but I know she hears me call out her name. The sound of shuffling feet on grass grows closer.

"Adeline? Where are you?"

"I'm down here." I stand on my toes, as if it will help her hear me better.

She moves closer again, but I still don't see her. "I knocked on the door, but you didn't answer."

"Sorry, I didn't hear it. I'm down in the basement."

"With all the spiders?" she asks, and I imagine her nose scrunched in disgust.

"I've been killing them as I see them." I laugh. "I'll be right up." I leave the laundry room and dash up the stairs.

When I reach the entryway, I unlock the front door and swing it open. Ember is standing on the front porch, a large pile of clothing bags draped over her arm. Her strawberry blonde hair shimmers in the sun, and her green eyes glint like two stones of emerald.

"It's been too long." She beams, opening her arms to wrap them around me.

It has been too long. The last time I saw Ember was a year ago, when she flew out to Los Angeles for a cosmetic event for a company sponsoring her.

"I'm so sorry I didn't answer when you called," she tells me.

"It's okay," I mutter over her shoulder.

"It's not. But I'm here now." She squeezes me tightly, and I squeeze her right back. She's always been a bright light in my life, especially in a place like this. Being back home.

Loosening my arms around her, I grab a few of the bags from her arms and help her carry them inside.

"We can take these to the living room," I tell her over my shoulder.

She closes the door behind me, I drape the bags over the back of the sofa.

Ember is slowly walking through the entryway, examining the building the same way I did the first day I got here.

"This house is huge." Her jaw drops as she spins in a circle.

Thankfully, I've cleaned most of the dust and cobwebs from the corners of the ceilings and walls. I spent all day yesterday wiping down every piece of furniture and sweeping the floors. When I take the time to look closely at the front room, it almost looks like a completely different room.

Ember joins me in the living room. She stands on the opposite side of the sofa and points to the bags. "I brought over every outfit I thought would fit you as well as your style."

My shoulders deflate and I eye them. "Thank you." My bottom lip wobbles. Suddenly, emotion swells in my chest and my throat.

Ember knows the reason why I'm here. Every bit of what happened flowed out of me when she called me back the other day. How I dropped my entire life back in Los Angeles, leaving Maddox without warning. She knows the truth of my relationship with him and how close I came to living in the same world as I did back home. She also knows the truth of what my home life was truly like growing up. In some ways, she knows more than my own brother.

"I'm just glad you got out when you did." She sighs. "I can't believe that asshole took advantage of you and the love you have. If you hadn't convinced me not to, I'd have killed him."

"I know. It took quite a bit of convincing." I give her a small smile of appreciation.

When I spoke to Ember about everything, I'd barely finished my sentence telling her what Maddox had done to me when she began threatening to race to the airport and hop on the next flight to Los Angeles. But when I told her I was already in a safe place, back in Boston, she conceded.

She grabs my hand and gives it a gentle squeeze. "I love you."

"I love you, too." I swallow back the tears lining my eyes.

"I'm sure it's difficult being back home, but I think you made the right decision in getting as far away from him as possible."

"I hope so." I shrug. "I'm terrified of running into my mom or my dad."

"You haven't seen them yet?"

"No." I shake my head. "And I don't want to."

"Not even your mom?"

I briefly close my eyes and take a deep breath. I see my mother standing in front of me, her kind eyes looking into mine. It's a memory that hasn't faded with time, but as with everything, there's always darkness beside the light. My mother's weakness was always the love she had for my father.

I open my eyes to my best friend in front of me. "I can't look at her without thinking of all the times she never stood up for me."

I don't fault her for anything other than loving my father

more than her resilience to stand up for me. Somehow, her love for me was never more than the love she had for him.

"I get it." Ember nods, biting her pink, glossy lip.

"Now, enough of that," I say, slapping my hands on my thighs. I look at the bags of clothes. "You didn't have to bring this many outfits over. I figured you were bringing a few shirts and pants, that's it. At least enough to hold me over until I can go shopping."

"How have you been getting around? I didn't see your car in the driveway. I'm assuming you don't have it since you flew here."

"Ruby has it." I swallow. "I'm not sure how I'll get it here, and I'm not sure I'll bother. So far, I've just ordered rideshares, but I can't keep that up for long."

I hide my true financial situation from her. Living as a freelance model in Los Angeles was already proving to be a challenge, but now that I've cut off all of my work, I'm living on the bits I have left saved from my last shoot.

"I'll do what I can to help," my best friend offers.

"Thank you." My chest warms as my eyes fall to the bags. "Now, about these clothes."

"These are only a few," she says, nonchalantly.

Ember is delusional when it comes to makeup and fashion, but I guess you could say I am, too. Though I like to believe I'm a bit more reasonable.

"Besides," Ember adds as she picks up the top bag and holds it up. Her mouth spreads into a wide grin. "This one is a little something special."

"What is it?"

"Now, I know you haven't been back long, and you're probably going to say no, but..." She lowers the zipper, revealing a small peek into the bag.

Silver sequins shine through the small opening.

I cross my arms over my chest and tilt my head at my best friend. "Ember, no." I know where this leads.

"Come on." She pouts, her shoulders deflating. "With my birthday in a few weeks, and yours only a few weeks ago, I thought this would be the perfect outfit to celebrate. I wasn't there for yours, and you'll be here for mine. We can celebrate together."

"I don't think I feel much like going out."

"How do you know how you'll feel in a few weeks?" She rocks from side to side, waving the garment bag in my face. "You never know," she sings.

I nervously look around the room. "I have a ton of stuff to do around the house still."

"You have plenty of time to work on it." She waves me off. "Just look at this dress, and maybe that will convince you."

She begins to pull the dress from the bag, slipping the bottom out from the base of the bag, but she stops when both of us snap our heads in the direction of the front door.

Cool air breezes in behind Micah as he steps into the entryway, shutting the door behind him. I haven't seen him since the night we ate peanut butter and jelly sandwiches in the kitchen on plates as old as this house.

My lips part, and I breathe in a quick rush of air at the sight of him.

He stops in the entryway, in direct line of sight of Ember and me.

"Hi," I say, stunned to see him here.

"Hi," he says back.

I feel Ember's eyes on me, bouncing back and forth between the two of us. She slowly lowers the dress down onto the back of the sofa.

"I just got back in today and thought I would make a list of everything that needs work upstairs," Micah says.

"Oh." I give Ember a side glance. "I'm sorry. Was I supposed to do that for you? I've been trying to work on the small things before I tackled the bigger repairs."

"It's okay." He rakes his fingers through his hair, making the muscles in his arms flex and tense. Muscles usually hidden beneath the sleeves of a collared shirt and suit jacket. Corded muscle strains against the dark blue sleeves of his fitted T-shirt. "It needs to be done either way, so I figured I'd get started on it."

"Okay." I nod.

Micah's eyes move to Ember. "Hi, Ember."

She giggles, casting me a glance before turning back to Micah. "I didn't think you'd remember me."

"Oh, come on." He jerks back. "You and Addy were always tied at the hip."

My stomach flutters at his use of my childhood nickname. I told him to only call me Adeline, but I guess old habits are hard to break.

"We still are." She elbows me.

I cover my ribs where she jabbed me.

"What are you doing these days?" Micah asks, crossing his arms over his chest.

"I'm a professional makeup artist and beauty influencer."

"Why am I not surprised?" He smirks.

She shrugs and points to me. "Only a few lucky ones like Addy and myself have been able to become what we've wanted to be since we were little."

"True." His eyes dart to me. "Not all of us are as lucky."

The storm I've come to see the last few times I've been with Micah has returned. My heart twists and aches at the sight of it. The desire to know his secrets swells inside me, ballooning in my chest, but Micah quickly pops that balloon with just three words:

"I'll be upstairs."

He leaves Ember and me, bounding up the stairs, his boots landing heavy on every other step as we watch him disappear.

I hold my breath, feeling Ember's hardened stare on me like a spotlight. The light brightens and grows in strength, shining like a beacon.

I may have told Ember everything, but I might have left out this one minor detail.

"Oh. My. God," she quietly says, craning her neck as if her head is on a swivel.

I chew on the inside of my cheek.

"I can't believe you," she hisses.

"Stop," I whisper, looking up the stairs where Micah went. "I was going to tell you but..."

"But what?" Her eyes widen as her jaw drops. "You just forgot to tell me?"

I wince. "I'm sorry."

Leaning closer, she whisper-shouts, "Holy shit," in my face before she playfully taps me on my arm. "You didn't tell me you moved into Micah Harding's house." She quickly glances back in the direction he disappeared. "And you're living with him?"

I widen my eyes. "No, he isn't staying here." My throat is dry, and my tongue sticks to the roof of my mouth.

"So, this isn't his house?" Her eyebrows knit, and she blinks. "I'm confused."

I roll my eyes, my patience wearing thin. I probably should have mentioned me living at Micah's house to my best friend, but I didn't, and I don't know why.

"This *is* his house," I whisper back, my heart racing. I feel like I've been caught with my hand in the cookie jar so to speak. "But he doesn't live here. He's letting me stay here as long as I help fix it up."

"Um." She smacks her glossed lips, pointing to the stairs. "But he's here, fixing it up."

"I didn't know that until today." I cross my arms. "He hasn't been here the whole time."

"Are you comfortable staying here? I don't mean just because you haven't talked to him in ten years, but because of his history. Didn't he just get out of prison a couple years ago?"

"He did, but I'm not going to hold that against him, Ember. It wouldn't be fair. Archer trusts him, and he's been a friend of our families for a long time. Just because he made a few mistakes doesn't mean he's a bad person."

I think back to the other night when we shared dinner. Even through the shield he holds up, I saw vulnerability and softness that made me feel more comfortable and more at ease than I've felt in a long time.

"I've only been here a few days, but I'm happy here," I reassure her.

She nods slowly, letting my confession sink in.

"Hmm." Ember twists her mouth in thought then rushes out of the living room and stands at the bottom of the stairs. She cranes her neck as if it will help her get another look at Micah, even though he isn't anywhere in sight. I follow her, tugging on her hand and urging her to return to the living room.

She resists, tightening her grip onto the wooden railing. I pull on her wrist again, but she's stubbornly glued to the banister.

Teasing, she scrunches her nose and giggles. "Damn, Micah's changed, hasn't he? How is it possible he's gotten hotter in his old age?" She's whispering, but she may as well be yelling. My insistence in trying to get her to move only makes her laugh louder. It echoes and bounces off the walls of the open-vaulted ceiling.

"He isn't old, Ember," I hiss. "Now, would you shut up and stop staring up the stairs like a creep?"

She laughs again, finally giving in to my efforts. Light on her feet, she stumbles away from the bottom of the stairs and falls back onto the sofa. "How old is he now? Thirty?"

I sit beside her and place my hands in my lap. We both keep our eyes focused on the front bay window. "Thirty-three." I'm still whispering, my cheeks redder at the thought of him hearing Ember's teasing.

"Right. He's twelve years older. I don't think it matters as much now than when we were kids."

"Doesn't change the fact he's Archer's best friend." I relax against the back of the sofa.

Tucking one leg under the other, she twists to face me. "Him being Archer's best friend never mattered before."

"You're talking about this as if I still have the same feelings I did for him when I was a kid, Ember. I'm not eleven years old anymore. We're two completely different people, and I've grown up."

"Exactly." She nods. A slow smile creeps along her mouth as she leans forward. "You can't tell me you haven't imagined how it would feel like to have him call you '*good girl*' with a voice like that."

"Oh, my God, Ember!" I squeal, shooting up to stand. With my heart pounding, I peek back up the stairs before my hardened stare slices back to Ember. "You are the worst."

"Why?" She stands, bringing her face close to mine. "Because I tell the truth and call it how I see it?"

"No, because you've never had any tact."

"You're right, but some situations call for honesty."

"Well, you may be honest, but your delivery is poor."

"I only tell you the truth because I love you." Her expression softens, and she reaches out, wrapping her hand around my arm. "You've been a sister to me, Adeline."

"And you've been mine."

Although my parents never had any other children after me,

I often wished I had someone to grow up with. Hours were spent huddled in my room after my father laid into me for being a disappointment. Because there were twelve years between Archer and me, he felt like I was born solely to hold him back. With me, he had to start over. With me, I was another expense. With me, he couldn't focus all his attention on moving up in the ranks of government. He may have made it to district attorney of Massachusetts, but he was always hungry for more, and he spent every single day of my childhood reminding me why he hated me.

While I used to be holed up in my room, I dreamed of having a sister, a friend. Even though I had a sibling, I couldn't confide in Archer. Our father made sure to stay in his ear, convincing him my life at home was just as beautiful as the one he was raised in.

But Ember was there when I felt alone. She filled the hole I felt when I stepped out of that house. A confidante and a friend; she's been a sister to me.

"I'm glad you're happy here." Ember's smile falls. "But still, I want you to be careful. A Harding will always be a Harding, no matter how much time has passed."

"Okay," I scoff, pushing her away. "One second you're teasing me about him calling me a *'good girl'*, and now you're warning me not to get too close."

"I'm familiar with their kind, Adeline. Micah is and always will be a rich boy, no matter how old he is. He's a product of the life he grew up in."

I bite the tip of my tongue and stay silent. I can't help but wonder if she thinks the same about me. Does she think I'm a product of my upbringing?

Ember comes from a family like mine: privileged. The only difference is Ember's parents constantly showered her with love.

Is she the product of her upbringing?

I may have only spent a few short hours with Micah, but it's hard for me to see him in the same light as his upbringing. Then again, I've always believed Micah was different.

Micah's heavy footfalls land on the stairs. When he comes into view again, his white shirt is stained with streaks of black and brown, and dust coats the length of his arms down to his strong fingers. He jogs down the stairs and heads straight for the kitchen without looking up.

The sound of rushing water fills the quiet.

I watch him from where I'm standing. His T-shirt stretches across his toned, corded back. My mouth waters, and I swallow, his voice suddenly in my ear calling me a '*good girl*'.

Damn Ember and her unfiltered mouth.

"I should go," Ember blurts out. She grabs her purse from the sofa and hooks it over her shoulder. "I have a client consultation booked for this evening, and another one next week. Would you want to come?"

"I don't know." My stomach twists as I shake my head. "I'm not sure I'm up for it."

"I'll text you the details and if you want to meet next week, I'd love to introduce you to my client," Ember adds. "She's a smaller influencer, but she's a model, too. Maybe she could connect you with photographers on the East Coast whenever you want to get back to work."

I twist my fingers. "Thinking about work right now is overwhelming. If I allow myself to think about it, my heart breaks."

We usually go out for drinks afterward. If you don't feel up for the makeup session, you can always join us after. There's this place not far down from the studio a few of us makeup artists like to go. Very lowkey and relaxed. It'll be fun."

There's a mirror located on the far wall of the living room. I've yet to bring myself to look at it or any other one in this house. I avoid them like the plague, afraid of what I'll discover in my reflection. Not in my appearance, but of the person I've become. Thrusting myself back into the modeling world this soon is the furthest thing from my mind and would only shine a light on my truth.

"I'll think about it." I give her a small smile, unsure if I should take her up on her offer. The thought of going out with my best friend is tempting. It feels like something I should do, but I'm afraid of being thrown back into the modeling world. Although Ember landed on the other side of it—the technical, cosmetic side—we exist in the same orbit.

Thankfully, it isn't for another week, buying me time to decide.

My best friend wraps her arms around me one more time. I rest my chin on her shoulder, looking behind her. My eyes catch the mirror for a moment before I quickly snap them shut. I still have a week to decide, but for now, I think I'll gladly stay wrapped in the bubble of Micah's old house.

NINE

Micah

"Two beers!" my best friend yells to the bartender, holding up two fingers.

She nods without uttering a word and digs two bottles from the cooler in front of her, pops the tops, and sets them on the small, square napkins in front of us.

Archer tosses her a twenty before turning around and leaning against the counter. He takes a sip of his beer but keeps his attention focused on the two couples playing pool on the other side of the bar.

"You know, I never learned how to play," he mutters, with his mouth against the edge of his bottle as he swings his gaze to mine, but I avoid it, taking another swig of beer.

I'm annoyed. Archer hasn't been in town for months and I don't know why he insisted on meeting here of all places. Every single time he's in town, we end up meeting at these shithole dive bars. It reminds me of Harley's Club, but this one is impossibly worse, called Traver's Back Hole, or some shit like that.

As soon as I stepped inside, I quickly understood why Archer picked it, aside from its name. Like Harley's Club, Traver's is dimly lit, with only a handful of unassuming customers. Plaster peels from the walls, and nearly all its neon signs are either turned off or broken. Old country music plays from a jukebox in the corner, and the smell of stale beer fills the air. Stains dot the carpet underneath two tilted pool tables.

This bar looks like garbage, and Archer sticks out like a flashing red light. His designer black suit, chrome watch, and the chain draped around his neck are dead giveaways he doesn't belong in a place like this.

I shove the sleeves of my forest green crewneck sweater up the length of my arms, thankful I don't look as strikingly out of place as Archer does. Still, my association with him doesn't help.

"Soren should be here any minute," Archer mutters against his beer in a hushed voice, as if the cracked-out couple practically fucking against the wall in the back corner of the bar can hear him from this distance.

"I'm getting fucking nervous, man." He blows out an anxiety-fueled rush of air and twists to place his bottle on the counter. "Soren is my largest supplier. I've been a little behind on getting his cut of the profits to him."

Instinct has my muscles tensing and my palms sweating. I hate that I'm even here, but if there's one thing I'm guilty of, it's supporting my best friend even when he's found himself in deep waters. Waters he often drowns in.

This time, I'm hoping I have enough strength to help keep his head *above* water.

Archer's green eyes dart to the metal door of the bar just as a customer steps in. I hold my breath, waiting to see if this is the man we're waiting on. Soren McGovern is well known in the drug trade. While keeping his profile relatively low, he and Archer have been in business for years, maintaining their relationship that has been watered down to one of convenience and money.

Soren provides a supply of prescription drugs. Archer sells them in exchange for extra profits.

I have yet to meet Soren in person. My heart hammers in my chest, knowing this is most likely more dangerous than Archer is perceiving it to be. He's visibly nervous, but he's downplayed his relationship with Soren for years.

Looking at my best friend, I try to pinpoint a time when it all changed.

I hardly recognize him.

"This meeting shouldn't take long." He spins around and swallows down the rest of his beer. "At least I'm hoping it won't so I can get the fuck out of here as fast as possible."

I narrow my eyes and ask him a question I already suspect I know the answer to. "Have you even seen your sister since you've been in town?"

"Not yet." He presses his mouth into a thin line. "I told her I was in town, but I was leaving tonight. We're supposed to meet for coffee later before my flight heads out."

"Didn't you just get in?" Irritation brews under my skin.

"Yesterday." He wipes the back of his hand across his mouth and waves to the bartender, for another beer. "But I'm not interested in staying long. I need to get back home."

By home, he means Austria. Archer landed a huge marketing deal for the tech company I helped invest in here in Boston, only to move its headquarters to Vienna.

I think about Adeline living in my house. I still don't know the reason for her returning to Boston, but I'm not an idiot. I see the loneliness in her eyes. I hear the sadness in her voice. She plays it off, pretending it doesn't exist, or I won't notice, but I do. Every conversation we've had over the past week, I've found myself wanting to learn more. She's easy to talk to, and something about her is comforting, like a bright, warm glow in this shit world.

Every day I'm at the house, I search for something to repair. I know I could easily call my brother Jude and his crew to help with the renovation, but until I feel it's out of my realm of expertise, I plan on helping Adeline myself. She hasn't yet begun to work on the structural parts of the house, but she's shaken off the cobwebs that once littered the walls and ceilings. She's started to breathe life back into the house in a way I wasn't expecting.

The work around my place has been a pleasant distraction from my reality, and the break Lennon forced me to take has been a little easier to swallow when I'm able to channel all my frustration into blowing out all the damaged walls and prying off broken floorboards.

Every day I'm there, I find it more difficult to leave than the day before.

"Don't you think you should have set aside a little more time to see her?"

"Why?" he asks, turning his head in my direction but keeping his arms resting on the edge of the bar. His eyebrows pinch together as he looks at me. "Is something wrong with her?"

"Well, no." I frown, avoiding his stare. "I just thought you'd want to see her for longer than an hour, considering she left Los Angeles in a hurry."

"I don't know why she did." He shrugs. "Adeline has always had this impulsive streak."

I don't know how accurate Archer is when he says his sister is impulsive. For as long as I've known her, she's dreamed of becoming a model, and she's done just that. She wasn't plastered on every billboard or magazine, but there were times I found myself scrolling through social media or on a news website and I'd come across a makeup ad with her gorgeous face on it.

"She didn't tell you why she left?" I'm careful with my questions. I've never pried into Archer's relationship with Adeline, and I've never brought her up with him. With their twelve-year age gap, I saw her very little compared to her brother. But getting small glimpses of her personality these past seven days has me curious now.

"Nope." He darts his attention to the front door again. "I didn't ask. She asked if there was a place she could stay, and I told her you might be able to help. That's when I messaged you."

"Oh." I frown, picking at the label of my beer. More curiosity eats away at me. The mystery surrounding Adeline's sudden departure from LA deepens. It's clear I won't get any answers from Archer, though. He appears to be as distant from Adeline as he's always been. I don't hold it against him, considering he moved out before Adeline even started kindergarten.

"Hey, but thanks for taking her in, man." Archer slaps me on the back. "I know she's in good hands at your place. I don't like to dig too deeply into my sister's life, but I know she's safe with you."

"She is." I raise my eyebrows. "I wish my house was in better shape, but I'm getting it there."

"I feel guilty for not being there as much when she was growing up, but she's done well for herself," he confesses with a distant look in his eye. "Her modeling career seems to be going well, and pretty soon she'll probably be more famous than either you or me."

He laughs, and I smile. He may be right, but from the look in Adeline's eyes, it doesn't look like it's happening as soon as Archer believes it will.

Either way, I hope he's right. Or I at least hope it's what Adeline wants.

"Don't worry, though," Archer adds, finishing off his second beer already. "She probably won't need to stay for long."

The squeak of the blue metal door swinging open has Archer and me darting our heads toward the front of the bar as a man dressed in a charcoal gray suit stops in the doorway. The door shuts behind him, and he surveys the room. None of the patrons inside bother to look up from their pool games, and the couple in the back corner are clearly not focused on anyone other than themselves. The man and woman are a tangled mess of limbs as the man grinds against the woman, pinning her in the corner.

I follow Archer's lead when he pushes off the bar top and turns around.

"Is that him?" I lean toward Archer, though I already know the answer when the man in question turns to look in our direction.

He lifts his chin in recognition and makes his way toward us. My stomach flips, and goosebumps dance their way down the back of my neck.

I don't have a good feeling about this. I tell myself Archer doesn't seem bothered, so neither should I, but this wouldn't be the first time Archer has pulled me into a situation I have no business being involved in. This entire thing reeks of the shit my father used to pull. Men like Soren played a hand in my father's death, taking advantage of those with addictions.

Memories and trauma from my past make the hairs on the back of my neck stand up. I have no business being here.

"We don't have to do this, Arch," I rush out before Soren and his men get close enough to hear.

"It'll be fine, Micah." Archer turns his head, his green eyes begging me to have his back just one more time.

"That's what you always say, and the outcome always takes

a turn. We can leave right now. We can put all of this behind us."

"Stop," he warns, his eyes narrowing. "I can't. I'm in too deep, and I need you on this. I need my best friend to have my back."

"I can help you," I offer. "Let me *help* you."

"Fuck, Micah. Please, stop."

I sigh and close my eyes. I've always had his fucking back. My teeth practically crack as I grind my jaw.

Alarm bells ring in my mind. I shouldn't be here. Archer shouldn't be here.

I see my oldest brother's eyes staring at me in disappointment. I see my father looking at me with admiration and pride.

"You've always been there for me," he adds. "And Adeline."

"Right." I turn so Soren can't read our lips. He hasn't reached us yet. "Think of her. How do you think she would feel if she knew what you were doing right now? Who you were meeting..."

"I can't. Not now." He immediately shuts me down, barely moving his lips. "He's almost here."

I turn back around to face the room.

Soren smiles in our direction, his silver tooth glinting in the light. The shamrock tattoo in the corner of his left eye scrunches when he holds out his hand to Archer.

"Archer Mayfield," he greets. Grasping onto Archer's hand, he wraps both around his as they shake.

"Good to see you, Soren," Archer replies.

While Archer and Soren greet one another, I find myself eyeing the two men standing behind Soren. They're each dressed in similar suits. If I were to guess, they could be twins. The only distinction is the snake tattoo wrapped around one of the men's necks, the head dipping below his Adam's apple..

Despite the snake tattoo, the men are clean cut and crisp.

Clearly, all of us stick out in this bar, but when I glance over my shoulder, the bartender appears unfazed. She dips a glass into soapy water, keeping her eyes trained on the boxing match playing on the small TV mounted in the corner.

Archer's hand claps my shoulder. "This is my best friend, Micah Harding."

"Holy shit, Mayfield." Soren beams, his twinkling eyes dancing between Archer and me. "I didn't realize you cozied up to corporate fuckers like the Hardings."

I stiffen, straightening my back and holding my breath. I'm not unfamiliar with the hate that is tied to my name, but I certainly don't want to hear it from a man as intimidating as Soren.

"Hey, hey." Archer holds his hand up, grinning. "Micah is all good, man. He's a family friend."

"Is that so?" He raises his eyebrows. "If he has the reputation of his father, I don't think it was wise for you to bring him with you."

My throat swells. Soren must not be aware of my past. If he is, he doesn't mention it. What situation has Archer gotten himself into? This meeting with Soren is more dangerous than anything we've done in the past.

"Micah isn't anything like James Harding," Archer reassures him.

"For your sake"—Soren leans in, his voice deepening as he lines his sharp, harsh glare at Archer—"you'd better hope to fucking hell he isn't."

"Hope isn't necessary when I've known him all my life," Archer reassures him. He's attempting to portray confidence, but his neck bobs as his hands shake. He stuffs them into his pockets, attempting to hide his nervousness.

"Good." Soren claps his tattoo-covered hands. "Now, down to business. What's the status of my supply?"

"Business is good." Archer nods, a small smile playing on his mouth. "I've got a few of my connections set up for transactions this week."

I don't like hearing about Archer's business dealings and how he's gotten himself into this mess. Years spent trying to get ahead or come up with other means of earning money has landed him in a web he can't seem to get out of.

"What about the money you owe me?" Soren asks, bringing his fingers to his mouth. "I give you my largest inventory for you to resell, and I have yet to be paid for any of it. You see, when it comes to this type of business, time is money."

"I told you I'd have it to you by next week." Archer straightens his back and tries to appear casual and relaxed, but the pulse in his temple rapidly speeds up. "You have my word."

"You know..." Soren's face transforms. His mouth straightens, and it's clear the pleasantries are gone. He doesn't take his eyes off Archer. "Here I was worried you'd brought a Harding with you, but it's clear I was mistaken. Your word doesn't mean shit to me, Mayfield. You told me you would have it to me two weeks ago."

"We've been doing business for years, Soren," Archer argues. "You know I'm good for it."

"Hmm." He lifts his hand and scratches at his clean-shaven chin with a sneer as he steps closer to Archer, bringing his nose in line with his. "If your word is as good as you say it is, I'm going to need some reassurance."

My stomach twists into knots. Like an anchor dropping into the sea, I feel sick.

Soren nods his head to the man flanking him on his right. The large man moves around Soren, sliding between him and me. In the time it takes me to blink, he clutches Archer's lapels, fisting the silky fabric, and pulls him to his chest, rearing his ring-laden fist back. Driving his fist into Archer's face, he delivers a solid, quick blow, knocking him to the floor. The broken barstools fall back as Archer topples against them and lands on the sticky tile.

I stuff my balled-up fists into the pockets of my jeans, even though instinct tells me to intervene. I want to fight back and defend my best friend, but I'm outnumbered. The other man behind Soren side steps, closing in on me in silent warning to not get involved. My heart leaps out of my chest when I watch Soren step forward and hover over Archer. He's curled into the fetal position on his side, covering his nose as he groans. Blood spills onto his hand and drips onto the floor.

The patrons in the bar appear unfazed. The bartender continues cleaning glasses. Her eyes lift only briefly to see what's unfolding on the other side of her bar, but she doesn't intervene. One country song ends, rolling right into the next. A happy tune starts playing, drowning out Archer's moans and groans of pain.

Soren pulls something from his pocket. It doesn't hit me right away what it is until I hear the sharp click of a blade popping out from the handle. He grips Archer's jaw, tugging his face to look up at him.

Archer groans again, looking up at Soren with hooded eyes as Soren brings the blade to Archer's throat and presses it against his skin. He kneels lower, pushing his nose to Archer's. Archer writhes under Soren's firm grip, twisting his head from side to side.

Clicking his tongue, Soren disapproves, seething with anger. Veins bulge and pulsate from his thick neck. I don't dare move knowing the bodyguard standing in front of me won't hesitate to put me in the same position as Archer.

"Brave and bold Archer Mayfield," Soren practically sings, teasing. "Son of a district attorney. Tech millionaire. Let's get one thing straight." He smooths his hand over Archer's face, pushing back his brown hair. Fear spreads across Archer's broken face, and my heart cracks. Soren adds pressure to the knife he's wielding. One quick slip, and I'll be witnessing my best friend's murder. "If I don't get my fucking money by the end of the month, it'll be more than your little pussy Harding friend over here who will suffer. One by one, I'll take out every single person you care about."

"You'll get your money," Archer tries to reassure him.

"I'd better." Soren soothes his hand over Archer's face once more before clasping his jaw again. "Or else that sweet baby sister of yours will unfortunately never be able to model again."

Archer grunts as blood spills from his nose. He kicks under Soren, anger building behind him. "Don't you fucking touch her," Archer spits, blood spraying from his mouth.

My heart pounds, clawing to jump out of my chest. I tighten my fists at the mention of Adeline. I want nothing more than to lunge forward and take down Soren for even mentioning Adeline's name. She doesn't need to be brought into this.

"Oh," Soren says, raising his eyebrows and tilting his head to the side. "You didn't think I knew about that baby sister of yours. Hard to ignore a sweet cunt like that one."

Archer grunts again, his eyes flaming with anger. "Fuck you."

"No, no, no." Soren shakes his head in disapproval. "I'd watch that mouth of yours if I were you." He slowly drags the sharp edge of his blade across Archer's lip with a sneer. When he's satisfied with Archer's silence, he slaps Archer's cheek in approval and stands. He closes his blade and drops it back into his pocket. Fixing the ends of his sleeves, he steps back and smooths down his dark brown hair. "Have a safe trip back home to Austria, Archer. I look forward to hearing from you by the end of the month."

Soren's bodyguard moves to stand behind his boss again.

Soren glances at me. "Harding." He nods. "It's been a pleasure. For your sake, I hope we don't need to meet like this again."

I stay planted where I am, panic slithering down the length of my spine. Soren's threat to me isn't what has me worried. It's the one he's put on Adeline.

Once they leave the bar, Archer moves to stand. He rolls onto all fours, taking a moment to catch his breath. I don't help him stand, too angry to do anything. I've tried to help Archer for years. He's the best person I've known and has been there for me in times I needed him, but I don't recognize him now. Not anymore.

I don't recognize the man in front of me—the one willing to put the safety of his sister and everyone he cares about at risk.

And if Archer can't protect Adeline...

I will.

TEN

ADELINE

"I'm sorry, hun. It's closing time.

I'm staring at the bottom of my empty coffee cup before swinging my gaze up to the waitress standing in front of me.

She's wearing a bright yellow apron, and her braided pigtails rest on either side of her shoulders, draping down the length of her chest. Behind her, the reflection of the streetlights shimmers on the wet, cobblestone sidewalk.

The emptiness in my chest expands when the lights of the coffee shop dim.

"I'm all finished," I tell her, sliding my empty mug and plate across the table. Crumbs dot the small saucer-sized plate, the remnants of the croissant I munched on over an hour ago.

The waitress sets my bill upside down on the table, but I immediately hand her my card, knowing she's wanting me to leave so she can close out her drawer for the night.

When she walks away to swipe it, I check my phone as anxiety and sadness fill the emptiness inside. I read back through my messages with my brother, ensuring I hadn't misread our meetup time and place.

I haven't seen him since I've moved back to Boston, and

while he doesn't live in the country anymore, our visits have become scarcer. But with him in town on business, I was happy when he set aside the time to meet with me before heading back home.

But he hasn't showed.

I spend the next minute trading glances between the window facing the street to my phone. I send Archer another text before giving in and messaging Micah.

Is Archer with you?

Aside from the few times I've seen him at his house this week, we haven't spoken much. Micah has maintained his distance, keeping himself busy with the unusable bedrooms upstairs and the bathroom. Although we haven't talked much, I've noticed him coming over more often and staying longer. Taking a break from work must have triggered his need to work on the house.

Micah quickly responds.

No. He told me he was meeting up with you before heading home.

He was supposed to, but he never came.

After typing my message, I place my phone on the table just as the waitress returns.

She hands me my card with a frown.

"I'm so sorry, but your card was rejected."

"What?" I ask, sitting up in my seat.

"It was declined," she repeats, speaking low. The café is completely empty, but her voice is quiet, as if someone might overhear us.

"Oh no." My cheeks heat with embarrassment. "I'm so

sorry." I swallow my shallow breaths and reach for my purse. The waitress stands patiently, but I feel her eyes on me. I dig through my purse, hoping I can find another way to pay. I sigh with relief when I find a twenty folded and stuffed in between a few old receipts. I hand it to her. "You can keep the change."

"Thank you." She smiles. "Have a great night."

"You, too." I force a smile and slide out from behind the table to gather my purse and phone before pushing through the glass door.

The street is dark and desolate. I'm deep in the heart of the city, but this street is littered with residences. Several blocks stand between the livelier side of Boston and me.

My stomach wavers while I decide what to do.

I took a rideshare here, but with my card declined at the coffee shop, I'm not sure I can get one back home.

I'm miles from Cambridge.

I begin walking toward the brighter lights in the distance. Small trees line the brick sidewalk. One after another, I pass house after house. The sky is pitch black and the wind howls through the branches of the trees. The air isn't as cold as last week, bits of spring finally peeking through, but the eerie quiet causes a shiver to sliver down my spine.

Unlocking my phone, I check my bank account. Since I work freelance modeling, my pay isn't consistent. Before I left LA, I was working on signing with a modeling agency, and the job I walked out on that day was one that would have helped me achieve that goal.

When I sign in to my account, I stare at the negative balance and feel sick.

I scroll through my transactions, wondering how it's been spent so quickly.

A payment is pending for a photoshoot I did a few weeks ago, but it won't clear for another two days.

Closing out my phone, I keep it in my hand while I figure out what to do. I shouldn't be walking these streets alone at night. I'm not familiar with this part of the city, and I have no idea why Archer wanted to meet here.

It's desolate and far from anywhere I would have chosen.

I stare at my phone, considering who to call.

Ember is working with a client, so I know she's unavailable. I wouldn't want to bother her anyway. There's no shot in hell I'm calling either of my parents. I haven't spoken to my father in years, and my mother and I rarely talk.

Before I talk myself out of it, I call the last person I expect, but the only one I can ask for help.

"Adeline?"

Micah's deep voice travels through my phone and lands against my ear. Goosebumps prickle across my neck, and my heart skips a beat. Ever since my conversation with Ember, I haven't been able to push the thought of him out of my head. Memories of how I used to litter the pages of my diary with doodles of my first name followed by his last play in my mind. Heat returns to my cheeks, as if he can read my thoughts.

"Hey, Micah,." I breathe out. I didn't realize I've been widening my steps and walking faster.

"Is everything okay?" he rushes to ask. "Why do you sound like that?"

"Sound like what?"

"Worried. You sounding worried is making me worried."

"Um, well..." I bite my lip. I'm too embarrassed to admit the truth, but I have no choice. It's either ask for Micah's help or risk the dangers that come with walking the streets of Boston alone at night.

"What is it, Addy?" he demands.

Heat spreads between my legs at his use of my nickname again. He seems to use it when he doesn't realize it, as if it's instinct to him, falling from his mouth without effort or thought.

"Well, since I don't have a car, I grabbed a rideshare here and figured Archer would have driven me home. But since he never showed, the café closed, and I was forced to leave."

"Where are you?" I hear what sounds like him swiping his keys from the entryway table, followed by a door slamming shut behind him.

My chin wobbles and my vision blurs. Until now, I've kept my emotions in check. I realize I'm not heartbroken over Maddox or love lost. I'm heartbroken my life has dramatically shifted into one where I find myself broke and stranded in a city where I don't feel welcome.

I swallow back the tears threatening to spill and look around. "I don't know."

"I'm coming to get you," Micah says, an engine roaring to life in the background. "I need to know where you are, Addy."

"Um," I swipe my hand across my forehead and tuck my hair behind my ear. "I don't..."

"Tell me where you are." His voice solid in my ear.

I read the nearest street signs out loud to him and stand on the corner, under the streetlamp.

"Fuck!" Micah yells over the rumbling engine. "That's not exactly the best neighborhood, Addy. Why the fuck did Archer want you to meet him there?" He doesn't give me the chance to respond before he says, "I'll be there as fast as I can. Is there anyone around, or are you close to anything?"

"No." I quiver as a tear slips from my eye. "I don't see anyone, but it's kind of dark. I'm standing under a streetlamp."

"Stay there," he orders. "I'm coming to get you."

He abruptly ends our call, and anxiety replaces the void. A chill creeps down the length of my spine. Silence overwhelms me.

Over the next ten minutes, I try my best to keep myself distracted. I scroll through social media. I play one of my phone games. All the while keeping my ears trained on my surroundings. From the corner of my eye, I keep my attention on the road. Every car that passes makes my heart race and my palms sweat.

I check the time on my phone. It's been almost twenty minutes since I spoke with Micah, and my mind is starting to spin in all directions. I imagine the worst scenarios, frightened I'm going to be stranded alone, yet again. Or worse... I've watched too many crime documentaries and know what happens to women in my situation.

A loud rumble down the street fills the silence. I take a chance and peek up. A single headlight turns onto the street from another two blocks away. It races down the residential road faster than any car has up to this point. The blood drains from my veins and down to my feet. Goosebumps spread down the length of my legs, and my heart beats against my chest.

The headlight grows closer, slowing as it nears me. The man on the bike is wearing a blacked-out helmet, completely shielding his face from view. I take a step back off the curb, creating as much distance between us as possible. My heel hits an uneven brick, and I stumble, rolling my ankle, but I quickly steady myself, retreating until my back hits the ivy-covered brick wall dividing the sidewalk and the yard of the house behind it.

The man climbs off his motorcycle, leaving the engine running.

I place my hands on the wall behind me, clamoring for what to do.

Relief slams into my chest as soon as the man takes off his helmet.

"Adeline," he breathes out. "What are you doing?"

I snap my mouth shut and sweep my tongue across my lips. "I didn't know you had a bike."

I look over his shoulder, and he follows my gaze before swinging his back to mine. His usually bright eyes are black in the dark of the night, even beneath the streetlamp we're under.

"I have several vehicles," he tells me. "I knew this was the fastest way for me to get to you, and if I hit traffic on the way, I would be able to weave in and out easily."

"Oh." I step away from the wall.

Micah backs away, his heavy black boots beating against the brick. His dark jeans are covered in streaks of paint, and his scent surrounds me: mint, laundry, and the old wood smell permeating his house.

"Here." He grabs another black helmet from the back of his bike. "Put this on." He holds it out for me to take, but I don't move.

He shakes it, his frustration getting to him. "Come on, Addy."

"I can't get on that." I shake my head.

Micah presses his mouth into a tight line.

I'm grateful he rushed here to pick me up, and although we're still standing on the same corner, I do feel a million times safer being with Micah... but when I look down at my half-naked legs, I can't help but feel self-conscious.

"You're getting on the bike, Adeline."

"I'm not."

"Yes. You are."

I look down at the black mini skirt I decided to pair with my hot pink, scoop-neck sweater.

"Micah..." I cross my arms over my chest with a huff. "I can't get on that bike wearing this skirt."

His eyes move to my legs. I cross them, heat pooling and

spreading in places even I haven't bothered to touch in entirely too long. It's apparent my body is telling me I've been neglecting myself. Sirens and warning bells sound off in every cell, telling me the look in Micah's eye is enough to make me soaking wet. I'm worried he'll be able to tell my reaction once my legs are wrapped around him.

Micah's eyes flash with darkness. His chest expands with heavy, heated breaths as he takes a step forward, cutting the space between us.

"Get on the bike." He growls.

I look up. Our faces are entirely too close; closer than we've ever been. It's an unfamiliar yet comfortable feeling. The sadness and darkness I've seen on his face over the past week has multiplied. His pain is up close and personal, begging to be seen, but then he blinks, and it's gone.

"There has to be another way to get home," I tell him. I know I'm being stubborn. I know I should be grateful. I'm broke, and Micah has driven all the way out here. He didn't hesitate, and the urgent way he climbed off his bike tells me he was worried for my safety. He didn't know if I would still be standing when he finally made it. The thought of his concern is comforting.

Still, I stand my ground. For now. I've never been able to give into Micah's demands easily.

His demand reminds me of when I was eleven years old. Lungs burning and heart broken with embarrassment.

"There's no other way home," he says between clenched teeth. His sculpted jaw ticks as he shoves the helmet in my direction again. "Get on the bike." He shoots me another piercing glare when I don't move. "If you don't take this fucking helmet right now, I'll throw you over my shoulder and place you on the bike myself. Everyone in this neighborhood will think I'm kidnapping you."

I suck in a sharp breath, my insides turning to molten lava. My nostrils flare as I rip the helmet from his grip.

"Good girl." He smirks.

White knuckled, I suck in another breath. It shoots to the back of my throat and slams into my lungs, nearly knocking me off my feet. Hearing those two words catches me and my body off guard.

Did he hear Ember teasing me about him calling me a good girl, or is it purely coincidence?

My fingers tighten their grip on the helmet. I place it on my head and stomp my way over to the bike, thankful when the helmet hides my expression. Micah is quick to follow, practically pressing his chest against my back before climbing back onto his bike, as if he's prepared to follow through on his threat to toss me over his shoulder if necessary. He waits for me to get on behind him. I carefully and quickly lift my skirt high enough to straddle the seat. At least I was smart enough to wear my converse. Once on, I fix my skirt, lifting myself high enough to pull it underneath me, and I slide forward, pressing the inside of my thighs against his sturdy frame.

The front of my soaked panties presses against him. His body tenses when I slide my hands around his waist. His muscles harden under my touch, even through his thin T-shirt. I clutch onto the fabric, fisting it with my small fingers, and press my whole body against his. I feel small next to him but protected and safe. He's solid and warm.

The engine rumbles and vibrates beneath us. My body hums in response, the heat from Micah's body between my legs emanating. The sensation on my skin, vibrating against my flesh, only makes me wetter.

I inhale a sharp breath and work to adjust myself again. My skirt slips back up my thighs, and I groan, knowing this will be difficult to keep down on the ride home. My skirt will be bunched around my waist by the time we get there.

With me shifting behind him, Micah freezes. His ribs stop contracting with every breath, and his muscles swell. I glance over his shoulder, wondering why he hasn't moved and why we haven't left yet since he seemed adamant about getting us out of this neighborhood.

The corded muscles of his forearm twitch.

He removes his hand from the handle and flexes his fingers, stretching them before placing his hand back on the bike. Finally, he takes in a deep breath, revs the engine, and drives us home.

ELEVEN

Micah

"I'm thinking we tear the whole thing down," I tell my brother, gesturing to the oversized, broken-down shed in the backyard.

"Are you wanting to build a new one?" Jude asks, wiping the back of his hand across his sweat-covered forehead. "Or leave this area open?"

His best friend and business partner Cain joins us, standing between Jude and me.

"I'm not sure yet." I stare at the broken sinking pile of wood.

The shed in the backyard looks almost as old as the house. By my guess, it was probably built to be a living space while the main house was being constructed.

The wooden planks bend as they near the foundation, as if the building is literally sinking back into the earth. The mustard yellow painted planks are peeling and littered with splinters. I've done my best to preserve the history of this place, but sometimes I don't have a choice.

I cross my arms and swing my gaze back up to the house. Specifically, Adeline's window. I can't help it. They gravitate toward her, and the longer I've stayed here, the more I find myself being conscious of her presence. Slowly, I started bringing over more of my clothes. Then the next week, I brought my toiletries. First, I was sleeping on the couch before switching to the bedroom next to Adeline's two weeks ago. After removing all the damaged parts, Jude came over to help add in new floorboards and finish patching the lower half of the drywall. I've tried to save as much of the original flooring and preserve as much of the original character of the house as possible. Having all the money in the world, a bottomless bank account, allows me to stay wherever I want. After Lennon forced me to take a break from work, and before I began moving into the house, I'd stayed at the most expensive room possible. But the claws that have a grip on the pockets of my mind exposed themselves. No matter how hard you work to leave the past behind, it still has a way of appearing in the unlikeliest of times. The good. The bad. Regret. All of it rears its ugly head, threatening to consume you.

I couldn't continue to live in solitary silence.

My moving into the house full-time was a subtle, gradual process—one I thought Adeline would have noticed or mentioned. If she has noticed or cares, though, she hasn't brought the subject up.

For weeks, I've told myself my staying here is for her safety. With Soren's threat constantly playing on repeat in my mind, I've stayed close to Adeline. The need to protect her has always been there. I want to say it's because I've always seen her as my best friend's little sister and there's this natural urge to protect her, but the feeling she gave me the night she was stranded in the middle of Boston told me otherwise. The panic and anger I felt went beyond care for my best friend's little sister's wellbeing.

I wasn't protecting his little sister. I was protecting Adeline.

Me moving into the house wasn't just for her protection. I liked being around her.

Her bedroom faces the back of the house, and from here I see her standing in front of her closet. She reaches inside, pulling out one of the hangers. Her arm stiffens as she holds the dress out in front of her, examines it, then drapes it against her body, looking down at how it looks on her. Frowning, she shakes her head and stuffs it back into the closet before pulling another one out.

She isn't standing in front of a mirror, only the closet.

I have yet to see her this morning, but from the window I see her. Her brown hair is braided and swept to the side, resting over her bare shoulder, her smooth skin catching the bits of sunlight peeking through the window.

My dick twitches, remembering what it was like to have her body wrapped around mine the night I picked her up on my bike. We haven't spoken about that night since. I haven't spoken to Archer much, either.

After making it home that night, I called him, even though I knew he was on his way to Austria and didn't have cell service. In a voicemail, I laid into him for leaving his sister vulnerable, especially given the fact Soren had threatened him with Adeline. He called me back once he'd landed, apologizing and thanking me for protecting her. He said he'd make it up to Adeline somehow, but I didn't ask for details. I didn't want to press him for more, especially given I was having thoughts about my best friend's sister. Ones that involved her long thighs wrapped around me and her near-bare pussy pressing against the small of my back.

"We'll need to take everything out of here before we can get started," Jude says, breaking my attention away from Adeline.

"Do you even know what's inside?" Cain asks, leaning in and prying the front door open.

"A few pieces of furniture and old tools," I tell him. "Mostly garden items."

"So, trash?" Cain raises his eyebrows.

"What's trash?" Adeline yells from the back of the house.

Not only has she caught the attention of the three of us, but she's also caught the attention of Jude and Cain's crew working on the back patio. Raised bricks and dirt pile around the area. The men are covered in dust and grime, exhausted from the early summer heat creeping in.

Adeline is clearly thrilled for summer to show its face.

The curves of her body are on full display with her fitted white tank top and her long legs greeting the sun with her cut off jean shorts. The men's heads swivel in her direction, following her as she makes her way toward us.

An inexplicable feeling comes over me, similar to the one I had the night I picked Adeline up from the street corner. I ball my hands into fists, and my nostrils flare. It's unreasonable and brash but something I can't ignore.

I suddenly feel the need to do... *something*.

Adeline treads through the overgrown grass and weeds toward us, not noticing the attention she's drawn. She slips between me and Jude and pries open the door, poking her head inside. She steps back out a few short seconds later. "This furniture looks vintage."

"Really?" Jude steps closer to a small window on the side of the building. He cups his hands around his eyes, peering through the dusty glass.

"There's a desk in here." She bounces on her toes, the muscles in her legs flexing. "And a dresser." She glances over her shoulder and looks directly at me with a smile. "It would be fun to try and restore it."

I want to tell her no. I don't believe it's a good idea, considering we have an entire house that needs renovating, but the glimmer in her eye and the excitement spread across her full pink lips weaken my resolve. I also think about Soren and the threat he could still be posing. Archer has stayed relatively silent.

A month ago, I'd sent him a text asking him if he was able to pay Soren what he owes him. After reassuring me he was, I relaxed with only a bit of relief. If Archer is telling the truth, it doesn't mean Soren's threat isn't still looming. Men like him in circles like theirs don't let those types of betrayals go so easily. Not even when the debt is paid.

I'm also not foolish enough to believe Archer hasn't continued to do business with Soren.

I considered sending Archer the money he owed, but I didn't want there to be a thread or connection tying me to Archer and Soren's business dealings. I didn't need to be involved, and I didn't want to be.

I'd paid the price for that lifestyle already. I didn't need to do it again.

Restoring furniture along with this house might give Adeline a reason to stay longer than she intends. However long that might be.

Heat pools in my stomach, radiating down to my cock. I cough, clearing my throat and the inappropriate thoughts running in my mind. I scratch the back of my head and lower it, surrendering. "Fine. We can pull it all out and go through it later."

"We're going to need to get our compact excavator back here to start on the demolition." Cain turns to his crew, who are working hard at loading shovels full of broken brick and crumbled dirt into their wheelbarrows.

He lifts his arm in the air and waves them over, and they drop their shovels and join us. Cain explains the plan of unloading every item from the shed and where we're going to put them. Adeline stands beside me, listening carefully. I try to keep my focus on Cain, but I can't help watching her from my peripheral. She's impossible to ignore. Her clean scent hits me, counteracting the pungent smell of the sweaty crew surrounding us.

Her arms are folded, pushing her breasts up, the soft, pillowy flesh swelling over the top hem. My hand twitches again, and my dick swells.

Get a fucking grip, Micah.

Once the crew breaks, they spill into the shed and begin emptying it out, starting with the items closest to the entrance. The shed is packed from wall to wall, but I don't have the patience to go through the items now, only tossing ones that are clearly trash.

Jude nods to Cain before walking over to me and Adeline. "Victoria and I have a date set up tonight." He holds the bottom hem of his shirt out. "I better get home and shower or else Victoria might want a divorce if I attempt to go out like this."

"She would never divorce you," I tell him.

"You're right." He grins. "Cain is going to get the excavator over here tomorrow. That way we can begin demolition on the shed. The crew will start unloading this stuff today so you can go through it. They'll be back tomorrow to work on the patio."

"Okay." I nod. "Thanks, brother."

"Of course." He nods, too, sweat dripping from the ends of his hair. He looks down at his feet before looking back up. "I know Lennon made you take this break, but I think it's been good for you. I'm glad you're finally working on this house."

My attention gravitates to Adeline again. "I agree."

"Take it from me: it's never too late to start over."

I'm not certain his words bring me comfort, though.

He claps me on the shoulder and walks over to gather up a few of his tools by the back door, then Jude and Cain head out.

They've already made their way to the gate on the side of

the house leading to the front yard when Adeline stands in front of me, grinning.

"What is it?" I ask, laughing under my breath.

She looks down at her feet, dragging her toe along the grass. When she looks back up, she squints against the bright sun. "I just wanted to say thank you."

"For what?"

"For agreeing to go through this stuff." She points to the shed. "I just think it would be a shame to throw it all away instead of giving it a second chance at life."

Warmth spreads in my cheeks. It could be the heat from outside or it could be the sight of Adeline standing this close to me. My body vibrates with the memory of her behind me on the bike. A twenty-minute ride home I'll never forget.

"You're welcome." Seeing her happy sparks a light in me. A piece of my soul that's been dead for the longest time is suddenly revived, and she's the one holding the paddles.

I'm terrified of what it means.

Her smile fades when she reaches out and swipes her thumb across my jaw. The small soft pad of it grates against my stubble-lined chin.

"Dirt," she says, pulling her thumb away.

I lift my hand and wipe the same place she just touched.

Leaving me, she spins on her heel and heads into the shed. I walk over to the patio and grab my work gloves.

When I step into the shed, the crew is already hard at work getting everything done before evening hits. Two of the men are lifting an old, dark blue, velvet upholstered sofa. The fabric is torn and weathered across all three cushions. It isn't salvageable. I tell them it's trash before turning my attention elsewhere.

They carry it outside but place it in a separate area from where the other items will go.

I spin around to get a view of what I'm in for when I find

Adeline on the opposite side of the shed. She's climbing a rickety old ladder propped against the wall. I don't know how old it is, but I can see the weathered, fragile rungs from here. Every other one is crooked, barely hanging on to the supports. She looks up at a framed picture of a beach, with a lighthouse in the distance hanging on the wall, keeping her eyes on it as she steps onto the next unsteady rung.

A member of Cain's crew drops the large clock he was working on carrying out, weaving in and out of the furniture to get closer to Adeline.

He slinks his way through, all the while keeping his attention on her. I step closer, too, and with my hands fisted, I walk around a large dresser, bumping my hip into it. I groan, the pain shooting across the right side of my body.

The crew member asks Adeline if she needs help, his attention dropping to her legs. She glances over her shoulder long enough to give him a smile, telling him that she has it.

He's now standing less than a foot away from her, in front of the ladder, offering to spot her in case she falls. He has a perfect view of her from where he is. Her ass cheeks peek out from the hem of her shorts. The man shifts on his feet, tilting his head to the side as he examines her like a piece of meat.

Again, my body is telling me to do something. I don't know what, but it needs an outlet. The way he's admiring her isn't sitting right with me. Fury rages inside me.

"Hey!" I yell, my vision turning red.

Adeline reaches up, trying to reach the frame, not hearing my booming voice. Her tank rises up the length of her stomach, exposing the small of her back. The man shifts on his feet again and leans forward, placing his hands on either side of the ladder. They slowly slide up the sides, growing closer to the backs of her legs.

"Addy!" I say, blood draining from my face. My pulse races,

watching as he slips his hand low, between him and the ladder, adjusting the hard on I'm certain he has.

What in the actual fuck?

My feet move, and before I know it, I'm standing directly behind him.

"What the fuck do you think you're doing?" I yell, seething with anger.

He spins around, lifting his hands up like he's innocent. "Nothing. I was just keeping the ladder steady for her... in case she fell."

Fucker stands in front of me, panicked and wide-eyed.

"Micah?" Adeline says, standing on the ladder about eight feet from the ground. She's looking down at us, half turned. Every curve of her body is on full display at that angle, while the picture remains hanging on the wall, untouched.

I cut the man in front of me a sharp glare. "I have it handled over here. I'm sure your help could be more useful elsewhere."

He sighs, pressing his mouth into a thin line, and his nostrils flare. The fucker knows I caught him in the act and now he's pissed he can't finish what he started. Fucker.

Without a word, he stalks away, his cheeks red with embarrassment.

Adeline is still looking down at me.

"Get down from there, Adeline."

"What?" She gapes, her mouth falling open. "Why?"

"Because," I clip. I know I'm being short with her, but after catching that asshole practically beating his dick to her in front of her, I'm at a loss for words.

Her eyebrows shoot up. "Because...?"

"Because I said so."

Her eyes flare with anger before she makes her way down the ladder, her feet landing on each rung with deliberate force. I know I've taken it too far the second her Converse land on the dusty, wooden floor.

"What the hell is wrong with you?" She glances at the man who was eye fucking her only seconds before, as if he wanted to devour her, and now I'm the asshole.

With a fiery glare, her cheeks flame red.

I step closer to her, closing the space between us. The men filter out of the shed, carrying varying pieces of furniture.

"That guy was about to touch you," I tell her in a low voice, my face close to hers as she looks up at me.

"No, he wasn't. He offered to spot me. He was being nice."

I inhale a deep breath. My neck tightens, and my veins bulge. I step closer, drawing myself to Adeline like a magnet. My resolve wears thin, practically disappearing. I've broken a barrier between us, crossing over into her circle. I expect her to push me away or step to move around me, but she doesn't. Instead, she takes a step back.

I step forward.

She takes another back until her spine lands against the broken ladder, and her hands wrap around the loose rung, pushing her chest out.

I press my chest into hers, towering over her as she looks up at me with wide eyes. Two glassy, caramel-green flecked eyes stare up at me. I get lost in them, savoring the sensation they give me. My anger dulls to a simmer, and the fury I had is replaced with another kind of heat. The type that wants more than the inch of space between us. Her eyes soften slightly, her anger with me transitioning. Her breath deepens. I'm fully aware of how close we are, how this is the closest we've ever been, but I don't care.

"I watched him, Adeline." I growl. "That guy was a fucking pervert. He was practically jerking off to you."

She scoffs, blinking and shaking her head in disbelief, naïve to her beauty. "Come on. Why would he do that when you and all the other guys were in here?"

"You tell me." I pop an eyebrow, keeping the truth to myself because Adeline is stunning. There's no denying her beauty, but I can't help feeling this possessiveness over her. Like she's mine.

"I'm not a child, Micah." She breathes out, the redness fading to pink. "Not anymore. You don't have a right to tell me to get off this ladder just because you demand it."

"Trust me," I sneer. "I'm fully aware you aren't a child, Adeline."

"Then, stop treating me like one." But the shift in her voice isn't a simple command. She's challenging me. Silently daring me to show her the truth of the thoughts I've clearly been thinking.

The jealousy. The desire building inside me.

She clouds my thoughts and my judgments. I shouldn't be feeling this way about my best friend's sister. I know she's a woman, but I can't give in. Heat pools in my lower belly again. The pressure builds, and I want nothing more than to sink myself into Adeline.

My eyes fall to her mouth, wondering what it would feel like to crash mine against hers. I want to devour it and every inch of her body.

I reach up and wrap my hand around the ladder, gripping onto the wood for support. My mind is going a mile a minute. I'm supposed to protect Adeline, not want her. But fuck, how I want her.

I need to get out of here before I do something I might regret.

"Are you going to stop?" she asks, her eyes searching mine.

I'm not sure if she means stop treating her like a child or stop what I'm doing right now. Something tells me it's the latter.

Dammit.

I inhale a deep breath, expanding my lungs with as much oxygen as possible.

But a loud crash snaps us out of the trance we're in. My hand falls away from the ladder, and I snap my head toward the front of the shed. The crew is carrying out one of the large dressers, with one of the guys kicking the door open with his foot. The fragile wooden door claps against the wall. I didn't even realize they'd come back into the shed. The man who was starting to beat himself off to Adeline is nowhere in sight. The rest of the men carry the dresser out, leaving the two of us alone again.

When I turn back to Adeline, she's already moved around me and away from the ladder. Her back is the last thing I see before she disappears out of the shed, returning to the house.

While I'm left with my chest split wide open, and the truth staring me directly in the face.

TWELVE

ADELINE

I must be losing it.

It's been two months since I've moved into Micah's house, and I haven't stopped thinking about him. Things have changed between us.

Ever since the night Archer ditched me, Micah has stayed in the house. He won't speak much during the day, keeping busy with the parts of the house I had yet to touch, such as the more physical jobs I had absolutely no skill set in even trying to attempt.

We've grown a little closer, though, despite our distance. Most nights, I cook dinner for him after he finishes with his work. We sit together in the living room, kicking off a marathon of watching a bunch of old movies from the eighties. We sit on opposite sides of the sofa. It's funny seeing him out of his element.

Some nights, I fall asleep during the movie, then wake up in my own bed. Only because the couch has become Micah's bed.

Until he moves into the bedroom next to mine.

I lay in my bed with my eyes closed for as long as I can. The sun refuses to let up, but I'm thankful it's here. It's been sunny all week, a clear indication the cold, blustery days of winter are behind us for the next four months.

I stretch my arms above my head, sore from yesterday's work. My phone rings from my nightstand, forcing me to roll over and open my eyes and see Ruby's name lighting up the screen.

"Hey, Ruby."

"Oh, Adeline." She sighs, relieved. "I've been so worried about you. I haven't heard much from you since you left."

"I'm sorry." My heart warms knowing she's been thinking of me. I do feel guilty for not messaging her as much as I should have after leaving Los Angeles, but the past is easier to let go when you're able to shut the door on it completely. I learned my lesson when I left Boston three years ago. Unfortunately, me closing the door on the past has included those I loved. First, my mom. Now, Ruby.

I'm working on finding the strength to not take my rough past out on those I love.

"I didn't mean to make you worried."

"Oh, honey." Her voice wobbles. "I'm just glad to hear you're okay. Are you safe?"

"I am." I nod, wondering how much information I should divulge to Ruby. Other than Ember, I don't have many friends I can confide in. Although Ruby is more like a mother to me, loving me in ways my own mother never could. "I'm staying with a family friend. Well, he's actually Archer's best friend."

I bite my lip. My anger with Archer is still strong, festering into a tightly woven knot in the center of my chest. I haven't been able to bring myself to talk to him since the night he ditched me, but he also hasn't tried to contact me, either. I guess we're both at a stalemate.

"You mean the one who went to prison years ago?"

Shit. I forgot Ruby heard about Micah's past with drugs.

"Yes," I wince, rolling onto my back. I lift my arm over my head, resting it on my pillow as I stare at the ceiling. "But he's clean now, and he's changed." I glide my finger over my lips, thinking back to yesterday when he pinned me against the ladder. "It's been great living with him, actually."

"Just be careful, Adeline," she warns, her tone cooling.

"I am being careful."

"I wanted to give you an update on what's going on here." She changes the subject, and my stomach sours. Ruby has just kicked open the door I've been holding shut on the past.

"Trending Runway reached out and wanted to see if you'd like to book a shoot this fall for their upcoming spring catalog. I told them I'd speak to you and get back to them with an answer. I didn't know when you were planning on returning, so when would you like to schedule it?"

Sickness overtakes me again. I try to picture a life where I go back to Los Angeles, pretending as if the past several years haven't happened. It's been months since I left, and being here in Boston has made it easy to forget. My modeling career, my disastrous relationship with Maddox, and bursting out of the trailer that day all feels like a lifetime ago. A life I don't recognize.

Trending Runway magazine would once have been a dream. Nearly thirty years ago, my mother had an entire spread in one of their summer issues. At one point, it was a dream of mine, but dreams constantly change.

"I don't know when I'm coming back, Ruby." My confession filters into the still air, and I try to picture her reaction. Her silence is enough of an answer to know I've taken her by surprise. She was expecting me to return.

"Oh," she finally says quietly.

Tears well behind my eyes and line my lashes. I blink them

back, but I'm unsuccessful. Slipping from the corner of my eye, one drips down my temple. I sniff and wipe it away.

"I'm sorry," I whisper, blowing out a breath as I turn my head on my pillow and face the long, body-length mirror propped up in the corner of my room. The sheet I tossed over it the first night I stayed here hides my reflection.

"I understand, Adeline," she reassures, with an underlying tone of sadness. She wants to beg me to come home—Ruby has always been supportive in every job I've taken—but she's also very opinionated. This is one opinion she knows she can't have. This is something I must do on my own.

"There's something else."

"What?" I sit up and clutch the blanket to my chest.

"Maddox has disappeared."

"What do you mean?"

"Well, after you left, he rarely showed up to the studio. After about a week of him not coming in, he finally showed up one morning completely drunk. He started throwing things around the studios: cameras, lights, props. You name it, he destroyed it."

I cover my mouth, gasping. I was worried Maddox might take me leaving out on others.

"He didn't hurt anyone, did he?"

"Thankfully, no." She swallows. "But after that, the management company he worked for fired him. There have been rumors going around that he completely emptied out his apartment. No one knows where he went."

"Oh, my God." I don't know where Maddox could have gone. From what I know, he doesn't have any family around, and the few distant members he does have don't speak to him.

"I wasn't certain I should tell you, but I wanted you to know."

"Thank you." I inhale a shaky breath, wanting now more

than ever to end our call. "I love you, Ruby. I'll try and keep in touch more often."

"Message me when you can. I'm still here for you. Always."

"I know you are." The tears dry, the sadness leaving me as quickly as it came. "I'll keep in touch."

"Goodbye, Adeline," Ruby breathes out before hanging up.

I drop my phone onto the bed and stare at the ceiling for a few minutes to gather myself. Ruby's conversation leaves a weight on my chest. A weight I've been keeping just above the surface of my flesh and bone. Keeping the distance between my life in LA and the one I have here has been growing easier by the day. Every day, the abuse and trepidation of my relationship with Maddox has been fading in the rearview. Her telling me about his sudden disappearance concerns me only slightly. Ruby wouldn't tell him where I am, and I doubt Maddox would take the time to figure it out.

Besides, I've never felt safer than I do here, living with Micah.

After I've taken a few minutes to gather myself, I wipe my conversation with Ruby from my mind and head downstairs to grab a bite to eat.

In my Nirvana T-shirt and shorts, I tiptoe down the stairs and grab a granola bar from the pantry. Reaching into the refrigerator, I swipe a can of soda and pop the top.

Micah saunters into the kitchen wearing a simple white T-shirt and faded, worn jeans—an outfit I've become accustomed to seeing him in.

It feels like it's been years since the last time I saw him wear a suit.

"Morning, Addy," he says before grabbing a mug from the cupboard and pouring himself a cup of coffee.

He's kept up his use of my nickname, and I haven't had the energy to correct him. Or maybe I haven't wanted to. Something about the way he says it is different than the way he used to say it when I was a kid.

"Morning," I mutter around a mouthful of granola.

His heated stare falls to my legs.

I sit behind the counter and cross them, thankful I was mindful enough to make sure I was wearing more than just my T-shirt downstairs. The first time I came down here with just my sleep shirt on, I was completely bare underneath it.

We haven't spoken since yesterday, when he yelled at me in front of the entire crew. I couldn't confirm whether he was telling the truth about the man jerking off behind me, but it didn't matter. He scolded me like a child, and I was thrust back to that day at the pool when I was eleven years old.

I want to be angry with him now, and I open my mouth to call him out on his behavior but stop when he lifts his leg and places his foot on the stool beside me.

He bends over, lacing up his boot. "I'm going to get started on the garden today." Once he's finished tying the first, he does the same with the second. He flicks his gaze up to mine.

Fine. We're pretending yesterday never happened. Got it.

"Okay," I choke out. Granola hits the back of my throat, and I cough.

"Thought you might want to help." He shrugs one shoulder. His blue-gray eyes deepen, still heavy with secrets, but I'm beginning to see the cracks.

"I'm meeting Ember for lunch," I tell him. "I was just about to go shower."

He drops his foot and stands with his hands firmly planted on his hips. "Do you need a ride?"

"No. She's picking me up."

"Okay." He sighs. "Well, have fun."

Short pleasantries, but the silence speaks loudly.

"Thanks."

My eyes fall to his mouth. He sticks his tongue out and sweeps it across his bottom lip.

Electrifying heat pools between my legs. It hums across my skin.

"I should get going or else Ember will kill me." I need to get out of this kitchen and away from Micah. My thoughts are going to places they shouldn't be going.

"Oh, yeah." He wraps his hand around the back of his neck, then turns around and places his hand on the handle to the sliding back door.

"Wait!" I blurt out, walking over to the refrigerator. I grab one of the bottles of water I'd placed in there earlier this week and hand it to Micah. "For when you're thirsty. There's supposed to be record heat today. You should stay hydrated."

His eyes fall to the bottle before he reaches out to take it from me. Our fingers brush against one another.

He doesn't respond. His Adam's apple bobs as he swallows and delivers me a small smile of appreciation.

I let him take it and leave the kitchen before I explode. I picture him following me and lifting me up to wrap my legs around his waist. I imagine him whispering in my ear, telling me I'm a '*good girl*' for finally listening to him.

I imagine the taste of his lips on mine, practically stealing my breath away. I reach the top of the stairs and stop. My legs are wobbly, and I feel like I'm losing the strength to stand. Pressing my back to the wall, I close my eyes and breathe, listening to the sound of the back door sliding open before it shuts again.

Once I've regained my bearings, I head straight for the shower. Since all the other bathrooms in the house are undergoing some sort of renovation, Micah and I are forced to share the one connected to my bedroom. His towel hangs off the hook bolted into the wall. His razor sits beside his toothbrush and half-used tube of toothpaste on the large, marble vanity.

I strip down and step into the shower almost immediately. Once the water is scorching hot, I allow the heat to beat against my skin, and I bury my face in my hands to force the sinful thoughts of my brother's best friend away.

Once I'm all wet, I wash my hair, run my razor quickly over my legs, and move onto washing my body. I grab my bright pink pouf and reach for my body wash but stop when I see Micah's next to it. The tall blue bottle sits in the corner of the shelf. I pop the top and bring it to my nose, breathing in the scent of cedarwood.

This is exactly how Micah smells every time I see him, when he's finished working outside before he joins me for dinner. This is Micah's signature scent.

I squeeze a dollop onto my pouf and pop the cap back closed before returning the bottle back to its home next to mine.

Bubbles cover my pouf within seconds, and I start to wash myself. Washing myself with Micah's body wash doesn't exactly stop the thoughts running through my mind. If anything, it solidifies the way I'm feeling. The truth is, I'm falling for Micah. I shouldn't be, but I am.

As each day passes, I envision a life with him here in his house. One where we don't tiptoe around one another or sit in our highly covered secrets.

I'm swiping the pouf over my peaked nipples, the image of Micah's anger yesterday playing on my mind. I squeeze my eyes shut, the fire in his blue-gray eyes sparking with jealousy.

Jealous because he caught another man looking at me.

Right?

I hear his voice telling me to get on his bike.

The space between my legs tingles, and I'm about to slip my

hand where my body is begging to be touched when I hear the back door slide open.

I gasp, dropping my pouf as if it's suddenly burst into flames.

The door shuts then again, and I breathe out, thankful I didn't hear Micah's footsteps coming up the stairs.

With the moment gone, and a chill replacing the heat, I pick up my pouf and rinse off the rest of Micah's body wash. I rinse the rest of the suds off my own body and shut the water off.

Stepping out, I wrap a towel around myself, tucking in the front, just above my chest. I pad my way into my bedroom before shutting and locking the door. Water drips from my hair onto the floor as I make my way across my bedroom, and Micah's grunting from outside the window pulls me to the opposite side.

Peeking around the old curtain, I place my hand over my beating chest at the sight of him down below. He's bent over the garden bed, ripping out dead flowers and broken branches. Long vines and stems with thorns cover the dry soil. He tosses them behind him, tearing and pulling with all his strength.

His hands are covered in dirt as he reaches forward and grabs onto one of the longer vines. He tears it out and tosses it into the pile he's building on the other side of the wood.

Broad shoulders swell, and the muscles across the planes of his back flex. His tan skin is covered in a thin sheen of sweat. He's removed the white T-shirt he was wearing this morning.

The sun glints and shimmers off his skin, highlighting the muscles my hands wish to touch. I close my eyes, the heat returning between my legs.

I sigh and open my eyes. Micah paused long enough to take a drink from the bottle of water I gave him earlier. With one foot resting on the edge of the wooden frame, he presses one hand on his knee and lifts the bottle to his mouth, tilting his head back as he takes a long swig.

With my hand still pressed to my chest, I drag my fingers down the center of my towel. Tingles spread down my legs and my hardened nipples. They're hidden under the towel, but the soft fabric hugs my skin, radiating the warmth I'm getting from watching Micah.

I part my towel and slip my fingers between the gap, finding my center. I part my folds, the pads of my fingers landing over my swollen clit.

Micah sets the water bottle down on the ground beside him, and he bends over again, resuming his work. Two dimples press into the small of his back. My fingers circle my clit, watching his fingers wrap around a large, dead branch.

Good girl.

Tell me you're going to be a good girl.

I circle my clit faster, parting my legs to get more access. I plunge two fingers inside myself, gasping when I press my thumb to my clit. I pump my fingers faster and harder.

Micah stomps his way over to the pile of furniture we set out in the middle of the yard yesterday and fishes out a shovel. He doesn't look up, not noticing me standing in front of my window. Heat blooms in my cheeks.

What do you want, Addy?

Do you want to be mine?

Yes. God, yes.

I roll onto the balls of my feet, standing taller. My mouth falls open as I breathe in a shuddering breath. Tucking in my bottom lip, I bite down on my pillowy flesh, wishing it were Micah's.

My body hums and vibrates from my own touch.

I watch him as he stabs the shovel into the dirt, lifting out the root to one of the bushes. After digging up half, he walks around the box to dig out the other half. He stabs the pointed end of the shovel into the ground again, pushing down to leverage it out.

Tiny bursts of electricity spread across my damp skin as I pull my fingers out to circle my clit again. I draw them along the length of my slit and add more pressure. My fingers are soaking wet. They move over me with ease.

Tell me you're mine, Addy.

Micah drops the shovel on a loud grunt. It vibrates from his broad, solid chest.

Tell me you're my good girl.

My orgasm slams into my body, and I shudder and vibrate, moaning as I reach the top of it, squeezing my eyes shut. The feeling is so intense, I fall forward, catching myself on the window. My hand slaps against the glass.

My eyes snap open.

Micah is staring directly at me.

Down below, in the garden, he's watching me. The shovel lays at his feet. His hands are balled into fists at his sides, his body on full display.

His torn, dirt-covered jeans rest just above the dents of his perfectly sculpted hip bones. It's a body that should be considered illegal for a man in his mid-thirties.

Solid as a statue, he stares up at me with a hardened expression. His jaw ticks as his dark brown eyebrows set in a firm line above his narrowed eyes. His arms are at his sides, but his hands are noticeably clenched into tight fists.

I gasp, the breath catching in my throat. I bring both my arms to my chest and spin around, hiding behind the safety of the curtain. I lay back against the wall and tip my head back, squeezing my eyes shut.

I want to die of embarrassment.

I wonder how much Micah heard... or *saw*.

I cover my eyes with my hand and sink to the floor. My wet hair clings to my shoulders, but my body is still humming from my orgasm. I haven't been with anyone in such a long time. I tell myself I only touched myself because I'm desperate for touch. I'm desperate to *feel*. Anything. Something. Something to remind me I haven't lost all sense of awareness. Something to remind me that my heart isn't completely shut off.

Maddox made it easy to fall for him, but I was numb. With the way I'm feeling now, after simply touching myself to the thought of Micah, I hadn't realized how numb I'd become. My heart jolted to life watching him in the garden just then, and although we argued yesterday, and I was furious with him for what he said, I was grateful. Grateful because my heart felt more than just numb.

This was proof. Proof I'm not completely unfeeling.

But I'm lying to myself if I think this was innocent. There's meaning to what I've done. The relationship between Micah and me has shifted. He made that clear yesterday when he didn't answer my dare for him to stop.

The problem is, I know I should be embarrassed. I just finger-fucked myself while watching my brother's best friend work in the garden.

But I'm not embarrassed. The truth is, I want it to happen again.

Only next time, I want what I know I can't have.

I want it with him.

THIRTEEN

Micah

Adeline is curled up on the sofa when I step into the living room. Her long legs are tucked under her, a throw blanket draped over her lap. The heat has only worsened this week, reaching new records for this early in the summer, but the air conditioning is on full blast. Thankfully, I had a technician come out and replace the entire system before the heat made its way to the Northeast.

Addy is scrolling through her phone while an investigative crime documentary plays in the background—something about a husband who found his wife lying in a pool of blood in their basement.

I catch her attention when I sit in the chair opposite the sofa, and she looks up from her phone. Her eyes drop to my clothes.

"Can I be honest?" she asks, a little smile tugging on the corner of her mouth.

"Aren't you always?" I toss back.

She shrugs. "I try to be." She points to my chest. "Honestly, I forgot what you look like in a suit. It's a little odd."

"Bad odd or good odd?" I raise my eyebrows.

She considers me a moment and clears her throat. "Good."

My heart flutters at the sight of her sitting here in my house, comfortable. Months ago, this place was a ghost house, covered in cobwebs and dust, only breathing through the memories that had been left behind by the family who sold it, and the ones I refused to create. Now, this house is breathing with life. The walls are painted a warm cream color. The floor is restored to a rich, hardwood brown. There are small bits of Adeline littered throughout the living room; decorations I've seen buried in boxes or left in the old hutch between the living and dining room. Pieces that have always been here but forced to stay hidden.

"I only meant I was getting used to seeing you in jeans and a T-shirt," she clarifies.

I pinch my tie between my fingers and glance down at it. I drop it and lean against the arm of my chair. I study Adeline, focusing on the way her eyes shimmer in the sunlight.

"Breakfast with my brothers."

"Do you normally meet them for breakfast?"

"Ever since our father died." I clear my throat, allowing Addy's stare to consume me. "We've always been close but even more so after he passed. It's tough because no matter how much my brothers made me feel like I was one of them, my father reminded me daily that his support for me only came from obligation."

Her eyes turn down at the corners, and her gorgeous mouth frowns. "Obligation?"

"Aside from money, my father only cared about one thing: image. He could lie and cheat his entire life as long as his image wasn't tarnished. When it came out that my mother was pregnant with me after an affair he'd had with her, he couldn't deny me. My mother threatened to expose all his lies and the illegal activity she'd witnessed during her time with him. Unlike his wife—my older brothers' mother—mine was a stripper. Her career was ruined when she'd found out she was pregnant, and without James Harding's support, we would have been living on the street. Apparently, James couldn't have that."

Adeline sighs, pressing her mouth into a thin line as she nods. "So, he cared for you out of obligation?"

"Yep. Though I guess you could say I was lucky. Better to have him claim me out of obligation than to be raised in some back alley under a tent, sleeping on a bed of cardboard boxes."

An emotion washes over her face that I can't explain, and It tugs on my chest. I want to cross the room and wrap my arms around her.

"I'm familiar with the feeling of being loved out of obligation." Her shoulders rise and fall on a heavy breath. "When, deep down, you know the truth and how it isn't true love."

Her confession slams into my chest like a ton of bricks. I understand her, but the deeper part of me wants to know who she's talking about.

Is she talking about Archer? Someone she dated? Her parents?

I realize I don't know much about Adeline personally, despite having known her most of her life, but these glimpses she's given me the past few months have opened a side of myself that's laid dormant for quite some time.

My heart hurts knowing there's been a time when she felt someone didn't give her honest love.

"Do you ever feel like you've wasted time?" she asks me, her voice heavy and weighted. "Like your life should be on a different path if you'd just changed one thing?"

The pile of bricks on my chest grows heavier. I look into her eyes, and my heart fractures. The cracks widen, exposing the feelings I've locked away for years.

"I do." I sit back in my chair, loosening my tie. "When I got out of prison, I struggled to find my footing. My place. Spending the time away from the life I was building set me back. Every breakfast I meet with my brothers is another reminder of where I should be at this stage of my life. At my age, they were already married, their wives pregnant with the first or second—"

"You aren't that old," she cuts in.

I chuckle. "To you. But when you reach your thirties, it's like, suddenly, you're more focused on where you should be in life than any other time. Your twenties are spent discovering yourself. You aren't really looking too far into the future, or thinking what the consequences will be of the choices you make. When you're in your thirties, you've already discovered who you are."

Her eyebrows pinch together. "Says who?"

I pause, unsure of how to answer her question. "I don't think anyone says it should be that way." I attempt to explain, reaching and grabbing at the first thoughts that come to mind. "I think it's more about how everyone's lives around yours constantly shifts. Most people in their thirties have kids and are married. Then there are the stragglers, like me, who feel we've somehow been left behind, or we've missed out on some secret password to get into their exclusive club."

"I don't think you've been left behind or missed out on the password. There's no magic wand or secret to getting there," she argues, tucking her long brown hair behind her ear. "Everyone's lives move at different paces, Micah. Not everyone is the same."

I give her a smile of appreciation, but it's hard to accept her comment when I've sacrificed so much for the ones I love and all it's gotten me is feeling hollow.

"Consider yourself lucky," I tell her. "You're twenty-one. You're still in the process of discovering who you are."

Her mouth twitches. I want to kiss it away, but I hold myself back. Again.

She tilts her head to the side and grins. "How do you know I haven't already discovered who I am?"

I smile back. "I don't, but I'm sure I could find out."

What the fuck does that even mean?

I'm certain Adeline can hear my heart pounding in my chest. For the longest time, I've been living in the dark, but now that I'm sitting here in the sunlight with her, I've opened my heart to her, sharing parts of my soul I've never shared with anyone before now.

"I don't know about not knowing who I am," she confesses. "But I do know I've been unfortunate to live in the existence of constantly feeling alone. I know what it feels like to have been treated a certain way by almost everyone in my life, which has left me with the privilege of constantly questioning everyone's intentions."

"I've heard LA has that effect." I tap my finger on the arm of the chair. "It's a city full of people wearing masks."

"It isn't just LA. I've felt that way here. In some ways, I think I've felt more alone at home than anywhere else." Darkness clouds her eyes, the weight of our conversation weighing heavy on her. I can't describe the shift. How and when did this become a topic of feeling alone?

I understand her in a way I never have, and again, I'm left wanting to know more.

"Do you feel alone here? With me?" I dare to ask. My voice deepens, carrying with it the weight of my question. The words fall from my tongue before I'm given the chance to swallow them back.

Her sparkling eyes widen. The air turns thick, and my chest stills. There's a magnetic pull to Adeline. I want to examine her soul. I want to let her in. But there's a part of me that holds back, afraid of what it might mean if she says she doesn't feel alone here with me.

Sensing the tension and heat in the air, she tosses the blanket aside and stands, folding it without answering my question. She turns her back to me. I study her, knowing there's something building between us. I just don't know what it is yet, and I'm not sure I'm ready to admit it. All I know is that every time I'm around her, I don't want her to leave.

I consider my own question. Do I feel alone with *her?*

The answer is an easy no, but I keep it to myself.

I stand as she drapes the folded blanket over the back of the couch.

"I was going to head to the bath remodel store to pick out some tile for the upstairs bathrooms. I thought you'd like to come with me."

Her shoulders visibly rise before she turns around. She smiles. "Sure." Her focus shifts to my hands undoing my tie and top button of my shirt. "I'll go change, then we can head out."

She swallows, her throat visibly bobbing. She blinks and brushes away her hair. "I'll go and freshen up."

After getting changed into jeans and a T-shirt, I meet Adeline out in the driveway, sighing with relief when I see she's still wearing her black leggings and fitted white shirt.

I walk over to my bike and grab the helmet sitting on the back seat.

When I turn around, her eyes are spread wide. She chuckles, but her eyebrows are knitted as she shakes her head and takes a step back. "Oh, no. Not the bike again."

I laugh, loving the way I make her squirm. Heat pools in my lower stomach when I look down the length of her legs and close the distance between us.

"You aren't wearing a skirt this time," I say, standing in front of her. "You'll be fine."

My cock jumps at the thought of having her thighs wrapped around me again.

Her dark lashes rest above her cheeks as her eyes flutter on a sigh. She opens them again, her mouth falling open, too, before she surrenders, standing still in front of me.

I gently slip the helmet over her head. The visor is propped open, revealing the top half of her face. Her eyes stare into mine, and I'm crumbling on the inside. It's been years since I've felt this way when looking at someone. I adjust the helmet on her head and bend my knees, lining my face with hers.

"How's that? Is it okay?"

"Yes," she says, quietly.

I spin around and place my own helmet on before straddling the bike. Adeline climbs on behind me without another word, then she slips forward, pressing her body to mine.

I close my eyes and focus on my breathing when she slinks her arms around my waist, gripping onto my chest. She doesn't fist my shirt like she did the first night she rode my bike. Her hands are pressed flat against my chest this time, one hand pressed to my right rib, the other over my heart. Her body is still warm behind me, but it's different. She isn't bare like she was before. Her leggings provide an extra barrier between us, and I'm thankful for it. I don't need the distraction again.

But who am I kidding?

It doesn't matter what she's wearing.

She's always a distraction.

FOURTEEN

ADELINE

I can't get the conversation I had with Micah back home out of my head. I think about it the entire time we walk up and down the aisles of the bath remodeling store.

Now, he rambles on, asking me which ones I like and which tile I think will go with which flooring. Several times he's caught me so deep in thought I had to ask him to repeat his question. He doesn't press me on it, though, and I don't divulge my thoughts.

The air is thick between us, the conversation in the house leaving us riddled with unanswered questions. I want to know more about Micah. I want to know why he feels left behind in a world of thirty-somethings. Does it have to do with him going to prison?

Temptation dared me to ask him back at the house, but I didn't want to bring it up when he'd already felt comfortable enough to share certain pieces of himself with me.

After picking the tile and placing an order, Micah and I head back home.

Thunderous dark clouds roll across the sky in the distance. The farther we drive out of the city, the closer we crawl toward the storm ahead. I glance over my shoulder while Micah races down the street and turns onto the highway.

The city grows smaller in the distance, stealing the sunshine and clear blue skies with it. We're only halfway home when drops of water start to fall from above. They're slow at first; the thunder rumbling into the ground beneath us. Water from the road kicks up at our legs as another round of thunder crackles in the distance. I shift my hold on Micah's body and close my hands around his shirt, clutching onto him firmly. His muscles move beneath my touch with every breath.

We're taking the exit to our neighborhood when the rain picks up even more. Quick pelting drops of water cover us in sheets of rain, the sound of it drowning out the traffic and the loud rumble of the bike's engine. We pull to a stop light, waiting to turn left, when Micah takes the opportunity to pop open his visor and look over his shoulder.

"Normally, I would stop and pull over to wait out the storm!" he yells. "But since we're almost home, we'll just keep going. Hang on."

I nod, letting him know I heard him and tighten my grip.

I catch one more glimpse of his blue-gray eyes before he snaps his visor shut, revs the engine, and turns when the traffic light switches to green.

I concentrate on my body pressed against his as he weaves through the streets of our neighborhood. The tiny bits of rain splash and bounce off every parked car we pass. Water wicks and slaps against the exposed parts of my skin. The front of me is almost dry, but my shoulders and back are drenched with cool rain.

I flex my legs around his thick frame, thinking back to yesterday when I'd seen him out in the garden. I wasn't just watching him work. I was thinking about him differently. I was seeing him in a new light.

I was a woman falling for a man.

I still don't understand my feelings for him, but something has changed over the course of these months living with him. Micah has allowed me access to the parts of himself he doesn't share with the rest of the world. He looks at me differently, talks to me differently, treats me differently.

My stomach flutters at the idea of there being more to us than simply roommates. I loosen my grip on his shirt and dare to feel his chest once again. My wrinkled fingers press against him. I wish the barrier of wet fabric wasn't resting between his beating heart and me. I want to know if I have an effect on him at all.

Does he react to my touch the way I do to his?

I squeeze my eyes shut and will myself to calm the thoughts running rampant in my mind. I haven't been able to shut them off.

Micah's touch has awakened what I thought were dormant parts of my soul. It amplifies across my body, sending shockwaves to my heart and stomach. Every time we connect, I find myself wanting more. I want to see how far this feeling can go.

The house comes into view, and Micah takes a sharp turn into the driveway. Eventually, he comes to a stop, and I look over at the flower box below my bedroom window. All the weeds and dead branches are cleared out. A puddle of water now floods the soil, spilling over the edges and onto the green grass. I climb off the bike and remove my helmet, placing it on the seat, then stand beside Micah's bike and stare at his back. He hasn't turned off the engine yet. He hasn't made a single move to climb off his bike, which is strange given how hard it's raining. White knuckled, he tightens his grip on the handles and remains on the leather seat.

For a moment, I think he might leave me here. Maybe he forgot to run an errand. Maybe he wants to put distance between us, considering the last several weeks. He knows something is different with me.

Rain continues to pour from the sky in sheets. I look up at the near-black clouds, squinting against the raindrops. My shirt and leggings cling to me like a second skin. My hair sticks to my cheeks, and water drips from my eyelashes. It's completely ridiculous that we're still out here instead of rushing inside to the comfort of our warm, dry house.

My heart feels like it's going to rip right out of my chest, as if Micah's opened it himself, barely hovering his hand over the organ that keeps my body running.

I silently beg for him to turn off the engine.

To do something.

To say something.

But he doesn't.

Unsure of how to will the feelings inside me to fade, I chance another look at the garden. My gaze immediately lands on all the furniture we left in the yard, still sitting in a large pile from when we emptied the shed days ago.

"Shit," I hiss, immediately jogging through the side yard.

I push through the half-broken, wooden gate separating the side yard and leading to the back. My feet smash into puddles along the way, and water soaks into my shoes, saturating my socks.

"Addy!" Micah yells behind me. I hear the creaking of the wooden gate opening and closing behind me again.

I don't waste time stopping or turning around. "We have to get these covered!" I yell back. "The rain will ruin them!"

"Addy, wait!" his voice booms over the sound of rain, but I don't stop. I'm almost to the furniture when I come to a screeching halt. Lighting strikes in the distance, several houses down. An icy chill slithers down the length of my spine, and the ground vibrates with electricity. My heart jolts, but I still don't stop.

The dresser and large grandfather clock I've fallen in love with are doused in rain. The rational part of my brain tells me they're a lost cause. They can't be saved or salvaged now. The chance of restoring these antiques is gone.

Anger boils under my skin, and I wished I'd moved them sooner. Why did we leave them outside this long? Why did I allow these fragile pieces to get damaged?

I stalk over to the grandfather clock and place my hands at the top. Micah charges through the yard, following me. His hair is drenched, the ends sticking to his forehead. Water drips from his bottom lip as he stands on the other side of the clock, catching his breath. His shoulders and chest rapidly rise and fall, and his shirt clings to his skin like cellophane. His dark lashes are clumped together, the blue of his eyes standing out against the gray-black sky above.

"We should have moved these somewhere else," I tell him, my voice quivering. "We shouldn't have kept them out here." I don't want to cry, but a tight knot has formed in my chest.

I feel constricted, the truth of how I'm feeling begging to be set free.

I'm tired of ignoring my feelings. I'm tired of pretending as if my feelings for Micah are the same as they were when I was a kid—a meaningless childhood crush—because the truth is, I'm not a child anymore. Any feelings I have for him now are valid and powerful. Ones that can't be ignored.

But my fear is laced with the desire.

Fear, because the last time I allowed myself to get close to someone, I nearly lost myself. I was catapulted back into a life of pain. But as I look into Micah's eyes, I know he's different. He's not Maddox. He's different than all those who have told me they loved me but failed to show up when it mattered most.

Micah is standing in front of me in the rain, pulling me back from the cliff I'm teetering on the edge of, and I shudder when another round of thunder and lightning cracks. I harden my stare and direct it at Micah.

"Help me move this under the patio." I grip the sides of the clock, my fingers slipping on the wet varnish. The edges have bubbled, and spots of discoloration litter the surface.

"It's too late," he argues, refusing to help.

"It's not." I shake my head.

"It is, Addy."

"No," I grind out, grabbing the clock again. I try to pull it down enough for me to hold it at an angle and slide it across the grass.

But Micah's hand wraps around mine, stopping me. Air rises from my lungs at his sudden touch. He tugs my hand, pulling me to him, and my wet body slams against his chest before he presses me against the clock.

"Let it go, Addy." His voice vibrates against me as he looks down into my eyes, and I want to cry. It's as if he's opened the windows to my soul with only his voice, exposing every irrational thought running in my mind.

I haven't told him about Maddox and the pain he caused me. I've never even told him about my dad. But he can see the scars I carry with me. The crucial evidence of those who have wounded me. Mixed with the hurt I feel, I'm certain he can see the desire I have for him, too.

"I can't let it go," I confess.

My eyes fall to his mouth as another drop of water slips from his bottom lip onto his rain-soaked beard, and up close, like this, I can see bits of blond and silver strands peeking through his otherwise dark brown hair.

I stare at his beautiful face, wanting nothing more than for him to give in, to take the leap.

"You asked me earlier if I felt alone here with you." My voice is suspended within the small space between us, shaky and uneven with my confession. "I'm not. Not when I'm with you."

Another round of thunder rolls in the distance.

Micah's body stills. He's holding my hand between us, running the pad of his thumb against my palm. A small gesture that ignites my entire body into flames.

But my heart sinks when he winces. His eyes fill with sadness and regret as he shakes his head. "I can't, Addy."

"I know you feel this," I say, pressing my hand to his chest. "I know you feel this like I do."

Lighting cracks again, bringing on another surge of rain.

He's surrounding every inch of me, consuming the bit of air I'm able to squeeze into my lungs. I beg for him to touch me. I crave it like my body craves oxygen.

Then suddenly, he leans forward just an inch, bringing his mouth above mine. His eyes are hard, at war.

I hold my breath, anticipation building inside me. Heat returns to the space between my legs, and our breaths are heavy and measured, each one more laborious than the last.

"I *shouldn't*, Addy," he admits. My nickname has never sounded sweeter.

"Why?" I ask, unable to focus on one thing long enough to pull myself together. I'm vulnerable and broken, surrendering to the truth buried inside me.

"Because," he whispers, "this can't happen."

"It can't happen, or you don't want it to?" I focus on my hand wrapped up in his as his other hand falls to my waist.

His fingers dance along the waist of my leggings, slipping under the elastic band. I hold my breath, imagining the pain I'll feel with his rejection, but I don't want him to stop. The space between my legs is begging for his touch, building with need for him. My heart hammers in my chest, begging for something I know won't be easy.

"What I want doesn't matter," he says, his eyes resembling the storm above. The vulnerability I feel inside is the same as what I see in Micah's eyes.

I press my hand against his chest, over his heart and watch my fingers move slowly over his hardened muscle. He's warm and comforting, and I practically melt just from touching him.

I want this. I want him to kiss me. I want his hand to explore more than just the waistband of my leggings.

"What you want *should* matter," I tell him, my mouth running dry.

"It never has." He swallows. There's pain laced in his expression, too. A battle turning into all-out war in his heated gaze.

His hand slips around the arch of my hip, his fingers grazing deeper below the elastic. He presses his fingertips to the curve of my lower back.

"Tell me to stop." He breathes harder.

"I won't." I shake my head and sweep my tongue across my lips.

"Tell me to stop," he begs, his eyebrows drawing in.

"Don't stop."

"Dammit, Addy." He groans, resting his forehead against mine.

"You asked me if I've felt alone living here with you," I start, concentrating on his hand on the small of my back. "But what about you? Do you feel alone?"

Releasing my hand, his fingers ghost along the curve of my neck, moving to tangle in my wet hair and grip the back of my head. I lean into it.

We're incredibly close when we shouldn't be, but how can Micah's touch be wrong when it makes me feel like this?

The way I'm feeling could be from my circumstances. Leaving Maddox was an easy decision, but the damage left behind is one I've swept under the rug since I left. I've been determined to move on with my life, burying myself in the tasks of renovating Micah's house. Somewhere along the way, Micah has done the same. Taking a break from work has him filling his days with the satisfaction of restoring the old house he's ignored for years. With me here, I'm someone to fill the void. The parts of his life he's hiding from.

We're one and the same.

But I know I want this. I want Micah.

I squeeze my eyes shut and drop my head back against the grandfather clock. A moan escapes my throat while I savor Micah's touch.

"Fuck, Addy." He tightens his grip on the back of my head.

I crack my eyes open to find him staring at me with a heated gaze. His hungry hands have started to explore more of my skin. His resolve is crumbling.

"Tell me to stop." He growls, anger sparking with his plea.

I simply shake my head, slipping my hand across his chest and over his shoulder.

"Always so fucking stubborn. Don't you ever listen to me?" he barks, his jaw clenching. "You don't understand. I can't do this."

"Why?" My pussy is begging for the sweet relief I know his touch will bring. Heat pools and spreads between my legs the farther he lowers his grip on the small of my back. I didn't realize until now that he's pressed his hips against mine. His words are telling me one thing while his body is showing me another.

I wasn't imagining his jealousy and possessiveness. He wants this as much as I do. Fear stands in the way of allowing him to completely surrender.

His swollen cock presses into my lower stomach, and I whimper, relishing in the feel of the size of it against me. Every move makes me want more. I'm greedy and hungry for a man who was never out of reach… until now.

"Why can't we do this?" I manage to squeak out.

He closes his eyes on a heavy breath, his lips parting. Slowly, his eyes open again, hooded with anguish. "You're my best friend's little sister."

"I'm not a little girl, Micah. I'm so tired of you telling me I'm something I'm not."

"I know you aren't a little girl, but I don't want to hurt my best friend. I don't want to hurt Archer."

"You won't, and you aren't." I push my hips forward.

His eyes flutter shut again, a heavy groan rumbling from his chest and up his throat.

When his eyes snap open this time, they've changed. With a heated glare, he grips onto the back of my head, pulling me impossibly closer. "I know you aren't little anymore."

I melt under his touch.

Yes. This is what I've been craving.

Kiss me. Please, I silently beg, inhibitions completely gone.

"I can't do this to my best friend," he says weakly.

"You won't be doing anything to Archer," I point out. He doesn't understand the dynamic between my brother and me. Then again, I may not fully understand his friendship with him, either. In some respects, I guess you could say they're friendship is stronger than our siblingship.

I don't want my brother to be a reason Micah holds back.

"Dammit." He hangs his head lower, moving his face away from mine before he leans forward and presses the top of his head to the side of mine while the rain beats against his back. It feels like we've been out here for an eternity. Time stills as Micah concentrates on his heavy breathing. He removes his hand from the back of my head and grips the top of the grandfather clock.

I slip my hand between us, hooking my fingers under his chin, forcing him to look me in the eye.

"I've spent so long pushing away what I want," he confesses. Streams of water drip down his face, falling from his mouth with every word. I hang on to them, the desire in me building with anticipation of what's coming next. "It's never mattered what I wanted."

"So, what?" I ask, frustration getting the better of me. "You plan on spending the rest of your life doing what everyone expects of you? Doing what everyone else wants? Is that why you neglected this house for so long? Was it your way of maintaining control, or was it your way of avoiding the truth?"

Anger and fury flame in his narrowing eyes. "You have no idea what you're talking about."

"Why?" I ask, my eyebrows pinching in anger. "I must not be able to understand because I'm only twenty-one, right? There's no possible way I can have an opinion because I haven't lived through any true hardships?"

There it is.

The truth laid bare. In all its glory.

Micah doesn't believe I have any hard experiences. He doesn't believe I've lived through true heartache. But he doesn't know our heartache is one and the same.

"That's not what I'm saying." He closes his eyes again.

"Then, *make me understand.*"

Silence.

"Please..." I beg.

Another quick rush of air fills my lungs before Micah's eyes snap open, flashing with heat before he grips the back of my head again and slams his lips to mine, stealing the bit of oxygen I have left in me.

The taste of him makes me grow weak in the knees, and I whimper against him, my brain and heart struggling to catch up with my reality.

His fingers twist and tangle through my wet hair while he slips his other hand down the back of my leggings and across my skin before his entire palm covers one of my bare ass cheeks. He massages me, and the ends of his fingers play at the space between my thighs from behind. My breath catches in my throat, wanting him to keep going. I moan as I roll to stand on my toes. He growls against my mouth, lapping his tongue against mine.

"Touch me," I breathe. "Please, touch me."

Hungrily, he squeezes my soft flesh, pulling me toward him. My pussy tingles, hoping he doesn't end this. I arch my back, and my hardened nipples peak through my wet T-shirt, ghosting across Micah's abs.

He moves his other hand from my hair to the side of my face. Gripping me, he tilts my face up to meet his.

I wrap my hand around his neck, pulling him down as I stand on my toes. He tastes of rain, mint, and heat. Keeping his hand inside my wet leggings, he slips around my hip and finds my pussy. His fingertips slide through my slit, finding my equally soaking wet clit, and he presses his finger to it.

"Fuck," he gasps between kisses, then he starts to move his finger in circles, and another moan falls from my mouth. He rips away from me, stealing the air from my lungs with him. "We can't."

I catch my breath, my mind frantic. My body immediately feels his absence. My heart beats erratically, and I want to cry. I want to cry because what we just did is unlike anything I've ever felt. He lifted me into the air before allowing me to fall like an anvil from the sky. I crash and burn.

"Why?" I ask, biting back the tears threatening to come. I

don't want them to spill. I don't want Micah to see how much his rejection stings. "Why can't we do this?"

"I told you. I'm Archer's best friend."

"I don't fucking care about Archer," I blurt out, regretting the words as soon as they leave my mouth. I press both of my hands to my hot cheeks. "I didn't mean it like that."

"No," Micah says, backing away. The growing distance between us stings, pouring salt in the already open wound. "I know what you meant."

The rain has slowed now. What was once sheets of rain is now only a light sprinkling. The clouds above are still heavy, but the sun and clear blue skies are breaking out in the distance.

"I'm not good for you."

My chin wobbles as I hold back my tears. "Sounds like you're trying to come up with excuses or reasons to push me away. To fight this."

"You don't know me, Addy. Not really."

"And you think you know me so well? Enough to tell me what's right and what's wrong?" I ask, my heart fracturing. "You have no idea what I've been through these past three years or even what my childhood was like. You have no idea what my relationship with Archer is like. You think you know based on only the side *he's* told you. But everyone wears masks, Micah. We all become experts in hiding the truth. Archer included."

Micah doesn't answer. His eyes stare into mine, searching for the truth. I've already shared more than I have my entire life. I've never opened up to anyone about the hard truth of my family dynamic. My childhood was centered around wearing a mask to bury the truth. Years were spent conditioning me to stay silent. But as the saying goes, old habits die hard.

I look into Micah's eyes, knowing there is more to what he means when he says I don't know him the way I think I do.

"You're right." He swallows, his neck bobbing with nerves. "Everyone wears masks. Including me."

"Are you talking about when you went to prison?"

His eyes widen and his jaw ticks. He looks off into the distance, even though he's still standing in front of me, close enough to touch. I don't move, though, instead curling my hands into fists, respecting his decision in the moment to keep space between us. I push through the pain of his rejection, knowing, deep down, he wants this. He just doesn't know how he can cope when his demons are as dark as mine.

"I know what happened," I tell him, chewing on the inside of my cheek. Nerves bundle inside me. I wish I could reach out to him and place my hand around his. "I read about you going to prison. The judge was harsh on you. But I also know that man isn't who you are anymore. I can see that. I don't judge you based off what's happened in the past. A few bad decisions don't make up who you truly are."

His far-off look softens, his defenses crumbling, but the wall remains. It may be small, but it's still there, standing between us.

"It doesn't matter what you think you might know." He finally turns back to me, his face filled with pain. "This can't happen, Adeline. Ever."

FIFTEEN

Micah

I can still taste Adeline in my mouth.

It's been three days since I kissed her, and the sensation of her mouth still lingers. I imagine her legs wrapped around me, and me buried inside her, fucking her sweet cunt. I haven't been laid in months, so when I step into the shower and jerk off with her strawberry-scented body wash coating my dick, I chalk it up to that simple fact.

After I watch my cum swirl down the drain, I lather myself up with my own body wash, hoping it will erase the scent of Adeline on me.

When I step out of the shower and get dressed, I check my phone to find a missed call from Archer. He's left a message, so I dial my voicemail, type in my passcode, and sit at the edge of my bed, slipping on a pair of socks.

"Hey, man," Archer breathes into the phone, his voice low and sad.

I already know where this is headed. I stop with only one sock over my foot and stare at my phone as my heart sinks into my stomach like an anchor cut from the rope. "I wanted to give you a heads up. I'm in a bit of a bind again, so I won't be able to make it out to the states for a while. It's safer if I keep my distance. Especially for yours and Adeline's sake. But don't worry. I don't expect you to intervene. I don't want you to. I have this handled, and it shouldn't be much longer before it's all straightened out. I did want to thank you for keeping an eye on my sister for me, though. I know she's safe and protected with you... so, thanks for that, man. All right, I'll talk to you later and let you know when I'll be able to come back out for a visit."

The voicemail ends, and I jab my finger on the red button, not even bothering to delete the message. A tight knot forms in the center of my chest.

I lean forward and rest my elbows on my knees. Rubbing my fingers against my forehead, I hold back a scream. I wish I could knock some fucking sense into Archer. For years, I've protected him, even taking the fall for his mistakes. And it's nearly cost me everything.

The claws that have made a home in my mind have weakened over the past few months. I wish I could say it was because the root cause of them has been erased, but it hasn't. The voicemail left by my best friend tells me they are alive and well, but Adeline's presence in my life has dulled their sharpness. The pain isn't as agonizing with her around.

Now, he's not only put my life in jeopardy, though, but he's put Adeline's in jeopardy as well.

We've spent the past three days avoiding one another. The silence has been apparent, and so has her avoiding stare. She's remained holed up in her room, even going as far as only going downstairs long enough to make herself dinner before shuffling back up to her room and shutting the door behind her.

Her silence has been loud and clear.

She's accepted my decision in telling her that what happened in the rainstorm can't happen again.

But fuck me if that wasn't the best fucking kiss I've ever had.

One kiss with her three days ago, and I still haven't been able to wipe it from my memory.

Good, because I don't want to forget.

Still, guilt ebbs its way into my anger and desires.

Guilt for crossing a boundary with my best friend's little sister when he's under the pretense of me protecting her. Which I am, but I want to offer more than protection to Adeline.

I want *her*.

After slipping on my other sock, I step into my favorite pair of jeans and quickly slide on a gray T-shirt. I swipe my toolbelt from the top of my dresser and carry it out of my bedroom. I haven't assessed the damage done to the vintage pieces of furniture from the shed yet, but I make it my mission this afternoon to see what can be salvaged. Anything to keep me busy and get my mind off Adeline.

After jogging down the stairs, I make a beeline for the kitchen and open the refrigerator to grab the bottle of water Adeline leaves in there for me every morning. My head is buried deep in the refrigerator when I hear Ember's voice carrying down the stairs.

"It's going to be a blast!" Ember sings. "They have dancers in cages and platforms throughout the entire place."

I swipe the water bottle and grab a stick of string cheese before shutting the door. When I spin around, Ember is standing in the threshold between the kitchen and hallway.

"Oh, hey, Micah." Ember grins. She saunters across the room before leaning over and sliding her arms across the kitchen island counter. She crosses them and picks at her bright pink nail polish, then she whips her pin-straightened hair over her shoulder, looking up at me with glittered shadowed eyes.

"Good to see you, Ember." I nod my head as I rip open my string cheese. I toss the wrapper in the trash bin and bite the end.

"You as well," Ember comments, still smiling. Her eyes dart to my toolbelt. "Working hard, I see."

I wonder how much of what happened the other day Adeline has told her.

Adeline's comment about how we all wear masks has landed right in the center of my chest and refused to budge. I've played our conversation in my mind repeatedly… but I know she spoke the truth. We all walk around wearing masks, only allowing others to see what we want them to see. Does Adeline wear a version of a mask around her best friend?

I'm guilty of this; taking the fall for those I care about at the expense of my own reputation and keeping the heart of the truth buried under a mountain of masks.

"A lot of work to do around here," I say around a mouthful of cheese.

"Understandable." Ember nods. "I'm glad you were able to get rid of all the fucking spiders and cobwebs around here." Her eyes roam over the kitchen. "Doesn't scream *Addams Family* or *Haunting of Hill House* so much anymore."

I laugh. "Thanks, I guess."

"Oh." Ember waves me off. "That was totally a compliment."

"Right." I smile, fishing back into the refrigerator for a beer. If I'm going to make it through all this furniture without thinking about my moment of weakness with Adeline, I'm going to need to loosen up a bit.

I crack open the can and take a swig before setting it back down on the counter, which I lean against and finish off my early dinner snack consisting of one stick of string cheese.

I swallow the last bite when Adeline steps into the kitchen, and I nearly choke as the nugget of cheese slips down my throat.

"Okay, I'm ready." Adeline taps her fingertips against her

bare thighs. Two strappy high heels dangle from the ends of her fingers.

Ember's head whips around as she pulls herself back to a stand.

"Holy fucking shit." Ember gasps. "You are stunning."

Adeline's cheeks blush red as her eyes swing up to meet mine.

Heat blooms in my chest, and my body feels like it's bursting into flames. I suddenly feel exposed, like my session in the shower earlier is somehow common knowledge. As if Adeline knows I haven't been able to shut the thought of her out of my mind, and I fucked myself with my own hand, using her body wash to help.

The flecks of sage green in her eyes are amplified by the purple eyeshadow painted across her lids. Bright glitter dots the inner corners, and smooth, crisp black eyeliner is swept across the top of her lashes. Her hair is pulled high and tight into a ponytail, the pin-straight ends dancing across her bare back. The thin straps of her silver sequined dress sit across her glittered skin. Flecks catch the light in the kitchen. Glitter is sprinkled across every inch, highlighting her bare breastbone and the curves of her shoulders. The moving shimmering fabric dips down to rest above her belly button, and when she moves to stand beside her best friend, her back is completely exposed.

She's worn skirts and shorts, even tank tops before, but something about this dress is different. It's as if she's been hiding her body, her true silhouette.

And fuck me, she's stunning.

"I was so right to give you this dress." Ember beams at Adeline. She circles her, holding onto Adeline's hand as she examines her. "Fits you like a glove. Isn't she beautiful?" Ember tosses me a look.

I cough, turning around to take a sip of my beer. I tip the can higher, savoring the fizzy liquid down my throat.

"Ember," Adeline hisses. "It's fine. You don't have to ask him a question like that."

"Why shouldn't I?" Ember asks, an edge lacing her voice. "The answer is easy. Any straight man with a working dick can see you look fucking phenomenal in this dress. Besides, you are a supermodel, so I feel like it's a given."

I grind my jaw, a conflict of emotions brewing inside me, so I clear my throat and turn back around, not wanting to raise suspicion.

"Thank you for doing my makeup." Adeline turns to Ember with a softened expression. "I haven't looked in a mirror, but I know you did an amazing job."

"You *should* look in a mirror," Ember says, wagging her finger over Adeline's face. "This is some of my best work."

Adeline's sweet mouth turns upside down while she avoids looking at her best friend... and the mirror hanging on the wall down the hallway.

"We should get going." Adeline inhales a deep breath, puffing out her chest. She presses her hands to her bare thighs before bending down.

I watch her carefully as she slips one foot into her black heel. She rolls it to the side while she works the clasp.

My cock twitches as I survey the length of her legs. Her dress hitches higher, the fabric stopping just before it reveals everything underneath. Her back is bent in my direction, displaying the pale pink flower tattoo peeking out from across her ribs.

Adeline moves onto working on her next shoe when Ember breaks my attention.

"We're celebrating our birthdays."

"What?" I snap my head up to see Ember staring at me.

There's a playfulness in her expression. She glances at Adeline before turning back to me. Still, I don't know how much Ember knows of what happened or if she knows anything at all. Something tells me she's usually like this, regardless.

"Well, Adeline's birthday was a few months ago, but my twenty-first is today." She presses her hand to her chest. "We're celebrating."

"Oh," I choke out. "Happy birthday, then."

"Thanks." Ember giggles.

Adeline's finished strapping on her shoes and moves to stand next to Ember. She's standing on the other side of the island from me, but she may as well be in front of me. I itch to touch her again. A part of me wants to throw her over my shoulder and carry her back to my room, not allowing anyone else to see her.

The thought of other men getting the privilege of seeing her dressed like this makes my blood boil at a temperature I didn't know was possible.

I flex my fingers, willing the tension to leave. I want to hit something or go out into the backyard and tear up the furniture I allowed to get ruined.

"All right, you ready?" Adeline asks Ember, tucking her matching sparkling clutch under her arm.

I pin my eyes on Adeline, letting them move up and down. I can't stop looking at her, at everything, from the way her hair is pulled high and tight, revealing all the angles of her beautiful face to the way her dress clings to the curve of her hips. I hadn't noticed until now, but Adeline hasn't been wearing makeup since the day she moved in. Her lashes are noticeably darker than usual, and her lips are painted a matte purple-red color. She's always beautiful, but with makeup on, she's slipped into model mode—a mode I've seen plastered online and in magazines.

"You should come with us," Ember blurts out.

"Ember!" Adeline gasps, shooting her best friend a glare.

"What?" Ember asks. She lifts her arm in my direction. "He's your roommate, and he's Archer's best friend. It's not like we're asking a stranger to join us."

"Really. I'm sure Micah has a ton of work he wants to get done here." Adeline shakes her head, her shoulders slumping. She plants one hand on the island and swings her gaze to mine. "You don't have to go."

Something about her pleading, embarrassed eyes relights the spark inside me, much the same as the insatiable sensation I got when sitting on the bike the other day before kissing Adeline in the rain. I should say no and walk away. I should stalk out to the backyard and take all my pent-up, sexual frustration out on vintage furniture now turned to garbage.

But I know it won't be enough. All I'll do is spend my time worrying about Adeline. I'm supposed to protect her. I know she's strong and she can protect herself in some capacity, but another quick glance at her long, bare legs and her fully exposed breastbone has me rethinking my decision to stay here.

"Where are you going?" I casually ask.

Adeline sighs, and I see the annoyance. She's tried hard to keep me at a distance since I stopped what we were doing before it went too far.

"Exodus." Ember leans forward, bringing her face into view.

Well, fuck. Exodus is one of the city's most popular nightclubs. VIP sections, dancers in cages, and a maze of a platform running across the entire dance floor. Exodus is a club for the elite and most prominent figures in Boston, especially their spoiled college kids who've never struggled a day in their life.

It's a place Archer and I used to frequent when we were in our twenties.

It's also a place I know will be packed with men salivating over themselves with the way Adeline and Ember are dressed.

"Is it just you two going?" I ask Ember, swallowing down my urge to object.

"No, we're meeting a few of my classmates at Empire Beauty School. Some artists and photographers. We've reserved a booth." Ember shrugs. "It'll be fun. You should totally come with us."

Adeline avoids my stare, keeping her gaze on the counter while I focus on her chest as she breathes.

My heart sinks, and although I'm frustrated, I don't want to keep pushing her away. I want to respect her for keeping her distance.

It's for the best.

Despite what my heart and body is telling me, I'm not good for Adeline. Not when I'm keeping so much of the truth from her.

"It's okay," I tell Ember. Adeline snaps her head up. "You two go celebrate."

"Okay." Ember sighs. "Well, if you change your mind, you know where we'll be."

Adeline keeps her gorgeous, glittered eyes on me while my gaze falls to her mouth. It takes everything in me not to change my mind. I want to kiss her. I want to know what her lips taste like when they look as sinful as they do now.

But I can see she doesn't want me to go. I'll only be a distraction.

"Thanks." I give them both a tight smile before setting my unfinished beer on the counter. "Have fun."

Ember makes her way down the hallway, checking herself in the mirror before opening the front door. She steps out, leaving me and Adeline to ourselves.

She doesn't speak a word to me. Silence lingers between us.

If I could, I'd cut the tension with a knife, but I'm at a loss for words. My need and want for Adeline are crystal clear, but all the ramifications that come with breaking this line with her involve crossing into unknown territory.

She knows it, too.

Not caring whether I'm crossing that line right now, I walk over to Adeline and place my hand over hers. She inhales a sharp breath and holds it, staring at our hands.

"Happy belated birthday." It's the only thought that comes to mind.

Adeline doesn't give me a smile. Her chest quakes with a shivering breath before she slips her hand from under mine. "Thank you."

Her words stab me in the chest. She's giving me the cold shoulder, and I deserve every bit of it.

With those two simple words still lingering in the air, I watch her walk out of the kitchen and down the hallway to meet Ember in the driveway. I watch her climb into the back seat of a black car, casting one more look up toward the house.

I swipe my toolbelt from the island and leave the kitchen before I give myself a chance to change my mind and follow her. I slide the back door shut with more force than I intend. My chest squeezes, and my blood pressure rises.

Stalking over to the pile of furniture, I stop in front of the grandfather clock Adeline desperately tried to save. The varnish is bubbled, and the stain is faded. The intricately crafted hands of the clock are frozen in time.

I don't know when they stopped working. Was it years ago, or was it the day I found myself feeling something for the first time since I could remember? I rip the hammer from my toolbelt and wrap my fingers tightly around the handle.

Pressure builds behind my eyes, and I find myself looking back at the sliding glass door connected to the kitchen. A tight sensation tugs at my chest, and I know I'm only fooling myself. I've been fooling myself for days.

The vision of Adeline walking away from me in that dress refuses to leave. I imagine a different scenario—one where I said yes to Ember's invitation.

I imagine Adeline's eyes if she had looked over her shoulder one last time before pushing through the front door.

The hammer slips from my grip and lands on the ground with a dull thud. I leave it and the grandfather clock behind, and head back into the house, knowing I won't be able to shut my mind off otherwise.

Then when I jog up the stairs and back into my room, ripping off my T-shirt and jeans, replacing them with one of my suits, the spark I felt when I'd kissed Adeline the other day lights in my chest again.

THE BOUNCER STANDING outside the front door to Exodus immediately recognizes me. It's been years since I've stepped foot in this club, but he acts as if no time has passed.

Everyone standing in the line wrapped around the building whines and groans when the bouncer unclips the rope barrier, allowing me inside without paying or checking my ID.

I give Hank the security guard a curt nod, remembering him from the days Archer and I would come in here after a long night of flying from one side of the country to the other. After signing a few business deals, we'd snag a flight on my private jet and meet a few of our college buddies here for an all-night bender, sometimes waking up the next morning just to do it all over again.

That life seems so long ago, and I try to push it from my memory as I step into the club. Sectioned off VIP booths surround the expansive dance floor. A large crowd of hundreds of people fills the center. Between each of the VIP booths runs the length of the elevated dancing platform. Each runway leads to one of the dancer's cages. The club is completely packed. Blue flashing lights pulsate across the entire club, and the DJ set in the back raises his arms in the air as he bobs his head to the beat playing over the loudspeakers.

The sea of party goers jump along.

I narrow my eyes, hoping to see Adeline and her group through the darkness. I scan each of the booths, remembering Ember said they had a VIP section reserved, so I weave through the sea of people passing through the space between the VIP sections and the bars, growing closer to the booths.

When I push through to the other side and catch Ember's strawberry blonde hair in one of the booths in the distance, I see she's standing between the seat and the table, swaying to the music as she holds her drink. The bartender serving their section another drink for one of their friends. Beside Ember, a couple is kissing, unable to keep their hands off one another.

My heart sinks when I don't see Adeline anywhere near Ember or their section. I scan the crowd again, surveying each of the booths, hoping to catch a glimpse of her shimmering dress.

I start making my way to the other side of the club, toward Ember, when I see Adeline on the opposite side. Her shimmering dress catches the blue and white strobe lights swinging over the length of the club.

Her long, dark hair sways back and forth as she bends her hips while dancing to the music. With her eyes closed, she runs her hands down the length of her body, tilting her head to the side. She's lost in the music, not caring who is watching. I stay where I am and watch her for a few moments, the knot in my chest tightening again.

My feelings for Adeline are fragile, and ones I can't ignore for much longer. I'm a fool for continuing to pretend as if our kiss in the rainstorm didn't amount to more than a kiss. I touched her. Touched her in places I'd never imagined before. But she'd also awakened a part of my soul I thought had died. Watching her now, though, I'm certain I want her. I just don't know what to do about it or where to start.

I push my way through the crowd, taking the three steps down to the dance floor. Elbowing my way across, I finally make a break through the crowd, but I screech to a halt when I see the man Adeline is dancing with.

I tilt my head to the side and narrow my eyes, blinking to make sure I'm seeing him correctly. He's vaguely familiar. With his sharp, clean-cut look, and his dark black suit, I take a moment and try to place him. An icy chill slithers down my spine when he closes in behind Adeline, reaching around her to place his hands on the front of her thighs. He's closing the space between them, but not before the bright strobe light swings over him, shining a light on the snake tattoo wrapped around his neck.

Soren's associate from the bar.

Heat simmers under my skin, injecting itself into my veins. I grind my jaw and take a step forward, ready to lunge at him and rip her away, but I don't want to cause a scene. Adeline has constantly gotten onto me for interfering when I shouldn't, but the need to get her away from him overrides my sense of reason.

I run my hand over my mouth and take a deep breath before shoving it into the pocket of my suit. I curl my hand into a tight fist and wait for the right moment. Adeline hasn't seen me yet, but I wait until the next song plays before making my move.

The song effortlessly rolls into the next one, and Adeline slips her hands over the man's and pushes them off her. He takes the hint and backs into the crowd a little more. He hasn't taken his eyes off her, but I take my shot and elbow my way through the few people dancing between us to grab onto Adeline's hand.

She yelps with my sudden touch as I pull her into the crowd. My heart is pounding, and I have no clue whether Soren's associate sees us or not.

When I'm certain there are enough dancers between us and him, I stop.

"Micah," she says, her jaw dropping. "What are you doing here?"

"Ember invited me, remember?" I look over her shoulder. "But it's clear you were preoccupied."

"I was dancing." She's clearly annoyed I've shown up. The pain and regret I saw in her eyes in the kitchen has returned. "You know, it's what people do at clubs like this."

"I thought you were here to celebrate your best friend's birthday." I can't help it. Seeing Adeline dancing with Soren's associate has me on edge and raging with jealousy. I'm furious with Archer, and I'm angry at myself for not being here to protect Adeline. I doubt him dancing with her was pure coincidence, especially given Archer's voicemail earlier.

"I am celebrating. Is this what you came here for? To ruin my night?" She seethes with anger. "I was having a good time."

"That man had his hands all over you."

"So did you the other day. But apparently, it doesn't have to mean anything. I must not mean that much to you if you allowed me to walk out the door earlier. You don't have the right to get upset with me for dancing with someone else."

I take a step forward, eliminating the space between us. "You have no idea how it fucking killed me to watch you walk out the door dressed like this." I lower my voice, not wanting others to hear.

"Seriously?" She gapes, crossing her arms over her chest.

Her breasts spill out of the fabric. "You're going back to this? Treating me like a child?"

"No," I growl, leaning close enough to bring my mouth to her ear. "I'm treating you like a fucking woman. Trust me, the images of what I want to do to you in this dress haven't gone away since you walked out that door. But I must admit, it's getting pretty fucking exhausting trying to protect you and warn you about fucking assholes who just want to fuck you." I fight to keep my hands off her. Her body is like a magnet. Especially in this fucking dress.

"You don't need to protect me. Or rescue me!" Adeline yells over the pounding music, jerking back, her cheeks flaming red and eyes lining with tears. "I'm fully capable of taking care of myself. I've been doing it all my life."

"Sounds familiar." I scoff, thinking back to the day she claimed she didn't need me to rescue her at the pool.

"I meant it then, and I mean it now." Her eyes narrow.

"You have no idea who that man was that you were dancing with."

"And you *do?*"

I look past her shoulder, watching Soren's associate disappear behind a curtain toward the back of the club. His eyes catch mine before he fades into darkness.

"I'm not doing this with you, Micah," Adeline mutters. "I can't." She holds her hands up and spins back around in the direction of where Soren's associate disappeared.

"Adeline, wait."

She pushes her way through the crowd and ignores me. I'm quick to follow, but I struggle to keep up. The crowd swells, and the deeper we go onto the dance floor, the more people there are between us.

"Adeline!" I yell, keeping my focus on her long ponytail.

I finally catch up to her before she makes it to the spot she was dancing in earlier. She spins around, and when her eyes find mine, they're fueled with more anger.

She crosses her arms beneath her chest. "You can't just come in here, demanding I listen to you, and tell me you want to do all these things to me then not act on them. I don't think that's why Ember invited you."

She turns on her heel, but I wrap my hand around her wrist; the crowd surrounding us forces us together. Our faces are less than an inch apart, with her nose practically touching mine. The heat radiating off her body surrounds me.

I look into her pleading eyes—ones that tell me she wants me to finally break down the remainder of the wall I've had in place between us. The crowd grows impossibly thicker when I bring my mouth to her ear. She shivers next to me, resting her cheek against mine.

"We can't." My voice rumbles in her ear. "I'm not good for you."

She jerks back, stiffening her spine, her eyebrows slanted in frustration. "Suddenly you're not good for me? You act like I care you went to prison or that you've been through some shit in your past. I don't care about that, Micah."

"I'm not good for you." I chance another glance up to the black curtain.

The man with the snake tattoo emerges from behind it. But this time, he isn't alone. He's with his twin; the other one of Soren's associates. They both stand at the edge of the dance floor, looking down. The man with the snake tattoo points to the spot where he and Adeline were dancing earlier. Unease grows in my stomach, and another chill slinks down my neck.

Why are they here? Was the man with the snake tattoo dancing with Adeline on purpose? Are they keeping tabs on her because Archer has found himself in Soren's debt once again?

The lengths to which Soren will go to get even with Archer

are unknown, but I know tonight isn't a mere coincidence. My stomach turns.

"We need to get out of here," I tell Adeline.

"What? No."

"Can you just trust me?" I ask desperately.

Secrets. I'm tired of keeping fucking secrets. But I need to get Adeline out of here. Right now.

"Give me one good reason why I should trust you?"

"Because..." I swallow, eyeing the men stepping closer to the dance floor. I swing my gaze back to Adeline's. "I just need you to."

Groaning with frustration, Adeline pushes me back. I don't go far, considering we're squashed in the crowd like a can of sardines.

"Go home, Micah. Go home and figure out how to get over whatever secrets you're hiding and battles you're struggling with. Leave me out of it." She shoulders past me, heading in the direction of Ember's VIP booth.

The men haven't spotted me, but I can't take any chances. Flashes and memories of Archer curled into the fetal position on the floor, with blood spilling from his mouth as Soren hunched over him, vowing retribution if he didn't pay up are all I see

I curl my hands into tight fists and follow Adeline. She's more than ten feet in front of me, and I'm unable to keep up. When I reach the three steps leading back up to the VIP section, Adeline leans over and whispers into Ember's ear. Ember nods and gives her a soft smile before Adeline swipes her clutch from the table. She gives everyone a quick wave goodbye before turning on her heel and heading toward the front of the club.

I don't bother wasting my time looking over my shoulder to see if Soren's men have spotted her or me.

I just know I need to get Adeline out of here.

I don't know where she thinks she's headed, but I'll be damned if she leaves with anyone other than me. Not when the threat of Soren and his men is so close.

I don't catch up to Adeline until we're both in the pitch-black tunneled hallway leading to the front door.

People pass us, but it isn't as difficult to navigate as it was back in the club. I jog the rest of the tunnel, catching Adeline before she pushes through the large glass doors. My fingers wrap around her wrist, pulling her to a stop. Her back falls against the wall, and I pin her with my hips.

Tipping her chin, she pins with a sharpened glare. "What the fuck, Micah?"

"Where are you going?"

"Nowhere." She presses her lips into a tight line, her nostrils flaring. "It's none of your business."

"It is my business."

"You aren't mine," she points out. "And I'm not yours."

My dick twitches, and jealousy settles into my bones. I want to make her mine. "You aren't leaving here with anyone but me."

She laughs with an unamused smile. "For someone who claims to be wiser because they're twelve years older than me, you sure are acting childish, making demands when it isn't your place."

My heart hammers in my chest, and my nerves are still on high alert. I don't know what Soren's men planned on doing with Adeline, but something tells me if I didn't show up when I did, she wouldn't be standing here with me now.

"I'm leaving," Adeline says. "But I'm not leaving here with you." She crosses her arms over her chest, planting her heeled feet to the marbled floor.

I stare into her eyes, and my heart flutters. With a tilted smile, a laugh escapes my throat. "We'll see about that."

I bend down and quickly wrap one arm around her waist and the other around the back of her thighs, then I hoist her over my shoulder as a loud yelp shoots from her pretty little mouth.

"Micah, stop it." She grunts, kicking her feet. "People will think you're kidnapping me."

"Let them." I push through the door with my free hand and head toward the curb where the valet parked my car.

"Wait," Adeline says, catching the attention of Hank the security guard.

Hank gives both of us a wave, and I give him a smile. "Have a great night, Hank."

"Have a good night, Mr. Harding."

Adeline grunts again, her arms relaxing as she gives up her fight. "Ugh, you're so frustrating."

SIXTEEN

ADELINE

My bare ass lands against the cool leather of the passenger seat. I'm struggling to catch my breath as I watch Micah walk around the front of his car. Silence lingers in the air, and there's a palpable heat sticking to my skin.

I wasn't really trying to leave. I wanted to stay with Ember longer. I was only trying to get some air and put some distance between Micah and me. Him showing up to Exodus has me confused. Was it his plan to come here and make me leave? Although I didn't have any intention of going further with the man on the dance floor, a part of me is delighted to know it made Micah jealous.

He swings his door open and quickly slips into the driver's seat, slams the door shut, and presses the button to the ignition. The engine roars to life, but when his hand wraps around the shifter, he stops and swings his heated gaze to me.

"Put your seatbelt on, Addy."

I refuse to move. I refuse to let him drive me anywhere without him explaining why he tore me away from Exodus, so I place my hands on either side of bare naked thighs and grip the edge of the seat, waiting.

Frustration boils over, and Micah's nostrils flare as a deep growl vibrates out of him.

He's being ridiculous and over the top. I'm still embarrassed by the way he acted in the club. Inside, I know there's a reason behind the way he's behaving, but I won't give in to his demands easily. Not until he tells me the secrets he's hiding or why he struggles so badly to give in to whatever is going on between us.

He's still grumbling when he leans over his seat and reaches behind me for my seatbelt. His scent immediately hits my nose. For a moment, I swear I smell a hint of my strawberry-scented body wash, but then again, Ember doused me in flower-scented body glitter before we left the house. I'm lightheaded and knocked off balance by his proximity. Micah jerks on the seatbelt, the sharp sound of him yanking on the strap filling the heated silence between us. His hands press against my body as he clicks the metal into the buckle.

But my attention falls to his mouth. I search his face while his eyes are pinned on mine. His hands are two red hot coals pressed against my body making the space between my thighs tingle again.

"There," he says, yanking on the strap once more and tightening it.

After sitting back and revving the engine, he shifts it into drive and whips away from the curb. I keep my hands gripped to the edge of the seat as I watch Micah. His firm set jaw is clenched tightly, and his white-knuckled grip squeezes the pristine leather steering wheel.

"I don't understand you," I say, breaking the silence as he whips through the traffic riddled streets of downtown Boston, where fancy cars and bright lights surround us. Micah's gaze constantly flickers up to his rearview mirror before falling back onto the road.

I avoid looking at myself in the side mirror. I still haven't looked at one in months in fear of what I'll see. It's strange given how I used to make a living off caring what I looked like. Everything rode on putting on my best face... or mask, as Micah would call it.

I didn't even bother looking into a mirror after Ember did my makeup for tonight.

My heart sinks into the pit of my stomach, and I feel myself frowning.

"I don't understand you either," Micah says, cutting me from my thoughts as his playful smirk forms.

"No." I grind my teeth together, squeezing my seat tighter. "I don't understand why you just get to show up at Exodus and suddenly demand I get in the car with you. Ember invited you to celebrate with us, but instead, you interrupt me on the dance floor, and for what? Because you were jealous I was dancing with someone?"

"You shouldn't have been dancing with him." His eyes narrow. He rings his hands on the steering wheel as he turns down another road, heading in the direction of the highway, but we're too deep in the city, and traffic is heavy, making it take longer for us to get there.

"Unless you've claimed me as yours, I can dance with whoever I want," I argue.

"What do you want me to do, Addy?"

"I want you to do something."

"Do something?"

"Yes. I want you to make up your mind." I only had one drink at Exodus, but my inhibitions have collapsed. I don't give a fuck anymore about holding back. This cat and mouse game Micah and I are playing is tiring.

"Make up my mind about what?" he asks.

I don't know how to be any clearer, but maybe this is what Micah needs. I see the resistance. He wants me, but he feels loyal to Archer. I need to be as honest about my feelings for him as possible.

"About me." I raise my voice, frustrated with the entire night. With the past three days. "I want you to make up your mind about me."

He remains focused on the road. His thick, muscled arms stretch under the sleeves of his suit.

"Do you want me?" I ask.

He doesn't deny it. Instead, his breathing grows heavier, and his eyes harden.

"Clearly, me dancing with another man made you feel something. I want you to admit it."

His nostrils flare.

At a red light, he hits the brake hard; his hand still clutched around the wheel, the other resting on the shifter. Every few seconds, he flexes his fingers.

Thirty seconds of silence lingers before the light turns green. Micah hasn't answered my question when he slams on the gas, and the engine roars before taking off. He weaves in and out of cars, then takes an unexpected sharp turn. Whipping the car into an underground parking garage, he blasts through the open gate and swings into the first vacant spot he finds. The tires screech and the engine vibrates as he stops.

My heart pounds in my chest, and my breathing is shallow. I've never seen Micah this way, and the sight is both exciting and terrifying.

"What do you want me to do, Adeline?" he asks, his voice deep and heavy. His shoulders and chest rise and fall with every breath, like each one is a struggle. "I'm *trying*. I'm trying to warn you that I'm not good for you, but I can't help feeling like this—"

"What do you feel?" I ask him, knowing he's so close to removing the mask he's expertly placed over his face.

"I don't know..." He raises his voice. "All I do know is that every time I watch you with someone else, it feels like you've torn this hole in my chest, and every time you resist me, or someone looks at you like a piece of fucking meat, I want to bend you over and fuck you until you scream my name and tell me you're mine." He slams his hand against the steering wheel, staring through the front windshield. His jaw clicks with frustration, but there's a sense of relief when his shoulders fall slightly.

My lungs starve for oxygen when my entire body stills. Micah's confession suspends in the air, heavy and thick, pulling me down with it.

I open my mouth, but snap it shut.

"But I shouldn't. I shouldn't. I told Archer I would watch over you and protect you!" he seethes, yelling. "So, what do you expect me to do, Addy?"

"What do you want me to do?" he asks again, his voice lowered.

I steel my chest and force the words to come out. "Instead of watching me, do something. Instead of yelling at me, do something. Instead of pretending like there isn't something between us, *do something*."

"Like what?"

"Touch me," I breathe, the words spilling out of me like a breaking dam. "Every time I'm around you, I'm so fucking wet. I touch myself, imagining you between my thighs. When you touched me the other day and stopped, I ached for you. My clit pulsated for hours afterward, wishing you'd given it relief. I want you to touch me, Micah. I want you to touch me like you did before, only this time, I don't want you to stop."

He snaps his head to the right, pinning me with his stormy blue eyes, and my breath catches in the back of my throat.

"Fuck it." A quick breath falls from his mouth before his hands are on me. I barely register what's happening before he's unclipping my seat belt, and Micah's hands land on my hips, tugging me in his direction. He pulls me hungrily, moving me as if there's nothing between us.

I climb over the shifter and straddle him in the driver's seat. My back hits the steering wheel, and my ass lands on the horn, but he doesn't let it stop him.

"I want you." He growls, running both his hands over my hips. My dress is already slipped up to my waist. It doesn't take much considering how short it is.

His hands are frantic as they explore my body. I plant both of mine on his shoulders, my pussy wet for him already, and I grind against his swollen cock.

"Give me this pretty fucking mouth." He hisses. He grasps my chin, pulling me down to him. My lips meet his and I moan, savoring the taste.

I rock my hips against his hardened length, hungry for more as I slip my hand around the back of his neck, combing his hair with my fingernails. His lips part just enough for me to gasp for air as I cry out. The ache inside me swells.

I need Micah.

I need to feel him inside me. My heart is racing at a speed I'm not certain I'll survive. It isn't until he growls hungrily against my mouth before moving his lips down the length of his neck do I realize I'm not only hungry for Micah—I'm starving for his vulnerable soul. Every time he shows me this possessive or protective side of him, I want him more.

He pulls at me, and although I push a little back, my heart constantly boomerangs back to his.

"Fuck, yes," I whimper, grinding my hips a little harder.

Micah's mouth finds the swell of my breasts. It isn't difficult, considering there's barely any fabric covering them. He nudges his face against the fabric, hoping to push it aside but is unsuccessful.

"Clothing tape," I mutter on a heavy breath, looking down at him. "Couldn't risk showing too much skin."

"This fucking dress." He snarls, and with a quick heated glare, he pinches the fabric of my dress between his teeth and tears it away from my skin. A yelp escapes my throat before his teeth find my peaked nipple. He sucks and kisses and nibbles. He teases me, inching me ever so closer to the edge.

"What's wrong with it?" I ask, knowing the answer even before he's said anything, smiling to myself. "You don't like it?"

"All night. It's been testing me," he says against my skin. "Taunting and teasing me. I don't like how it made others look at you. Like you were a meal for them to feast on."

"Is that how it made you look at me?" I ask him, my breath hot.

He clutches my breast and flicks the pad of his thumb across it as he pins his hardened stare on me. "Yes. But unlike them, I want to be the only one invited to this meal, and I intend to savor every bite."

I smile, a fluttering sensation tickling the bottom of my stomach. Uncontrollable feelings stir inside me. My hands are wrapped around his thick neck when I roll my hips even harder, tilting my head back. I bite down on my bottom lip, ready to come right now if he keeps touching and tasting me like this.

Heat radiates from my body as his hands splay across my bare ass, my swollen flesh filling his large palms. His long fingertips are deep underneath me, playing with my slit.

"You're so fucking wet." He moves to the other breast, repeating the same motion with removing the tape pressing it to me. "I can't wait to slide my cock into you."

"Do it," I beg, my lower stomach fluttering with the idea of him being inside me. "Please."

It's all I've been wanting.

The lights from the garage illuminate the inside of the car. If a security guard or anyone else were to walk by, they wouldn't have to question what we're doing. But I don't care.

Micah's touch has made me come alive.

Removing one hand from behind, he slips it between us and under the hem of my black, lacy thong, quickly finding my clit. He slides his fingers along my wet slit, pressing his fingertips against the swollen bud.

I move with his hand, not wanting him to stop.

"Oh, my God."

"Fuck," he groans. "You're so fucking slick. I won't have any trouble burying myself inside you."

"I've wanted this for so long," I breathe out, rocking in time with Micah's hand. "I'm going to come if we keep going like this."

I move my hands from around his neck and try to work his belt. Micah stops moving, watching me as I work to free him. I manage to unbuckle his belt, and my fingers frantically undo the button to his black slacks before sliding down his zipper to free him from his black boxer briefs. His cock springs to life, and I wrap my hand around his thick length, my eyes widening at the sight of it.

"Take me," Micah grunts. "Take all of me."

I'm staring into his eyes as I lift myself off my heels and center myself over him. My heart swells at him asking me to take him. Micah places his hand back on one of my ass cheeks, guiding me down his length. My mouth falls open, and I dig my fingers into his shoulder, my nails cutting into his collared shirt.

I gasp when I lower myself completely, feeling stretched to fit around him. I take him inch after inch. When I think I'm close to taking all of him, I'm wrong. I hold my breath as my body adjusts to fit him inside me.

"That's right, Addy," he moans. "Fuck, you feel so good and tight."

I lift myself again and lower my head, watching myself move above him. I watch the space where we're joined, concentrating on Micah's hot breath mixing with mine. He slips in and out of me with ease, even though we're squeezed between the driver's seat and the steering wheel.

I feel myself tightening around him. I'm already close to coming all over him. It's as if the past several months of pent-up frustration is finally being released and my body isn't wasting any time getting there.

I'm still looking down when Micah hooks two fingers under my chin, lifting my gaze.

The corner of his mouth lifts into a satisfied grin. He rests his head back as his hand continues to massage the flesh on my ass cheek. With his other hand, he traces my jawline, slowly dragging his finger down the center of my chest. I'm completely exposed, and my dress is spread wide open.

There's no way in hell Ember is getting this dress back after tonight.

Micah leans back in his seat and watches me with his heated blue-gray gaze. "You're so fucking beautiful."

My pussy tightens around him. His words are an arrow straight to my heart. While Micah pushes my buttons, and definitely pushes the boundaries of being possessive, it's different with him. I know with him, I'm safe. I know he'll never lay a hand on me. Not the way Maddox did, or anyone else who has ever treated me unkindly.

Micah's touch is gentle and healing. He's the kind of man who lifts me up without ever putting me down. He sees the beauty in me when I struggle to see it in myself.

I tilt my head back and let Micah watch me. My hands glide over my own body. I touch my clit, the feeling of him inside me and the feeling of my own hand sparking a renewed sensation. It's electric. While working myself, I slide my other hand along my stomach and ribs, gripping my breast. Between my thumb and forefinger, I pinch my nipple. Another jolt of electricity passes through me, and I open my eyes on Micah.

His grip on my ass tightens, and I let him guide me.

Moisture clings to my skin when he grabs the back of my head, pulling me to kiss him. My hands fall away from myself, and I press my forehead to his, wrapping both of my hands around his face. My pussy clenches as I lift myself, moving over him faster. The sound of me moving around him mixes and mingles with our heavy breathing. I press my lips to Micah's, tasting him once more. His tongue slips inside my mouth, and I moan, savoring every second. My mouth can't stay on his for long before I'm closing in on the edge. I can feel it building inside me. My orgasm presses against my insides as Micah's cock pumps inside me, pulling it out with every thrust.

"Right there," I tell him. "Don't stop."

"Oh, I'm not stopping." He grunts. "Fuck me, Adeline. Fuck me like the good girl I know you are."

I place both my hands on his chest and work myself over him faster. My entire body tingles. Whether it's the heat from being inside the car, crammed in this small space, or from Micah, I don't care. Everything about this moment with him feels good and I don't want it to end. But at the same time, I do.

"I'm going to come," I confess.

My entire body tenses as I lower myself over him a few more times. My orgasm rips through me. My thighs clench on top of him, and my pussy pulsates, reaching the top of my orgasm. A high sensation rocks through my body as I cry out Micah's name.

My pussy is contracting, and I've slowed my movements when Micah follows me, reaching his own orgasm. His teeth are clenched, and he lets out a sharp hiss, spilling into me.

The way his cock pulses and the feeling of his cum spilling into me heightens my orgasm.

I've never experienced this with anyone else. The sensation of this moment crashes down on me all at once.

Walking out of the house with Micah's heated stare.

The club.

Micah pulling me back away from the stranger.

Him throwing me over his shoulder and carrying me out to his car.

I'm still panting, recovering from what we've just done when I open my eyes and sit back on my heels.

He traces the side of my face with his fingertips, tucking my hair behind my ear.

Fear slips in, mixing with pleasure.

Was this it? Was this the moment Micah was wanting and it'll be our one and only time? Will reality hit him, and he'll suddenly feel like this is wrong? Will he think he made a mistake?

I stay on top of him, with him inside me as I look into his eyes.

He must sense my hesitation or hear the hiccup in my breathing when he places his mouth to mine again. The motion is soft and gentle—a stark contrast from when he pulled me on top of him a few minutes ago.

His mouth moves over mine gently before he pulls back. I smooth my hand over his tie and smile.

"That good, huh?" he asks.

My legs ache, and I know they're going to hurt tomorrow. His hand continues to massage my ass cheek. My thighs are still quivering, aching to start moving again with Micah still inside me, but I know we can't stay here, like this.

"I think the same could be said for you." I roll my hips, and Micah grunts, softly closing his eyes.

"What are you doing to me?" he asks, opening his eyes on me again.

I smile as he tugs on the end of my ponytail, and I lean forward as his mouth lands on my neck, leaving a trail of kisses. Steam clings to the windows, blurring our view to the outside and blocking anyone from peeking in.

His mouth doesn't leave my neck as his fingertips hook under the thin straps of my dress before slipping them back onto my shoulders. He adjusts the fabric over my breasts, attempting to re-stick the tape.

I giggle. "It's okay." I cup his face, pulling him to look up. "I'll fix it when we get back to the club."

"Get back?" His eyes narrow.

"Yeah." I nod, swiping my tongue across my lips. "It would be rude of me to leave Ember hanging on her birthday."

"Oh." His forehead creases. "I thought you told her you were leaving."

I shake my head, running my thumb over his lower lip. "No, I told her I was stepping out for some air."

"I'm sure she'll understand, or at least she assumes you aren't coming back."

"Maybe." I twist my mouth in thought and kiss him again. I keep my mouth to his and breathe him in. He's still inside me, and I feel his cock growing harder again. My chest swells, and I pull away. "Not to mention I still have a dance to finish. It was kind of disrespectful of me to disappear on my dance partner like that."

He shoots me a stern look. "What did I say earlier?" He slides his hands around my waist, palming my flesh again. He jerks me against him. His fingertips press into me, and my body hums in anticipation.

I roll my hips. "Remind me again. What did you say?"

"When you resist me, I want to fuck you until you scream my name..." He grits his teeth. His eyes fall to my mouth.

"Right." I give him a devious grin. "Well, after I finish up my dance, we can get on that." I bite back my laugh, knowing I have no intention of being anywhere other than where Micah is.

He senses the humor but keeps his jaw clenched. With his hands still on my ass, he pulls me against him, grunting. "You're a brat, you know that?"

"No." I shake my head, ghosting my mouth over his. "Why don't you show me?"

I'm about to kiss him again when a bright light shines in my face, forcing me to jerk back. I inhale a sharp breath and look up. Two headlights beam into the car.

I tilt my head, trying to get a better view of who it is or how far back they are. The back windshield is clear, despite the other windows covered in steam.

The blacked-out car is parked two rows back, but other than a van in the far-right corner, we're the only vehicles here.

Micah's hands tense against me, holding me still. He holds his breath as his eyes dart up to the rearview mirror.

"Uh oh." I smile, pulling his attention back to me. "Looks like we've been caught." I kiss him, expecting him to let our kiss linger, but he surprises me and cuts it short.

"We should go." His eyes nervously dart to the mirror again with a stern look.

My shoulders fall, and I wonder if this is the moment he cuts this off. He's gotten what he wanted. The desire and excitement surrounding us is gone. And the person in the car has just pulled him back to reality.

He's already begun to pull away, the distance growing in his expression.

Every worry and fear plays in my mind.

"Okay," I whisper, finally pulling myself off him. His cock

slips out of me, and I lift my leg to climb off him when his hand wraps around my wrist. He stops me and looks up at me with hooded, satisfied eyes. I relax against him as he lifts my wrist to his mouth, and his lips press against my delicate flesh.

"I'm not finished with you yet." The words vibrate against my wrist, directly on my pulse. The corner of his mouth curls. "In case there was any doubt."

Heat pools between my legs. "Then, take me home."

SEVENTEEN

Micah

If I could stay here forever, I'd die a fucking happy man.

I lay in my bed, staring at Adeline. There's a small space between us, and I'm arguing with myself on whether to close the gap and sink into her, or stay here a little longer, admiring her.

Adeline Mayfield is naked in my bed—a sentence I never thought I would say—with my sheet wrapped around her waist, stretched out on her back, with her hand draped above her head, and her breasts on full display. The cool air blowing from the air conditioning system breezes across her skin, making tiny goosebumps break out and her nipples peak like two hard pebbles. Her lips part, allowing a small passage of air between them, and her long, dark lashes rest against her pinked cheeks. Remnants of the body glitter she wore last night are still sprinkled across her body. Every now and then, the sun catches the tiny specks, shimmering in the light.

An arrow shoots straight to my heart. I've slept with many women—if I'm honest, I'm embarrassed to admit how many—but I've never felt this way about a single one. I've never had a woman force themselves into my life, steal my heart, and hold it hostage while I gladly stood by and let it happen. But with Adeline, it's a feeling I welcome with open arms.

I lay outstretched in my bed and stare at her, knowing if anything were to happen to her, I'd hunt down who was responsible and kill them before they took another breath.

A chill slithers down the length of my spine, thinking back to last night. Soren's men were close to Adeline—too close—and when the car behind us in the parking garage shined their headlights on us, I was almost certain it was one of them.

I don't know their intention with Adeline or their reasons for being at the club last night, whether it was by chance or with purpose. Either way, I can't take any chances. I won't risk Archer's reckless choices spilling over into Adeline's life, putting her safety at risk.

She still hasn't shared with me her real reason for moving back here, but part of me knows it must be serious. There's a vulnerable part of her life—one she hasn't shared with me. Archer, either, I suspect. But something tells me she came here for solace, for change, even if it wasn't ideal. She came here to run away from her life back in LA.

Beneath the surface image Adeline puts on, the one of a model with the perfect life, lives a vulnerable, fractured woman. She's shown me glimpses over the past few months, and now we're closer than we've ever been, I'm hoping she's willing to let me in just a little more.

My cock swells when I feather my fingers across her skin. I start at her breast, circling her hardened nipple. She squirms, slowly awakening under my touch.

"Mm," she moans, her eyes shut as her mouth lifts into a satisfied smile. "Keep going."

"You don't like it when I stop, do you?" I tease, flicking my fingers over her nipple. Her legs shift under the sheet, pulling it farther down her hips, revealing what's underneath. She's completely bare and open for me.

Good.

"No." She shakes her head. "I don't." Her eyes are still closed, but her mouth falls open. Arching her back, she writhes, her body begging for me.

"Aren't you sore?" I ask her.

"Very."

"But you don't want me to stop?"

"Absolutely not." Her eyes open, and she rolls her head to the side. "I like the way it feels when you touch me."

"Tell me where," I demand.

"Where?" Her eyebrows dip, and her breath hiccups as I circle my finger around her belly button. Her eyes flutter closed before she rolls her gaze back on me.

"Tell me where," I repeat.

I drag my finger over the curve of her hip, already knowing she's soaking wet for me. Liquid heat fills my groin. My dick is already hard as a fucking rock. It isn't difficult to pull this reaction out of me when I'm around Adeline.

"I like it when you lick my nipples and touch my pussy."

My cock twitches. Well, her confession is a pleasant surprise.

"Your pussy, huh?" I raise my eyebrows and slip my fingers between her thighs. I don't quite reach her slit just yet. I'm loving this game we're playing.

Her arms slink across the pillow underneath her head.

"Yes." She sighs, her eyes widening. "But I like it more when you're inside it."

I chuckle. "I love how bold you are, Adeline Mayfield."

"I haven't always been this bold." She blushes.

I play with her slit, sliding my finger between her soft flesh before I lean forward and lap my tongue over her hardened nipple. I want to press her further on why she's suddenly bold with me when she hasn't been in her past, but I don't want to ruin this with her. I want to savor this moment.

I circle my tongue over her nipple, then sink my teeth into her supple flesh.

"Oh, God. Yes..." she whimpers, arching her back. Her chin is tilted high, and her head is buried in the pillow. "Please, Micah."

"Are you sure you're not too sore?" I ask her.

Once we left the parking garage, I sped through the rest of downtown Boston, attempting to get home as fast as possible. Part of me wished I'd taken my motorcycle to keep me from hitting as many red lights as we had, but I still made it home faster than usual. We barely made it inside the front door before I bent her over the kitchen counter and fucked her from behind.

Afterward, I'd carried her upstairs, where I pulled her into my room and we disappeared for hours, only to wake a few minutes ago to the morning sun.

"No, I'm not too sore." She moans. "I can handle it."

"I have breakfast with my brothers this morning," I tell her, moving the bedsheet away from her body. "But I'm hungry now."

I slip my fingers between her slit, and she arches her back in response. She's slick and wet and fuck, I want to plunge my dick inside her so badly.

But I want to enjoy this with her.

Her eyes sparkle, and she fists the pillowcase, gripping onto it as I move my fingers in circles across her clit.

I plunge two fingers into her, coating them in her wetness.

"More..." she pants, pulling on the blue pillowcase.

I add one more finger, then another. Every finger leaves her with another gasp, another moan. I press my thumb against her clit, cupping her sweet cunt.

She pants and slides her feet across the bed. "Fuck, Micah. I'm about to come."

"Not yet." I deny her the satisfaction, ripping my hand away from her body.

"What?" She gapes, her jaw dropping as she catches her breath. "Don't stop."

I pull my fingers from inside her and scoot closer to her, lifting my hand to my mouth. Licking and sucking on my fingers, she looks up at me with sparkling eyes.

"You taste sweet," I tell her. "And I'm starving."

Without another word, I climb over her and part her legs with my knee, then bury my face between her smooth thighs. My tongue slips between her wet cunt, landing on her clit. She arches her back and grips onto the back of my head.

"Oh, my God."

I bite on her swollen bud, relentless, and I don't let up, the taste of her overwhelming me. I hook both of my arms under her legs, and she drapes them over my shoulders as I pull her closer to press my face to her once more. She bucks, riding with the rhythm of my mouth, and I slip both of my arms under her, cupping her ass cheeks.

I growl against her pussy, sending a vibration through her body. She whimpers and moans. My cock is solid, begging to be inside her.

But I know she's close to coming.

My heart splinters watching her. I know this is wrong, but how can it be wrong when it feels this fucking good?

Adeline is Archer's baby sister, but where he sees her as someone fragile, as incapable, I see her as a strong woman. My need to protect her hasn't faded, but she's proven to me she can handle her own.

I don't want to let her go.

The threat of Soren and his men is more apparent than ever.

I've tried to protect her from the truth. I've tried to protect Archer from those he loves. But when is it my time? When do I get to finally have what I want?

"You taste so fucking good," I tell Adeline, keeping my mouth pressed against her. "I'm going to keep tasting this precious cunt until you've screamed my name."

"Micah," my name falls from her mouth on a soft breath.

I pull her closer, pressing my fingers into her flesh.

"Louder." I grunt, sucking on her swollen clit. I move my arms from under her, plunging four fingers inside her. She cries out when I slide my other hand across her stomach and palm and massage her breast. I hook my fingers inside her, pulling at the special spot that brings her over the edge. Her body quivers under me, her legs vibrating.

I feel her everywhere, all at once. Her moans and her fingers in my hair tell me she wants this.

"Micah!" she screams.

I smile against her clit, continuing to kiss and suck as she rides out her orgasm.

Burning heat rests at the bottom of my stomach. I plant kisses along her pussy, moving to the space inside her thighs. I kiss along her lower stomach, planting a trail all the way up to her face. I slide my cock between her wet pussy.

"Better?" I ask.

"Yes," she breathes, lifting her hips. She bucks them against me, clearly wanting more.

"Good." I part her legs farther.

She reaches down, grabs onto my cock, and slides her hand up and down my length before she places her fingers on my shoulder, pushing me. I fall back onto the bed, my heart ready to beat right out of my fucking chest.

"Now it's my turn to satisfy you." She brings herself to her knees, whipping her long, brown hair over her shoulder.

With a sly grin, she places a kiss on my cheek before climbing on top of me. She straddles me, pressing her shins into the mattress. Her thighs clench around my waist, and she centers herself over my swollen cock.

I watch her move freely above me. The pink flower tattoo I'd seen peek out of her dress last night is on full display. The petals wrap around her ribs, the ends stopping just below her breast. I run my fingers across them as if they were real.

"A symbol of rebirth," she moans, rolling her hips over me slowly. This time is different. She isn't rushed. She takes her time, and I don't press her. I tilt my head, studying the petals, memorizing them before the pleasure overwhelms me.

I close my eyes and tilt my head back into the pillow. My hands fall to her hips, moving her with me.

"Open your eyes," she commands. "I want you to watch what you do to me. I want you to see how your cock makes me feel."

My eyes snap open. She tilts her head back, the ends of her hair dancing gracefully across her lower back. The veins in her neck stick out as her pussy tightens around me.

"I'm close to coming again," she says. Her eyes are squeezed shut, and her hands are on her breasts. She's fucking beautiful. I've never seen someone so open, so vulnerable with me.

I roll my head, catching the mirror standing against the far wall, stretching practically from the floor to the ceiling, and I watch what Adeline is doing to me from a new perspective. I run my hands along her thighs, watching her this way, adding more fuel to the fire between us. Her eyes open as she looks down at me, looking at her through the mirror.

Her skin glitters with the morning light pouring in through the gray, linen curtains.

"Watch us," I tell her. "Look at the way you fit so perfectly above me."

A sweet moan falls from her mouth before she squeezes her eyes shut and leans forward, catching mine. I let her take control, paying me back for the pleasure I've given her.

Every lift and every thrust vibrates through my cock, and I'm buzzing from the high she's giving me. A feeling of euphoria washes over me as she breaks our kiss, straightening herself on top of me again. She lifts herself even higher, driving in and out of me. I look down, watching the space where our bodies meet, where my cock disappears inside her.

"Fuck, Addy." I groan. "I don't want this to stop."

"Me, either," she whimpers.

But I already feel myself reaching the edge. My body lights on fire, heat pooling in my stomach. My cock hums with every thrust.

"I'm coming again," Adeline whines, and I feel her pussy tighten around me. She stills, with only her thighs vibrating and quaking with her orgasm. I pump my hips, pounding into her, feeling myself getting there. My cum spills inside her when I drive my cock into her once more. Tilting my head back, I close my eyes, squeezing them shut as I struggle to catch my breath.

Like I said, if I were to die like this, with Adeline surrounding me, naked in my bed, I'd die a happy fucking man.

When I've rode out my orgasm, Adeline rolls off me, tucking herself against me and under my arm. I lie back and work to catch my breath before turning to look at her.

I sweep her hair away from her face and kiss her deeply.

She lifts her hand and cups the side of my face. Her eyes wander as she sucks in her bottom lip.

"What is it?" I ask.

She pops out her bottom lip and sucks in a breath, clearly nervous.

"Addy, what is it?"

"I was just curious." She looks up at me, wide-eyed, and fuck, I feel myself falling harder and faster for her.

I smile. "Curious about what?"

"I realize I don't know much about your dating history. And with the way you are in bed, it got me thinking..."

I raise my eyebrows. "Are you asking how many women I've slept with?"

"Sort of." She lifts one shoulder, curling in on herself. A hint of pink touches her cheeks. "Or just serious relationships in general."

"Oh, man." I sigh, and stare at the ceiling. "Unfortunately, if you're asking for a number on how many women I've slept with since I lost my virginity, I won't be able to give you one."

"Micah Harding, a Playboy?" Addy mocks, pretending to gasp. "No..."

"Stop." I laugh, her sarcasm a slight pin prick to the chest. But she's right. I've had a reputation for years as the menace little brother of the Harding dynasty. Up until last year, I wore it like a badge of honor, sporting it proudly. And up until a few months ago, I'd slipped back into old habits, delicately balancing on the line of wanting to be the person I know I am to the person I once was.

"It's okay," Adeline says, disappointment lingering in her voice. "I kind of expected that. But what about relationships?"

I rest my hand on my forehead and shove the ends of my hair back. "The last serious relationship I had was right before I went to prison. I was with Calista for almost two years when I cut things off with her the day before my sentencing."

I close my eyes and remember the day I'd bought this house. Calista stood on the front porch and told me about the life she'd envisioned here with me, but that dream died the second I stepped into my prison cell. I'd considered asking her to marry me but wasn't sure I was completely ready to take that leap at the time.

I've been dealing with the loss of that dream ever since.

"You didn't think she'd stay with you until you got out?" Adeline whispers.

I roll my head back to her. "No," I sigh. "I noticed the way she looked at me, and I didn't want to be with someone who looked at me with disdain, because even after I got out, it would always be a point of contention with us. It would always be an issue."

Guilt and regret make a home in my bones.

Silence lingers before Adeline breaks it. "Did you want children with her?"

A knot tightens in my chest. "I've always envisioned having children. I still want them, but I don't know if it'll ever happen."

"Do you regret leaving Calista?" she asks, as if reading my mind.

I cup the side of Adeline's face. Heat spreads down the length of my arm, warming at the place we're connected. I haven't talked about Calista in a long time, but the feeling I'm having now isn't what I expected.

"No," I confidently say. I lean down and kiss the corner of Adeline's mouth. She smiles against me. "I don't. I only regret the time I've lost in moving on from my past." I feather my mouth above hers, allowing my breath to dance against her heated skin.

"What about now?" she asks. "How do you feel now, here with me?"

I grin, gripping the back of her head tighter. "I like where I am right now." I kiss her. "No regrets."

It's the truth.

I don't expand on the Calista conversation for much longer. I pull away from Adeline far enough to let my head fall back on the pillow. It's strange yet surprising to feel a weight lift from my chest.

There are parts of my past I'm still keeping from Adeline, especially the ones about Archer, but the load doesn't feel as heavy now. Talking about my relationship with Calista feels like a weight has been lifted off me.

"Didn't you say you have breakfast with your brothers?" Adeline asks, threading her fingers through my hair.

The gesture is small and insignificant, but it heals a part of my soul I didn't know was broken. It's intimate and personal. A silent message I'm not even certain she knows she's sending.

"I do." Though I'm tempted to text Lennon and Jude to say I won't be able to make it today. I never want to leave.

I also don't want to leave Adeline here alone. I doubt Soren and his men know Adeline is staying here with me, but I don't want to take any chances. If they tracked her down last night at Exodus, there's no telling what they know. And I haven't spoken to Archer yet about what happened. I've been with Adeline ever since last night, but I intend on calling him later and see if I can figure out what's going on and what he knows.

I roll onto my side and face Adeline. "I can always cancel."

"No." She shakes her head, a small smile growing on her pretty mouth. "I don't want you to back out because of me."

My stomach dips. "Did you have any plans for today?"

"I did want to talk to Ember." She pulls her bottom lip under her teeth. "I feel bad for leaving last night. I want to treat her to breakfast or lunch... if she isn't too hungover." She giggles.

I open my mouth to protest but stop myself. I have no right to tell Adeline what to do, and I can't tell her about Soren. Not when Archer clearly hasn't filled her in on the truth.

I won't deny that it frightens me a little knowing there's a chance Soren might be following her, waiting to catch her in a moment when she's vulnerable.

But I can't tell her not to meet up with Ember.

I offer her the only other form of protection I can when I can't be there.

"My driver can give you a ride if you want."

She raises her eyebrows. "You have a driver?"

I laugh. "Of course."

She lifts herself up and rests on her elbow, looking down at me. "I've never seen him."

"Well, Ray's been our family's driver for decades. He mostly works for my older brother Lennon, since I'm usually in and out of the country several times in a month." I clear my throat. "I'm usually working in the UK or Europe. But when I'm home, he'll drive me around sometimes. When I don't take my car or bike, that is."

"I don't know." She shakes her head. "I'd hate to put Ray out. Or your brother."

"You won't. He's probably going to drop Lennon off at the restaurant, but other than that, he should be available," I tell her, grabbing my phone. I text Ray, asking if he's free this morning, then drop my phone back on the table. "There, I've already asked him if he's free."

She rolls her eyes at me before playfully slapping me on the chest. I catch her hand before she's able to pull it away and bring it to my mouth to kiss the inside of her wrist, pressing my lips to her pulse.

"I need to shower before meeting my brothers. Would you like to join me?"

"Is that a real question?"

I laugh, my heart swelling at the twinkle in her eye.

AFTER SHOWERING WITH ADELINE, I quickly get dressed in one of the suits I keep at the house. I wait until Ray picks Adeline up before jumping into my car and driving into the city. I toss the keys to the valet and step into Eclipse, heading straight for our usual booth. Even after all these years, I'm surprised my brothers and I have kept up with the tradition of eating at my father's favorite restaurant, at his favorite table.

At first, I thought it was some sort of sick torture the three of us were putting on ourselves. Like a punishment, carrying out my father's obsession with power and control long after he's been dead.

But as the years have gone by, I think of it more as a chance for us to rewrite our own script. Where my father used dinners at Eclipse to control and manipulate, the three of us Harding brothers use it as a way of checking in with one another.

Meals at Eclipse have brought us closer.

I slide into the booth beside Jude.

He's wearing a simple, short-sleeve, collared shirt. The forest green fabric is thick, and the two buttons are undone at the top, just below his neck. His shirt is tucked into his black slacks.

"Play at Abbey's school later," he mutters against the rim of his glass of water, as if he already knows I was going to make a comment about his outfit.

"You should have mentioned it," I say, waving to the waitress for her to grab my usual drink: a gin and tonic. "I would have come."

"It's not a huge production or anything." Jude frowns, sitting back in the booth, draping his arms across the leather backing. "It's a re-enactment of *The Wizard of Oz*, and it's all taking place in the classroom. Apparently, they think all the parents will fit on one half of the room while the play takes place on the other."

"Sounds like a blast." The waitress sets my drink in front of me, and I take the first sip. "Who's Abbey playing?"

His grin reaches his eyes. "Dorothy."

"Of course, my girl gets the lead." I smile. "Make sure you take pictures."

"We will." Jude smiles back.

"What did I miss?" Lennon asks as he walks up to the table. He undoes the top button of his black suit and slips into the booth, opposite me; Jude in the middle.

I've talked to Lennon several times since he forced my break on me. We haven't talked about when I'll return to work, but we have dabbled in conversation about some of the accounts I was running before my break.

Olivia, Lennon's secretary, has emailed me weekly updates and reports Lennon has sent her to forward on to me. Other than that, and our family meetups, we haven't talked much. At least not about the nitty gritty truth.

"Abbey has her *Wizard of Oz* play today." Jude fills Lennon in.

"Oh, right." Lennon nods, waving to the waitress. Once again, she disappears and comes back seconds later with his drink. "Excited to hear about it. Lucy has a concert next week."

"I won't be able to make it." Jude frowns, his forehead creasing. "But Victoria said she'll make sure she's there."

A knot in my chest tightens listening to them talk kids back and forth. Jude goes on about how proud he is of his daughter Abbey, and how his son Cade took his first steps today. Lennon talks about how his kids, Lucy and Holden, got into a big fight the other day, causing them to be grounded for a week.

I think back to when I told Adeline I feel left behind, like I missed out on the passcode to get into their exclusive club. If there were any moment where I feel left out or behind, this is it.

School plays and concerts. It's a world completely out of my orbit.

I sit in silence, sipping on my drink while my brothers chat about their family lives. Every now and then, I catch a glimpse of the front door, and my body itches to leave. I think about Adeline and watching her climb into the back seat of Ray's car. I find my mind wandering, wanting to know where she is and what she's doing right now. The urge to hop in my car and find her swells and inflates in my chest.

But the balloon pops the second I hear Lennon's voice.

"So, Micah," Lennon says, swallowing a bite of his roasted asparagus and eggs. "How's the break been going?"

"Honestly, I'm surprised you've waited until now to ask me."

His eyebrows slant. "I've asked you how you're doing."

"Not really. We've talked about the work I left unfinished and Jude helping out with the shed a few weeks back, but nothing about my break."

He wipes his napkin across his mouth and takes a deep breath. "I'm asking you now, then. How has your break been? How's the house coming along?"

"Fine." I try to brush off the bitterness I feel toward my brothers. It isn't their fault my life has turned out the way it has. My decisions have been mine alone, and the consequences of my choices, too. "The house is almost finished."

"I told you we could have had the renovations done in, like, two months," Jude interjects. "You could have had it listed and sold at this point."

"I thought that's what you wanted," Lennon says, sipping on his drink. "You wanted to move on. Get your life together." His eyes dart to my drink. "Though, I see you haven't tried to stop drinking."

I purse my lips and chew on the inside of my cheek and my eyes dart to Jude, but he simply keeps his focus on his plate.

"We all know drinking was never an issue of mine." I grit my teeth and pin my eyes on my older brother. I chance a look at Jude again, hoping he doesn't take my comment as a dig at his sobriety. I'm proud of his ability to overcome his past and his struggle with alcohol, but I can't stand it when Lennon assumes my issues are just like his, even if he doesn't know the whole story or the truth.

"You're right." Lennon drapes his arms over the table. "Pills were."

There have been few times since our father died where I've seen rare glimpses of him in my brother. There are even times I've seen him in myself.

The times I've seen him in me have been when I've caught myself looking in a mirror after I've just destroyed someone's life over money. When I catch others at their most vulnerable. Weak and broke, the Hardings come in like dark knights, delivering the worst news anyone can receive. Ripping their livelihoods out from underneath them.

But then there are these moments when I see my father in Lennon. As the eldest son, I know he's fought hard to put as much distance between our father's reputation and the one he has made for himself. But then there are these moments, where he stares at me with skepticism, like a disappointment, unable to let go of my past, never believing I can truly change when the truth is, I've always been the same.

"It's different now," I lie, holding back the desire to spill the truth to my brothers. "I haven't sold the house yet because I'm thinking of keeping it."

"What made you change your mind?" Lennon tilts his head.

"Does it have to do with Adeline staying there?" Jude questions.

"Adeline?" Lennon's eyebrows dart across his forehead. "You mean Adeline Mayfield? Archer's sister?"

"Yeah." I swallow, relaxing in my seat. I don't want to give too much away. "She needed a place to stay after moving out here from LA. I don't know how long she's staying, but I'm helping her out."

"I've told you to be careful around the Mayfields." Lennon switches into lecture mode, the one where he acts like he's my parent. "Considering your past with Archer, I don't think it's a good idea to stay close to Adeline."

"She doesn't really speak to her family." I brush his concern off. I know Adeline. She isn't as transparent as everyone believes her to be.

"Her father is a powerful man in this city." Lennon leans forward, lowering his voice. "The last thing I need is him to come back and say you've influenced his daughter in any way. He knows every bit of trouble you and his son caused years ago, and despite what our family knows about you, the rest of the world doesn't. They're waiting for one hint or rumor of a hint that you've slipped back into your old habits. And if you think the publicity was hard the first time around was bad, it will be much, much worse this time. I was barely able to help the last time."

I narrow my eyes and look away from Lennon. I hate that he's defending Lachlan Mayfield as if he's some well-respected, highly-regarded saint. The man is as corrupt as any politician.

"You're always so fucking worried about what everyone will think. Why can't you just trust what I tell you?" I turn my head and pin my eyes on him. "I'm your brother."

Lennon's shoulders drop as he falls back against the booth. His hands fall into his lap, and he looks at me with sympathy. "I'm sorry. I just care 'cause you're my baby brother. And you're thirty-three now. I think I speak for me *and* Jude when we thought you would be in a different place by now. I want to know you're okay."

"I am," I assure him. I'm more than okay, in fact.

Fuck, I want to get back to Adeline.

"So, what does this mean?" he asks. "Are you not selling the house anymore?"

"I'm not sure." I scratch at the stubble on my chin. I haven't thought about selling the house. Not with Adeline there. Not with the looming threat of Soren and his men. I can't risk Adeline not having a place to go. Kicking her out would be like throwing her to the wolves.

"You don't have to come back to work anytime soon if you want more time with the house," Lennon offers as a truce. "From what I remember, the place was on the verge of being condemned. I understand if it's taking longer than expected."

I look at my brother with conflicted feelings. He's right. The house was on the verge of being destroyed, and deep inside, I know I've given it another shot at life. I've given it another chance. But I can't take all the credit.

Adeline brought life back into it before I even laid a finger on it.

I owe it all to her.

"Thanks," I tell him, knowing at some point I'll want to get back to work, but now isn't the time.

The rest of breakfast goes by quickly without another mention of me and my past drug history. Neither Lennon or Jude bring up Adeline again, and I'm thankful. The last thing I need is for them to have any hunch that I'm sleeping with her.

After saying goodbye to my brothers, I head home and pull into the driveway, unsure whether Adeline is back from meeting up with Ember. I hold back on texting her, not wanting to interrupt her again. If Adeline needs me, she'd reach out.

I park my car in my driveway beside the house and start to

make my way toward the back door but stop when I see someone peering through the back window. The gate is swung wide open, and the man is standing on his toes with his hands cupped around his face. He's dressed in a dark gray suit but doesn't seem fazed by me being here. Either he didn't hear me pull in or he doesn't care.

I step through the open gate, quickly making my way through the yard. I make my presence known, making sure to make as much noise as possible as I shuffle through the yard. I swipe the hammer I left out here yesterday from the top of one of the dressers, gripping it tightly in my hand as I carry it with me, gaining on the asshole peeking into my house.

"Excuse me," I say, lifting my chin, catching his attention. "Can I help you?"

My throat thickens. Could this be one of Soren's men?

The man's spine stiffens before he spins around.

My breath catches in my throat, and my hand loosens around the handle of the hammer. He looks the same as he did three years ago. The only difference is the silver strands of hair peppered around his ears. The top of his head is still a rich, dark brown. His eyes are a familiar hazel color with specks of sage.

"What are you doing here?" I grind my jaw and aggressively take large steps toward Lachlan Mayfield, retightening my grip on the handle.

He holds his hands up innocently. "Sorry, Micah. I didn't mean for you to–"

"Catch you snooping around my house like a fucking creep? How *dare* you show your face here!" I can't help it. This man is the root cause of why my life took the turn it did.

"No, I wasn't." He holds his shaking arm out toward the window. Fucking asshole is tweaking. "I heard my daughter was staying here. At least that's what Archer told me."

I narrow my eyes and look up at Adeline's bedroom window. "You haven't talked to her?"

He shrugs, his eyes hooding over with sadness. "My daughter and I haven't always been close. She doesn't let me in as much as Archer does."

I look at Lachlan skeptically. What does he mean by that?

I straighten my shoulders, an icy chill prickling down my spine. "She isn't here."

"Oh." He nods, running his shaking fingers over his jaw.

"Go home, Lachlan," I say, moving past him to get inside.

I'm pulled to a stop when his hand wraps tightly around my arm. "Wait," he breathes. Now I'm standing closer, I have a better look at his eyes. His pupils are wide, and the whites surrounding his hazel irises are bloodshot. "I was hoping you might have a few pills you can spare. Like the ones you've given me before. You know..."

I rip my arm from his grip, stepping back. "I don't have anything for you." I swallow, memories of the past ten years digging their claws in, once again. "You know I don't."

"Please," he begs. Part of me feels sympathy for him. The grips of addiction are white-knuckled on this man, but my sympathy is short lived.

I point my finger toward the open gate, down the driveway. I have no clue how he got here. I don't see a car other than mine in the driveway, and I didn't see one out front. Quite honestly, I don't give a fuck how he got here. I just want him gone.

"Get the fuck off my property... or I'll call the police."

"You wouldn't dare." He steps up to me, shooting me a sinister glare. "Besides, do you truly believe the police will be on your side? With your history?" My brain practically explodes, and he laughs. "You wouldn't dare turn in your best friend's dad. You're too loyal to risk losing Archer. You'll always do what's best for him, regardless of what the cost is to you."

I curl my hands into fists. My chest twists and aches. Poisonous hatred and resentment bubbles in my white-hot veins. I shove Lachlan, and he stumbles back, the withdrawal evident in his lack of balance and strength.

"Fuck *you*," I spit. "Even if I had pills to sell, I wouldn't give them to you. You haven't done a fucking thing for me."

He falls back onto the asphalt and props himself up on his elbows with a groan. I lean over him, bringing my face close to his.

His swallows, his eyes twitching. "I couldn't do anything for you."

"You were District fucking Attorney. You could have done something—anything—but you kept your mouth shut."

"I couldn't," he says, sniffing.

"You make me sick," I tell him, the claws in my mind digging in again. I lean down even closer. "Now, I'll only say this one more time: get the fuck off my property before I turn you in. The truth always has a way of revealing itself, Lachlan. Oh, and you might want to tell your son to get his shit straight before he ends up getting us all killed. Tell him to leave me out of whatever bullshit you and him have going on. I'm done hiding the truth. It's getting pretty fucking exhausting."

Lachlan rolls to his side and pulls himself to a stand. He smooths his disheveled hair and inhales a deep breath, his nostrils flaring.

Without another word, he saunters out of the yard and down my driveway, disappearing down the street. It isn't until he's out of sight do I feel the massive, weighted rope knotted in my chest finally let up.

No matter how hard or how much time has passed, I was right about one thing.

The truth always has a way of revealing itself.

One way or another.

EIGHTEEN

ADELINE

I clung to the house like one of the hundreds of vines of ivy. Resting my head back against the brick, I squeezed my eyes shut, willing myself to wake up from this nightmare.

This was all a daydream. A figment of my imagination.

A truth that holds no water.

My father in Micah's backyard.

Ten minutes ago, I'd come out back in the hopes of planting new flowers in the garden box Micah had cleaned out. The sad, pathetic dry dirt was calling for new life. Some of the furniture we'd pulled out of the shed was beyond saving, but the garden box was different. I could see the potential. I could envision what it would look like flourishing with full blooms, new life breathed into what was once viewed as a symbol of death.

But I'd stopped when I heard movement from the far end of the backyard—someone climbing over the half-broken fence. I knew it wasn't Micah, considering he'd taken his car to meet with his brothers. Ray had dropped me off after breakfast with Ember.

Then my heart plunged deep in my stomach when I spotted

the man climbing over the fence and falling to the ground. He'd barely looked up when I saw who it was.

Lachlan Mayfield.

My father.

Quickly, I'd ducked and ran to the side of the house. I knew he was on the other side of it, peering in through one of the windows.

I was about to step out and demand to know why he was here when I heard Micah's car pull into the driveway.

He'd barely asked him what he was doing here when I'd decided I couldn't, no wouldn't, stick around long enough to risk being seen, or hear what they were saying.

My breath caught in my chest when I gathered the strength to turn my head to my right. The door leading to the butler's pantry was beside me.

Panic set in. I needed to leave. I swung the door open and ran up the stairs as fast as my feet could carry me.

And now, before I give myself a chance to rethink my decision to leave, I'm breathlessly racing through the door to my bedroom. The wooden plank creaks under my step as I race across my room. I reach up to the top shelf of my closet and pull out my duffel bag. I'm on my toes, unable to fully wrap my hand around it. It slips from the shelf, and I duck my head as it falls to the floor. Picking it up, I carry it back to my bed.

Tears line my eyes as I drop it on the foot of my bed. As quickly as I can, I cross my room again and pull as many shirts as I'm able to fit in my arms out of my dresser.

Flashbacks to months ago crash into my mind with unrelenting force. The vision of me storming out of my work trailer, with only the clothes on my back and this very duffel bag, plays like a movie on repeat. A movie I don't want to rewatch.

I swallow the bile in my throat and take a breath.

When I close my eyes, a river of tears flow down my cheeks. I don't know where I'll go, but I can't stay here.

I chance another look out the window, hoping my father is truly gone.

He knows I'm here.

Maybe it was a foolish notion to believe I could have come back here without running into him or my mother. But Boston isn't exactly a small town. Even though Micah's house is in Cambridge, a neighboring suburb, technically, it's all a part of the same ecosystem. Cambridge can't exist without Boston. With hundreds and thousands of people here, I didn't think I'd see my father.

Especially not out in this backyard.

With Micah.

I shove the rest of my clothes and toiletries into my duffel bag and zip it shut. Leaving my room, I shove my hands into the pockets of my sweatshirt and jog down the stairs.

"Hey," Micah says, catching me before I make it halfway down the stairs. His eyes fall to the strap of my duffel bag before swinging back up to mine. "Where are you going?"

I open my mouth, counting the breaths I take.

I know I'm panicking, possibly overreacting, but the ghosts of my past haven't afforded me the luxury of remaining calm when it comes to my father, nor anyone else who's burned me in the past.

Sniffing, I look down at my feet.

Micah places two fingers under my chin, pulling me to look up at him. Through my watery gaze, I see his eyes soften, panic etched into his forehead.

"Why are you leaving?" he wearily asks.

I swallow thickly and breathe in a shallow, pain-stricken breath. "I heard you talking to Lachlan outside."

"You heard us?"

"Only a little. I didn't stick around long enough to find out why he was here. After Ray dropped me off, I thought I'd get started on replanting the garden box out back. I saw my father climbing over the back fence. I was going to confront him until I heard you, then I ran up here."

His eyes widen as he takes a step back, and my heart fractures. I don't know the depth of his relationship with my father.

Are they friends? Associates?

For years, I watched my father pop pills and snort cocaine, sometimes finishing a line before he barged into my room in the middle of the night to remind me of what a disappointment I was. From what I've also heard over the past few years as I've gotten older, Micah isn't unfamiliar with my father's type. He had a father like mine.

And knowing Micah went to prison for drug possession and drug addiction, it's all starting to click into place.

I told Micah I haven't judged him for his past addictions or his time served in prison, and I haven't. Everyone makes mistakes, and I know it doesn't define him. But with my father in the mix, I'm not sure it's a fact I'm willing to overlook.

Anything involving him is something I'm not willing to be a part of. A pain too great.

"I haven't seen him in years, Addy," Micah explains. His voice is smaller, as if he's afraid the truth will cause me to leave, and it just might. But the fear in Micah's expression makes me stay for now. I want to listen.

"I told him to leave," he adds.

"Why was he here?" My voice quakes. I'm afraid of his answer. Anything involving my father can't be good.

"I don't know." He blinks, but I know he's holding back, only giving me a partial truth.

"You're lying." I sniff, wiping my hand under my nose. I feel myself slipping away. "If he was here, there was a reason."

"I'm not lying." He takes a step up to the one below me.

"Was he here asking you for drugs?"

His face pales. If my father is involved, it must involve drugs, too. I swallow, scared of the answer to my next question. "Are you his dealer, Micah?"

His shoulders fall, and he swallows. I feel the blood drain from my face and pool at my feet.

A heavy breath leaves his chest. "Not anymore."

My bottom lip wobbles as I take in a shaky breath. Chills slither down my neck, making my heart race. "But you were?" My lungs squeeze, forcing the words to leave my mouth.

Micah runs his hand down the side of his face, clearly conflicted with how to answer.

"Yes," he admits, so quietly, I almost don't hear him.

A sob rattles in my chest.

"But that was a long time ago," he's quick to add. "I guess he came here thinking I still had some pills for him."

I cover my mouth with my hand. There's truth to what Micah is telling me. I see it in the way he's desperately and silently begging for this to not cause me to walk out the door. He's holding his breath, anticipation thick in the air.

I want to cry. I want to scream. My past will forever haunt me.

"I'm sorry." His eyes swim with genuine regret.

"I believe you, but I know you aren't telling me everything. The world of money and drugs has many secrets, Micah. You know that better than anyone. And I can't stay here. Not anymore."

"Addy, no," he pleads, with a softened, wounded expression.

"He might come back," I tell him, blinking away the fear, hoping it will leave, knowing it won't. "And I can't risk that. I don't want to see him."

I slide past him, but he stops me when my foot steps on

the landing. I'm only five feet from the door, and Micah is desperately pulling me back. He wraps his hand around mine, and

my back lands softly against the wall. He presses his body against mine, towering over me, lifting his arm above me. I tip my chin higher.

"Where are you going to go?" he asks.

"Ember's." I'm not confident in my answer. I know Ember can take me in maybe for a few nights, but it won't be permanent. The same fear that propelled me to leave the first time is back with the same force.

I wish there were some island I could escape to—one where no one could hurt me.

"There's nowhere safer than here with me." He brings his mouth close to mine.

"Micah..."

I want to stand on my toes and give in. I want to taste him and feel him. I want his touch to numb the pain coming back to life inside my soul. I want to stay in this bubble we've created, where Archer doesn't know I've fallen for his best friend, and where my father hasn't shown up, asking for me. Deep down, I know that if he knows I'm here, it means he'll tell my mother, and the vicious cycle of emotional abuse will wash, rinse, and repeat.

I avoid looking at Micah. If I allow myself to stare into his blue-gray eyes, I'll give in.

"Addy." My weakness for him using my nickname crumbles my defenses. I look up into his eyes. "I truly don't know what made him come here, other than him asking for the pills before I told him to leave," he whispers. "Maybe it was for you. Archer told him you were staying here. Did you not want him to know? Why are you so afraid of him?"

The pain and trauma of my childhood rears its ugly head. It

mocks and taunts me. Memories I've repressed for years have come back, consuming me like a virus.

Tears sting the back of my eyes. It's not that I assumed Archer would tell our father where I was, but I didn't realize how afraid of facing my past I was until I've been faced with this very situation where my father knows where I am.

I want to be angry with Archer for telling him, but I should have known. I should have suspected he would tell him when he doesn't know the whole truth.

"No, I didn't want him to know." I shake my head, unable to look at Micah. This is the part of my life I've tried to run from. I've tried to bury the past. I've locked it in a chest, tossed the key, and buried it under cold, hard dirt. But the sight of my father in the backyard has brought everything back up to the surface.

"Trust me, I get it. Your father isn't perfect, but Archer's never indicated he was bad enough to make you want to leave like this."

I roll my eyes. "Of course he hasn't."

"Outside..." His velvet voice lingers between us. "Outside, he told me you and him weren't close."

"We aren't," I grind out. "You don't understand."

"Then, make me understand it. Talk to me, Addy," he begs. "You're right; I only know Archer's side of the story—the one he was willing to tell me—but I don't know yours. My history with your father isn't more important than the truth. I want you to tell me *your* truth."

Tears slip from my eyes, pressure building behind them. My chest is split wide open. Micah's demand to hear the truth to prevent me from leaving is breaking me all over again.

"I can't." I close my eyes and take a resolving breath before I slink out from under Micah's body. "I'm sorry."

I feel my back pocket for my phone, but it isn't there. Fuck. I left it on my bedside table, and I need to call Ember to see if she'll pick me up.

I run back up the stairs, but Micah is quick behind me.

"Why are you running?"

"I'm not," I tell him, crossing my room. I swipe my phone from the table and spin around, but I slam into Micah's wall of a chest.

"You are." He's looking down at me. "Five minutes of seeing your father in my backyard has you running. There's a reason."

"Micah, please don't do this." I gulp, staring at his chest. Water fills my vision, emotion heavy in my chest. "I think it's best if I go." I step back, trying to walk around him.

"I can't let you go." He growls, closing in on me. "I won't." He cups his hands around my face again, forcing me to stop, and this time, I see his determination to make me stay.

All I want is this, with him. But how can I when he's right?

One glimpse of my father, and old habits return. The instinct to flee and move on is burning through my veins. I'm acting on impulse. But despite the need inside me, seeing Micah begging me to stay makes me hesitate.

"Let me go." I try my best to stay strong, to say it with conviction.

"If you think I'm just going to let you walk out of here without putting up a fight, you're sorely mistaken, Addy." He narrows his eyes but the softness in them remains.

His touch anchors me, keeping me from floating away. Escaping and running is easy. Facing the demons of your past takes bravery.

"Why are you here?" he asks calmly, running his thumbs under my eyes, catching my tears. "What are you running *from*?"

I look over his shoulder, catching my reflection in the mirror hanging on the wall. I inhale a sharp breath and dart my eyes away.

"See?" he continues. "That right there. You won't even look in the mirror. Every time you've been confronted with one, I've caught you looking away."

Him admitting to catching me and my aversion to looking at my own reflection hits me in a way I'm not expecting. It's as if I've been knocked down with a feather. My deepest, darkest secrets exposed. The truth is, I haven't been able to look at myself in the mirror because my face is a reminder of everything I've lost. It's a symbol of my hopes and dreams, shattered by the people who were supposed to love me.

"You were right." I swallow, not able to tell Micah the truth. "We don't know each other well. You're my older brother's best friend, and I'm just his silly little sister."

"I was... wrong."

"You weren't." I tighten my hands into fists. "You said you weren't good for me, but maybe I'm not good for you. You're Archer's best friend, and I can't jeopardize your relationship."

"I don't think you understand what you're doing to me, Addy." His velvety voice hits my ear. "I told you about Calista and my past with her. I thought I wanted a future with her, until the day I decided I didn't. She wasn't my future, nor any other woman for that matter. Because this, with you, is different. You make me feel things I've never felt with anyone else. You push my buttons and get under my skin. When you aren't near, I wonder all the fucking time what you're doing, who you're with. If you aren't with me, I immediately start figuring out the quickest way to get to you. I want you. I want you so fucking badly sometimes, it hurts, but we can't *be* if you don't tell me why you're running."

Micah's confession breaks the dam.

"All my life, I've struggled, blaming Archer for what he

doesn't know." I swallow the tears, though they keep flowing. "But I've also blamed him for ignoring the signs, for never taking the initiative to listen."

"What do you mean? Signs of what?" Micah asks, tracing his finger across my jaw line. He hasn't let up, clearly unsure whether I'm still on the verge of fleeing.

"There are twelve years between Archer and me," I start. "My mother used to tell everyone the story of how I was their *surprise* baby... but my father liked to call me the mistake. He had a vasectomy a couple weeks after Archer was born. One child was enough, and as soon as my father found out Archer was a boy, he solidified his decision to only ever wanting one child. My mother was a famous model, and I know, for her, she was worried going through another pregnancy would force her to leave her career behind. Back then, pregnancy was essentially a modeling career death sentence. And after she'd had Archer, she practically lived in the gym and starved herself just to be able to go back to work."

I swallow, the tears only stopping momentarily, but my chin quivers as the next words spill from my mouth.

"She was able to work for twelve years after having Archer, but then she got pregnant with me. And while she was older and her career was dwindling in the eyes of society, she was still forced to leave on their terms, not hers. The older I got, the more my dad made me aware of the resentment he held for me. For her losing her career. For me holding him back to raise a child all over again. When Archer left for college, everything got worse. I found myself counting down the days until I got out, and the second I was old enough, I did."

"It isn't your fault," Micah says, cupping my face. I lean into his hand, allowing his warmth to wrap around me, but the feeling is only temporary, the pain of never being wanted ripping through me.

"Don't you see, though?" I look up at Micah with tear-filled eyes. "It's all my fault. I'm the cause of everyone's pain. My father's for having to raise me when he clearly didn't want me. My mother's for being forced to quit her career before she was ready."

"Addy, stop." Inhaling a sharp breath between his teeth, he wraps *both* of his hands around my face now, forcing me to look into his eyes. "You are not the cause of everyone's pain."

"I am." I squeeze my eyes shut. A sob rattles my chest, forcing me to shake.

"Addy," Micah soothes, willing me to open my eyes. "There is no justification for abuse. Ever. You are not the reason he treated you that way."

Micah loosens his hands from around my face and wraps his arms around me.

He's a blanket of safety. A warm light in the darkness.

I wish I could hide here in the comfort of his arms, but being here with him isn't reality.

"As I got older, I wanted to tell Archer about the way I was treated at home, but I didn't think he'd understand. Then when I was old enough and brave enough to tell him, he didn't want to hear it. He's been too consumed with his own life to fully care about mine."

"Archer loves you."

"I know he does." I nod. "I know if he knew, he would have done something. He's only wanted what's best for me. And I know it isn't right, but there's shame in me not telling him the truth. I should have said something, but back then, I knew the only person I could count on was myself. Then I made it to Los Angeles, and I found myself in a relationship headed down the same path. One of fear and manipulation. Control." I pull my face away from Micah's chest. His shirt peels away from my skin, wet from my tears. "I left him before it got worse. I didn't want to end up like my mother."

"Oh, Addy," he says, soothing me. He tenses his jaw, clearly the idea of a man hurting me angering him, but he keeps his hatred close to his chest. He buries it, comforting me instead.

I don't dive further into my history with Maddox. I realize the pain I feel isn't from leaving him. It's the pain from allowing myself to walk into a relationship of abuse again so easily. It's pain and disappointment in myself.

"Looking in the mirror only reminds me of what I left behind. I invited another man into my life. He used me and punished me by hitting me where it would hurt most. I can't look at myself in the mirror because I know the eyes I see looking back at me aren't the same as the hopeful ones I saw before him. My face was my career, my passion, and my livelihood. And now, what do I have?"

Micah pushes my hair away from my face. "I know what it's like to look in the mirror and hate what you see." He swallows as his eyes search my face. "But we can't move on when we're afraid of looking at the past and acknowledging the kind of person it's made us become."

"I'm terrified," I whisper, closing my eyes.

Tears slip through my lashes and stain my cheeks while I listen to his voice.

"Stay," he says above the shell of my ear, sending a shiver down the back of my neck. The sensation slinks down the length of my back and to my front, splitting off. A piece of it shoots straight for my heart, the other settling in my lower belly. The warmth of him surrounds me, the echoes of my past vibrating in the air between us.

His hand finds my stomach, trailing around my waist. He slips under the hem of my shirt, touching my bare skin, leaving an invisible trail that gives me strength I didn't know I needed.

"If there's anything I've learned since you barged your way into my life, it's that we aren't victims of our past, Adeline." He wraps his hand around the back of my neck and gently tightens his grip, pulling me to look up. "We're fighters and survivors."

"I don't feel like I am."

"It took courage to walk away. Don't ever doubt or question your decision in doing what was best for you."

"I don't know if I know what's best for me anymore." I shake my head, my voice still uneasy. I feel like I'm standing on the edge of a cliff, my toe reaching the edge. I can't go back, and I can't go forward.

"You don't have to figure it out right now. But I can't let you go. You make me feel something no one else has, Addy. I may not know what this is between us, and I'm scared as fuck, considering you're my best friend's sister, but I'm tired of pretending we're the same people we used to be. I'm tired of pretending that all the other bullshit matters." When I don't answer him, his eyebrows knit as his eyes soften. "Just stay. Will you stay?"

I look into Micah's eyes and try to read his thoughts. I search for them in the storm clouds that make up his blue-gray irises. Something tells me he needs me just as much as I need him. He's filled a void in me that otherwise would still exist. Walking away is scary, but so is staying.

Either way, I'm left confronting parts of my life I'm not exactly ready to face.

I inhale an unsteady, shaky breath. "I'll stay."

NINETEEN

Micah

I sit on the edge of my bed and stare at my reflection in the mirror.

Adeline is still asleep, the sound of her breaths hushed and barely audible. Her gorgeous face is pressed against the pillow and her eyes are closed.

As quietly as possible, I slip on my shoes, quickly tie them and tiptoe out of the bedroom. I hate the thought of leaving her alone in the house, so I messaged Ray and asked if he didn't mind staying parked out front, just in case he saw anything or anyone suspicious lurking around. I don't need Lachlan coming back, and the best I can do is hope that my threat will have kept him from wanting to return.

Undoing the button of my suit, I climb into the driver's seat of my car and back out of the driveway, waving to Ray before putting the car into drive and pulling out of the neighborhood. It takes twenty minutes longer than usual before I make it to Harding Holdings, and when I stroll into my brother's office, he's already tapping his finger on his desk—a clear indication I've fucked up his schedule.

"Traffic," I tell him, falling back in the chair opposite his desk.

"There's always traffic, Micah." He taps his finger again. "This shouldn't be a surprise to you."

"It's not." I nod once. "I was just stating a fact."

"Right." He purses his lips, annoyed. "I don't have time for this."

"You called me down here," I point out. "What's going on?"

He taps his fingers a few more times before looking out the window. "I was thinking about our conversation at breakfast two weeks ago."

I sink deeper into my chair and lay my hands in my lap. I can't explain it, but I'm nervous. My oldest brother has always been intimidating. More so to others than to me but intimidating, none-theless. There are moments like now, where I see the care and concern in his eyes, but he hides them behind his serious exterior.

"Which part?" I ask.

"All of it." He sighs. "You haven't talked about your time in prison very much, and I never asked. Part of me feels respon-sible for not having been there for you. Even though the judge didn't offer any leniency, I still feel like there was more I could do."

"Don't blame yourself." I clear my throat. "You shouldn't, and there's no reason for it."

A tiny hint of a smile plays on his lips. "Easier said than done."

"Yeah, you're right." I chuckle.

He rests his elbow on the arm of his chair and scratches at his chin. "I've given it a lot of thought these past couple of years since you were released, and despite knowing why you went, I also know it isn't who you are. I don't need to know all the details. But I know you, little brother. You're a good person."

His words hit me like a sledgehammer. His serious expression and the silence in his office overwhelms me. It swells and suffocates, and I choke on the truth.

I open my mouth, wanting to tell him. I want to tell him his intuition is right. But I don't. I force it back down, swallowing it and fighting the urge to vomit it back up.

"Thank you." It's all I manage to say.

"With that said..." He sighs. "I want you to come back to work."

"What?" My eyebrows rise, and I sit up in my chair. "Really?"

"Yeah." He nods. "Considering what I just said and what I know to be true, I don't think you need a break anymore. Unless, of course, you don't *want* to come back to work."

"No," I blurt out. "I do. I'm just caught off guard. I don't know what I was expecting, but I guess I wasn't expecting you to give me a straight offer to come back."

"I did offer last time. At breakfast. I just left it open ended."

I laugh. "You're right."

"I left it open last time for you to return, but an opportunity came up with a client that I think you would be best suited to handle." He slides a blue folder across the desk.

I pick it up and open it, reading the first page before flipping through the other papers.

"PharmTec is a startup pharmaceutical company based in Connecticut. Right now, they're manufacturing plant needs expansion, and I've decided to throw my name in the hat of those willing to take on investing in their goal."

"Pharmaceutical?" I ask, giving him a confused expression. "We aren't exactly experts in the medicinal field, Len."

"We aren't," he agrees, nodding toward the paper. "But they're main mission is to find a cure for cancer."

I hold my breath and freeze. Sadness fills my brother's usually hard eyes.

Finding a cure for cancer has incredible meaning to Lennon. After losing both his mom and sister-in-law to the disease, I understand why this means a lot to him.

"I guess you could say this endeavor is more personal than it is business," he adds.

I clear my throat. "Okay." I nod, closing my mouth and swallowing. I scan the paper again, reading over every single itemized objective and mission statements, along with their sales data from previous years, then I look back up at Lennon. "What do you need me to do?"

"I'd like you to go with me to check out the plant in New Haven." He stands from his chair and looks out the window, his black suit a stark contrast to the city outside. He half-turns. "I've scheduled a meeting and tour with the CEO and founder. He's going to explain what their next project is, and we'll also get to see the laboratories."

"I don't know what to say." I blink.

He shrugs. "You don't have to say anything. I would just like my brother on this project with me."

"Of course." I shake off the weight of what this means. For years, my brother has worn a mask—one of strength, but also one of secrecy. Vulnerability isn't exactly one of the words I would use to describe him, but I see it now.

A warmth spreads across my chest. My brother wouldn't want me to be a part of this if he didn't see value in me. If he didn't believe I was in a better place.

"There's a reason I want you on this job with me," he adds.

I open my mouth to ask him what reason, but he answers me before I have the chance.

"I was harsh in forcing you to take a break months ago, but I'm glad I did." He stuffs his hands into his pockets and faces me fully. "Whether it's you renovating the house, or if it has to do with Adeline Mayfield staying with you, you've changed. It's good to see."

"Thanks," I croak around the lump in my throat. For once, I feel seen. Lennon doesn't even know the whole truth about why I went to prison, but he's given me the benefit of the doubt. His confidence in me, regardless, makes life not feel so hopeless.

"Those copies are for you to keep." He nods toward the folder in my hand. "Look them over and make sure you get a good grasp on the numbers and products. We aren't scheduled to head out there for a few weeks."

"Sounds good." I stand from my chair with more pride and hope than when I walked in here. My life finally feels like it's on track, heading in the right direction. I button the jacket to my suit and tuck the folder under my arm. Excitement bubbles in my chest at the thought of telling Adeline about this trip and me going back to work.

I'm thankful the visit to Connecticut isn't for another few weeks, though. That gives me more time to beef up security at the house for Adeline when I'm not there. I can't take the chance of Lachlan or Soren showing up.

I'm almost out of my brother's office when he stops me. I stop and turn, looking over my shoulder.

"You seem happier, Micah." He smiles. "It's good to see you smile for once."

"You know..." I laugh. "I said the same about you at one point in time."

"What do you mean?" His smile falls, immediately disappearing. His eyebrows pull together. "I smile. I've always smiled."

"Sure, Lennon." I slap my hand on the doorframe. "I'll see you in New Haven."

TWENTY

ADELINE

I hold my breath and tug on the front door, only briefly getting a glance of my reflection in the sparkling clean glass door, but in a flash, it's gone.

The buzzing sound of the studio immediately floods my ears, replacing the busy sounds of the city traffic outside. I stop just inside the door and remove my sunglasses. It takes a moment for my eyes to adjust as I stuff the glasses inside my purse and search for my best friend.

"Addy!" Ember's high pitch squeal calls out from across the room. With her arms tucked against her, wearing the largest grin, she shuffles over to me. The squeal never leaves her, even as she wraps her arms around me.

"Ember!" I laugh. "You act like I haven't seen you in weeks. I just saw you yesterday."

Her arms dig into my back, holding me close. Resting her chin on my shoulder, she doesn't let up. "Doesn't matter. I'm glad you showed up."

"I told you I would."

She pulls away, keeping me at arm's length before she tucks my hair behind my ear, and I know exactly what she's thinking.

She's working to convince me to do a photo shoot today. Unease rests at the pit of my stomach, remembering why I came here today: to support my best friend and watch her in her element.

"I know you did." Her smile fades slightly, her eyes still lit with fire. "But I know it probably wasn't an easy decision."

She's right. It wasn't.

"It's going to be a blast." She bounces on her toes and continues to tuck my hair behind my ear before she traces my jawline. "Fuck. Do you remember me telling you that you had the cheekbones of a model?"

I roll my eyes and groan. "Yes."

"Well, I would just like to point out how smart I was back then." She shakes her head in admiration. "Because I was fucking right, and your face hadn't even fully matured all those years ago."

"Stop." I hitch the strap of my bag higher on my shoulder.

"I'm just saying." She shrugs innocently.

I dart my eyes over her shoulder toward the staging area. "So, what's going on today?"

"Oh..." She flips her strawberry blonde hair when she turns back to face me. "Small photoshoot for a local makeup company centered here in Boston. They hired me to do the makeup for their ads that they're going to use in their first storefront."

"Wow." I smile.

A warmth spreads and fills my chest. I won't lie, seeing the white backdrop surrounded by lights and photographers pulls me back into the life I left behind in LA. It's a mixture of emotions, with a haunting feeling dominating a small glimpse of the dream I once had.

Various types of makeup and hairstyling tools are littered across the stations, all organized and glinting under the bright lights of Ember's studio.

"This is your studio?" I ask Ember in awe.

"Yep." She plants her hands on her hips and looks around. She keeps the makeup brush she carried over with her wrapped up in her long fingers. "I don't always have photoshoots here, but for the smaller companies that hire me, I offer it to them. It's great, isn't it?" She scrunches her nose, giggling with pride.

"It's wonderful." I grin.

"Come on." She grabs my hand, pulling me further inside. "I'll show you around and introduce you."

After Ember shows me around her small studio and introduces me to the crew and makeup company's team, I sit in one of the chairs set up for the models. Ember walks to each of the model's chairs, inspecting her assistants' work.

"Oh, my God." The blonde model sitting in the chair beside me presses her hand to her cheek, with her jaw dropped. Ember's assistant is working on her contouring, forcing the model to talk to me through her reflection in the mirror. I avoid letting myself look into the mirror in front of me, instead focusing on the blonde model through hers. She grips onto the wooden arms of her seat with her eyes widened. "You're Adeline Mayfield."

I feel the heat rush to my cheeks. "Hi," I say, giving her a small smile.

"I followed yours and your mom's careers all my life." She beams, her voice reaching an excited pitch. "You're the model who made me want to be a model."

"That's very sweet of you. Thank you. What's your name?"

"Merit." She smiles. "This is only my second photoshoot, but I'm hoping it will build up my portfolio to pitch to agencies."

"Everyone starts out somewhere."

"Right." She sits back in her chair and closes her eyes. The makeup artist working on her sweeps a brush across her face, blending in her contour. "Are you taking pictures for the campaign also?"

I open my mouth to object, when Ember sidles up beside me.

"Yeah, Addy," she teases, digging her elbow into my shoulder. "Are you in the campaign, too?"

"I wasn't planning on it." I wince, nervously looking up at Ember. When she doesn't let up on her grin, I narrow my eyes, kicking myself for not being more prepared to resist her persistence.

"Not to put any pressure on you," Merit says, "but it would be amazing if I could say I did a photoshoot with *the* Adeline Mayfield."

Her admiration warms my heart, but I don't feel like I deserve it. As with any creative field, I've battled with imposter syndrome. I'm no stranger to adoration of fans. I watched my mother get it all through my childhood. But me... I don't feel like I deserve it.

I give Merit a smile through the reflection in her mirror.

"Maybe next time," Ember answers for me.

I sigh with relief, thankful Ember didn't press me in front of Merit.

Ember stays standing beside me while her assistant finishes up Merit's base makeup, taking over to do her eyes and lips. I sit and watch, occasionally pulling out my phone to check for text messages from Micah.

I have one sitting on my screen, unread. I click on it and immediately blush.

> Sitting here in my old office, imagining you bent over my desk, wearing nothing but my blue tie resting between those supple breasts. I can't decide which part of you I'd want to fuck first. Your tits or that delicious pussy of yours.

"Holy shit, I'm going to need to splash some cold ass fucking holy water on my face after reading that text."

I snap my head up and see Ember standing over me.

Merit isn't in her seat any longer. She's moved over to the hair station on the other side of the studio. It's just Ember and me now.

Still, fiery hot heat engulfs the length of my body. Ember's eyes are bugging out of her head and her jaw has dropped lower than I've ever seen on her before.

I shut the screen to my phone and drop it into my lap. "What are you doing?" I ask.

"I didn't mean to spy," she says, unable to wipe the grin off her face. "But I had to know what text it was that got you smiling like that." She waves her brush in the air like a wand. "I can't remember the last time I saw you this happy."

I rest my elbow on the arm and cover my face with my hand, too embarrassed to look at my best friend. I hear her take a seat next to me—the one Merit was sitting in. The wood creaks under her weight. She taps my knee, and I slowly remove my hand from my face.

"Was that Micah?" she asks, clearly stunned.

I tuck my bottom lip under my teeth and scrunch my nose. "Yes."

"Oh, my God." She puffs out her chest and rocks back in her seat as if the wind has been knocked out of her. It reminds me of our summers spent at the pool, when she'd come running over to me, giggling with excitement and gushing that Teddy, her secret crush, had glanced in her direction.

"I can't believe this," she whispers as she sucks in a breath, then leans forward. "Are you sleeping with Micah?"

I snap my mouth shut and simply give her a look.

She gasps, and I fight the urge to laugh. She's right, though. I am happy.

"When?" she blurts out. "How?"

I shrug, thinking back to when Micah gave in the night of Ember's birthday, but knowing it didn't start then. It's been a slow build, and if I think about it, I don't know exactly when it began. My feelings for Micah have always been locked inside a vault, but at some point, Micah cracked the safe.

"I don't know." I blow out a heavy breath. "It just kind of happened."

"Just kind of happened?" Ember presses both her hands to her cheeks before she holds her hand out, pointing to my phone. "Sleeping with Micah Harding doesn't *just happen.*"

"It's a long story." I look around at the dozens of people buzzing in Ember's studio. I don't mind having this conversation with my best friend. In fact, now that I'm with her, I think I could use some girl talk. But not here. Part of me wants to keep what's going on between Micah and me between us.

"We don't have to talk about it right now." Ember senses my hesitancy. "But we definitely should meet for drinks. I have a feeling I'm going to need one. Especially if he's been sending you texts like that." Her eyes widen. "I can only imagine how he is in bed."

"Ember!" I scold, embarrassment still consuming me.

"I'm only teasing." She winks and then her smile fades, her face turning serious. "Does Archer know?"

"No." I shake my head. "We haven't been talking very much lately. And anyway, I'm a little upset at him." I swallow thickly. "He told our dad I was back."

"What the fuck?" Ember huffs. "You've talked to him?"

"Micah caught him scaling the fence in the backyard. I was working in the garden when he showed up, and I went in the house before I could hear what they were talking about. But Micah told me he'd said Archer had been the one who told him. I think he was there to see me. And buy pills from Micah."

"He doesn't still sell, does he?" Ember asks, worry etched into her brow.

"No." I shake my head, confident in my answer. I have no reason to believe Micah would take that risk. Not after he shared his experience with me. I see how happy he is now and know he wouldn't want to risk losing it all for the sake of selling drugs again.

"Good." Ember gives a small smile. "Hopefully, you don't run into your father again."

"I hope not." I feel tears sting the back of my eyes. "I almost thought about leaving, but... I don't know." I shrug, looking around before landing back on Ember's kind eyes. "There's something about where I am that makes me feel safe."

Ember gives me a closed-mouth smile.

"Ember." One of the photographers steps up to us and leans in. "Sorry to interrupt, but we're ready to start."

"Perfect." Ember bounces out of her seat and slips between our chairs but stops before she joins the rest of the crew. "Are you sure you don't want me to style you? We could do a quick, small shoot."

I look over Ember's shoulder, watching Merit sit down on the single barstool set in front of the white backdrop. She's unmoving in her seat, patiently waiting for Ember to join her and make a last few finishing touches to her makeup. My palms sweat, and I inhale a shaky breath, wrapping my hand around my phone still in my lap.

"Not today." I tilt my head, focusing back on my best friend. "I think Merit deserves this day all to herself."

Ember glances over her shoulder. When she turns back, she's wearing a smile. She softly nods. "If you change your mind..." She wags her brush back and forth before backing away.

I respond to Micah's text before following my best friend and joining her.

Watching Merit's photoshoot is more enjoyable than I expect it to be, and by the time she's finished, my chest feels a little lighter. I realize my love for this world isn't completely gone or diminished.

The joy on Merit's face gives me a boost—one that reminds me why I fell in love with this profession. Somewhere inside me is still the little girl who would sneak into my mother's vanity and steal her lipstick.

Once the photoshoot finishes, I chat with Merit before saying goodbye to Ember and her team.

While hitching my purse over my shoulder and heading toward the front door, I'm texting Ray a message to let him know I'm done and plan to meet him out front when I slam into a wall. Well, it isn't so much a wall as it is a person.

"Oh, I'm so sorry," I yelp, grabbing onto the woman's arm, steadying both of us.

Three gold bangles jingle on her wrist, and a distinctive sapphire diamond ring is wrapped around her index finger.

One I recognize.

It pulls at my memory, and it takes everything I have to gather the strength to look her in the face. Slowly, my eyes move up the length of her arm, then up her neck before they land on her all-too gorgeous smile.

"Mom." I swallow.

She tilts her head to the side and relaxes her shoulders. Lifting her hand, she runs the back of her index finger down the side of my face. "My Addy girl."

I cringe, jerking away and giving her a scowl. "What are you doing here?"

"Well." She licks her lips and flips her long, wavy brown hair with her hand, flashing her signature smile. The one she gives when she's trying to come across as confident. Inside I know she's uncertain about seeing me. "I heard Ember had a studio, and I wanted to come by and see it. Actually, I was going to ask her about you."

She pulls me in for a hug. Her long, thin arms wrap around me, tugging me without waiting for an invitation, my arms pinned at my side. She's warm and familiar. I look over her shoulder, searching for Ember, but I don't see her. She must still be hiding in the back.

"I was just leaving," I mumble.

She releases me. Her fingertips play with the ends of my hair before she finally let's go. "I've been worried about you."

"Have you?" I ask, tilting my head with narrowed eyes.

"Yes." She blinks. A small humorless laugh escapes her. "Of course, I have. You're my daughter, Addy. Your father and I will always worry about you."

"You know, I haven't been home in three years, but I already know at least one thing hasn't changed." I bite back the tears threatening to spill at the sight of my mother standing in front of me. "You're still lying for him."

"I'm not sure what you mean, Addy."

I close my eyes. "Stop calling me Addy."

"Fine." She sighs the moment I open my eyes. "Adeline."

I try to stand my ground and not allow my mother to see my emotions—it's never worked for me in the past—but I can't help it. Seeing my mother brings back every memory. All the times she would tuck me in at night. All the times I felt her fingers in my hair as she braided it before dance class. All the times she sat across from me at the dinner table in silence while my father yelled at me, telling me how pathetic I was. The times I'd come home from school wearing makeup, only for him to slap me across the face before telling me to wash it off because I looked like a whore. Seeing my mother standing at the end of the hallway. Silent.

While I've felt my mother's warm touch and loving embrace, it's only ever been empty displays of affection.

"The entire time," I manage to say, swallowing back the emotion threatening to spill over. "The entire time, you never spoke up. You never said a word."

"I've told you before." Her voice is soft and calm. "He was never like that with me. Your father is a good man."

"Just stop." I raise my voice. "Don't you see how fucked up that sounds?"

Her eyes widen and she takes a step back, clearly wounded by my words and my sudden change in tone. But I'm tired of pretending with my mother, dancing around the shards of glass laying at our feet, preventing us from growing closer to understanding one another.

"Your father loves you," she reassures me.

I want to scream and yell. I want to kick my feet and pull my fucking hair out.

"You say it so casually as if it makes everything okay. As if I'm supposed to accept that his love will override everything he ever did. And if he does love me as you say, well, he had a great way of showing it." I grind my teeth together, almost certain they're going to crack. "And so did you."

"I took care of you, Addy-" She clears her throat, wiping her hair away from her face. "*Adeline.*" Her bracelets clank against one another. "I did everything I could to give you the best life possible."

"And you also stood by and did absolutely nothing!" I cry. I can't help it. The feelings I have for my mother are complex and difficult to reconcile. The anger and hatred I have for my father is clear. Every breath I drew was one he resented. With him, he's easy to hate.

But it's difficult to love someone who took care of you, loved you, and nurtured you from birth. The one where when you look into their eyes, you see your own. But they also stood by and basked in their complicity, all while you were left wondering why they never had the courage to stand up for you.

No. Those feelings are much more difficult to reconcile.

A tear spills from my eye, and I'm quick to wipe it away.

My mother's gaze softens again—her empty way of consoling me.

"There's nothing I could have done." She nervously sweeps her tongue across her red-painted lips. Her chin trembles, and for once I see her show emotion. Like her heart isn't completely surrounded by armor made of steel. "I did the best I could with what I had. With both you and Archer."

Her mention of Archer sparks something inside me. Like the far off look in her eyes tells me there's deeper meaning behind her statement.

I pity her, and the longer I stand here in front of her, the more I feel sad for her. The sadness clings to the warmth I feel from her. Staining it and dying it with frigid, black darkness.

She reaches out, and with her shaking hand, grabs onto mine. "I'm proud of you, Adeline. You've turned out better than I could have ever hoped for."

"How so? I haven't talked to you in months, Mom."

"Your modeling." A tiny smile tugs on her lips. "I've seen your comp card. So beautiful."

My eyebrows pull together. "You saw my comp card?"

"Well, yes." She blinks. "Of course, I have."

"How did you see my comp card?" My comp card contains all my info and the best images I've taken throughout my modeling career, along with my stats. The only ones who see them are me, my manager, and any modeling agency or firm when I send it to them in hopes of hiring me.

I never sent it to her.

When it finally clicks who, the blood drains from my head down to my feet.

"Maddox sent it to me months ago," my mother finally explains, casually and nonchalant, without consequence.

"Maddox?"

"Of course." Her dark brown hair shines in the light pouring through the front of Ember's studio. Her sunglasses rest on top of her head, pulling back her long waves. "Ever since you and Maddox began dating, I've gotten to know him very well. He calls me several times a week. He told me what happened between you two."

I want to vomit.

Bile fills my throat, and I bite my tongue, holding back my gag. I feel sick.

"What did he say happened?"

"That you had an argument over some little misunderstanding." She flicks her hand. "He said he mistook your photographer for someone else, and when he confronted you, it sparked a little spat between you both."

"That's what he told you?"

"Yes. You really shouldn't make such big fusses about these things. Maddox admitted it was all a misunderstanding and said you overreacted, and I agree." She nods, pressing her mouth into a thin line. "Coming out here and everything. You can't run from your problems, Adeline."

Tears cloud my vision. "You have no clue what you're talking about." I inhale an unsteady breath, forcing myself to regain my bearings. "I'm not going back."

"Oh, sweetie." She pouts, frowning and looking at me with sympathy. "Your father told me you were staying with Micah Harding. Considering who he is, I'm guessing you're well taken care of living with him. But this won't be forever. I told Maddox maybe to give you some time, and that staying with Micah wouldn't be permanent."

A chill trickles down the length of my spine.

If Maddox knows I'm staying with Micah, he isn't as dismissive about it as my mother is making him out to be.

I gasp for air, forcing the oxygen to fill my lungs as the room spins. "You told him I was staying with Micah?"

She shrugs. "I didn't think it was a big deal. I figured he already knew, since you told him you were getting away to visit family and take a few months off work to regroup. You've found a good one with Maddox. Don't let him get away, sweetie."

I curl my hands into fists and force the tears to stop. I close my eyes and inhale another deep breath, refusing to let my thoughts run away with me. I refuse to let my mother undo the past few months.

It's as if her mere presence and the sound of her voice has pulled me back to three years ago. My parents let me go without resistance. They didn't ask if I needed support or a hand. They simply let me go. My father held the door open, and my mother gave me a hollow hug disguised behind her soft, soothing words telling me how proud she was of the woman I had become.

I used to think my mother wanted me to follow in her footsteps, to take on the dream she lost when she brought me into this world. But when she loosened her arms around me, I saw the altered sense of reality she lived in. The one where she didn't see me for who I was. She only saw herself.

I wipe the wet tears from my eyes and open them to see her still in front of me. Over her shoulder, I see Ray pull up along the curb.

"I love you, Mom," I tell her, swallowing down all the words I wish I could say knowing she wouldn't hear any of them. This is the way our relationship has to be. My heart breaks, wishing we could be different. I wish my mother was able to push her love for my father aside to see the scars they've both left on my heart, but I know it won't happen. Love can be unconditional, but sometimes love can also be foolish.

"I love you, too, Adeline." She grins, the smile reaching her eyes briefly before disappearing.

"You deserve better," I tell her, wrapping my hand around hers. "I hope you know that." I look into her eyes, ones that look like mine, and I see her fractured, beautiful spirit, and find it easy to envision an alternate world where we can be each other's best friend.

I give her hand a gentle squeeze, then I walk out the door without looking back.

TWENTY-ONE

ADELINE

It's nearing the end of summer and I'm adamant about finishing the garden box. I don't believe Micah ever envisioned what to do with it, but it seems to be a recurring theme around this house. He never had an intended purpose or plan in mind on the renovation, only deciding on its fate until someone confronted him with it, or surrendering when I barged in to tackle it.

I feel Micah's eyes burning a hole at my back as I bend down into the box, digging my fingers into the soil. I'm covered in dirt up to my elbows, but I haven't let it stop me. The cold soil is therapeutic in a way. My nails are lined with black dirt, and my hair is piled into a sweaty mess on the top of my head, but digging through the dirt touches a dormant piece of my soul. One that is a far cry from the life I've lived before coming here. Far from the limelight and glamorous lifestyle of the modeling world.

The day I had the run in with my mother at Ember's studio, I spilled the entire story to Micah as if I were recounting a summary of a book I'd read. I felt disconnected from my mother, realizing I'd come to terms with the fact I will never meet her with mutual understanding. At least not for all the ways she's defended my father, even at her children's peril. Micah held me while I cried. He didn't speak much, allowing me to spill my conflicted feelings about seeing her again. I was thankful he held me, not feeling the need to offer his thoughts, only allowing me to feel every emotion.

When I was done telling Micah about my conversation with my mother, I told him about my mother's relationship with my ex. I kept my fears about Dad coming after me to myself, but I did tell Micah about my mother's defense of Maddox.

The thought of seeing him again turns my stomach sour, but I've been in constant contact with Ruby, and she's assured me that he was seen a few days ago at a party in The Valley, with his arm wrapped around a model visiting from Paris.

I can't say I'm certain, but I feel the threat of Maddox showing up at Micah's doorstep is slim. Perhaps he's moved on like I have. Perhaps he's let go of the idea of him and me. Perhaps I never meant enough for him to chase after me.

Good.

I've pushed away the tiny bit of fear about Maddox coming for me, not wanting to give it any credence. I don't want to live in fear or paranoia anymore. I refuse. Not when I'm finally happy and at peace.

My life in this bubble with Micah isn't worth losing simply because I'm living in constant anxiety.

Instead, I've turned my focus on what brings me joy.

Seeing my mother brought up old wounds—ones I've since been able to heal since running into her.

I'm determined to plant as many flowers in the garden box as possible. Over the past few weeks, I've been researching different types of soils, and which ones are best for certain plants. I even went as far as creating a vision board and drawing up a sketch while playing my favorite crime shows in the background.

Although Micah and I have crossed a bridge in understanding one another when I tried to leave several weeks ago, we're still existing in this bubble of our own creation.

I left my career behind in Los Angeles and with that comes a sense of insecurity. I've mostly been avoiding my bank account, only spending money when absolutely necessary, but I know this can't last forever. I can't hide from my responsibilities. I'm not certain if modeling is my future anymore, and that realization is terrifying. Modeling is all I've ever known. All I've ever wanted. A life without modeling is like standing in a pitch-black room, feeling for the light switch, hoping to find what brings light to my life.

While gardening may not be a passion that leads to a lucrative career, for now, it brings me joy. But living in this bubble with Micah is like holding a needle above a balloon, waiting for the moment it will burst.

How long will this fairy tale last?

Telling Micah the truth about the life I lived at home with my parents has also stirred up feelings of my big brother. A deep longing filled with regret tugs at my stomach. A million different scenarios played in my mind, wondering and imagining if even one single moment had changed, how different would our relationship be? Would we be closer? Would we talk more?

In recent weeks, Archer's messaged me and shared pictures of his travels across Europe. Envy tugs on the same string of regret. Envy for a life he's living. The freedom from a trauma only I experienced, simply because I was born twelve years later.

Archer's messages are filled with false promises of meeting

up with me, spending time with me to make up for the time he didn't show up for coffee before flying back home. I haven't held my breath, knowing my brother isn't the most reliable.

Micah stands against the house now, watching me tend the garden. I stuff my hand into the bag and grab a fistful of dirt, then sprinkle it over the last remaining corner before bending over and spreading it out. I sweep my hand across the dirt, closing my eyes as the scent fills my nose. I listen to the sound of the birds in the trees. The warm, sticky, sea salt breeze dances across the branches, reminding me of the day I showed up on Micah's doorstep.

I bend down again and hear Micah make a sound behind me. Smiling to myself, I picture his face. I know exactly what he's thinking. His stare burns a hole in my back, and my thighs hum in response.

Still grinning, I stand and inhale a deep breath while wiping my hands along the front of my bare legs. Streaks of wet soil are painted across my thighs, but I don't care. The sun beats against my skin as more dots of sweat stream down my face to my shoulders, a drop slipping in the space between my breasts.

"There." I huff, planting my hands firmly on my hips. I point to the garden box and glance over my shoulder. "I've taken out all of the bad soil and replaced it with new, and I've removed all of the roots that were buried deep."

"I told you." He grins while leaning against the house, shielding himself from the beaming sun. "I could have hired a landscaper to take care of all of this."

Squinting against the harsh sun, I turn and cross my arms. My heart flutters as if it were stuffed with a bundle of feathers.

"And I told you," I tease. "I'll appreciate it more now knowing I was the one who brought it back from the dead."

"Is that what you're doing?" he asks, wiping the back of his hand across his forehead.

A drop of sweat trickles down the back of my neck. "Yep." I pop the 'p', exaggerating the sound it makes coming off my lips.

We simply stare at one another, the sound of the ocean breeze creating a symphony with the birds and trees.

Finally, Micah pushes off the wall, closing the space between us. He glances at the neighbors' houses briefly. Last week, he hired Jude to install a new security fence, changing out the rotted wooden paneling with a taller brick fence that had an additional wrought iron detail wrapping around the top. Not only does it fit better with the house and the surrounding neighborhood, but it also offers a better sense of privacy and security.

I guess after my father trespassed his yard, Micah lost a sense of safety here. Along with the fence, he's gone one step further and installed the best security system possible, with cameras located at every corner of the house, recording every angle of the outside perimeter.

He says his next job is installing a front security gate within the next couple weeks.

The steps Micah's taken to increase my sense of comfort and safety since my father's unexpected appearance has made it easier to fall for him... as if I wasn't already.

Slow and torturous. That's how my love for Micah has blossomed. But there's beauty in the pain of falling in love with him.

And that's what I've done. I've fallen in love with Micah Harding.

A fantasy I never believed would come true.

His devastatingly beautiful eyes search around the yard and the neighbor's houses on each side. Gerald, the old man in the house on the right, is spending the summer with his grandchildren in Maine. Heidi, the one who lives in the house on the left, has a line of tall trees separating her property from his, making it impossible to see into the yard. A similar boundary of trees run along the rear of the house, thick and wooded, meaning there's no one who would be able to see in.

When he reaches me, he immediately presses his hands to my face.

Rolling onto the balls of my feet, I stand on my toes, trying my best to bring my mouth above his. "I'm dirty, Micah," I breathe over his lips.

"Do you think I care?" His fingers dip into my hair and grip the back of my neck.

His hands are on me, and he doesn't stop. A sense of euphoria washes over me, his touch burning my skin in the best way.

"Is that how you want me?" I ask.

He presses his hips into me, his hardened erection against my stomach. I feel the length of him, and the space between my thighs hums with need.

"I want you in every possible way," he confesses.

I smirk, then I press my mouth to his, nibbling on his lip until I pull my mouth away. I look down at my feet before casting my eyes back up. "Tell me what you want me to do."

"I want your mouth on me. I want to watch your pretty mouth sucking on my cock."

"How do you want me?" I ask softly.

He massages the back of my neck before tilting my head up. "On your knees."

I do as he says, falling to my knees in front of him, heart racing.

My face is in line with his erection, the outline of it evident beneath his dirty jeans.

Nervously, I take another look around, ensuring no one is watching. The last thing I want is old man Gerald to be sitting on his second-floor balcony, sipping on his cup of coffee while watching me on my knees in front of Micah.

My cheeks heat, but there's no sight of Gerald.

Two fingers hook under my chin, pulling my focus and attention back to him. "Eyes on me."

A heavy breath falls from my mouth when I look back at his erection straining against his jeans. I unzip and free him. His cock springs straight out, hard as a statue. My eyes widen at the sight of it, stomach fluttering and my pussy getting wetter with need. It isn't the first time I've done this with Micah, but it's the first time we've done this outside.

I wrap my hand around his length, running the pad of my thumb over the mushroomed tip. A deep sigh falls from Micah's mouth followed by a deep, hungry growl. His hand is on the back of my head, massaging me as he patiently waits for me. Slowly, I slide my hand all the way down to the base while looking up at him with hooded eyes.

His jaw ticks, and his neck swells. Sweat coats his skin, a dot dripping down his neck. Keeping my eyes on him, I open my mouth, taking him in. His hand on the back of my head guides me. He groans the second my tongue slips against the tip. Letting go of him, I move my hands to the backs of his thighs, and he slides himself deep into the back of my throat.

"I love watching you on your knees for me."

I don't move as he stares down at me with darkened eyes that flutter as he groans.

"Your mouth feels so fucking good. It's even prettier when it's wrapped around me."

I suck my cheeks in and pucker my lips while he threads his fingers back through my hair, pulling me back.

I moan as I continue to suck and lick, pulling him in, then pulling him back out. Keeping my eyes pinned on him, I flick my tongue across the tip. "You taste so good."

"Fuck!" He hisses between clenched teeth when I go back

in for more until he hits the back of my throat again. "Just like that, baby."

He thrusts into my mouth over and over again. My jaw falls open, relaxing to allow him to move faster, but the more he fucks it, the tighter I get. I take him inch for inch, moaning and sucking, licking and tasting. Every time I allow him back in, he slams the back of my throat harder than the last time. His cock pulsates in my mouth.

"Fuck, baby." He groans, full of pleasure, stiffening. "I'm going to come."

I grip the back of his thighs tighter, holding him in place as I swallow, the muscles of my throat forcing him over the edge.

His orgasm slams into him with full force, and his cock pulses and vibrating. I hold him as he comes in my mouth and it lands at the back of my throat, making me widen my eyes and swallow. When he's finished, I pull out and lick the corner of my mouth. Micah watches me with fascination, and something in him clicks. He's suddenly hungry for more, not wasting any time when his hands are on me again. He leans down and wraps his arm around me, lifting me high enough to fall back into the garden bed. My back meets the cold, damp soil, but I don't care.

My hands are immediately on him, too, sliding under his shirt. I frantically lift it over his head and drag my long, pink-painted nails down the length of his chest and abs. His rock-hard muscle under my fingers adds to the wetness between my thighs.

"I want you so fucking badly, Micah."

"How bad?" His mouth lands on my neck, tasting me, where the tip of his tongue grazes the length of it. When he reaches my shoulder, he bites down, and I let out a small whimper.

Filled with need, I wrap my legs around his waist and pull him against me.

His cock presses against my dripping wet pussy. Disappointingly, I'm still wearing my shorts and panties—a barrier between us.

"This bad. I want you this bad," I whisper. "Can you feel how wet I am through my shorts?"

"Not yet." He groans with a devious smile. "But let's find out."

He makes quick work of popping the button of my shorts. With his knees pressed into the soil, he falls back on his heels and slips them down my legs. Once they're gone, he tosses them over his shoulder, discarding them on the ground outside the garden box.

He grinds his hips into me, his stiff cock pressing against me again. This time, the feeling is more intense. The only remaining barrier left between us is my black lace thong. The fabric adds another tickling sensation, intensifying my need and hunger for him.

"You're fucking soaked," he says, feeling my wetness seep through the thin fabric. He reaches down and hooks his fingers under the material, grazing them along my folds. Then without much effort, he tears them from me.

I gasp.

He tosses the shredded thong aside, and now there's nothing left. My ass is pressed into the dirt, but all I care about right now is having Micah as close as possible. I want to feel him inside of me, filling my heart in places no one else ever has.

Wrapping my hands around the back of his neck, I pull him down to me. He moves his hips back and swiftly slides himself into me.

My head falls back into the dirt as my mouth falls open on another gasp. The air is knocked from my lungs as he pounds into me.

"Oh, my God, yes," I breathe out, tipping my chin back

down. My nails dig into the back of his neck as he pulls out nearly all the way before driving back into me.

I move my hips in time with his, matching him thrust for thrust, meeting him with as much power as he's giving me. Our movements are rough and rushed in the soft dirt. I can't get enough of him. I feel like I'm chasing a high—one I know I'll withdraw from later, only to chase my next fix. But this is an addiction I don't want to recover from.

His large hands press into the wet soil on either side of my head. We're completely dirty, every inch of our bodies littered with dirt, but we don't care. My bare ass is pressed into the fresh garden bed I just finished laying out. Luckily, I haven't planted any seeds yet.

The scent of damp earth fills my nostrils as white-hot heat blooms. My legs tighten around Micah's frame, my orgasm coming. I hold him against me, his lower stomach grinding against my clit. I cry out, the feeling of him inside me sending a shock through my body, then he slams his mouth to mine, catching my moan with his kiss.

He pounds into me harder. Deeper. My body tenses, and my breathing is shallow, the vibration of my orgasm reaching fever pitch. I shudder when I fall over the edge.

My body is wracking with my orgasm as he thrusts a few more times before he falls apart inside me. His cock pulsates, and his jaw tenses, the feeling more intense with this second orgasm. His cum spills inside me and he falls against me, burying his face in the crook of my neck to catch his breath.

Once he's regained some control, he pulls himself out of me and looks over his shoulder for my shorts before grabbing them and carefully slipping them back up my legs. Lying still with my back in the dirt, watching him admire me, I feel myself smiling.

"I hope I didn't mess up all your hard work," he says, reaching the bottom of my ass.

I raise my hips as he slides my shorts the rest of the way up and over my curves. Once they're back on, I lift myself up onto my elbows, and he sits back on his heels.

"If you did, I'd say it was worth it."

The smile he gives me reaches his eyes.

I love Micah Harding. I've always loved him. But unlike when I was a kid, with just a hopeless, meaningless crush, this feeling I know won't disappear.

TWENTY-TWO

Micah

I thread my fingers through Adeline's hair as I hold the shower sprayer over her head, massaging the soap through her long, dark strands. Her strawberry-scented shampoo mixes with the brown dirt. Suds swirl at our feet as evidence of what we did in the backyard disappearing down the drain. Bubbles trail down the length of her back and over the flower tattoo inked into the skin along her ribs.

My chest expands looking at her, and I think back to how long I've known Adeline. I remember the first time I met her when Archer invited me over to his house during freshman year of high school. Adeline was only two years old at the time. Her mother had her strapped into a stroller, just having come back from a run in the neighborhood. Adeline's hair was pulled into two braided pigtails. I'd barely given her any notice, and when I think back on it, neither did Archer.

Granted, we were high as a fucking kite, about to head out for a movie, but I think back to that day and wonder if Archer noticed the contempt their father held for Adeline—even a hint or an inkling.

I don't think he did or else he would have done more to

protect Adeline. Either he lived in ignorant bliss or was too afraid to speak out, because despite the shit my best friend has put his family and friends through, and despite what he's put me through, I know he has a big heart.

But mine breaks for Adeline now. She's had to endure years of pain and neglect, feeling alone. I wish I'd known the truth even then.

If I had, I wonder if there was anything I could have done. *Would* I have done anything?

Guilt stabs at my chest for thinking I was doing the right thing when, in reality, my need to protect her was misguided. Maybe if I hadn't done what I did, Adeline wouldn't have suffered for as long as she did.

My fingers slide over her skin now, tracing over her pink flower. She steps back, nearly bringing her back to my chest. I lean down, pressing my mouth to the hollow of her ear.

Goosebumps rise and prickle her skin.

I want to drop the showerhead and sink back into Adeline, but I hold back, admiring her and savoring this moment instead.

"Do you feel better now you've repaired the garden box?" I ask.

She inhales a shaky breath, shivering again when my mouth moves over her ear. She leans into me. "Yes."

"Good." I trail my fingers down her ribs. "You can do whatever you want."

"With the garden?" She turns in my arms. "Or with you?"

Hook, line, and sinker. Adeline's completely hijacked my heart. She holds it in her hands with the ability to do with it what she pleases.

"Both," I tell her, surrendering to this feeling.

Two years I spent in prison rethinking the decisions I made throughout my life. There was nothing for me to do but sit in my cell alone, wondering if I'd made the right decision. My sentence was harsh, and I spent every single day angry at the judge for using me to send a message. But I also spent my time thinking my life was lost. Every hope and dream vanished in the matter of days.

I thought my life was over.

Adeline may be twelve years younger than me and in a different phase of her life, but I see a future with her. I see the future I thought was ripped away from me.

Adeline is a gift. A gift I wasn't expecting.

I wrap my free hand around her neck and bring her in for a kiss. Her mouth is warm and molds to mine as if she was made for me.

"What are you doing to me?" I ask her, pulling away.

The corner of her mouth lifts and she falls back against the tile. "You might not know, but I know what you're doing to me."

I drop the showerhead and tower over her, placing my hand above her head. "What am I doing?" I ask, my voice low.

"The same thing you've always done." Her eyes search mine. "I fell for you a long time ago, Micah. There was a time I never thought this would be possible, chalking it up to a meaningless crush. But all the days my heart hummed in anticipation at the thought of seeing you weren't meaningless. I know you never paid attention to me, but I've always noticed you. You stole my heart a long time ago."

I inhale a deep breath, the cold air hitting my skin after the absence of the hot water spraying on us, and I lean in and kiss her. We don't speak again, instead allowing her words to sink into both of our souls. They make a home, healing both our souls.

I still haven't told Adeline the real reason I went to prison, but I push it to the back of my mind right now.

I want to take my time with her. I want to live in this moment, knowing I deserve it. Telling myself I deserve it.

Life is full of heartache, but life with Adeline isn't.

I fall to my knees in front of her and lift her leg over my shoulder, then bury my face between her legs, dipping my tongue between her slits. She's warm and wet, tilting her head back against the tile on a gasp.

I flick my tongue and suck on her swollen clit while her fingers tug on the ends of my wet hair.

She's quick to reach her orgasm this time, her body shuddering, and her leg clenching my back. I taste her and hold my mouth to her, even as she rides out her orgasm on my face.

Panting, she lowers her leg from my shoulder. I stand and grab the showerhead as

I place my lips to hers, kissing her before she turns around and plants her hands on the shower wall. I finish washing her hair. We don't talk. We simply finish cleaning each other in silence. It's slightly comical watching her stretch to reach my head when it's her turn to clean me, her nails barely meeting my scalp, so I bend my knees, giving her better access.

"Will this ever fade?" she asks, sliding her hands across my chest, fixated on where her skin touches mine.

I place my hand over hers. "Will what fade?"

"The need inside me to always be with you. To touch you."

"I don't know," I breathe as she slips her hand between us, grabbing my cock. It swells under her touch. Heat pools in my stomach. "But I can't imagine it fading right now."

Her hand slides easily down my length. A heavy, deep groan rumbles from my chest as I lift her and wrap her legs around me. I'm about to spin around and plunge into her, with her body pressed against the wall, when a loud banging sound comes from downstairs.

Both Adeline and I turn our heads in the direction of the bathroom door as the steam billows inside the shower, clouding and fogging up the glass holding us in.

We hold our breath under the streaming water.

"Micah!" The faint sound of Archer's voice echoes through the house. "Addy!"

"Fuck!" Adeline hisses, covering her mouth. Her legs loosen from around my waist as her feet land on the shower floor.

"Micah?" Archer yells again after hearing no response. "I know you're here. Your car and your bike are in the driveway. Unless you're with Ray."

Fuck, does Archer keep tabs on me?

I look down at Addy. Her eyes are wide, and she tucks her lips between her teeth.

I haven't spoken to Archer in weeks, and Adeline hasn't talked about him, either, which tells me she's as perplexed by him showing up as I am.

Panicked, I keep my eyes on her when I finally do respond to Archer.

"Hang on, Arch!" I yell. "I'm in the shower. Be right down."

"What are we going to do?" she whispers, doe-eyed, her skin suddenly pale.

I cup my hands to her face. "I'll step out first and go down to talk to him. I'll see if I can get him out of here."

"He probably expects that I'm here, too," she whispers, her obvious fear taking hold. "I don't want to lie to him."

"It's fine. I'll take care of it."

It's not that I expect to keep my relationship with Adeline a secret, but I didn't expect Archer to find out today. I haven't thought too much about how this conversation will go when we do come to it. I'm caught off guard, trying to appear strong for Adeline.

"I'm an adult, Micah," Adeline whispers, pulling my attention back to her. "We shouldn't be expected to keep this a secret forever, even if you are his best friend."

"I know." I nod. "I just don't want to hurt him, and I know he won't be too thrilled to know we're together."

Closing her mouth, she swallows nervously. "All of my clean clothes are in my room."

I lean in and kiss her. "It'll be okay. Wait until I'm downstairs to go change."

"Okay." She stands on her toes to kiss me again.

I turn off the shower and hand Adeline her towel before wrapping mine around my waist, then I step into my room and slip on a pair of sweatpants and a plain T-shirt.

Before I leave my room, I give Adeline one last look. Her towel is wrapped around her small frame and another towel is wrapped around the top of her head. Her eyebrows are set in deep concern. I wish I could take it away from her, but the expression on her face is the way I feel inside.

Eventually, I jog down the stairs and find Archer sitting on the sofa, his arm draped over the back. He turns his head my way, and I sit in the chair opposite him, placing my feet on the edge of the coffee table as I flick my gaze to the front entryway. "How did you get in? The door was locked."

"Did you forget I have a key?" he asks, jingling the keys dangling from his finger. His eyebrows are knitted as he tosses them onto the coffee table.

"Oh, yeah." I scratch the back of my head. "It's been so long."

Archer takes in the living room. "It looks great in here." His gaze falls back to me. "Let me guess: Adeline."

I laugh. "Definitely."

He grins but doesn't add to the conversation.

"So, what's up?" I ask him, pointing at him.

"What's up?" he asks, his eyebrows rising. "I haven't seen you in months, and you ask what's up?"

I tilt my head to the side, confusion marring my expression.

"Well, the last time you texted me you said you weren't able to make it to visit because it wouldn't be safe."

"I've got everything handled for now." He waves me off. "You shouldn't be worried."

"I shouldn't be worried? Did you know I've seen Soren's men?"

"What?"

"Yeah, I saw one of them dancing with Adeline at Exodus. I don't know why he was there, but he was clearly keeping tabs on her." I rub my forehead. "Luckily, I pulled her out of there before he was able to do anything, but I'm almost certain he's been following me. At least, he *was*. I haven't seen anything recently that would make me think they still are, but I'm not under the assumption that they've suddenly stopped for no reason, either."

"Dammit." He looks out the window and exhales heavily. "It wasn't supposed to be like this."

"What the fuck, Archer?" Just how deep into this are you with Soren?"

"Soren?" Adeline's voice carries from the staircase. Her feet land on the bottom step before she steps through the opening to the living room. "Who's Soren?"

"Nobody," Archer says, turning to Adeline.

Her gorgeous eyes bounce back and forth between us, and I can tell she isn't buying Archer's lie. I wouldn't, either.

"Who is he talking about Micah?"

"Seriously, Addy," Archer interrupts. "It's fine."

"No," she bites back. "I heard you upstairs. Why wasn't it safe for you to visit before? Is Soren the reason you haven't shown up in months?"

"I'm not kidding, Addy," he barks. "Drop it."

Anger sparks in her eyes, and she takes a few more steps

into the living room to stand above Archer and cross her arms over her chest.

"Dammit, Archer. Stop treating me like a child. If there's something going on, then we should know about it."

A drop of water from the ends of Adeline's hair splashes onto Archer's leg. It soaks into his jeans, causing him to follow it with his eyes before looking back up at Adeline.

Her hair is still wet from our shower, hanging in waves, framing her face. She's dressed in a pair of loose sweatpants and a form fitting tank top.

But when Archer's eyes move from Adeline to me, I know exactly what he's thinking.

I told him I was in the shower when he came in, and now Adeline is in front of him, with soaking wet hair, the scent of her strawberry body wash filling the room, mixing with my cedar-scented one.

In one breath his eyes turn wild.

"My sister is right," he says to me. "If something is going on, I should know about it."

Adeline half turns my way, her arms still crossed over her chest. Suddenly, this conversation is no longer about the secrets Archer is hiding. It's about the ones Adeline and I are keeping from him.

Both of which I'm keeping from the other.

"Archer.," I say, sitting forward, resting my forearms on my knees. I lift my gaze to Adeline, watching the panicked expression on her face.

"Fuck you!" Archer yells, standing from the couch. He bounces off and charges toward me. I straighten my back and look up at him towering over me. "Are you fucking my little sister?"

"Archer," Adeline cuts in behind him. "Stop it." She places

her hand around his arm, but he isn't having any of it. He jerks away from Adeline's touch and keeps his attention on me.

"I fucking asked you to take care of her and protect her," he spits with venom. "And this is how you fucking repay me? By fucking her in the shower?" He spins around, looking at his sister. "How long has this been going on?"

I ball my hands into fists, fury building within me. I've stayed silent for far too long. When I look at Adeline and see the fear in her eye, I see the little girl who used to hide from her father. The one who never felt seen or heard or loved. Her relationship with Archer is delicate, sure, but I see the pain inside her soul. Pain for hurting someone she loves despite how he's kept her at a distance.

I also can't help fixating on one single word that fell from Archer's mouth. All the pent-up frustration of the past ten years ignites like a powder keg. The rope is lit, the fire climbing up its length, ready to explode.

"Repay you?" I look up at my best friend with more anger than I've felt in my entire life. My vision turns red. "What exactly do I owe you, Arch? Because I think you might have forgotten what I did for you. How I ruined my entire fucking *life* for *you*."

"What do you mean?" Adeline asks, wide-eyed. She turns to her brother. "What does he mean he ruined his life for you, Archer?"

"It doesn't matter," he answers. "He's twelve years older than you, Adeline." He looks at me, curling his hand into a tight fist. "She's my baby sister, you fucking asshole. I trusted you."

Adeline screams, and stars fill my eyes when Archer's fist connects with my face. I fall to my right, on my side, and lift my hand to my face. Radiating pain shoots across my cheek, and I let out a groan, blinking away the ache.

"Archer, what is wrong with you?" Adeline yells, falling to

her knees in front of me. She wraps her hand around my arm. "Micah," she cries. "Are you okay?"

"I'm fine." I nod, taking a second to gather my bearings.

"So, it's true, then?" he asks. "You're fucking her?"

"Shut up, Archer!" Adeline yells. "You have no idea what's going on, and it's none of your business. My relationship with Micah has nothing to do with you."

"The hell it does!" he yells. "He's supposed to be my best friend."

"I am." I grind my teeth together, massaging my jaw, and when I finally look up and find Adeline looking into my eyes, I decide it's time for her to know the truth. She deserves it. Regardless of what she might think of me or Archer afterward.

I sit up and remove the mask I've used to conceal the truth for so long.

"You talk about protecting family, but you've done nothing but constantly put them in danger. Why don't you tell your sister the truth, then?" I ask him. "She deserves to know."

"What are you talking about?" Adeline asks, frustration bubbling in her expression. She stands and turns to her brother. "Stop with all the fucking secrets, Archer. What is Micah talking about?"

The silence drags on far too long before Archer finally gathers the courage to declare his confession. His eyes don't move from his sister.

"It was me." Plain and simple. His voice is deep and straight to the point. My jaw echoes with the pain inflicted by Archer, but the real pain is inside. I can feel the safe cracking and unlocking, allowing air into my soul that's felt crushed by secrets for far too long.

"What was you?" Adeline's voice trembles.

"I was the one selling and distributing illegal drugs." He swallows and takes a deep breath, knowing the truth will add fuel to the fire. I see the fear in his eyes. Fear for losing his sister... or at least what little remains of the relationship they do have.

"Wait." She lifts her hands in the air, her mind working around the truth Archer is telling her. "From what I read all the drugs were found in Micah's bag. They found a trail leading back to him."

Archer shakes his head. "When Micah and his family's company invested in my tech company, we made incredible amounts of profit, exceeding expectations. I was able to pay back the loan they'd given me to startup within months. But after a couple years, profits started to dwindle, and I couldn't understand why. I'd gone to Dad for help, and he'd introduced me to some associates of his. At that time, Soren wasn't involved. It was someone else running their ring. They told me if I'd help them move some inventory, I'd be able to keep my business afloat, and it worked. Then, once I'd helped and seen what money could be made, I wasn't able to stop. I just went in deeper and deeper until I couldn't see a way out."

"But that doesn't explain how Micah took the fall for you and Dad," Adeline points out in a tight voice.

"When I'd introduced myself to them, I gave them Micah's name."

An audible gasp passes Adeline's mouth. "How could you?" she asks him, her mouth gaped in horror. "Why would you think that was a good idea?"

"I don't know," Archer says, guilt clear across his face. "Maybe part of me thought his father's reputation in the drug world would help keep them off my back. Or... I don't know, maybe I'm a fucking coward."

"So, you just let Micah take the fall?" she yells.

"You have no place to judge me, Adeline," he argues, clearly frustrated this is how his visit here is turning out, but I'm thankful the truth is finally being ripped open and exposed. I didn't realize how suffocated I'd become from keeping everyone's secrets. "I'm not saying what I did was right, but I panicked. Micah was never a part of it."

"Stop," she says, closing her eyes, not wanting to listen to another word. She finally turns and looks at me. "Why would you lie for him?" Tears stream down her face. I want to stick my hand out and wipe every single one away. "Why would you go to prison for them? Why didn't you tell the police the truth?"

"I thought I was protecting Archer. I thought I was protecting Lachlan." My voice is shaky and weak, knowing how foolish my decision ended up being. "I thought I was protecting *you*."

A sob rattles Adeline's body as the truth settles inside her.

"I didn't know then," I explain. "I didn't know how protecting your father only brought you more suffering. If I had, I wouldn't have made the same choice."

There it is. The truth. I'd taken the fall for the Mayfield family, believing I was protecting all of them. "The Mayfield family going down for drug trafficking would have been devastating. A Harding going down for drug possession would be history repeating itself."

Adeline's heart seems to break in front of me. Her eyes turn down, as well as her mouth, and her chin trembles. "Micah..." A shaky breath passes her lips, and I know this is the moment I know I'm in love with her. I want to gather up every moment she ever felt less than or felt betrayed by those she trusted and shield her from them.

"How did you going to prison affect Adeline?" Archer asks, his brows slanted. "What do you mean by suffering?"

Adeline's tears stain her cheeks as she looks at her brother. "You have no idea what life was like living at home, Archer. You have no idea what it feels like to live in the nothingness, to exist in the shadows. To be neglected and overlooked. Then when you are given attention by the ones who are supposed to love you, you're constantly told you're a waste of space and oxygen."

"Addy," Archer says, wide-eyed. "I had no idea. If I did, I would have..." He's looking at his sister with pity and regret.

"Don't. I know you didn't know what was going on." She swallows. "I don't want your pity. I've had enough of it. I'm telling you this because, yes, I should have told you what was going on. Maybe it would have made a difference, maybe it wouldn't. It isn't your fault for not assuming what was going on. You didn't have any reason to believe that I wasn't okay. You had no reason to believe I wasn't living with the same loving parents you'd experienced. I did what I could to survive, and I got out of there as soon as I could. But when I got to Los Angeles, I ended up in the arms of someone just like Dad. He made the promise to love me, but in the end, he hurt me. That's why I'm here. That's why I came back. I left my entire life and career behind. I had to because I knew what would have happened if I'd stayed."

"I'm sorry you were with someone who hurt you, and I'm glad you were brave enough to leave him, but it wasn't all sunshine and roses for me at home, either, Addy." Archer sighs. "I'm sorry I wasn't there for you. While I may not have dealt with the same issues, Dad always looked at me like I was one step or one breath away from disappointment. I guess since the day I was able to leave, I never looked back and never thought to make sure you were okay."

Silence inflates the air while the three of us stand among the truth. It's heavy and weighted, crushing us all.

Adeline swallows as she sheds quiet tears. "There's no point in living in the past." She finally breaks the silence. "But I don't understand how you could let your best friend spend two years in prison for you. And now..." She hiccups on one of her cries.

"And now you're worried about this Soren person coming after us?"

"Soren shouldn't be a problem anymore." Archer clears his throat, but he doesn't sound convincing. "I wouldn't be here if I thought he posed a threat to you or Micah."

"You shouldn't be here," I tell him. It hurts to say, but it's true. If Soren is still a threat, I don't want Archer to give him any reason to make me or Adeline a target. My need to protect Adeline comes in at full force. "You need to leave until you're certain Soren can't hurt any of us. You shouldn't have come."

Archer opens his mouth to object, but instead snaps it shut. He knows there's nothing he can say that will make this right. He also knows *I'm* right.

"I'm sorry," he says to Adeline. For the first time in all the years I've known Archer, tears line his eyes. "I'm sorry for all of it, and I'll make it right."

"I hope so." She holds her breath.

Archer trades glances between us and then without another word, he walks out the room, leaving behind his sister, his best friend, and the truth.

TWENTY-THREE

ADELINE

The truth will set you free.

I've heard the saying time and time again, but I mull over the words now, dissecting them, wondering if they're true. Do I feel set free? Or is the weight of the truth too overwhelming?

I realize I haven't taken a breath when I feel Micah's hands on me. He moves to stand in front of me, breaking my attention away from the front door, where I saw my brother disappear seconds ago.

Micah's hands wrap hold of my face, grounding me. I gasp, allowing a sharp breath of air into my lungs when I look at him.

"Are you okay, Addy?"

His words echo in my ears, but all I hear is the rushing sound of water, the sound flooding my ears, protecting me from the outside world. The burn from holding my breath permeates my lungs.

"Addy?"

I blink my swollen eyes, the tears drying on my hot cheeks.

"Yeah," I croak, working around the emotion in my voice. "I'm okay. I just need a moment." I look at Micah, and my heart breaks again for what he sacrificed. It aches thinking about every day he spent in prison carrying the truth with him. The truth of his innocence.

My brain works around the facts and all the unknowns I have yet to learn.

"How?" I ask him. "How could you have let the police believe you did this?"

"It wasn't difficult for them to believe." He shrugs. "Like I said, I'm a Harding. I'd already built a reputation of petty crime, then add my father's name and reputation in this city, and you have the perfect suspect. Archer has been my best friend for nearly two decades. He was there for me when I needed him most." He runs his thumbs over my cheeks. Over the dried tears. "I didn't hesitate in letting them believe it was me. I didn't fight back or argue that the bag wasn't mine. I let them believe it because I care for Archer. And I care for you. I didn't want your family to have the same reputation as mine. I know what that life is like, and you and Archer don't deserve it."

I inhale a shaky breath, a round of fresh tears burning my eyes.

"But it cost you everything." I look into his eyes. "Your life, your relationship, everything. Something like that doesn't ever leave your record." My heart hammers, the fractured pieces rattling against my ribs. The amount of love I feel from Micah is indescribable. Words I feel but can't voice.

Every moment shared with him up until this moment living in the truth begins to click. Why he said it's never mattered what he wanted. His trouble in seeing this house as anything other than a dying dream. I get it, and I wish I could fix the way he's viewed the world, as if it's wronged him but by his own hand. Almost as if he's fallen on his own sword.

"Adeline." His voice saying my name sounds so sweet, and I melt into it, closing my eyes, allowing myself to feel it.

"I need you to look at me when I tell you this," he pleads.

I slowly open my eyes. My legs feel numb, almost as if they aren't keeping me grounded. All I can focus on is Micah's hands on my face, and his eyes staring into mine.

"You gave up everything," I repeat, my voice cracking. "You gave up everything thinking you were protecting me."

"Ten years ago, you said you didn't need me to save you. Or anyone to save you. But I can't help it, Adeline. I would save you over and over again if it meant you were safe and felt well-loved. My feelings for you were different back then. I was protecting you because you were my best friend's little sister. You're his family. You and Archer are my family. But now you've blossomed into something more, and now that I know how I feel about you, I don't regret a single moment in jail. I only regret that if I had turned in your dad, it would have saved you years of heartache."

I think back to that day at the pool, the words I'd told him ringing in my ears.

I don't need you to save me. I don't need anyone to save me.

My vision was red when I spouted off to him. I meant those words then, but now, looking into Micah's eyes, I realize they've taken on a new meaning.

"I was a foolish girl back then with a foolish dream, and I only said that to you because I was embarrassed." I need Micah to understand the evolution of my feelings for him. "You were the boy I dreamed of being with but knew I could never have. You were my brother's best friend and twelve years older. I used to doodle my name with your last name in hearts, for God's sake. And when you pulled me out of that pool, I wanted to die of embarrassment. What I really should have done was thanked you. You were the one thing I looked forward to during the summer. You were the light in my dark world."

Micah's loyalty runs deep—deeper than I could have ever imagined—because the fall he took to save Archer wasn't an easy one to take, and the sacrifice he made that day for Archer was one that will forever leave a mark on his life.

"I spent two years in prison thinking about what I'd done, the choice I made," he says. "There were days I regretted giving in as easily as I did. I cursed myself for not putting up a fight or standing my ground. But I don't think I realized the weight of my decision until I heard those cell bars close. One day I was flying from London back home, the next I'm lying in my jail cell, wearing a bright orange jumpsuit. I'd lost my identity; a prisoner identification number stamped across the chest. I'd given up my life for your brother's. For yours." His thumbs gently run under my eyes, catching the tears I can't seem to shut off. But I don't want them to stop. They're a reminder of how hard I've fallen for Micah.

He leans forward and brings his mouth close to mine. His fingers thread through my still-wet hair. My back is wet, too, and my shirt clings to my skin, but I don't care.

"I gave up my life back then for you, Addy," he adds. "And I'm so sorry it ended up doing the opposite of what I wanted for you. If I had known..." He shakes his head.

"Don't apologize." I grip his shirt, fisting the fabric, hoping I don't wake up. The reality of my brother's crimes weigh on me. I haven't been able to wrap my head around the damage he's caused. If I do, I'm afraid I'll fall apart.

For now, I'll cling onto Micah.

"You can't blame yourself for what you didn't know, just like Archer can't. I don't hold it against him, and I don't hold it against you. You care about Archer, and that's why you did what you did. You have a massive, protective heart, Micah Harding. Don't ever apologize for it." I press my forehead to his and look down at my hands. His mouth ghosts mine, and my heart races. Heat radiates down the length of my body, and every breath of his that passes my lips injects life deep in my bones, down to the marrow.

His hands are still wrapped around my face when he pulls me to look at him, somehow keeping his mouth impossibly close.

"I love you, Addy."

He whispers the words I used to dream of hearing, and I feel all four feather across my skin before he steals my mouth into a kiss, and I sob into it. I melt into him and, fuck, every kiss is a solvent to my open wounds.

"I love you, too," I say back, meaning every single word.

IT TOOK a ton of convincing for Micah to finally agree to go to Connecticut with Lennon. He didn't want to leave me, especially after the situation with Archer. But I know how important this visit to the pharmaceutical factory was to his brother, and I didn't want him missing out on it because he's worried about me.

Four days have passed since we watched Archer walk out the front door. I've messaged him telling him I'd love to meet up and talk with him about everything when he has the chance.

He said he will make it right with Soren, and I'm not entirely certain what that means. Fear for my brother's safety plays in my mind. I'm angry with him for allowing Micah to take the fall for him all those years ago. Micah made the ultimate sacrifice for his friend, yet Archer hasn't been the best support for Micah since he was released. If anything, my brother hasn't been able to dig himself out of the hole he's gotten himself into. Over the past four days, I've tried to place myself in my brother's shoes. My father's influence as both our father and District Attorney is strong. If Archer felt he was drowning in his business, I don't blame him for going to our father for help. But at some point, the water became too high for Archer to swim in. The waves of the drug trade my father had pulled him into became too turbulent. Eventually, Archer struggled to stay afloat. Then like the current, the tide constantly shifted, pulling him farther adrift from the shore. Archer must not have been able to find a way back. A way out. Once he pulls himself out just a little, he gets sucked right back in, deeper every time.

I'm waiting for Archer's message when Micah's name flashes across the screen. I immediately answer, my stomach fluttering with excitement, despite the thunder crackling outside—a prelude to the storm coming.

"Hey, everything okay?" he's quick to ask me. His paranoia about my safety is over the top but sweet.

I smile, humbled by his protective streak. I love it, and I love him.

I giggle. "Everything is fine. Where are you now?"

"We're about forty-five minutes out from the house. I should have driven myself, but Lennon insisted Ray take us together. I told him to run through every red light once we get off the highway and to drive at least twenty over the speed limit just to get there faster." He laughs.

"Please don't do that." My cheeks turn red. "A storm is coming, and the last thing I need is for you to get into an accident. Tell Ray to obey all traffic laws."

I stand in front of the kitchen sink and rinse my coffee mug from this morning. I see my reflection through the glass of the window overlooking the backyard. It's out of focus, and I still have yet to look myself dead in the mirror, but I'm getting closer.

Every day I put my past in the rearview mirror, the more I'm embracing my new life. I'm learning to fall in love with myself again and learn who I want to be. After Archer showed up the other day, I've gotten a better sense of those around me. Not everything in my life is painted in black and white. It doesn't have to be. My life can be full of color even when surrounded by truth.

I feel whole and complete with Micah. His house has become our house, and I've never felt more at peace than I do here with him.

Micah lowers his voice, whispering into the phone. His voice in my ear sends shivers down my spine. "I can't wait to get back to you and bury myself in you. I'm going to fuck you so long and hard, I'll make it so you'll never want to leave our bed."

Our bed.

My heart flutters in my chest as another round of thunder rolls through the sky. The trees begin to violently sway, the moon hanging overhead casting a white glow on the backyard.

I grip the edge of the counter. "I can't wait for you to come home, either."

"I heard that," Lennon mumbles in the background. "Did you forget I'm sitting right next to you? On the side you're holding the phone?"

I laugh again as the lights in the kitchen flicker. I look up at the ceiling, and they flash a few more times before shutting off completely.

"Oh shit." I groan.

"What is it?"

"The power just went out."

"Fuck." Micah sighs.

"I'm fine," I reassure him, trying my best to stay calm. "The storm is getting worse, but it's not like I can't handle a little power outage."

I know he worries about me—mostly because he's worried the risk of Soren is still present—but the security system Micah put in place several weeks ago has worked. The fence surrounding the property offers more protection along with the cameras.

"There's a generator on the side of the house," he tells me. "It should kick in any minute. The security system is also programmed to run even when the main source of power gives out."

"Good," I breathe out, relieved. The wind howls outside, blowing against the side of the house. I stand on my tiptoes, peering up at the night sky.

Micah left this morning, but it takes more than two hours to drive down to Connecticut from where we live, and when you factor in Boston traffic, you can count on adding another hour. Going to Connecticut wasn't going to be a quick day trip. It's already past nine, and he still isn't back.

But since he didn't want to leave me as it was, Micah made sure the security system was put in place the best he could. We're still waiting on the front gate to be installed, but we at least have the other systems installed. It's better than it was before.

Dark clouds roll over the blanket of midnight blue, covering the moon. I'm still leaning over the counter, peering up, when another round of thunderclaps erupt, followed by bolts of lightning. I jump, and my breath catches in my throat.

Micah's in my ear replaying his whole tour of the pharmaceutical factory. I've gathered and understood bits and pieces of his story, only partially listening. The lights haven't turned back on yet, though, and I'm wondering if it takes longer than Micah said it would.

"The lights haven't come back on yet, Micah." I don't want to sound too paranoid because that will only worry him more than he already is. "I don't think the generators kicked on yet. Isn't it supposed to be by now?"

"That's strange." He clears his throat. I can tell he's nervous. "It should be on."

"It's fine. There are candles in my bedroom. I'll go grab

them and use those. The battery on my phone is charged enough, so I'm not worried about it dying before you get home."

"Okay," he says. "Do you want me to stay on the phone with you?"

"If it makes you feel better." I smile to myself.

"It does."

My cheeks heat, and my body aches for his. I imagine the warmth of his body against mine, the feel of his hardened muscles under my fingers. I'm imagining his kiss, but then another crack of thunder rolls above, this time it's louder, and shakes the house.

I'm still looking out the window when a sharp bolt of lightning strikes one of the trees still violently swaying with the wind. Then without warning, a torrent of rain falls. Heavy sheets of it pour down in weighted sheets, the sound drowning out the thunder above. I'm scanning the backyard when my gaze falls on the garden box.

Puddles form in the dirt, with water spilling over the sides. The rain is falling so hard and so fast, the soil is splashing over the top. Having just planted the seeds yesterday, the soil is fragile.

"Oh, fuck, the garden box." I hiss, running to the back door.

"What about it?" Micah asks.

Pressing the phone between my shoulder and cheek, I slip on each of my garden boots. "I need to cover the garden box or else it'll flood."

"Addy," Micah sighs while I slip each of my arms into my coat. "Don't worry about the garden box. You can replant the seeds again."

"I can't. I've worked so hard on it."

I push through the back door, allowing the screen to slam shut behind me. The metal bangs against the doorframe as I dash from out underneath the covered patio. I pick up the folded blue tarp I placed in the corner by my garden supplies and stand at the edge of the patio. I'm already out of breath, preparing myself to quickly run out into the yard.

"Micah, I have to go."

"No, Addy. Don't hang up." His voice cuts in and out, the phone losing signal.

"I'm not yet." I still have my phone pressed to my cheek and the hood of my raincoat pulled over my head. "But I need to get this covered or else all my work will have been for nothing. It'll only take a second. I just need to drape the tarp over the box so the seeds don't drown."

"Addy," Micah growls in frustration. He knows how stubborn I am when it comes to my projects. I already lost out on the furniture. I don't want to give up on this, either.

"I'll keep you on the phone," I tell him, running out into the yard. My feet pound into the puddles flooding the yard. Rain pelts my back and head, and by the time I've made it to the garden box, my legs are soaking wet up past my calves.

I'm quick to unfold the tarp, keeping my phone pressed against my shoulder. It would have been easier if I'd ended my call with Micah, but it's too late for that now. Lightning strikes again, and a figure in the distance catches my attention.

The tarp is only half unfolded when my breath catches in my throat.

"Adeline?" Micah asks.

"Wait." Another round of thunder crashes, and lightning strikes. Flashes of bright light shine across the backyard, highlighting the shadowy figure stalking toward me. I can't tell who he is from this distance. My legs are frozen in place, unable to move. An icy chill slithers down the back of my neck as he grows closer. I hear Micah's voice in my ear again, but he's choppy and unintelligible now.

The man continues walking toward me. Stiffly, his arms are

at his sides, and his boots pound into the soaking wet ground. I drop the tarp when he reaches the opposite side of the garden box. He moves around it and begins walking toward me again.

His face is covered in shadows, making him unrecognizable, but from what I can tell, he's tall and broad shouldered, towering over me.

I open my mouth, and the sounds of my heavy, quick breaths are drowned out by the rushing rain.

"Adeline!" Micah yells, cutting out again. "Tell me what's going on!"

"Someone..." I swallow, slowly starting to back away.

"What?" Micah asks. His voice fades when the phone slips from under my cheek. It falls from out under the hood of my coat and into the garden box.

I take another step back, but the man is quick to catch up to me, and my breath is stolen from my lungs when his face finally comes into view.

His name barely falls from my lips before a sharp pain hits my cheek and I meet the cold, hard ground. Then the world fades to black.

TWENTY-FOUR

Micah

I didn't want to leave Adeline.

Constant worry has made a home in my chest, refusing to leave. But with Archer's reassurance of settling his debts with Soren, I gave in when Adeline pled her case about why this trip was too important for me to miss.

Now I'm fucking cursing myself for leaving her alone. Panic has risen inside my body at an alarming rate. Ray has barely pulled into the driveway and parked the car when I jump out of the backseat. Lennon follows, his footsteps heavy behind me.

The rain is still pouring down in heavy sheets—a typical end of summer storm in New England. The tree branches sway angrily, the whipping rain falling against my face so hard it stings my skin. Trees slam against the brick exterior of the house, their leaves floating through the air and across the yard.

I stand in the driveway at the side of the house, but the house is completely dark now, with not a single light peeking through the windows. The gate to the backyard is wide open, and when a flash of lightning cracks in the sky, I get a clear view of the backyard.

Adeline is nowhere in sight.

I stand in a large puddle, the water soaking into my shoes and socks. The cool rain in the late summer heat mixes in the air, causing a chill to shoot straight into my bones. This doesn't feel right.

"Micah!" Lennon yells over the noise of the rain. I look over my shoulder at him. His suit is completely soaked, his tie clinging to his shirt. "Someone's in your house." He nods toward the back door, his eyes trained on one of the windows upstairs.

Both of our heads snap in the direction of the sounds coming from inside: shattered glass followed by muffled yelling.

"Have Ray call the police," I tell Lennon.

I don't even wait for his acknowledgement before sprinting to the back door. I make a quick run through the downstairs without any luck finding Adeline. I stop in the living room and listen for more sounds similar to those I heard outside. The floorboards creak upstairs, the muffled sounds of footfalls echoing through the ceiling. Following the sound, I run upstairs, unsure of what I'm going to find.

My mind plays over all different types of scenarios. Ones where Adeline is completely lost to me. One where I'll find Soren or Lachlan standing over her lifeless body. I'd be too late to save her. I wouldn't have kept my promise to protect her.

When I make it to the top of the stairs, I poke my head into each bedroom, calling for Adeline.

She doesn't answer, and each time I investigate a room, the claws of fear sink in deeper. The power is still out, making it harder to see. My eyes try to adjust to the lack of light, but every second that passes where I'm wasting time looking, I feel myself drifting farther away from finding her.

"Adeline!" I yell her name once I'm farther down the hallway and stop when I hear her groan coming from my bedroom.

I run the last few feet before I push through the partially open door.

My heart stops the second I see her.

Adeline is lying in the middle of the floor, curled in the fetal position. I sprint toward her, the blood draining from my face down to my feet. I'm weightless, and within a moment, my worst fears are realized. With shaky hands, I hold them above her, afraid to touch her. I don't know what to think or where to begin. I look her up and down. The tarp is lying beside her. She's wearing her dark green garden boots and her black rain-coat. I fear she isn't breathing until I stare at her chest long enough to see it move. Her hood is shielding half of her face, and I push it back, my fingers grazing her skin. Blood drips from her mouth, and a large cut stretches from her jaw back to her ear.

I swallow the thick lump in my throat. "Addy?"

She groans, and I momentarily breathe a sigh of relief. My heart thumps in my chest at the sight of her. She squeezes her eyes shut, and I wrap my hands gently around her. I place one on her back. With my other, I hook my fingers under her chin, gently lifting it so she's looking up at me. Cracking her eyes open slowly, she takes me in.

"Micah?" she croaks.

"I'm here, baby."

She tries to move by lifting herself up onto her elbow, but she winces in pain. A sharp hiss slips between her gritted teeth, and her hand flies to her ribs.

"Don't move." Fear slips into my voice.

She's still groaning in pain when I lift her gaze to mine again. She falls back onto the floor, still holding her hand to her ribs.

"Who did this to you?" I ask.

She moans again, her chin trembling. If tears are spilling

from her eyes, I'm unable to tell. She's still sopping wet from the rainstorm.

Her shoulders wrack with a sob and she squeezes her eyes shut. She rolls, burying her face away from view. The tip of her nose presses into the hardwood floor.

"Addy," I repeat, louder than the last. "Who. Did. This. To. You?"

She opens her eyes again, tears clumping her long, dark lashes. Thunder crashes in the background, vibrating the house. Addy's eyes meet mine and my heart tightens.

"Ma..." She quivers, widening her eyes, swallowing down her pain. "Maddox."

I wrap my hand around her jaw. My thumb catches the blood spilling from her cut.

Repeating his name in my head, it takes only seconds for me to remember who Maddox is.

Adeline's abusive ex. The one she left back in Los Angeles when she came to live with me.

My first instinct had been that Soren was responsible for this. Archer never confirmed he no longer posed a threat, but when I think about him coming back here four days ago, he must have truly settled his debt. At least enough to where it didn't put us at risk. My best friend has his issues, and I've taken the fall for him probably more than I should have, but he wouldn't have shown up if he knew his sister could be hurt.

"Oh, my God," I whisper as I run my thumb across Adeline's cheek. Blood streaks her skin, and I try to lift her head, but she hisses again in pain, crying out.

"He's still here," she whispers, her eyes wide with fear.

"We'll be okay." I try to reassure her. "I'm going to get you out of here."

"Step away from her."

A man I've never seen before steps out from behind my

closet door. I catch his reflection in the mirror on the opposite wall. His dark eyes are piercing in the blackness of the room. Lightning strikes again, highlighting the shadows of his face. He looks young—several years younger than me—with a boyish look to his face. Fucking weak.

My eyes drop to the knife he's holding, the blade glinting in the bit of light from the lightning.

When Maddox steps out from behind the door completely, I turn around and stand, shielding Adeline as much as possible.

"Get the fuck out of my house." I curl my hands into tight fists at my side.

"I think you must be confused." He lifts his hand to his chest, pointing the knife he's holding at it. "I'm not leaving here without Adeline paying for what she did."

"My patience is very limited, so I'll only tell you this one more time." White-knuckled, I tighten my fists even more. "Get the fuck out of my house, or you won't live to see the end of this storm."

"I don't think you understand what this little bitch did," he spits, waving the knife in my direction. He closes in on me, crossing the room to where Adeline and I are. I refuse to move away from her, but when he gets close enough to stick the knife to my own chest, I inhale a deep breath. One wrong move and he can stab me.

The tip of his knife presses into my tie.

I'm inhaling another sharp breath when his fist lands in the middle of my stomach. I hunch over, catching my breath. My mouth falls open and I fight the urge to vomit. Pain radiates across my body.

"No!" I yell around my constricted throat when I see Maddox moving toward Adeline. He bends down and grabs her by the back of the neck

She cries out when he lifts her up, forcing her to stand. Her head falls back, and her mouth falls open as he pushes her toward the other side of the room. He wraps his arm around her neck, holding her against his chest.

Looking up, I clutch my stomach, still trying to catch my breath. Fucking asshole hit me when I least expected it.

"Let her go," I choke out as I stumble toward Adeline, but I'm only a few feet away from her when I'm met with the tip of the knife pointed only inches from my face.

"Back the fuck up," he seethes, inhaling a deep breath. "I'm about to show this little girl exactly what she cost me and make sure she can never do it again." He keeps his arm outstretched as he sidesteps, keeping Adeline with him.

She stumbles on her own feet, trying to keep up. She's weak and injured, crying out in pain, sobbing while holding onto Maddox's arm with both her hands, trying to pull him away.

"Micah," she cries.

"Shut up, bitch!" Maddox booms.

My stomach wrenches, and my brain frantically searches for a way to get her out of Maddox's grip.

"Maddox," Adeline cries, switching tactics. "Please don't do this. It doesn't have to be this way."

Holding the knife to her throat, he walks over to the mirror and stands in front of it. The very mirror I managed to save from the pile of furniture salvaged from the shed out back. The wooden frame around the weathered glass is cracked in places, the stain peeling.

My eyes have finally adjusted to the darkness of the room, and the stars have cleared out. My vision is still slightly fuzzy as I work to regain my bearings, but I push the pain aside.

Maddox and Adeline are standing in front of the mirror. The glass is shattered, small shards and pieces of it lying on the floor. My eyes fall to Maddox's hand below Adeline's face. Blood drips from his sliced knuckles.

I stay where I am and think of what to do and how I'm going to get Adeline out from his grip. I know Lennon has called for help, but I start to wonder where he is. My eyes dart to the door opening, trying to hear for footsteps, but aside from the rain and thunder outside, the house is eerily quiet.

I glance around the room, searching for a weapon. On top of the dresser is my toolbelt, with my hammer still tucked inside one of the pockets.

I swing my gaze to Maddox and Adeline, making sure I don't lose them from my line of sight. Slowly, I sidestep toward the dresser.

"Shh. Hush, sweetheart," Maddox whispers into Adeline's ear as he runs a hand down the length of her cheek over the cut. "Open your eyes."

"*No*," she cries out, squeezing her eyes shut. "Please."

He presses the knife harder against her throat. "Open them!" he yells, his veins bulging from his neck.

Adeline only cries harder, her shoulders wracking with fear. She shakes her head, refusing.

I step closer to him, everything in my body wanting to do anything I can to get him away from her. My heart breaks seeing Adeline in his grip.

His eyes shoot to me in the reflection. "Don't you fucking dare try it."

I stop, and Adeline's eyes finally open, but she doesn't look at herself or Maddox. She looks at me through the reflection in the mirror, her gorgeous eyes spread wide with fear.

I want to vomit.

"Oh!" Maddox snidely laughs. "You love him, don't you?" He snickers and clicks his tongue. "That's so sweet." He looks at me again. "Don't let this girl's beauty fool you. Don't let her suck you in like she did me. She uses her looks, then flips it around on you, making you seem like the fucking fool." Every word he spits grows louder, his anger consuming him.

"How so?" I ask, hoping if I keep the conversation going, he won't go through with his threat on Adeline. I'm hoping Lennon or the police will be here any second to back me up or end this.

"Let me tell you about this little slut." He lifts the knife and drags it across her open wound, tracing the line he's already placed on her face. Adeline's eyes are still squeezed shut, but she screams in pain. "She's just like every other model. She moves to Los Angeles, thinking she's some hot little shit, like she's going to make any kind of difference in this big fucking world. Instead, all she's doing is selling her fucking body and making horny men more feral. She doesn't give a shit about you or your livelihood." He leans into Adeline, pressing his cheek to hers. "You made a promise to me, didn't you?"

I take another step to my left, seizing the opportunity to move closer to the hammer. Maddox's eyes are still on Adeline when I finally reach the dresser and slip the hammer quietly out of the pocket. I hold it behind me and take a tentative step back to my right, returning to where I was before.

"What was your promise, huh?" Maddox asks Adeline, curling his lip.

"Maddox, please," Adeline begs. "Just let me go."

"What was it?" he barks.

Another sharp gasp escapes Adeline, and she shakes before she opens her eyes to find Maddox in the reflection. "That I wouldn't hurt you. That I would never look at anyone else."

"That's right." Venom slips into his words, fueled by his anger and hatred. "But what did you do?"

"Nothing," she whispers. "I didn't do anything."

"Don't lie to me!" He sniffs, wiping the spit hanging from his mouth from yelling. "After I caught you flirting with that photographer, you honestly thought I would believe it was innocent?" He scoffs, narrowing his eyes. "Women like you always play the victim, but after I confronted you about it in your trailer, you made a promise not to do it again." He clicks his tongue again in disapproval, still running his knife over the cut on Adeline's cheek. "Then look what you did. You came here and spread those long, pretty fucking legs and fucked your older brother's best friend."

A tear slowly spills over Adeline's lashes, sliding down her bloodstained cheek.

I hold my breath, the pain in my gut radiating with sickness.

"Oh, I know all about the little Harding brother here." He smirks. "She has a sweet little cunt, doesn't she?" He narrows his eyes to me through the mirror, tipping his chin higher. "Sweet like candy."

He traces his tongue over his mouth.

White-hot anger injects into my veins.

He focuses back on Adeline's reflection. "Mommy was more than willing to tell me all about how he opened his doors and offered to take care of you. It was so easy for you to move on, wasn't it?"

"You hurt me, Maddox," Adeline forces out. I can tell she's holding back her sobs, and I take another step closer.

I'm moving toward her when I see movement in the reflection of the mirror. Down the hallway, I catch the quick flash of Lennon's watch. I'm guessing he's sticking close to the wall, not wanting to give Maddox any hint of his presence, but knowing Lennon is close by gives me strength to make a move soon.

"I didn't hurt you," Maddox tells Adeline as he grips her cheek. "*You* hurt *me*." With his knife, he drags it along her cheek once again. "I lost all my clients the second you decided to leave. My entire career has been destroyed because of what you've done. Now I'm returning the favor." He smiles at his handiwork on Adeline's face. "And now, I'll make sure you never seduce anyone else with this pretty face of yours."

He starts digging the tip of his knife deeper into Adeline's cut. She cries out in pain, and I decide to take my chance. I can't wait any longer. Adeline's pain tears into me, pumping me with adrenaline. I fought with others in prison. I know men like Maddox. They beat women because they're weak on the inside.

I lunge at Maddox. Pulling the hammer from behind my back, I slam it as hard as possible on the back of his arm—the one he's holding to Adeline's cheek. A loud bellowing scream leaves him as he stiffens. When he doubles over in pain, Adeline takes her chance and slinks out from his hold. She falls to the floor and crawls backward on her elbows, scrambling to get away.

Maddox spins around, eyes wildly fixed on me.

He's holding the back of his arm, groaning in pain when I switch the hammer to my left hand and rear my arm back to deliver a blow to his temple with my fist. He falls back onto the broken pieces of glass littering the floor in front of the mirror. The bones in his face crunch and crack under my fist.

He takes a second to catch his breath.

"Come on, asshole," he spits up at me while on his knees. "Do it. I dare you. I dare you to kill me. Kill me and you'll go straight back to prison, but this time you'll fucking rot. Right where you belong."

"Shut the fuck up." I growl and deliver another blow, and this time he flies onto his back on the floor. It doesn't take him long to try to roll to his side, but I'm quickly on him, holding the handle of the hammer over his chest, below the base of his throat, to keep him down.

He gasps for air, his eyes widening in shock.

My vision turns red, and the claws that once haunted my mind have returned. Every cut that's healed over the past few months reopens the second the claws expand. They slice into my mind, telling me I'm this person. The one full of vitriol and anger and resentment. The one who has a record and ruins the lives of those who care for him. The one who tells himself he's worthless and everything is lost. The one who swore he would do anything to protect those he loves, even if it cost him his own life.

I slide the hammer farther up Maddox's chest. Sweat drips down his face and neck, making it easier to hold against him.

His face turns purple, the veins bulging under his skin.

Seconds go by, and my vision turns black. I'm straddling Maddox while he struggles underneath me, and I add pressure on the hammer, leaning into it. His legs violently kick across the floor, and he grasps for the hammer. With gritted teeth, he stares into my eyes, challenging me, taunting me.

"Micah!" Adeline cries behind me. "Stop." I catch her reflection in the mirror, but she isn't looking at me through that anymore. Now, she's looking at *me*.

Her shaking hand lands on my back, and I'm thrusted back to the day I saved her from the water, thinking she was drowning.

Her eyes are wide, even as the blood spills from her cheek. Dark strands of brown hair saturated in rain and dirt frame her face. She's still gorgeous, and the claws in my mind that tell me I'm like him, that I'm worthless like my father, that I'll die just as vile of a human being as him, pull back. The more I concentrate on her hand on my body, the more I slip back into reality. I look down at Maddox and immediately pull away, dropping the hammer and crawling off him before moving to Adeline.

"Addy." I say her name in a tight voice, not fully realizing I have tears streaming down my face now. My chin quivers, and my throat swells.

"It's okay." She presses her hands to my cheeks, staring straight into my eyes. "We're okay."

I nod and look over my shoulder at Maddox. He's coughing, his body wracking and trying to recover. He's rolled on his side, clutching his neck just when the police barge into my bedroom.

It's soon chaotic, and panic settles in. Countless police officers enter with their guns pointed and their voices raised. I stare at the floor, afraid to look up. I hear Lennon's voice on one side of me, Adeline's on the other.

My body is tense, though, my muscles hardened and my breaths shallower. I feel myself inching closer to the edge of panic, remembering the feel of the cold, metal handcuffs locking around my wrists.

I hear the familiar click, and I swallow, trying to catch my bearings as I squeeze my eyes shut, willing the memories to disappear.

But a soft hand presses against my face once more, urging me to look the other way. I crack my eyes open and see Adeline, and my heart splinters at the sight of her.

"Addy," I whisper, but I'm unsure if she hears it.

Her eyes search my face before finally meeting mine.

A mixture of caramel and brown with flecks of sage green.

The breath is knocked from my chest when she leans forward and presses her forehead to mine.

"You saved me."

TWENTY-FIVE

Micah

I held my breath until the last police officer stepped out of my house.

Having a record and serving two years in prison leaves you with a permanent fear of the police or anyone who has the ability to send you back into a five-by-five cell. Especially when your record will forever tell a lie.

The fear of never being believed will always live within me now.

But with Lennon as my witness, and the security cameras surrounding the house catching Maddox tampering with my generator before the power shut off, the police were easily able to gather a picture of what happened.

Maddox shut off the backup generator knowing that if the power went out, he'd be able to attack. They found his car parked on the street behind mine. It looked exactly like the car I'd seen in the parking garage the night I'd taken Adeline home from Exodus on Ember's birthday. The feeling that washed over me when they walked out the door after taking our statements and with Maddox in tow was indescribable.

I run my fingers under the heavy stream of water now,

making sure it isn't too hot. While sitting on the edge of the claw foot bathtub in the spare bathroom, I glance over my shoulder and eye Adeline. She's leaning against the vanity with her arms crossed, staring at the floor. The cut on her cheek is stitched shut, with a white bandage taped over it. For now, we're avoiding the bedroom we've been sharing the past several weeks, and the bathroom connected to it. Once the tub is filled, I shut off the water and unbutton my shirt. I slip it off and remove my pants. In only my boxer briefs, I cross the room to Adeline.

She hasn't spoken much since she came home from the hospital. Shock has settled in, and now that the adrenaline has worn off, the world has come crashing down around us.

I still haven't worked my head around the fact Maddox did this.

For months, I thought Soren posed a threat, but I was wrong.

"Archer caught the soonest flight out of Austria." My voice breaks the silence in the room. "He should be here by morning."

"Wha—" Her voice catches in her throat. She clears it, never looking away from the floor. "What about Soren?"

"Archer assured me he paid off his debts and they both mutually agreed to end their business dealings."

Adeline scoffs, shaking her head. "Hard to believe he would let go of Archer that easily."

"Agreed." I blow out a hot breath. The metallic scent of dried blood and wet earth fill my nostrils.

"I'm glad he's out of that life, though." Adeline's bottom split lip quivers. "I hope he means it this time."

"Come on. Let's get cleaned up." Gently, I run my thumb down the side of her face and wrap my hands around the bottom of Adeline's shirt before lifting it over her head. Dried blood and dirt cover the blue fabric. I peel it away from her body, making sure not to scrape her cuts and abrasions.

I stifle a sharp breath when I see the bruises on her skin. A blue and purple bruise blooms across her ribs, over her flower tattoo. She wraps her arm around herself, covering it. Her brown eyes line with tears, and I want to destroy her pain. I wish I could reach inside and take it away. I see the grief in her expression, what she's lived through. Adeline isn't new to abuse, but seeing it up close ripped my soul to shreds.

I kneel in front of her and slide her jeans down her legs. The knees are torn, and mud is caked from her calves down. She allows me to undress her, never uttering a single word.

Once we're both completely naked, Adeline climbs into the bathtub after me. She sits between my legs and slides into place until her back is pressed against my chest, then she bends her legs and pulls them to her chest, wrapping her arms around them. Turning her head, she rests her cheek on her knees, letting me wash her.

I dip her pouf into the soapy bath water and squeeze it over her back, watching the water stream down her spine. A million thoughts run through my mind. I want to say so many things to Adeline. I want to ask her questions. But sometimes, I know there isn't a need for words. Sometimes silence is all we desire.

I continue to gently wash Adeline's back, watching the dirt wash away, but the bruises never leave.

"I'm sorry, Micah." Her whispered apology catches me off guard.

My hand stills on her back. I drop the pouf into the water and press my hand gently against her skin.

"You have nothing to be sorry for," I tell her, stunned she's apologizing.

"I do." She chokes back a sob and lifts her head before she spins around between my legs. She keeps her legs tucked and her arms wrapped around them. Her lip trembles as a tear slips from her beautiful eye. "I should have told you more about

Maddox." She shakes her head and her eyes dart back and forth, as if she's trying to rationalize what's happened. "I should have been more careful."

I tilt my head to the side, imploring her to look at me. "Don't blame yourself."

Her mouth turns down as she cries, her tears soaking the bandage on her cheek. "I feel so stupid. I feel so stupid for falling for someone like him. And now..." Her voice trails, the words eventually evaporating in the air as she lifts her hand to her cheek. She doesn't quite reach it, barely ghosting her fingers above the bandage.

"Addy," I say, scooting closer. I wrap my arms around her and hold her. "This isn't your fault. You couldn't have known he would do this. And we'll get through it. You're strong."

She sobs into my chest, giving in and unraveling her arms around her legs. I hold her while she cries. I hold her until the water changes from hot to lukewarm. Her face is still pressed to my chest when she finally speaks again, and I run my fingers through her hair

"Can I ask you something?" Her voice cracks, racked with sadness.

"Anything." She lifts her head from my chest, and we sit facing one another.

"When you held the hammer against Maddox's chest..."

I swallow the lump in my throat because I know where this is leading. I know what Adeline is going to say.

"I could see the pain in your eyes. The anger fueling you. You became someone else."

I bend my legs on either side of her and rest my arms on my knees, then I sniff and close my eyes, relieved to know the claws that once plagued me have gone. Maybe it's because I've crossed some path or bridge I've been standing in front of for the past several years. Maybe it's because of Adeline's love. Her love has set me free from the cage I've lived in for the past ten years.

"When I saw Maddox taunting me, my vision turned red," I begin to explain. "I slid the hammer down his chest and pressed it to his neck."

She inhales a shaky breath, and her lips part slightly.

My stomach flips, and I worry this will push her away, but she's asking me to be vulnerable, so I share the piece of myself I've never shared with anyone. The deepest, darkest pieces of my soul.

"As the days went by in prison, I was left with nothing to do but think about the choice I'd made. I thought about how the police and prosecutors barely batted an eye, believing I did all these things. All because I was a Harding. An endless, vicious cycle of thoughts ran through my mind about the ramifications I would face once I was released." I swallow, thinking about the first night I spent out of prison. "The first night after I was released, I spent it in my penthouse in the city. It's funny. I spent two years feeling completely isolated, but that night, I'd never felt more alone, more outside myself. I laid in bed, and when I closed my eyes, I felt them."

"Felt what?" she asks, wrapping her hand around my arm.

"The claws digging into my mind." I place my hand over hers, watching our fingers move together.

"Claws?" Her eyebrows pull together.

"My brother Jude used to say he feared he would end up like our father. He'd struggled with alcohol and the pressure of society, and at one point in his life, it cost him everything that mattered to him. I never understood him until the night I felt the claws in my mind appearing. They were worse when I looked in the mirror. Instead of me staring at my own reflection, I saw him. I saw that I was now existing in a world where I was closer to becoming him than I had my whole life. No one would ever see me as anyone else. I was the one others would look at, unsurprised I turned out just like him."

"But you aren't." Adeline tightens her grip on my arm. The bath water ripples as she pulls herself impossibly closer so the warmth of her body surrounds me.

"I lived with the claws and pain for years after I was released. All the money in the world couldn't erase them, though. I tried my best to return to my old life, but I wasn't the same person. Prison changes you whether you want it to or not. I admit, I made poor choices. When I told you I was taking a break from work, it was because I nearly cost our family's firm a deal we'd made. I was living in the past. Living in complete darkness... Until there was you."

Tears line Adeline's eyes, and the hint of a smile tugs on her mouth.

"I didn't realize it until earlier when I was holding the hammer to Maddox's neck," I confess. "I didn't realize the claws had all but disappeared, and when they returned, turning my vision red, I felt him. I felt my father, and saw him in Maddox. Anger and rage took over, and I pushed all my pent-up resentment into that hammer. I shouldn't have done it, but I couldn't stop. But then you touched me and pulled me back."

I press my hand to Adeline's wound-free cheek. She closes her eyes and leans into me, breathing me in.

"I love you so fucking much, Adeline, sometimes it aches," I tell her, and she opens her eyes. "You said you didn't need anyone to save you, and while earlier you'd said that I saved you, it's you who's truly saved me. You jumped in without hesitation and pulled me from under the water. You've given me back what I thought I'd lost, and a chance at a life I thought I'd never get to live."

She nods, and for the first time tonight, I see her crack a

smile. She winces and tilts her head to her shoulder, pressing her cheek against it. "You've done the same for me."

I wrap my arms around her and pull her close. All the pain I've felt in my life suddenly disappears. None of it matters when I'm with Adeline. Hope inflates my chest, overwhelming me. The darkness is replaced with light, and while I felt I'd missed out on the most crucial moments in my life, I see the opportunity with Adeline now. I may only be thirty-three and witnessed my brothers living full lives by the same age, but I don't feel left behind like I did before. I'm right where I'm supposed to be.

With my fingers under her chin, I tilt her face to mine and press my lips to her broken skin. She tentatively gives me a kiss, whimpering.

"You've given me a chance at life, too," she whispers against my mouth. "Let's start living it."

TWENTY-SIX

ADELINE

It took seven days for me to resume my work on the garden box and another seven to step back into Micah's bedroom. We both moved into the room I'd stayed in when I first came to live with Micah, keeping the door shut on his until we were ready.

I simply couldn't face the evidence of what Maddox had done to our home and the space I'd shared with Micah. I didn't assess the damage until after the police searched our house, and I'd returned from the hospital that night with bruised ribs and fifteen stitches on my right cheek to find broken furniture and picture frames scattered around the house. I'd stood in the doorway of Micah's bedroom, unwilling to step inside, afraid I'd have to relive the physical and emotional trauma caused by my ex. Shattered glass was sprinkled across the floor in front of the broken mirror, with blood splattered amongst the shards. I couldn't face it even after the cleaning crew came in and replaced everything.

But it's been nearly a month since the incident with Maddox now, and I've never felt freer than I do.

I'm bent over the edge of the garden box, trimming a few of the flowers I planted the week after the terrible rainstorm that flooded the garden. I had to start from scratch and remove all the seeds I'd planted before, but something about completely gutting it and starting anew sparks joy in my heart. Joy I almost lost the night Maddox tried to ruin my life.

My hands are covered in dirt as I place the last handful of soil around the pink flowers in the far corner. My knees are pressed into the cold ground when I glance over my shoulder and look up at Micah's bedroom window. He's standing in front of it, watching himself get dressed in the new full-length mirror he bought. Although we haven't been sleeping in his bedroom, he still keeps all of his clothes in his closet. Today is his first day back to work, and I smile, watching him take pride in his appearance.

Sweat sticks to the back of my neck despite the cool early fall weather settling in. We're in the strange period where there's a thirty-degree swing between morning and afternoon. I've shoved the sleeves of my shirt up my arms to allow the warm sun to beat down on my skin.

Once I'm finished with the garden box, I take a few seconds to admire my work before heading upstairs to shower.

After washing away all the dirt and sweat in the spare bathroom, I wrap a towel around my chest and tiptoe down the hallway to my bedroom, only to stop as I pass Micah's room. He isn't standing in front of the mirror any longer, and the scent of coffee permeates the house.

I pause in front of the doorway and peek in. My chest stills and I shove the memories of that night away. The room is drastically different than it was before. The curtains are pulled back, allowing the warm sun to pour into the room. The old mirror has been replaced with a more modern one with a thin, black frame, untouched and free of damage. It has no story to tell.

I step inside Micah's bedroom, the floor creaking underfoot. Slowly, I cross the room and walk toward the mirror. The moment I see my foot in the reflection, I come to a screeching halt. My breath catches in my throat, and I'm overcome with emotion.

Up until the night Maddox cut my face I hadn't looked in the mirror. I never even looked in one after having my stitches removed. The doctor told me there would be a faint scar, and I knew Maddox had accomplished what he set out to do.

Ruin my career.

He saw it as payback for standing up for myself and having the power to walk away from him.

Facing myself meant facing the truth. There were no masks for me to hide behind anymore. I knew if I were to see the woman I'd become, I wouldn't recognize her, and the thought of facing the new me was a terrifying notion—one I still haven't felt strong enough to deal with.

But something about the way the sun shines a light on the bed Micah and I sleep in and the reflection in the mirror being new gives me the courage to keep going. I think back to the pink flowers flourishing in the garden, like the one tattooed across my ribs.

Rebirth.

I close the remaining gap between the mirror and me. My breath catches when I see myself for the first time.

My hair is longer than I remember it being, and my eyes shimmer in the sunlight. The cut I'd felt on my bottom lip has disappeared. The bruises painted over my collarbones have faded to a faint yellow hue.

When my eyes drop to the scar on my right cheek, tears immediately prick the backs of my eyes. My chin trembles, seeing the three-inch scar stretching at the perfect angle from my ear to my mouth.

I lift my hand and ghost it along the raised skin.

Maddox got what he wanted. There's no way I'll ever be

able to model again. Not if this scar remains. But as my fingers trace the mark, and tears spill over my lashes, I realize he wanted more than for me to lose my career. He wanted to leave a lasting impression. He wanted me to look in the mirror and think of him every time I see myself.

He wanted me to never forget.

Even now, as he waits in jail for his trial to begin.

Unsteady, my fingers tremble across my skin, and I feel myself caving in. My vision turns watery and more tears stream down my cheek. Inhaling a sharp breath, my eyes dart up, catching Micah standing behind me.

"Hey," he whispers, touching the back of my arm.

I blink and sniff, clutching onto the towel wrapped around my chest. "I don't know why I came in here." I look at him once more before stepping away.

He stops me, his hand gently wrapping around my arm. I spin around to face him, with my chest pressed against him. He's dressed in his signature blue suit, with a pale blue shirt. His blue tie hangs loose around his neck, undone.

"Wait," he whispers, tracing his fingers along the length of my face. "Can I ask you something?"

I tuck in my bottom lip and bite down, unsure what he's going to ask. I'm glad I was able to finally face my own reflection, but overlooking the scar that now serves as a constant reminder of the past is proving difficult to bear.

When I look up, though, all my worries fade the second I meet those same kind, blue-gray eyes I've fallen in love with.

"Yes," I whisper back.

"When you were looking at yourself, what did you see?"

"Micah." I drop my gaze, clutching onto my towel tighter.

I can't answer him. I can't put into words how I feel. At my core, I know I love myself and the way Micah makes me feel. He never makes me feel less than. He never puts me down, constantly reminding me how beautiful I am. But a piece of something buried deep in my chest is fractured by pain, loss, and tragedy, and that pain may never completely disappear. It will forever live in me, attaching itself to me, becoming a part of me.

"Can I tell you what I see?" he asks.

My lips part and I look into Micah's eyes as he places his hands on my shoulders and slowly turns me around, back to my reflection. He towers over me, my head meeting his chest. My body shivers, and goosebumps dance across my skin when he reaches in front of me, unraveling my towel.

It slips from my body, pooling at my feet.

The ends of my hair are still wet from the shower, drops of water sliding down my bare chest. The cool air pumping into the room breezes over my nipples, hardening them into two pebbles. Anticipation bubbles inside me, bringing my body back to life. It's as if I'm suddenly being awakened.

He leans forward until his face is next to mine. I watch as he presses his mouth to my collarbone. I splay my palms flat on my stomach, telling myself to remain calm. I don't want this moment to end with Micah.

There are times where I still can't believe this is real. At one point, he was completely off limits and unattainable. Now, here we are.

With his mouth hovering in front of the hollow of my ear, he stares at me through our reflection.

"I see a woman," he whispers, the stubble on his jaw grating against me.

Heat pools in my stomach, replacing the fluttering. The tears are still coming, but they're coming from a different place. Instead of sadness and agony, I'm healing.

"I see a woman," he continues. "A woman who has survived

and fought. A woman who's always known who she was and who she wants to be."

"Micah…" My eyelids flutter, and my head falls back against his chest. I feel weightless, his words hitting deep in my soul.

He catches me, dragging the back of his index finger along my shoulder. I feel my body inflate, and I struggle to breathe. The oxygen feels tight in my chest, and I keep my eyes open, wanting to watch Micah.

"You're the most beautiful woman I've ever seen, Adeline." While he draws invisible lines down the length of my arm, he takes his other hand and traces the scar on my cheek. A tear rolls over my lashes and onto the scar. "It isn't just what's on the outside. It's your soul. You aren't simply measured by your outer beauty, Addy." He slips his fingers over my nipple before cupping my breast in his palm. "Although it definitely can't be ignored."

A smile tugs on my mouth.

His whispers send a shiver down my spine. "You are the most stunning woman, and some days I wake up next to you still not believing you are mine. *Mine*. Every beautiful inch."

He traces the scar once more before wrapping his hand gently around my neck. He angles my face up, but I keep my eyes trained on my reflection.

The way we're standing here together reminds me of the way Maddox held me hostage that night. I felt helpless and terrified then. But this is different. With Micah, I'm safe. He's commanding yet gentle, never letting me feel as if I'm not in control. He's showing me that I don't have to live in the darkness or run from it. I can tackle it and switch the narrative. He's giving me the gift of a new memory —one where I see the beauty in the woman I've become.

"This is what I see." His voice is velvet, coating every inch of me.

He keeps his hand around my throat and catches my breath with his mouth to kiss me before pulling away.

"Do you see it, too?" he asks. His eyes have darkened, set on a mission. He keeps his hand around my neck and removes his other from my breast to trail his fingers down the center of my stomach before settling them between my thighs. Parting my slits with his fingers, he finds my clit.

I jerk my hips back, rolling into the pressure, and I gasp as his fingers work me. His cock presses into the small of my back, and I'm suddenly begging to have him inside me.

"Watch yourself," he says. "I want you to watch and see how beautiful you are. Do you see it?"

"Micah," I say tightly. "Please. I want you."

"I want to hear you say it first." He rolls his hips into me, and I know he won't hold back for long. "Heartache isn't always pretty." He growls in my ear.

His words are an arrow straight to my heart. A jolt of electricity courses through my veins, and my entire body lights up. I stand on my tiptoes, reaching behind me to grip onto his shirt, my mouth falling open.

"Tell me you see what I see."

"I do," I tell him, and as I watch his hand working me, I know I mean it. I do see beauty in myself. And he's right.

Heartache isn't always pretty.

"Life is only ugly when you ignore the beauty," he says. "And you, Adeline..." He presses his mouth to my ear, biting on my lobe. "You *are* beauty."

His teeth graze my skin, and I feel myself reaching my orgasm. I moan as tingles spread across my lower stomach and between my legs. His fingers move faster, pressing harder against my clit. I roll my hips, lowering my feet, pushing into him.

My orgasm crashes into me, and I cry out, the feeling

vibrating across my entire body. Watching myself orgasm in the mirror gives me a feeling I have yet to experience. I catch Micah's fiery gaze in the reflection.

I'm still working to catch my breath, riding out my orgasm on Micah's fingers, when he pulls them from between my legs and spins me around to wrap his hands around the back of my thighs and lift me up. My legs curl around his waist, and he carries me over to his bed.

I feel as if my life has come full circle when his knees hit the bed and he falls back. I land on top of him, looking down at his face. My wet pussy is pressed against his crisp button-down shirt.

I know today is a big day for him, but I don't know when he's supposed to be at work or if he's going to be late. All I care about right now is that he's here with me, showing me there is beauty in the pain. That this life may not be perfect, but none of it matters. All that does matter is that I'm happy and whole.

I slip the tie out from under his collar and drape it around my own neck. The silky fabric ghosts along my breasts, perking my nipples back up.

My body is still humming from my orgasm, but the need to have Micah inside me is still strong. I unbuckle his belt and unzip his pants before effortlessly slipping his hardened cock inside me, and once I've lowered myself all the way down, I stop to allow my body to adjust to him. Our eyes meet, and my heart explodes, the heat in my stomach expanding.

Lifting myself up, I lower myself back down; his eyes watch me in fascination. I've never felt more beautiful. *More seen.*

My entire body ignites feeling his length slide against my insides. I clench around him, reaching my orgasm faster than expected. He does the same, gripping onto my thighs and matching me thrust for thrust. He never once breaks eye contact, and that's when it hits me.

Just as much as Micah has saved me, I've saved him. The love pouring out of him nearly takes my breath away.

He tenses as his cum spills inside me, and even after we've both caught our breath, I stay on top of him and lean forward, hovering my mouth over his.

"I love you, Micah Harding." I press my lips to his, knowing I'll never be able to say it enough.

You can't quantify a love like ours. One that's withstood secrets and truths, pain and tragedy.

"I love you," I repeat. "Now and forevermore."

EPILOGUE

Adeline

Four years later

"Okay, one last final touch, and we'll be ready."

Ember sweeps her makeup brush across my cheek once more, adding another layer of powder. She stuffs her brush back into her apron and pulls out a small, black bottle. She holds her index finger over the top and points it in front of my face.

"Close your eyes and mouth."

I do as she says, trying my best to stay still as she spritzes a layer of setting spray across my face.

"You can open now." She sighs.

When I crack open my eyes, she's fanning my face with her hands.

"Perfect." She drops the bottle on the vanity and plants her hands on her hips, studying her work. A slow grin grows on her face. "You look absolutely beautiful."

Ember steps aside and allows me to see my reflection. "You did an incredible job," I tell her, turning my face to the side to run my fingers gently over my scar, amazed with how she's able to apply the makeup without completely hiding it.

It took another six months after Micah first stood me in front of the mirror for me to consider stepping in front of a camera again.

I spent the first few months considering switching careers, maybe even diving into horticulture, but I couldn't deny the power that came with the idea of going back to work as a model. Deep in my soul, I couldn't let Maddox win. Even if he would never know, I couldn't spend my life giving him the satisfaction of getting what he wanted. I took back control of my life and was unafraid.

Ember's strawberry blonde hair shimmers in front of the vanity lights. Her white teeth are revealed behind her wide grin.

Large, round bulbs frame the mirror in front of me, making me feel like an old Hollywood starlet. Subtle, gold, shimmery eyeshadow frames my eyelids. My hair is curled and pinned like an actress from the nineteen-forties.

"I love this cosmetic brand." Ember holds up the gold tube of lipstick, reading the label on the bottom.

"I do, too," I agree, smacking my lips. "You did an incredible job making everything fit."

"Well!" She winks. "It is my job."

"Mrs. Harding, we're ready for you."

I roll my eyes and slide out of the chair.

"I'm not Mrs. Harding yet." I shoot Ruby a playful glare. She's been teasing me for weeks, calling me *Mrs. Harding*.

I raise my hand, reminding her that I don't have a ring, and I'm not keeping a proposal story from her or Ember.

She pouts, sticking out her bottom lip as we walk over to the studio backdrop. Ember's London studio is littered with photographers and makeup artists.

"I swear..." Ruby shakes her head in disappointment. "When is that man going to propose?"

I shrug. "I haven't really thought about it, Ruby."

"You've been with him for more than four years, Adeline. He's thirty-seven years old. You'd think he'd have proposed by now, especially since the man worships the ground you walk on and talks about making a million babies with you."

"He doesn't worship the ground I walk on. But I wouldn't mind making a ton of babies with him." I blush, suddenly hoping this photoshoot won't take as long as I think it will. "Besides, we agreed we weren't rushing things. All I did as a kid was rush things. I love Micah, but I don't want to pressure him just because we think it's what we should be doing."

"But you wouldn't be marrying him because you should," she argues. "You'd be marrying him because you want to."

"He knows that," I reassure her. I wrap my hand around her arm once I step onto set. "And I know that, Ruby. Of course, I want to marry him. I promise I will tell you when he proposes. And when he does, I already know I won't hesitate to say yes."

"Fine." She rolls her eyes and moves behind the photographer.

After I finish the photoshoot and leave Ember, Ray gives me a ride to the airport. He drops me off just outside the hangar, where Micah and Archer are waiting for me outside of the private jet. The stairs leading to the airplane door are ready for us. The stars are out against the backdrop of London in the distance.

I can't deny that I haven't gotten my conversation with Ruby out of my head.

"Fuck," Micah says, bending over at the waist with his hands tucked in his pockets. The sight of him still makes my heart flutter. "You look so fucking beautiful."

I changed my outfit at Ember's studio, but I decided to keep my hair and makeup intact. I always hated washing it off after a shoot, anyway. Feels like such a waste.

"Well, thank you," I coo, wrapping my arms around him

when he meets me halfway to the plane. My lips immediately land on his, and the familiar sensation of safety fills me. Micah is my home, and I missed him today.

He kisses me as if he hasn't seen me in days. Reality is I saw him this morning when Ray dropped me off at Ember's studio before taking him to a meeting with a client in the heart of London.

I moan when his hands slide down the length of my back, pulling me against his tall, muscular frame. He growls against my mouth and tugs my bottom lip between his teeth before he pulls away.

"I missed you," he says, pressing his forehead to mine.

I giggle. "I missed you, too."

"All right, all right." Archer groans behind Micah. "That's enough of that. No one wants to see it."

I pull away but keep my hands wrapped around Micah's neck, tilting my head to get a view of my brother behind him.

"Archer." I give him a pointed look. "We've been together for four years. You should be used to it by now."

"I know." His eyebrows flatten, creating a shelf above his eyes. "It doesn't change the fact he's still my best friend and you're still my little sister."

I stick my tongue out at him the way I used to when I was a kid.

I laugh, but Archer doesn't find it as humorous. He makes a face.

We've worked to heal our relationship over the past several years. Forgiveness didn't come easy. It took me several months to reach out to Archer after he'd confessed about Micah taking the fall for him. I couldn't get past the fact he allowed him to go to prison, knowing the lasting consequences it would have on Micah's record. But at some point, I let it go.

Micah's sacrifice came from a place of love and loyalty,

because if there's one thing that's well known about the Hardings, it's their determination and faith in loyalty.

And Micah Harding is absolutely loyal.

That's what I've focused on.

That, and the fact Archer's left his drug dealing life behind, even going as far as to cut our father off completely.

I pull away from Micah, and Archer pulls me in for a hug. "It's all good," he says, scratching at his chin. "This is where I leave you both, anyway."

"Oh?" I trade glances between him and Micah. "I thought you were coming home with us."

"No." He shakes his head. "I need to get back to Austria. This trip is just for you two." He looks at Micah once more before bringing him in for a quick hug, clapping him on the back.

Archer leaves us and climbs into his own car. Micah wraps his arm around me and ushers me toward the plane.

"How was your shoot?" he asks. We're still several feet away from the stairs when he starts slowing his steps.

"It was good," I tell him, eyeing him with suspicion.

"Just good." He arches his eyebrows and pulls us to a full stop.

I smile and laugh. "Yeah."

"You don't sound so sure." He bends at the knees slightly, his hands still dipped into his pants. I search his beautiful face, giving in to tell him what's been on my mind for the past several hours.

"Fine." I groan, stabbing my heel against the pavement, hating that Micah can see right through me, but also loving that he notices. "It's stupid, but I can't get something Ruby said at the photoshoot out of my head."

"What did she say?"

"It's dumb, Micah." Suddenly, I'm embarrassed—a feeling I'm not completely foreign to when it comes to Micah.

"I doubt it."

I roll my eyes and inhale a deep breath, blowing it out between my red-painted lips. "Ruby called me Mrs. Harding because she thought you'd proposed to me and I'd been keeping it from her."

Yep, I definitely feel stupid for bringing this up now.

My heart races, and my cheeks heat. I swallow my nerves, hating that I've brought this up. Micah has spent most of his adult life thinking he's behind. He's thirty-seven now, still unmarried, still childless. And while I've wanted to give him all those things, I didn't want to rush him. I wanted to marry him years ago, but I didn't want him to feel like he was only doing it to check a box off his list.

He's also thought it's what I've wanted since my early twenties. I constantly remind him that I don't care what age I am. Since he felt like he'd wasted his twenties, he didn't want me doing the same.

But I've always known I want to marry him, and as the years have gone by, I don't think I've ever been more ready than I am now. As I look into his blue-gray eyes against the backdrop of a city far from home, I realize this is all I've ever wanted.

"Huh." He frowns in thought. The lines in the corner of his eyes deepen as he jerks back, trying to get a read on me. "And how did hearing her call you that make you feel?"

"What?" I ask, my heart racing even faster.

"How did it make you feel? Her calling you Mrs. Harding?"

I smile, my nerves higher than they've ever been. "I liked it. It felt like it's been my name all along."

"Oh." He removes one hand from his pocket and rests it on his chin in thought. "Kind of like how you used to doodle

Adeline Harding in little hearts all over your notebook when you were eleven? That kind of feeling?"

"Micah." I gape, playfully slapping him on the arm, but he catches my left hand before I have the chance to pull it away and drops to one knee. "Micah?" My giggling subsides, but my cheeks remain heated. Tears immediately prick the backs of my eyes.

"I've loved you for years, Adeline, and when I look back on it, the only regret I have is not having asked you this before."

"Don't regret it," I whisper. "Any amount of time with you isn't a regret."

"It isn't," he says, staring up into my eyes. "Not one single moment. I used to spend my years counting the days of what I missed, thinking I had to check off milestones by this year and that year. But I don't. And then I thought because you were in your twenties, you shouldn't live your life tied down. You deserved to spend your twenties not rushing. But I'm only lying to myself."

"We are lying to ourselves." I giggle.

His smile hasn't left him. "You've given me more than I could have ever hoped for. So much of my life was spent living in the darkness, but all you've given me is light. You saved me. I don't need to count my days with you, Adeline, but I won't waste another pretending I don't want nothing more than my ring around your finger and my last name doodled in a heart in one of your notebooks."

I laugh as tears spill down my cheeks. Micah stands and pulls a box out of his front pocket. He lifts his free hand, wiping a tear from my scar with the pad of his thumb.

He opens the box, and the air is knocked out of me when I see the ring: a pale pink stone surrounded by hundreds of tiny diamonds.

Micah holds the ring between us and looks into my eyes.

"Will you marry me, Addy?"

The word doesn't leave my mouth before I'm frantically nodding, a sob escaping my chest. The light in Micah's eyes is the last thing I see before he crashes his mouth to mine, slipping his ring on my fourth finger, giving me the only thing I've ever wanted and known I've wanted my whole life.

To be a Harding, and to be loved.

READ AN EXTENDED BONUS EPILOGUE FROM ADELINE AND MICAH HERE

ACKNOWLEDGMENTS

First and foremost I want to thank my husband and my two boys. Without your love and support, I wouldn't be able to continue doing what I love. You three are my favorite people in the entire world.

Thank you to my amazing assistant, April. Your passion for me and my work extends beyond our daily work together. You've easily become a friend and confidante. I can't even begin to tell you what you mean to me.

My designer Amanda Shepard. As always, you kill it with these covers. Thank you for creating every one of the Harding Brothers covers. They are as stunning as you are!

My agent, Nikki for your constant encouragement.

My editor, Vicki James. Sometimes my work is a little more rough around the edges so I appreciate your patience with this one. Thank you for helping to make my work shine.

My betas team - Joan, April, Amy, Lori, and Ana. What can I say and where do I even begin? I can't tell you how much your feedback means to me. Throughout the writing process, the story begins to take shape and transforms multiple times before its final version. I took every critique you came back with to heart and in the end, you helped shape Micah and Adeline's love story to become as authentic as possible. I love you all!

And finally to my readers. Without you, I quite literally wouldn't be able to do what I love. I know there are a million amazing books out there and the fact you decided to pick mine up and dedicate your time to little old me, means everything. Thank you for reading Micah and Adeline's story. Thank you for reading and loving the Harding Brothers. Thank you from the bottom of my heart.

ABOUT BRITTANY

Brittany Taylor grew up all over the world including places such as California and England. Her love of reading started at a young age. Finally deciding to fulfill her lifelong dream, she took the plunge into the writing world and published her first book when she was twenty-eight. Today she resides in Maine with her husband, two sons, two cats and one dog.

www.brittanytaylorbooks.com

www.ingramcontent.com/pod-product-compliance
Lightning Source LLC
Chambersburg PA
CBHW022019310726
48972CB00006B/1718